I0826840

LABYRINTHINE

LABYRINTHINE

A THRONES OF THE FORSAKEN NOVEL

CJ HOLMES

LABYRINTHINE
Thrones of the Forsaken, Book 1

CITY OWL PRESS
www.cityowlpress.com

Cover Design by Sarah Rose at Gravewing Studios. All stock photos licensed appropriately.

Map by Alec McKinley.

Edited by Tee Tate.

For information on subsidiary rights, please contact the publisher at info@cityowlpress.com.

Paperback Edition ISBN: 978-1-64898-547-8

Digital Edition ISBN: 978-1-64898-546-1

To Isabelle,

The first story my heart ever wrote.
The girl who reminds me that any labyrinth is worth walking—for love.
This first book will always be yours.

Velastra
Nyxford
THRENOS
Varethorne
Echoridge

Evernight Hold
Elemere Cove
Crossroad Shrine
Silverbrook
STARSFALL

PROLOGUE

STARSFALL WAS ONCE SACRED. THEN, THE GODS ABANDONED IT, and us, to the mercy of a man who had none.

My father.

The priests say it was necessary. That the gods were merciful. Clever. Brilliant. That they saved Starsfall and Larksbind from the curse of magic and stopped the war that had turned into a feast of fire and flesh. From the blight that made our rivers run red with the blood of youth and choked our skies with smoke from the pyres that never stopped burning.

But it's what men don't say that tells the real story.

They don't speak of the way silence settled like ash after the gods turned away, or how my father stepped into that silence. How he shaped himself into the image of a savior, but there were always fractures in the mask—hairline cracks where his cruelty leaked through.

They don't say that binding the magic in Starsfall smothered the kingdom's heartbeat, or that even the gods could not unmake it. For even they don't hold that power. So the priests don't tell tales of sorcery that is more than mere destruction. More than spells and storms and fire. That is power born from pain, woven into the land and its blood.

They say the binding was a sacrifice.

But it wasn't made by them.

It was mine.

Made without my consent, breathed into me the moment I was born—for when the gods bound Starsfall's magic, they bound me with it. Because the curse they feared wasn't the land's fury or a king's wrath. It was his daughter's.

What lives in me is old and patient. Made of darkness and death. Power that remembers. Magic that seethes and rebels and waits. That doesn't forget the sound of screaming. That seeks the light—that hunts for it through the small hours of the night—to destroy it.

They say the gods locked Starsfall's magic away in a contest whose rules are written in blood. That the Reaping is the cost of peace. A sacred rite. The priests whisper that the gods found a way to contain two monsters who might ruin the world. My father, with his craving for power and his eternal quest for more. His child, with her magic that could destroy all the gods had created. But what they really did was put a blade in my father's hand and called it mercy.

Each year, ten men from Larksbind enter the Reaping. Ten lives offered like prayer, like tribute. They hope to win my hand in battle, and with it, the magic bound inside my blood. If I marry a man from Larksbind, the power returns to them. Peace, they say. Balance. But if a man from Starsfall wins my heart and earns redemption through love, our kingdom's magic stays with us.

And that makes my father hungry. A man who would bleed the world dry to have magic on his side.

The gods must have thought a balance had been found. That mortals would rise to meet the trials of combat or the heart. That someone would survive long enough to reach me, and that mortals would, somehow, learn compassion through suffering. Perhaps they even thought that my father's hunger would burn itself out.

But he is not the kind of man who fades with time. He is the kind that rots deeper.

Over the years, he's made certain no suitor survives the Reaping and none comes close to claiming me.

He's twisted the trials until they're nothing but slaughter. Changed the rules, the terrain, the odds. Turned them into a show of blood and fear. The people cheer. The priests bless the carnage. No one remembers it was meant to be anything else.

And each year, the outcome is the same.

I remain unmarried.

Unclaimed.

And with every failed Reaping, my father comes closer to claiming what should never be his.

Because long ago, he made another bargain. One hidden in the fine print of gods and law, a deal no one speaks of.

If no man reaches me before my twenty-fifth name day, the magic bound in the Reaping reverts to him. Not to the kingdom. Not to the land. Not to me.

Him.

So he waits. And bleeds them all dry.

Until only I remain. A crown with no court. A throne with no allies. A girl with no choices left but one.

Or so they say.

CHAPTER ONE

There's only one thing left to do.

Run.

I've served a sentence I never earned, locked in a palace I was never meant to survive. I won't stay for another Reaping—won't watch ten strangers die trying to win my hand like it's a prize the gods tossed into a pit.

Escape is the only path left. There's no honor in this. No bravery. Just the raw, aching will to live. If I had more courage, maybe it would let me face what's coming. But hope left me long ago and all that remains is the hollow where it used to be.

Let the gods be angry. Let them come.

I'm done being theirs.

My only way is out. Cowardice is all that's left. I've lived in the shadows of my father's palace too long, enduring nights that coil black around their halls like a curse we never learned how to lift. Torches flicker in their sconces, burning brightly and pretending the darkness isn't winning. Marble floors gleam beneath them, polished and proud, but I know the truth. These halls have held me long enough for the rot breathing through the stone to make my throat close off. The palace's stench feeds on all the things we pretend aren't there.

Columns rise like false idols—ornate, gilded, triumphant—bearing witness to centuries of blood and silence. Even the paintings along the walls are liars, dripping with color and glory, depicting victories that were never clean. My gaze snags on them as I pass. They do not look back. None of them ever do.

The shadows cover me as I creep with the caution of a creature used to being hunted. I've rehearsed every step, every pause, every breath. But when I slip past two guards slumped in drunken laughter, a new fear twists in my gut. Maybe it won't be precision that saves me, but luck. Maybe it never was about being good. Maybe it was always about timing and prayers whispered to gods who stopped listening long ago.

The palace watches. Its hunger gnaws at my back as I press myself into an alcove. The guards' laughter grows louder, then fades as they wait for their relief. The shift will change soon, and for the briefest moment, the corridor will be mine—emptied of bodies, filled with only cold opulence and the sound of my own heartbeat.

That's when I'll move.

When I'll run.

A hidden passage lies just beyond the royal wing, a secret kept by a trusted few, by those my father says are loyal enough to know of the escape his family will take in times of war. Or rebellion. Tonight it's both. My war. My rebellion. My father never thought I'd dare.

But I have earned this escape.

Earned it with silence. With obedience. With all the days I did not scream.

I will survive this.

More than that. I will escape this place—and never again endure captivity and its smothering protection.

The bell tolls. The guards stir. A burst of movement as they peel themselves from the walls, muttering and swaying as they stumble toward the barracks. I imagine they'll be thinking of wine. Of firelit celebrations. Of the feast the Reaping promises and maybe even the men from Larksbind who will die to appease the gods.

They don't see me.

I'll let them chase their hunger. Mine is older. Keener. Mine has fangs.

I move—through the doorway like a shadow unmoored, into a stairwell that spirals downward into silence. My hand trembles as I ease the door closed behind me, careful not to let the wood betray me with a slam. One sound—

too sharp, too loud—would be enough to shatter the silence and my safety. So I creep through the dark, my breath slow, my heart beating like it knows what's coming.

The stairs are uneven and ancient, half-carved into the stone like an afterthought. I descend them without doubt, each footfall an echo in my bones, before I break into a sprint at the courtyard, veering along the east wing where the manicured beds run beneath the palace windows. More gardens unfold ahead, their flowers all groomed and beautiful and drowning in moonlight. I tear through them, the scent of jasmine thick in the air, a cruel perfume meant to mask the stench of what festers beneath.

Even now, even as I flee its grasp, the palace shadows cling, a reminder that freedom will never be mine. Not truly. Not while the cursed magic coils inside me, waiting.

The grate to a supply tunnel eases back onto its hinges as a passing cloud erases my shadow. Left. Right. Clear. The cover settles on the cobbles, and I drop into the crawl, my hands and knees scraping in dust. Emerging onto the paved streets of Threnos, the capital's air hits me like a blade. Cold. Damp. Free.

I blink too long. I shouldn't have stopped to stare. Starsfall's capital is a jewel in the dark, its spires catching torchlight, its narrow alleys gleaming with secrets. But awe is a luxury for someone not being hunted.

I run.

My boots pound the stone. My cloak flies behind me, catching wind and trailing shadows. Streets blur around me. I cut into alleys toward the celebrations, praying my memory hasn't failed me. Threnos's veins wind and tangle, and I am a drop of blood trying not to clot.

A swell of music rises ahead—lutes and laughter and drums echoing off stone. I push toward it, toward the central square where the Reaping crowds gather, their joy oblivious to the price behind it.

The scent of roasting meat and spilled wine thickens. Voices slur in song. My pace slows, just enough for me to tug my hood lower and slip into the tide of bodies, letting their revelry swallow me whole.

Dancers twirl in silks that shimmer with every spin. Men lift tankards in toasts to death and destiny. No one sees me—not really. They see another girl in velvet, flushed from drink or song or sin.

I keep walking. Head low. Hood up. Heart pounding. I weave through the brightly colored cloaks, pretending to dance and sing along with travelers, drifting toward the bread ovens' gate, the workmen's entrance the city forgets.

Let them think I'm just another reveler come to watch the gods play with lives.

Let them believe I'm free.

The guards at the gatehouse are distracted by the women clinging to them, each trying to secure a husband by sunrise. The girls ply their charms and flutter their lashes—and I seize my chance, slipping past them, and finally stepping outside the capital of Starsfall.

My body begs to celebrate.

To run and laugh.

To breathe in the wild air of freedom.

I do not give in. Instead, I make myself walk steadily toward the trees that border Threnos. Their trunks are only meters away. All that is left is for me to hold my nerve and slip past them.

The wood swallows me whole and I sink into shadow. The glimmer from Threnos fades behind me, and the night presses close. Branches creak. Leaves whisper. The quiet should comfort me. It doesn't. It wraps too tight, too still, like smoke around a dying flame. The shadows shift.

My boots sink into moss. I take one more step—

A hand wraps around my throat and pain explodes through my side as I slam into a tree, hard enough to rattle bone. The guard doesn't let go, not even when I kick out. His weight pins me against the bark like I belong there, and I take a moment to collect myself.

There's no screaming. Or begging.

Just a girl saving her strength. Assessing his weaknesses.

The air reeks of sweat and sour wine. He leans in, breathing hot and heavy against my cheek. I turn my head, but he laughs as his hands drift downwards, brushing my cloak aside. His fingers reach for my hips, where my coin bag should be.

"What've we got here?"

He rocks back on his heels.

He acts like I'm cornered. Like I'm prey.

The fool hasn't recognized me. Hasn't found the blade strapped to my other thigh. He doesn't know I trained beneath Mallen, Commander of the

Royal Guard, whose drills carved steel into my bones. *Be swift. Be silent. Use your weight. Strike before mercy becomes a mistake.*

He's too drunk to notice me move.

Too slow to stop what's coming.

I twist. Drop. Strike.

His body hits the bracken, and blood spills onto ground that has soaked up worse. The earth drinks it down, unconcerned.

There's no time to waste breath on guilt.

But the noise will draw attention. It always does.

And my father ensures Starsfall is full of men in borrowed armor who like the taste of fear. Thugs turned into legal knives with no leash. Men who are paid too little to feed their children, so find other ways to earn gold.

I bolt deeper into the night, ducking under branches, racing into the darkness to widen the distance between us. The ground is slick, the underbrush dense. Twigs catch at my cloak and roots try to snag my ankles, but I'm small and quick. I dart around trunks and duck under limbs. Any guards who the commotion might attract will be larger—slower through the tight growth—but their strides are longer and they'll plow through everything in their way.

In a straight chase, they'd win. But Mallen taught me not to play fair.

His training reverberates through every movement, through every turn and breath. He was ruthless. He taught me to fight, to endure, to survive. I'd have been caught already without him. He made me strong enough to escape.

Strong enough to survive my father's moods.

And this, this is nothing compared to that.

My chest aches, my legs burn, but I keep going.

The terrain is rough, the forest thick, and the moonlight barely touches the path ahead. And then its silver lights a ridge ahead, and I know I'll reach the clearing in a few more meters.

My heart pounds.

I'm going to make it.

The clearing opens before me. My stomach clenches.

It's quiet. Too quiet.

The horses are tied, just where they should be. But the air is wrong. Still. Expectant.

Anya should be here. My maid. My almost friend. We weren't close. Not really. Anya was too kind, too soft, and I could never trust her enough to hold her closer than I absolutely needed to. We shared small secrets in the dark sometimes—two girls caught in a gilded cage—but there were walls between us. She served me. Obeyed me. Feared me a little. And I never told her no. She should be waiting—smiling, laughing, eager to know the joy of freedom.

But there's only the sound of hooves shifting and leaves whispering.

My fingers drop to my blade as I creep forward, every sense screaming. The horses are uneasy, snorting, stamping the damp earth. I start forward, ready to calm them, but something stops me.

Something primal.

This is too easy, too exposed.

Too wrong.

A trap.

I spin, narrowly avoiding the sword thrust at my neck. My blade catches moonlight as I draw it and drop low, throwing up an arm to deflect. My body pivots instinctively, moving just as I was taught. Mallen drilled these moves into my bones.

Strike. Balance. Move.

It's almost like dancing—if dancing demanded both blood and surrender.

A man steps from shadow, cloaked and hooded, a soldier's stillness in his stance and mail glinting at his wrist. My dagger flashes, clashing against a sword. He's fast. Too fast. He parries every blow with ease.

I grit my teeth and strike again. He dodges, shifting his weight, his blade moving like water. It gleams under the moonlight, and he forces me back. He advances in silence, methodical, relentless. I duck a wide slash and counter low, feinting right and spinning left. My blade catches the edge of his sleeve—just cloth, no flesh.

He grunts, annoyed now. I press my advantage. A quick jab. A pivot. He blocks, but I can see he's testing me, not fighting to win.

And gods, that angers me.

I lunge again, this time not pulling back. My dagger arcs for his side. He twists, faster than thought, and the clash of metal rings loud enough to wake the trees. His blade turns mine aside and traps it. One flick of his wrist and my weapon is ripped from my hand, sent spinning into the grass.

I twist and drive my fist into his ribs. Hard.

Steel kisses my neck. Just enough to make me stop. To hold me. Not enough to harm. We stand, both breathing hard. My gaze fixes on roped and scarred forearms, their cadence too familiar to deny. And I know those sword strokes. I've spent my life parrying them.

"Princess," he growls.

I sigh, shoulders slumping. "Mallen."

The Commander of the Royal Guards stands before me, amused. Taller than me by more than a head, all sharp angles and disciplined lines, in road-dark leathers and mail. Dark hair pushed back, jaw rough with stubble, a faint bruise shadowing his cheekbone. Starsfall green marks his shoulder and catches the light when he shifts. His eyes stay steady and measuring while his mouth tips into a small smirk. It is the look of a man who has caught me misbehaving again, and I loathe it. *That* look. The one that reminds me how much more experienced he is than me, even though he's only a few years older.

"You can sit and we can talk, Azhara. Or I can carry you back over my shoulder and let your father decide what's reasonable."

Flashes light up my vision, and I lock my eyes on his. His don't blink. Don't blur. Don't even flicker. I know better than to test him.

He's always protected me. But he's never been afraid to teach me a lesson, either.

And he's never hesitated to spill blood.

"Fine," I grit.

He nods, stepping back without hesitation, and gestures toward a fallen tree. I move slowly, keeping my eyes on him as he sheathes his sword—not with arrogance, but with the casual confidence of someone who knows he doesn't need it.

"You could've let me go."

He waits until I'm seated before joining me, his tone even. "You brought this on yourself. I've spent the evening killing to keep you safe."

Of course he did. Death follows me as it burns through my veins. It coils behind every step I take, lingers in my shadow, staining everything I touch. Even locked away, even sealed by the gods themselves, the magic inside me hungers. And people die. Whether I will it or not.

"Where's Anya?" I ask as I sit.

Mallen doesn't answer.

"Where is she?"

"Taken care of, Princess," Mallen says.

My breath hitches. Those words could mean anything from banishment to execution.

"What have you done?" I ask.

He exhales slowly, the way he does when calculating risk.

"I didn't lay a hand on her. I would have captured her, but a group of thieves got to her first. I assume they were targeting the celebrations—looking for coin, distraction, chaos. I made sure they won't bother anyone again. Let's hope it won't take any more sacrifices to keep you safe."

Maybe things are better this way. Maybe the gods were right to bind me. Because even shackled, my magic leaves bodies in its wake. And I don't flinch. Not like I should. Not like Anya would have. Her death doesn't hollow me out. It just confirms what I've always suspected: I was born wrong. A weapon pretending to be a girl.

His logic is always convenient. Cold. Effective. He's a blade honed for strategy, not sentiment—it's why my father made him Commander so young. He doesn't hesitate. He never does. And that's what terrifies me most—that somewhere in me, I'm glad he didn't.

But something about this feels...off?

"Why?" I press.

A flicker crosses his face—not quite regret, but something less carved in steel.

"Because it matters to you," he says simply.

His body shifts, muscles relaxing, and he leans just enough for his shoulder to brush mine. It's nothing like his presence during training—there's no force behind it, only weight and warmth. But it unsettles me more than his judgment ever has. I start to shake. He notices.

Without comment, he places his hand gently over mine, steadying it on my thigh.

"Azhara," he says quietly. "Why did you run?"

Those green eyes—they've always been sharp, unyielding, the kind that makes men fall silent in his presence. But now they're unreadable in a different way. Still intense. Still dangerous. But no longer aimed like a weapon. More like a question.

"I can't bear another Reaping," I whisper. "They're going to die. Again. It's cruel. It's pointless. I don't know how else to end it."

He doesn't speak right away. When he does, his voice is steady, not unkind.

"It's ten men a year. Men with no ties to Starsfall. It keeps Larksbind in check, and the rest of us safe. Peace comes with a cost."

I shake my head against him. Against the firm, solid frame I've leaned on too many times to count.

"I don't want it. I don't want to be the prize two countries fight over."

His chest rises with a quiet laugh. It's low and dry, more breath than sound. His arms wrap around me slowly, like they have all the times I've needed his calm before. Like he's offering something instead of taking it. And I don't know what it is. Comfort, perhaps. Or loyalty. Or something far more dangerous.

"Your father doesn't need you to control Larksbind," he murmurs. "And you won't be marrying anyone who isn't worthy."

I pull back, just enough to see his face. I'm confused. He's always respected the tributes, more than anyone in the palace. Yet here he is, dismissing them with uncharacteristic ease. He even narrows his eyes as he looks down at me and his lips part, his mouth curving down like he's trying to swallow the words he knows he shouldn't say.

"If the Reaping doesn't kill them, I will," he says. "I won't let you be forced into an arrangement you despise."

Relief washes through me. The emotion doesn't make sense because Mallen has always kept me safe, but it steadies the heat rising through me. Or maybe it makes it worse. And now he's brushing another loose strand of hair from my cheek and tucking it behind my ear with an unexpectedly gentle touch.

"Will you stop it?" I ask softly. "For me?"

His gaze meets mine, and there's something in his eyes I've never seen before. It's too potent to ignore, but I don't know how to name it. It isn't disappointment. It isn't envy or anger. And it isn't hunger. It's more resolute. Fiercer. Like Mallen's just been handed the reason he's been searching for.

Waiting for.

Like he's falling apart and holding on and he doesn't know which will prevail.

"That depends," he says, his voice low and sure, without threat. "On what it is that you choose to do next."

CHAPTER TWO

He lowers his head, and for a moment, I can't read him. My breath burns, caught in my chest.

There's a quiet fierceness in the way he looks at me—unflinching, unguarded. I don't understand it. I don't know what he's asking. After all these years, I should. But my thoughts have scattered like leaves in a storm, and my heart beats so loudly I swear he must hear it. My pulse flurries fast enough that my body turns light and all I can think about is how breathless I am.

I press my lips together—

And then he kisses me.

It's not sweet. Not slow. One hand anchors me while the other cradles the back of my head as Mallen grips my hair as though their strands might slip through his fingers. His mouth moves over mine and I'm startled. It's everything, but I don't know what I'm doing. Gods, I don't even know how to breathe.

My lips part out of instinct, not certainty, and I mimic him—clumsy, breathless, burning.

This isn't how I imagined my first kiss.

I imagined warmth. Certainty. A sense of readiness. Too many times I'd half-dreamed it would be Mallen, but now I'm swept away in him. By him.

I've stepped off the edge of a sheer cliff face and I haven't figured out if I'm falling or flying.

His teeth graze my bottom lip and I flinch. His tongue brushes mine and I taste him—smoke and winter spice and something I can't name. Something older. Something born before fire had a name. He is too much. Too close. And I can't keep up.

He pulls back slowly, like he's loath to end it. His forehead rests against mine and for too many racing heartbeats, neither of us moves. I don't want him to move.

I am shaking. Not from fear. Not from cold.

His voice is soft as he whispers, "Azhara. Have me instead."

My mouth falls open. My arms and legs seem heavy, barely responding. The world sounds muffled. His words don't make sense at first. They ring like a bell that hasn't finished echoing.

My breath catches. Mallen—protector, shadow, constant. He's never touched me like this before, never hinted.

"I..." My words tangle.

I didn't see this coming.

Not from him. Not like this. Not now.

He tenses, bracing. My hesitation is a storm he's already preparing for.

Mallen's expression falters. "I've wanted you for years," he says. "I've stood at your side, kept guard when you slept, and learned the shape of your silences and the weight of your courage. You've never been a duty. Just a choice I made a thousand times over. But if this isn't what you want—say so."

His arms don't tighten, but they hold firm while his gaze rakes over me like he's searching for a sign. For some proof I won't vanish. I'm not sure I'm built for this kind of tenderness, and one more breath from him might scatter me like dust. I've stepped into a moment too delicate to survive, and Mallen just stares at me, like he's waiting for just one word from me and he'll give me the world and all the stars.

I am small and trembling and unmoored.

And still—I don't want to run.

Because just like that, the world tilted. I could say no. I could walk away.

I could stay.

Or keep falling and let him catch me.

I reach for him, desperate for an anchor. His tunic bunches between my fingers and I'm half-tempted to cling to it. But my mind is pulling me in every direction. Duty. Magic. The Reaping. The man from Larksbind I'm meant to marry when they win. The peace that union would promise. The kingdom I'm meant to protect.

All of it feels brittle now. Distant. Like a future meant for someone else.

"We can't," I whisper.

He lifts my chin, carefully—never demanding, only asking. My eyes meet his and I see the ache he's been carrying. The devotion he's hidden behind distance. He's only four years older than me, but that's not what sets him apart. It's the grief in him. The depth of his restraint. He never speaks of the wound; he only keeps watch over what it made of him.

"Why not?" he asks. "You can choose a man from Starsfall."

"It would mean war," I breathe.

He gives a small, rueful smile. "Wars have been fought for less, Azhara. I've killed for you before. And I would burn a thousand kingdoms if they tried to take you from me."

I swallow hard. There's no fire in his voice. No posturing. Just quiet certainty. It chills me more than if he'd shouted.

My gaze traces the sharp lines of his face—the scars, the strength. The dark hair that makes him seem more menacing than he is, and the emerald eyes that pierce my thoughts. The way he moves like he was forged to endure and overcome. He's beautiful in a way that almost frightens me. Lethal in the way he holds it all back.

He's been my antagonist, my protector, my shadow, and my shield. I never thought he could be anything more. Never thought he'd want anything more. But now that possibility hangs in the air between us like lightning waiting to strike, like snowdrops daring to rise from the frozen earth.

"Why tell me now?"

"You ran. I thought I had more time. I didn't realize how close I was to losing you."

"You don't love me," I say, because I need to hear it.

His brows knit, a crease of disbelief drawing across his forehead. "You truly haven't seen it?"

I glance away. "You've mocked me more often than I can remember. You hate the parades and formal receptions where you're forced to smile at my side.

And let's not forget all the times you told me I wasn't strong enough. That I was soft."

"You were," he says, not unkindly. "I needed you to survive."

A breath leaves me.

His hand curls around my fingers. It dwarfs my hand, as his frame dwarfs mine. "I pushed you to make you harder. Stronger. Not to break you. Because I wanted you to endure."

I don't know what to say. I'm left sorting through memories that seem different now that he's told me this truth. And gods, I believe him. Because Mallen never acts without a reason. Now, what was cold and calculated has also become an act of devotion, and all those mornings he made me spar in frostbitten dawns take on an entirely different meaning.

"I didn't know," I murmur.

He leans in, presses his lips to my cheek with aching reverence. His fingers thread through my hair and a quiet sound escapes me. A whimper. Gods, it's small and helpless.

"You deserve to feel," he says. "More than duty. More than fear. I've never used or held your wants or wishes against you. I would die before I let anyone else try."

I try to turn away again, but he doesn't let me. Not with force. Just the press of his gaze. Just the steady warmth of his hand on the small of my back.

"Azhara. You must have known. The way I watched you. The way I never stopped watching."

I shake my head, too overwhelmed to speak.

And then he says it again, quieter than before. "Do you care for me?"

The words root me in place. His voice is low, and dark with a different kind of danger—the danger of being seen. Of being known.

Every path is a risk. Every decision comes with consequence.

And in a life of never having choices, I don't know how to handle having one.

"I don't know if I'm allowed," I say. "I'm supposed to marry someone from Larksbind. I don't know if I'm brave enough to want what will hurt this many people."

"You are," he says, without hesitation. "You know you can choose."

I wish I knew which one he meant.

My throat tightens. "You serve my father."

"I serve *you*," he answers, leaving no room for argument. Or doubt. "Always you. Only you."

He kisses me again—not hard, not wild. Just slow. And devastating.

And I let myself fall.

"Was that better?" he rasps as he breaks the kiss, and the words scrape over me like a knife sheathed in silk.

Mallen takes my chin, fingers firm but reverent, guiding my face back to his. He smiles like a man with the sun in his hands, like this moment is everything he's ever wanted. His gaze drinks me in slowly, possessively, savoring the effect he has on me.

There's no need to rush when you own the hourglass.

"You're serious?" I whisper. "What about my magic? We can't. It's too dangerous to release. Even the gods—"

He inclines his head, not in challenge but acknowledgment. Calm. Grounded. His gaze holds a storm, but it's not fury I sense. I cannot name this emotion, only feel it, like a thunderstorm running along the edges of my skin.

"The only force that could turn me from this path," he says, voice low and deliberate, "is you. Am I without hope?"

I shake my head, wordless.

His eyes search mine, fierce and vulnerable. As if he's bracing for impact and hoping, quietly, that I'll spare him.

"You're in every breath I take," he says. "You're not a need, Azhara. You're not even a want. You're a truth. A foundation I build my soul around." His voice softens. "I only hope I haven't failed in showing you."

His fingers graze my sternum, featherlight. A question, not a claim.

"I see no proof your magic is any more dangerous than your father's," he continues. "And if it truly is, I will face it. I don't think your magic is wicked. I think it simply is. And I would far rather bear the consequences of having you than I would have you bear any man, any army, or any fate that tries to cage you."

I blink up at him, speechless.

"I wasn't expecting this," I whisper.

"You expected to run," he says, almost playful. "You still can try, but we both know your father won't let you get very far. And if you stay, I won't trap you. I'll walk beside you, step for step, as long as you'll have me. Until you decide otherwise."

I believe him.

Not just because of his words. Because of the way he waits. The way he gives me time to decide. The way he needs me to know it's still my choice.

"Let me earn a future with you," he says. "I can't stop the Reaping this year—but I promise you, next year, there will be none. Let me show you what you can have. Let me prove myself. Let yourself feel."

And this is what I want.

It isn't perfect, but Mallen isn't asking for that.

He's asking for a chance. He's asking for me to listen to the part of me that still dreams, even after everything. The part that wants more than duty or survival. The part that wants him.

I nod.

He exhales a breath like it hurt him to hold onto it, and smiles. The kiss he gives me next is not to conquer—it's to remember. Gentle at first and then more. Enough to make me believe I'm standing on the edge of oblivion, and all I know is the possibility of him. His fingertips press into me as if he's been desperate for this and only now dares to take what he wants. And gods, I want this too.

"No others," he says, and there's an edge to it. Jealousy. "I won't stand in your way if you don't want me, but I won't watch as you let someone else win your heart."

I nod again, more slowly. It's a truth—or promise—we both share, even if we don't yet have the shape of it.

"I don't want to go back," I whisper, my voice barely more than ash.

He tilts his head, that wolfish pity softening his fierce eyes.

"Starsfall is your home. Threnos's walls and the palace keep you safe. Now is not the time to challenge your father."

I hate that he's right. Hate it with the kind of bone-deep fury that feels like grief. Because I want to fight back or run until the sky splits open and something *changes*—but there's nowhere left to go. Not really. My father is always ten steps ahead, and this time, I'm too tired to pretend I can outpace him. The truth tastes like rust and ruin, and I swallow it down like a blade.

Mallen's gaze is soft again, almost fragile. Almost tender. It disorients me. Mallen commands through fire and steel but he's softening, and the brush of his thumb beneath my eye nearly undoes me. It destroys me more than any cruel word ever could.

"What will you tell him?" I ask.

"The best lies lean on truth. I'll tell your father that Anya colluded with Moonsrise to kidnap you—and that I found and returned you. The bodies fit the story. It'll be enough to stop another war."

Moonsrise has been pressing our shores for months. Raids in the north, ships sighted off estuaries, envoys with smiles too sharp to be peace. It won't escape my father that this tale makes Mallen the hero. But maybe that's what Starsfall needs. A hero who isn't hungry for power but fights to protect it. Perhaps that's what I need too.

Mallen's hand lingers as he helps me to my feet, and I realize it's because I won't let it go. We mount our horses in silence, and I catch myself wishing I could stay here. With him. But wishes do not come true in Starsfall, and so we ride back to Threnos. To my father's palace.

And for once, I know I won't be alone.

At the main road, he guides my gelding beside his, keeping pace with me without taking control. We ride in silence until the gatehouse looms, and then he nods once and says, "Lower your hood."

I obey.

My hood falls, and our hoofbeats carry into the press of bodies. A few faces turn, then more, a hush widening like a ring on water. Laughter thins. The fiddles lose their measure as recognition takes hold. Gasps ripple through the crowd as faces turn toward us. Mallen rides with his back straight, his hand brushing my leg only to steady me. To anyone watching, the Commander of the Royal Guard is delivering a princess home. They wouldn't guess that he touches me with both possession and wordless worry.

The palace rises like a dream ahead—torchlit, golden, far too beautiful for the ache it hides. Its walls are perfection. Its doors are locked from within.

A gilded cage.

My throat tightens. I've never felt more trapped.

"You're safe now," Mallen says, just loud enough for the guards to hear.

The irony is sharp enough to draw blood. He's playing his part, while I play mine, letting tears fall. They think I'm crying from relief. They don't understand I'm mourning.

"Let's get you home," he murmurs. Then he slaps my horse's flank, and it surges forward. I don't have time to protest.

We gallop through the torch-lit streets, past shuttered stalls and lantern smoke, through the palace gates, up the marble steps. Sentries snap to attention. Stableboys scatter. We take the marble steps at a climb. Mallen dismounts first. He doesn't ask if I want help. Instead, he lifts me from the saddle like I'm fragile and precious, not because I'm weak, but because he's careful.

I let him and bury my face in his neck to hide from any gawking nobles. Courtiers have spilled from the east gallery, drawn by the clatter and the feast still roaring in the royal wing. Silk and jewels crowd the balustrades, eyes bright with news. Mallen doesn't care. He sets me on my feet and keeps a hand at my back as he takes me in through the colonnade, along the north passage, past guard posts and tapestries and the map room, cutting straight to my father's rooms.

Inside the royal chambers, my father stands from his chaise. His expression twists in offense, not concern, as we interrupt his dinner with the high-ranking lords.

"My King," Mallen says with a bow.

"My daughter appears to be a burden."

"The princess was nearly taken tonight," Mallen replies evenly.

I gaze at the murals and friezes adorning the royal chambers, letting my thoughts drift to the myths they depict. The stories of heroes and villains, of monsters and men, and of great battles and romances that tore the world apart. At the men who were worthy of Starsfall's greatest honor, who were brave enough that the crown bent for them, offering not just gratitude, but reverence. A gift my father has never learned to give.

He paces, presumably thinking of treaties, borders, and optics. Mallen receives no thanks as my father pours wine, his silence a verdict. His thoughts are not on me. They never are. I've lived here too long to foster such foolish delusions.

"Is she intact?" he asks finally.

"Unharmed, Your Highness."

It's a clinical term. A transactional concern that ought to make me flinch. Instead, it leaves me feeling nothing. That's what I am to my father. A commodity. A prize to be claimed. A bauble to dangle in front of kingdoms like Moonsrise and Mistsong and even Rivenmere.

The nobles fidget and I wonder if they're surprised by his callousness. I don't move. Let them see the truth. Let them know I'm not the adored daughter he makes me pretend to be.

"Azhara's had enough for one night," Mallen says quietly. "She could use rest."

My father blinks and then recovers, plastering on a smile. "Of course. You've had quite the ordeal. Come, dear girl—anything you need, just say the word."

He takes my hands like this is a fatherly gesture. We both know it's theater. I play along before excusing myself. As I slip away, my father and Mallen remain to speak—behind closed doors, where politics matter more than people.

I'm gone before the men notice I've stopped listening.

Before I can ruin my father's reputation, like I almost did the moment I was born. When the magic flared in me like a star exploding—blinding, beautiful, fatal. The gods bound it before it could destroy both the kingdom and its queen. But the ash of what burned stayed inside me, and its shadow never left. And neither did the bodies.

CHAPTER THREE

The palace guards escorting me to my rooms are as silent as specters, but I hear their relief when the door shuts behind me. They didn't speak a word the entire walk. They didn't need to. No one wants to witness a princess fall apart.

I don't cry. Not yet. I bite it back like poison on my tongue. I'm still swallowing it down when the servant girl enters—new, young, her voice trembling. It's the sound of her that shatters me. The way her auburn hair cascades over her shoulders.

She isn't Anya. She'll never be Anya.

And Anya is dead.

My heart claws for denial, insisting it's a mistake. But my head knows better. Starsfall is not a place that lets weakness survive, and Anya was never meant for this life. She was too naïve. Too easily manipulated. And I made her a target just by being close to her. My grief isn't clean—it curdles into guilt, bitter and thick, because she died for me. Because I was careless. And I should have known better.

Because my magic brings death, even when it is caged.

The girl introduces herself. Her name escapes me. She smiles as she offers a kind word; I return a glare so sharp it could draw blood. She stammers something about a bath and flees and I barely notice her go.

The magic inside me is rising again—hot and cold at once, pressing against my ribs. It ought to be dormant but it isn't. It's a darkness that doesn't belong here. It never did, because it came from somewhere far darker than even the depths of my father's ambitions.

My fingers trace the carvings on the table edge as I lean toward the ornate mirror and stare at the girl looking back at me. She's tired. So very tired. Her cheeks are hollowed, mouth pinched, as if every word she's swallowed has left a scar. There's a tremble in her hands she can't disguise, and her hazel eyes—once sharp, once shining—are now rimmed with exhaustion, dulled like glass buried too long in sand.

And somehow, I'm touching my lips. Absent. Thoughtless. Remembering the way his mouth met mine—how soft it was, and how hard it turned when I didn't pull away. The heat. The shock. The terrifying sweetness of being wanted.

Or maybe I kissed him. I can't remember quite how every kiss with him happened. Only that some of it was gentle. Some of it was not.

It was a reckoning. It was a mess.

A knock comes, followed by the servant's timid voice. "Your bath, Princess."

She leads me through the torchlit halls, chattering about herbs and salts and how everything's been drawn fresh for me. The guards flank us without comment. It is only three turns and one stair from my rooms, a short way that feels longer tonight. The unease sits too heavy for the simple ritual of a bath in the royal pools, and I know that even the warm waters of the royal pools cannot wash away the ruin of me.

We reach the bathhouse and the guards take their stations outside. Jailors, not protectors. Inside, the water steams like fog over glass. The scent of lavender and bitterwood curls through the air, earthy and calming. Light flickers across marble and shadow. The space is beautiful—ancient, serene, intimate—but I know none of its peace.

The servant girl helps me undress, her hands trembling. I lift my chin and unclasp the cloak myself, draping it over her arms. "I'll manage from here."

She opens her mouth, uncertain.

"Go," I say, gentler. "I need to be alone."

I keep the distance on purpose. Father plants eyes everywhere, and kindness can be mistaken for trust.

She bows and hesitates. "As you wish, Princess."

But she doesn't make it to the door before a low, unmistakable voice speaks. "I'll stay."

I turn—slowly—and there he is, framed in the archway like some carved sentinel from legend. Sword at his hip, and the night caught in the hollows of his face.

Mallen.

For a moment, I don't speak. The torches hiss. The steam curls between us.

"I didn't summon you."

He steps forward, his expression unreadable. "Your father insisted someone guard you after the attack from Moonsrise. I wasn't about to entrust that to the palace watch." He glances over his shoulder at the servant still frozen behind him. "Leave us."

Her gaze darts between us, unsure. But this time, she obeys.

Now it's only us.

Mallen closes the door behind her and remains there, upright and distant, as if chained by his own restraint. His presence pulls at me like gravity, though he keeps his distance as if one more step might shatter his control.

"He's insisting someone is with you at all times." He lets the latch click, the sound small in the steaming room. "Your father wants you watched carefully. Too closely for your liking."

"Mallen—"

"I won't look," he says, softly. "Not unless you want me to."

Only now do I realize how much my ribs ache. How much I needed to exhale. And how much I want to play with fire.

"You think I'm in danger?" I ask.

"Always."

"From you?"

His gaze lifts to meet mine, and his eyes are far too bright in the darkness. They glint, as if there's something wild beneath their emerald color. "If you choose it."

It's a cruel thing, the way my stomach flips at his voice. The way warmth pools where it shouldn't. Mallen is a man who's torn men's lives away. A king's blade in daylight, and a patient knife in the dark. But he's also the man who pressed me against him and kissed me like it might be the last thing he ever did.

And still.

Still, I want to know how much this means.

"I don't want a guard."

He doesn't move. "So bathe. I'll watch the wall instead."

My fingers play with the laces of my tunic as I hestitate. I've undressed before him a dozen times before. But it was never like this. Not with this weight between us. Not with the memory of his mouth still lingering on mine.

I turn slightly, keeping my back to him. My voice is steady now, clipped and cool. "You may stay. But if you look, I'll know."

There's the faintest sound—perhaps a breath, perhaps a laugh—but he says nothing.

I want to turn. More than anything I've ever known. He's only standing a few paces behind me, silent as a shadow, so I pretend the heat in my face is from the steam curling over the bath. This should be like any other evening. Routine. Unremarkable.

I step out of my sandals and trousers, curling my toes at the edge of the pool.

Think of the steps. *Just the steps.* Not the man behind you. Not the way my breath tangles in my chest. Just water. Just normal. Not the way I'm pulling at the knots in my hair as I let it fall over my shoulders like armor I never asked for.

When I finally glance back, Mallen's gaze is fixed on the torchlit stone—staring at the shimmer where the light hits the wall, as if the answer to every unspoken thought might rise from its surface if he watches long enough.

The water welcomes me, warm and calm. I pause at the waist, hands drifting to the tie at my hip, the last barrier between this strange new self and the man who's trying not to watch. I freeze, the water lapping softly at my hips. The tension pulling at me is like a drawn bowstring. Taut. Dangerous. A game I shouldn't be playing, but that makes it more exciting.

I take another step deeper into the heat.

And then I hear something else—his breath catching. Uneven.

A slow smile tugs at my lips. If this is what it feels like to be wanted, truly wanted, then I understand why people hunger for it. Why they chase it through fire. Why they surrender to its flames, offering their hearts as kindling.

I draw the knot loose and let the fabric slip from my shoulders. I turn to see it half-floating, half-submerged behind me. Entirely forgotten.

Mallen doesn't move. His chest rises and falls, heaving and controlled, like a man fighting a battle he refuses to lose. His hand curls at his sides, white-knuckled. His muscles tense, as if restraint hurts him.

"Maybe you should turn around," I mumble.

The water swallows me as I glide deeper and I close my eyes as heat seeps into my aching muscles. A moan slips from my lips. Not performative—just real. Honest. My fingers rub along my shoulder and neck, chasing away the tension, and for a heartbeat, I forget everything.

When I open my eyes again, he's gone.

Panic flutters in my throat. I'm alone, and Mallen said he wouldn't leave. Only now do I understand how much I need him. I turn, scanning the mist, and I'm disorientated when I find him standing at the edge of the pool—close now. Watching. Silent.

I inhale too sharply.

"Princess," he says.

"Mallen."

His arms fold across his chest, but not lazily, as though he's bracing against a storm only he's caught in. The motion makes his form more severe. Regal. Warrior-like. As if he's holding himself together through sheer force of will. There's nothing flirtatious in it. But his eyes—those piercing green eyes that trace the shape of me like a map he's memorized and can't stop revisiting—devour every inch of me with a reverence that makes me ache.

And this game—gods, this game—is a wicked kind of worship, a sacred tension drawn between us like a blade held at the throat of control.

"I told you. There's no escaping me."

His voice is rough, but the arrogance is tempered now, quieter. A truth, not a threat.

There's a difference between being looked at and being seen. And Mallen sees too much.

I square my shoulders and lift my chin, unwilling to flinch beneath the intensity of it. The corners of my lips curl into a grin I cannot hide as my fingers trace my collarbone. Mallen sees that too, and I realize he's also waiting. Not to win, but for me to want to play. This is invitation, not conquest. A challenge extended, not forced.

"A sponge," I say, extending a hand. "Unless you'd rather I ask one of your soldiers for help."

His lips press together. "We both know I'd kill them first."

There's no jest in his voice. But it's not possessive in the way that once made me hesitate. It's deeper than that. Protective. Instinctive.

He strides to a nearby table and returns with a sponge and a vial of oil. Instead of tossing them in, he crouches at the pool's edge and crooks his finger.

"Come here."

"I can wash myself."

"You can," he agrees. "But you don't want to."

He's right, and he knows it. I glare at him anyway.

I swim closer, slower than necessary, just to see the flicker of frustration in his jaw. He's still Mallen, after all. Still used to obedience. But he waits. His weight shifts a little, but he doesn't move. His shoulders tighten as his breathing quickens, and my heart races, desperately trying to keep pace with itself.

I duck under the surface and emerge just in front of him, water streaming down my face. When I wipe it away, his gaze rests on my lips. There's nothing soft in his eyes now—only heat and want and flame.

"A kiss," he says quietly, "for a sponge. Seems fair."

"You said you wanted to talk."

"I do. But you need this more. I need this more."

His voice dips, roughened at the edges, like it's been dragged over gravel. Not just with want—though that simmers in his gaze—but with something rawer. His eyes search mine, not demanding, but uncertain. Like he's offering something without knowing if I'll take it. Like he's asking for more than a kiss and doesn't know how to name it.

I hesitate.

"You don't want to?" he asks. But his tone is different this time—gentler, without demand. He watches me closely.

The game has changed. This is rawer. Harsher. Truer.

"It wasn't..." I glance away, humiliated. "Our kiss was...confusing."

He doesn't push. He waits.

That makes this worse. Harder.

"I've never..." My voice dies in the steam. "I didn't know what I was supposed to feel. Or do. And I did...feel something...and it was a lot, for a first kiss."

His brows lift, barely. Surprise flickers across his features and then something like regret.

"You've never—?"

I shake my head.

"Not even those smug little heirs who linger around the palace like vultures?"

"They saw a throne. Never me."

A shadow passes through his gaze. A growl coils beneath his breath. But he reins it in.

"I would have done it differently," he says after a pause. "If I'd known."

He reaches out, slowly, and I let him touch my cheek. His hand is warm and steady.

"I would have kissed you like this."

His fingers slide into my hair, cradling the back of my head. He doesn't pull me in—waits, close enough to breathe me in, his forehead nearly resting against mine. My heartbeat stutters. He could take. But he doesn't.

So I lean up and he meets me halfway.

His lips brush against mine, light as air, and I shiver. This time, I catch it. The soft press, the spark, the slow drag of his mouth as he moves in rhythm with mine. It's not urgent or overwhelming. It's like a dream I'm only now remembering, and when I open to him, trembling and willing, his tongue finds mine with aching gentleness, coaxing rather than claiming.

He finally draws back, and I can't breathe.

"Better?" he asks.

I nod, stunned. And then I lean in again, bolder now. This time, I kiss him.

I'm left panting. Wanting more. Needing more.

"Did I overwhelm you earlier?" Mallen asks.

I don't answer. I let the water swallow half my face instead, my gaze pinned to his, unblinking. He watches too closely. Too carefully. There's a hunger in his emerald eyes—not just desire, but the more dangerous kind. Possession masked as patience.

He smiles, slow and deliberate. "You're not used to being seen, are you?"

Heat creeps up my neck and over my cheek.

"Did you think I didn't see you, Princess?"

I've trained beside Mallen for years, fought against his blade, endured his bruises and taunts. I know the cut of his jaw and the swell of his muscle—not because I admired it, but because I learned how to break past it. Even so, he seems broader than I remembered now the candlelight catches on the breadth of his shoulders. Dark hair damp at his temples, a curl loosening in the steam. His gaze holds mine, steady, as if he has been practicing restraint his whole life. And now, under the flicker of the flame and the veil of steam, the lines blur. I can't tell if I'm watching him—or if I've been seen too clearly, and it's already too late to look away.

When I splash him, testing the weight of this new imbalance, he doesn't flinch. He just laughs. But it's not joy—it's calculation. A warning disguised as play. It says he will not be bait. If I want more, I will have to ask.

"Need help with your hair?" he asks, too casually.

What he means is: *Will you let me touch you? Will you give me that much?*

I want this game to continue, but I'm not ready to explore this. Not yet. Not in the way he wants. Not when the lens I view him through is shifting and I'm dazed by its changing colors.

I shake my head and reach for the bottle. He sets it in my hand at once and steps back to the edge of the room. The silence that follows is not still. It smolders between us, heat banked under iron, and I let it burn in me too. I comb the tangles from my hair while he keeps his watch.

"You should return to your chamber." Mallen turns his back, offering a moment's privacy.

I rise from the bath as if it's nothing.

As if I feel nothing. As if I don't want everything.

It's only as I dry myself that I remember my tunic is still adrift in the pool, waterlogged and silken where I abandoned it, the weight of it forgotten. I eye it and then glance at Mallen's turned back. There's no robe. No shift. No gown. The new attendant never brought them. So I wrap myself in the towel instead, clutching the corners with more dignity than grace.

"I'll walk back in this," I mutter.

Mallen turns and freezes. His mouth parts slightly, just enough to catch the breath as it stutters past his lips. His eyes turn to midnight, like he's seeing something precious left too close to danger, like a storm cloud sliding over the sun.

"No, you won't," he says, voice low.

He shrugs off his cloak without ceremony and drapes it over my shoulders with careful hands. It's warm, smelling faintly of smoke and steel, and far too large—swallowing me whole. Still, he adjusts the folds so they cover me fully, even tugging at the collar to shield my neck.

"You could have found something cleaner," I murmur, my tone caught somewhere between dry and grateful.

"It wouldn't be mine," he says, as though I've just given him everything he's waited for.

I don't quite know how to respond. To that. To him.

"You're not going anywhere in a towel, Azhara." His voice is low. A sound catches in his throat. "You're mine. Not because I own you, but because you're carved into me. Written in my bones. No one else sees that. No one else ever will."

The ferocity in his voice startles me. There's heat behind it, and command—and a tension that might break me open in the best, or maybe worst, way. My stomach flips, heat curling low and deep, and gods help me, I want to be claimed like that. I want to belong to something. To someone. Maybe even to Mallen.

Before I can think of what to say, he lifts me into his arms, gentle but firm.

"Mallen—"

"You're tired," he says. "And I don't want to argue."

His hold is careful, as if he's taking the weight of me. I rest my head against his shoulder despite myself. Neither of us speaks on the walk back. The silence is soothing. Nothing more needs to be said. There's peace here. Balance too. And I catch myself before I drift asleep in his arms, certain he'd never let me forget that my guard fell.

He sets me down at the edge of the bed and steps back immediately, putting distance between us that he doesn't seem to want but gives me anyway. He crosses to the windows and checks the bar, his gaze on the courtyard instead of me.

The girl rushes in and helps me dress for bed while Mallen looks away, her hands brisk. I sink into the sheets, exhaustion finally catching up with me.

"If you need me," Mallen says from across the room, "I'll be right here."

I open one eye and spot him dragging a blanket onto the small couch in the corner.

"You're not serious."

"Always," he replies, easing onto the cushions. "Especially about you."

"I don't need protecting."

"Your father said you're not to be alone. Not when you eat. Or sleep. Not even when you bathe. Always watched, always guarded."

He settles into a chair across from the bed and keeps his gaze on the ceiling, like one more word might be the drop that causes the dam to break. As if he'll say too much if he looks at me, and his collapse will lead to ruin.

"And I'll be damned if I let another man into your chambers."

I lie back down and pull the covers over my chest, staring up at the ceiling and asking the gods what I've done to deserve this. They don't reply, and all I hear is a sound dangerously close to a low laugh rolling off Mallen's chest as I shut my eyes and try to sleep.

CHAPTER FOUR

Evie adjusts my dress. A tug at the shoulder, a sweep at the waist. She adjusts the final fold of chiffon draped across me, her hands practiced, impersonal. The gown is pale gold, a soft shimmer that catches the firelight like bursts of starlight. The slit up my leg reveals just enough to keep the old men salivating. The fabric is too delicate for evening, too easily torn—a garment made for display, not battle—and the ornate belt that clinches my waist is more of a shackle than an accessory. My arms remain stiff, and I don't offer her so much as a glance.

I'm trying not to snap.

It's taken hours.

At least I know her name now.

My hair is braided, threaded with pearls. My skin perfumed. Lashes darkened. Gems pressed against my collarbones as if I'm some glass trinket made to glitter.

I watch the girl in the mirror with calculation.

She's pretty, I suppose. Too pale, too soft, too still. Her heart-shaped face makes her seem younger than she is, and her hazel eyes—my eyes—are wary even when they're lined with gold. This girl looks valuable. That's the point.

Because I don't get to choose what I wear. Or get to say no.

Not since I turned twelve.

Certainly not since my father found out about the failed escape that was officially an attack on Starsfall's ruling family. According to Mallen, Moonsrise nearly stole me. Slipped into my rooms, tried to whisk me from my bed. According to the palace guards, the attack was swift, brazen, and proof that our enemies will stop at nothing.

And now, those guards stand at every door. The palace wings are locked. Courtyards I used to walk through are now roped off as if the hemp could keep out armies. And Mallen. Always Mallen. He doesn't walk anymore, he stalks, like a creature who once lived in chains and is now set free to reap his revenge.

He hasn't left my side since the lie was planted.

And tonight, with the Reaping's opening reception just moments away, he's leaning against the door like he belongs there—arms folded, gaze heavy. He stares at me like I'm not just his charge, but his religion, his ruin, his one sacred obsession. Like he's daring anyone to come close enough to bleed.

Evie finishes with a flourish and smooths the fabric at my hip.

I resist the urge to move her hand away.

"Leave," Mallen says.

His voice is calm but firm, and Evie's hands freeze mid-motion. She glances at me and then at him.

There's no mistaking the tension in her posture. She dips into a shallow curtsy and withdraws without a word, but I catch the lift of her brow as she passes. A subtle flash of disapproval.

She shuts the door softly behind her.

I smirk, just barely, meeting Mallen's gaze through the mirror. "Still watching?"

"You look beautiful," he says.

I don't answer. My lips form a thin, unimpressed line.

He crosses the room in a few long strides, armor catching the candlelight, and slides his hands around my waist. The polished silver of his uniform gleams like moonlight, trimmed in forest green. It makes the emerald in his eyes burn darker, sharper.

"Like a perfect princess."

"Ready to be bled dry."

The taste of copper crawls up the back of my throat. For a moment, I imagine myself in the arena—barefoot, bloodied, free to die on my own terms.

The sand drinks me and lets me go. No vows. No throne. No hands shaping me into a myth I did not choose.

"They're going to die," I add, and my voice is dull, detached. Not mournful. Just true.

No one survives the Reaping. Not one man in its ten years.

I remember some making it past the first trial, but no one's ever made it to the third—the labyrinth. The maze beneath Threnos is a crypt. An ancient tomb woven with magic older than its walls, steeped in death. It isn't my father's design, but he added to it, made it impossible to survive. A fail-safe. No noble from Larksbind, no trader's son or wide-eyed soldier, will live long enough to claim me.

Mallen does not speak, but his jaw tightens. I know him well enough to read it. He will not let me be claimed by a man I do not want. He promised me that. Now that he has spoken his own wanting, he will not leave the choice to chance alone. If I say no, he will hold the doors. If I say yes, he will see every other claim fall away.

I stare at my reflection, fingers brushing the beads stitched into the silk. My magic simmers, uninvited, under my skin. It comes without invitation, cold under my ribs, like a room that waits on the night. It answers fear and anger and grief, but also wakes for no reason at all, a pressure behind my teeth that melts copper onto my tongue.

My magic is not a gift I can wield. It's not a gift at all. A blasphemy the gods sealed at my birth. They knotted it inside my bones, inside their bindings. I cannot cast or call it; only feel it pace the walls of me as it tests for a seam. It presses harder in the Reaping, as if the drums of Threnos thin the seal. It has taught me to live small and still, to swallow want before it wakes.

I was born cursed. Chosen. A vessel of death, a child of the dark.

My father would gild me in silk and gems, parade me through these halls like a prize horse, while the truth of me screams beneath the surface.

"I don't share, Azhara," Mallen says, voice low. "You shouldn't pity them."

I turn to him slowly and lie. "I don't."

Resentment coils tight—at all of it. The theater. The blood-soaked games. This torment masquerading as courtship.

The Reaping could have ended if I'd said yes. One word from me, and the drums would have stilled. Magic would be returned to Starsfall, and men from Larksbind wouldn't be forced into trials that my father ensures they cannot win. But I did not choose Mallen. I let silence answer for me. Time turned into a noose, and now men will die because I didn't speak.

Because possibility has a price.

Ten lives will be offered like coins—some foolish, some hopeful—and none are meant to survive. Larksbind stopped sending their best when it was clear that my father would not let them live. Perhaps this year, they'll find some men with hope left in that. That would be the harsher cruelty.

Mallen's armor looks ceremonial, but it isn't. Every piece is functional. Deadly. And he wears it like a second skin, like he's waiting for war.

"I know it's ugly," he says after a breath. "This thing in me that snarls at the thought of you with anyone else. But I've never pretended to be better than I am."

He raises his eyes to the heavens. There's no relief. For either of us.

"No other suitors," he says. "If one of them touches you—"

"I know," I interrupt, exhaling. "You'll kill them."

He's not being dramatic. Some of them forget themselves. They think being chosen means access, and they grab me. Hands at my elbow. Fingers at my waist.

"Mallen, they get excited—"

"They know the rules," he says, coldly. "My job is to keep you safe."

He steps back, heading for the door.

"Mallen."

My voice is sharper than I meant it to be, but it stops him. Instantly.

He glances over his shoulder.

"Allow them one mistake," I say, walking toward him. "Just one. You don't have to gut them for breathing near me."

His entire body stills.

He shakes his head, and the angles of his face sharpen.

I move past him slowly, dragging my hand across his breastplate as I go. My fingers catch the edge of the polished metal and linger there.

"I've watched this farce unfold for years," he says, voice tight. "You've suffered enough. They will not touch you without consequence." His gaze flickers, just briefly. "If they are suitably...repentant, I may grant mercy. But that decision is mine, Princess."

I don't push further. Instead, I nod, and he opens the door.

The corridor beyond is lined with banners, candelabras, and guards who stiffen at our presence.

This is the tenth time I've done this. The tenth Reaping. The tenth procession. The tenth evening that I've worn a gown like armor and walked these steps like a condemned woman to her own funeral.

I was ten the first time. Mallen had been almost fourteen—tall and gangly but already dangerous. I still carried the innocence of a child and hadn't understood then. It was only in the years that came after that I understood why Mallen had sat with me throughout every banquet. Why he'd stood between me and every man who came from Larksbind. Why he'd refused to leave me alone with them, standing guard while my father did not intervene.

Now I know.

As I know my hatred isn't only of the Reaping. Or even of its men. Nor is it because I know my father will whisper that I'm lucky to be loved, while their bodies are dragged past my feet.

It's the performance I hate most, pretending I don't know how this ends. A week of leading men to their deaths with grace and feigned laughter, while my magic presses like a scream behind my ribs.

"Princess?" His voice cuts through my thoughts.

I glance back as we descend the stairs. Mallen steps closer.

"You are stunning tonight."

The words are soft, reverent.

My palm settles against my stomach as I stop and inhale and ground myself in the rhythm of breath and blood.

The wind murmurs through the courtyard ahead. I think of running. I think of what it felt like, days ago, to almost be free.

Mallen places his hand against my back. It's too familiar. Too dangerous. Too right. It's not protocol. It's not allowed. But he does it anyway.

"I'm here, Azhara," he says, voice low. His breath brushes the edge of my ear as he leans closer. "This is the last time. I swear it."

He doesn't remind me of what I could have chosen. Doesn't mention peace or politics, or war. He doesn't say my magic could have cost less than it does now. His restraint says it all. His hand presses into my spine just slightly—not possessive, but anchoring. And despite everything, I breathe a little easier.

The doors open ahead. The music starts. The Reaping begins.

We face the palace's Grand Square, a lamplit basin of stone and water held within the palace walls. Balconies brim, banners lift, the fountain scatters torchlight into shards as the twilight colors dazzle. The cheers rise like a song, but I stand apart from it, untouched. Their joy moves around me but never through me—like a warmth I can no longer feel. Maybe it's because I know this ritual is built on blood and silence. A charade we all endure, because its truth would destroy us all.

Mallen and I descend the stone steps, pausing before the marble columns that flank the palace gates. Beyond them, the procession winds its way uphill. Ten cloaked figures, swathed in Larksbind blue, glide like wraiths through Starsfall's sunset streets. I watch them as I cross the threshold and take my place beside my father. One step behind him, as is expected. As required.

"You are late, Azhara."

His voice is mild, a velvet sheath. It cuts anyway. The court tilts to listen.

If I give him my maid took her time, he will break her. If I say it was my fault, he will find a way to make me pay for it later. So I find a third way. The one learned at his knee. The dance Mallen taught me the steps to: use praise as cover, silence as a blade, make the room your witness, and let him love his own reflection.

"Am I, Father?" I lift my chin and turn into the torchlight so the jewels do their work. "Perhaps the procession should wait for its prize to appear. You want me perfect."

Silk hushes. Goblets still. On my other side, Mallen sets his weight, a quiet shift that reads like a shield finding the ground. His jaw cuts hard, eyes on the king, and the smallest nod tells me that my father saw the move and will not challenge it.

"The next time, be here on time," my father says.

"Of course," I answer, smooth as poured wine. "The procession shall have what you want."

He turns away to let the crowd breathe again. Mallen does not touch me. His hand relaxes at his side, not quite to the hilt, not quite away. The moment passes like a knife sliding back into its sheath. Evie keeps her skin.

My pulse will not settle. The seam in the marble draws my attention and lets me count my breaths. My hands want to shake, and I refuse them. Mallen keeps his gaze forward, the line of his body quiet and ready, and still I feel the heat of his attention like a palm between my shoulders.

"Stop trembling," my father hisses.

"Azhara's unsteady after yesterday's ordeal," Mallen says, just loud enough to carry. "She won't faint tonight."

The court will believe any tremor in my hands belongs to the knife that nearly found my throat. They are always hungry for a story dipped in blood. Mallen knows better. He reads it in the way I cannot quite meet his gaze. This shaking is not fear. It is the aftershock of what just happened. And of his hands on my skin, the memory of his mouth, the echo of a promise that rooted too deep and has not stopped ringing.

"I didn't realize you were so upset, dear girl," my father says at last, his voice pitched to the lords. He takes my hand and pats it, playing the doting parent. "Always trying to be brave. Forgive me for not noticing your distress."

I manage a brittle smile and glance at Mallen, my throat tightening around words that can't quite escape it. Heat stirs low in my chest, unsteady and unexpected. Not just relief, not quite affection. Gratitude, edged and bright. He did not have to speak. He did.

His choice has kept me safe. Whatever we are now, it is already unraveling me, and still I want more, even if it burns past saving. So I stand beside him, wondering not just who I am, but who I could be. What version of myself might survive this Reaping.

Threnos plays its part well. Everyone knows my father loathes Larksbind. Every fiber of his being thrums with contempt for them. He wants us to think of them as hollow. Empty. Void. Most of Starsfall has fallen for my father's lies. But I know Larksbind is full. Full of everything this kingdom can't be trusted to hold.

So once a year, he's forced to smile for their emissaries as he extolls the virtues of peace. A performance the court is well-versed in applauding. An act the court sees as proof of my father's benevolence instead of duplicity. Wisdom, not malice. Redemption, not revenge.

But there is another performance few know is playing out. The one in which my father is a loving parent. A man who protects his only child. Who praises her, indulges her, adores her.

Only Mallen sees the cracks. Only he knows what festers beneath the golden crown.

My stomach coils with dread. I don't need to glance at Mallen to know his disquiet. He radiates it, a storm tethered only by discipline. My father, of course, assumes my discomfort is leftover fear. He prefers me brittle. Weak and malleable. Easier to control.

He turns and extends his hand.

The court sees a father offering reassurance. I see the grimace that flits across his face when our palms touch. Hear the disgust in the hiss of breath he swallows down. And I see him wipe his hand on his robes when he thinks no one is looking. Like touching me made him unclean.

I step forward, cast in my role, and smile through clenched teeth. I wave. I thank the gods and the people of both nations, and give the blessing that reminds us that while magic rolls like a storm in Starsfall, its winds die at Larksbind's borders. Then I descend to the midpoint of the palace steps and brace myself for the part I loathe most.

The tributes.

One by one, the men will step forward. One by one, they'll offer themselves for my hand, unaware they are sealing their own doom. None will survive. None meant to. Maybe they are aware of what awaits them. Perhaps that would be a mercy.

Mallen joins me, his presence a shadow at my shoulder. When the routine shifts subtly, his brow arches—a small, private warning. Follow the rule. Remember what we are. What we were in the woods and the water. Remember that I let him touch me. Kiss me.

That no one else may.

No one else may touch me.

The first man steps forward. He lowers his hood and bows. He's young. Far too young. A soldier, judging by his build. He murmurs his name and vows his fealty before retreating after I accept.

Four more follow. Two fishermen. A merchant. A smith. All older than the first, but still too young to die for a ceremony that means nothing.

Then comes the sixth.

He lifts my hand in both of his and presses a kiss to my knuckles, holding the contact too long.

I recoil instinctively.

And then, he is airborne.

Mallen has him by the throat, suspended in midair like a child's doll. The man kicks, gasps, and claws at invisible fingers, but it's hopeless. Mallen doesn't falter. Or forgive.

"Mallen," I whisper, barely audible.

"Don't. Touch. Her."

The words boom like a god's command. The courtyard stills. All eyes turn to the man holding death in his palm. Mallen's expression is unreadable, but the weight of his fury is unmistakable.

There is no chaos in him—only resolve.

He lowers the man with surgical precision and releases him with a final flick of power. The man stumbles, collapses, and then scrambles back to the others, his face pale with terror.

The remaining suitors hurry through their vows as I accept their offerings. One noble. Two soldiers. None dares to meet my eyes.

Then—the final man.

He kneels.

He does not remove his hood.

He's broader than the others. More assured. The set of his shoulders speaks of command, not submission. He speaks his prayer, recites the words, and then lifts his chin.

"Your answer, Princess?"

I stiffen. Protocol dictates that the suitor reveal himself first.

"Your hood," I say.

"Your answer," he repeats.

The voice is smooth. Confident. Mocking. And loud enough that Mallen hears what the rest do not.

Mallen moves. Quiet as snowfall, deadly as winter. His sword slides free, and the tip rests lightly—lovingly—at the man's throat.

He does not flinch.

"She will not ask again," Mallen murmurs. "Remove your hood. Or be removed."

Gasps ripple through the crowd. Rejecting a tribute would be tantamount to declaring war. No one has ever dared.

I don't look at the court. Or at my father. Only at the man who kneels before me, as he laughs. A slow, rich sound. Deep. Familiar.

"You are not the timid little mouse they say you are," he says.

Then he draws back the hood.

And I stop breathing.

His face is flawless. Beautiful in the way a blade is beautiful—honed, perfect, lethal. His lips curve in a lazy smile. Golden hair spills over his collar like silk. His eyes, when they meet mine, glint with knowledge.

He knows who I am.

He knows I'm already afraid.

"My offer, Princess?"

I take a step back. My hands shake.

I look at Mallen.

He is still. A pillar of calm. But I know that stillness. It is the quiet of an ocean before it drowns a city. The hush before a sword sings, before ruin breaks loose from its leash.

He is beyond fury.

And the smile on the stranger's lips deepens—as if he's been waiting all this time for me to notice him.

"Larksbind sent their prince?" I whisper.

CHAPTER FIVE

Mallen's hand brushes the small of my back as he guides me through the palace gates. It's a fleeting touch. Nothing the nobles clustered along the marble colonnade could mark as improper. But it's different from before. Protective, yes. But bristling too. Charged. He squares his body behind mine as we pass beneath the arched doorway, as if what happened might harm me.

And I don't know if what's burning is his touch or what happened with the prince from Larksbind. Darian.

I keep my head high, my spine regal, my steps measured and slow because Starsfall's heir must not let the terror. Or the nervous excitement either.

Inside, the cool hush of shadowed stone closes around us. But my pulse doesn't slow.

The heat of the night still clings to my skin—phantom flames brushing my calves, the echo of Darian's voice, as smooth as the gold of my dress, still curling in my ears. I try to push it aside, to silence it with the steady rhythm of my steps and the press of mosaic tiles beneath my heels.

But the memory lingers.

So does Mallen.

We walk in silence for three full corridors. A hush pools in the space between us, broken only by the distant flutter of banners in the upper halls and the murmurs of servants scurrying to prepare the reception chamber.

"What is Larksbind doing?" I murmur, low enough that only he can hear. "They sent Darian to face the Reaping. Their heir. He'll die. Unless they know something we don't."

Mallen doesn't answer at first. The tension in his posture tightens, the corded muscle in his forearm flexing beneath his bracer.

"I don't like guessing games," he says at last.

"That wasn't a guess." I glance sideways at him, keeping my tone mild. "It was a question. You usually enjoy those."

He exhales—sharply, but not with frustration. With control. Every movement Mallen makes is carefully banked, like a fire trained to flicker instead of roar.

"I don't know him personally," he says. "But his reputation precedes him. Cunning and polished. The kind who shakes your hand to count your rings, and only smiles when he is already winning."

"You don't like him."

This time, the flicker is sharper. Keener. Fiercer. "I don't know him. I know his type."

We round the final turn before the great hall. A long stained-glass window casts its fractured light across the corridor, splashing shards of gold and crimson across Mallen's armor. It softens him. Makes him look almost ethereal.

I stop beneath the window. Not because I need to. But because I want to see his face.

"You mean charming?" I press, just enough to test.

Just enough to feel the edge of what he's holding back. He doesn't smile. Not even a twitch. Only those eyes, dark and steady emeralds, glint, watching me like I'm something he's sworn to protect and been ordered not to touch.

"I mean gilded," he says. "He's forged for others to admire—not for truth."

A pause.

"He's been raised to make princesses fall," he adds, so low it would be easy to miss it.

My pulse skitters. The window overhead gleams a little too brightly.

"I'm not the falling type," I say, pivoting toward the open doors ahead.

"Good." His voice is rougher now, not angry—just raw, like its tone keeps him in check. "Though you are the hunted kind. For now."

I stop. He steps closer, close enough that I feel the heat of him at my back. His next words are quiet and measured.

"You cannot lower your guard, Princess. Especially with him. Keep your truth close and your lies closer, no matter the cost." His breath stirs the back of my neck. "Even if it tangles the court or causes friction with Moonsrise. You must keep that lie steady. You were afraid. They tried to take you. I stopped them and brought you back. Let it sound like a confession, not a defense. He needs to believe that."

I turn back. "Of course."

Mallen exhales, a little too loudly.

He doesn't follow at once. The space behind me stretches, as if Mallen's choosing whether to follow or fight. He shadows me instead, and his course is charted.

Inside, the reception chamber swells with sound and silk.

Candles float in golden rings above the vaulted ceiling, their light gilding the room in soft gold. Marble columns rise like frozen waterfalls along the perimeter, draped in seasonal greenery—late-autumn vines twined with burnished silver. Courtiers drift between tables laden with wine and honeyed fruit, their laughter brittle and rehearsed.

And every eye turns to me.

A ripple of silence chases me around the room. I see it in the sudden pause of a goblet mid-air, in the quick draw of fans, the collective sharpening of posture. I feel it settle over me like a second cloak. Every hall receives me like this, alone at the center of attention, a figure to be named before it's heard.

Azhara of Starsfall. Heiress to the throne. Nightborn. Unwed.

They're wondering if I'll be won this year. If I'll kneel for Larksbind, or if I'll release Starsfall's sorcery. But the Reaping will only bend to us if I choose a man for love, and my heart has not chosen.

They watch as I move forward slowly. My gown's gold and chiffon whisper as I move, offering hints of secrets that fall from the braided filigree at my waist. The jewels adorn my neck, catching the light like stardust. My braid falls to my shoulder, decorated with star-flung pins. And the slit in the skirt parts with every step, baring one leg to thigh. Enough to entice. Not enough to scandalize.

Every inch of me has been designed to make them doubt. To make them want. To make them fall.

There's power in performance.

That is what my father wants. What he wields.

And tonight he wants me to be an instrument of destruction. A beautiful weapon that the men from Larksbind will willingly impale themselves on while thanking him for letting them bleed.

I make it almost halfway through the chamber before I see him.

Darian.

The Prince of Larksbind stands at the far end of the hall, surrounded by foreign dignitaries and a flutter of pale-robed diplomats. He wears no crown, but he doesn't need one. His presence is a royal decree. He laughs with easy grace, and gestures with subtle elegance. The kind of manner that feels rehearsed but not hollow. Poised but not posed. Charming enough to cover any viciousness.

He sees me the moment I see him.

And parts the crowd like silk.

He moves without urgency but with the quiet force of someone who's always known people will move for him.

He bows when he reaches me—fluid, flawless, precise.

"Starsfall's beauty lives up to its name," he says, voice pitched low and warm, for my ears alone. "Though I find myself most dazzled by its heir."

It's the kind of line that should sound trite. But somehow it doesn't. Not from him. Not with that mouth, curved in soft amusement. Not with that voice, as smooth as water over stone.

I lift one brow. "Careful, Prince. I bite."

"Then I'll bleed gladly," he murmurs, straightening.

He gestures. A servant steps forward with a velvet tray bearing three offerings.

The first is a hairpin—moonstone carved into a single falling star, set in filigree silver so fine I can't see the seams. He lifts it delicately, holding it like something sacred.

"To light your path in darkness," he says.

I accept it with a nod, brushing his fingers by accident. Warm. Uncalloused. The hands of a man who's never held steel long enough to earn the scars.

The second is a book—slim and leather-bound, glinting with silver thread. The title gleams in old Larksbind glyphs, but they are easy to recognize: love poems, written for kings and queens who ruled by star and fire and devotion turned to ruin.

"I had it translated," he says with a sly smile. "Though some words are best in their original tongue."

This gift is clever, too clever—designed to charm, not unsettle. I set it aside.

The third gift is a pendant.

At first glance, it looks like glass. Fragile. Pure. But when he places it in my palm, the weight catches me off guard. It drags against my skin like a chain—cool and solid, with a coldness that sinks deeper than it should.

"Delicate," he says, "but unbreakable. Like you, I suspect."

Unbreakable.

But I feel like crystal. Both a brittle and transparent thing, made to gleam under candlelight and be admired from a distance. Something already fractured—hairline cracks hidden beneath polish and poise, waiting for the blow that will finish the shatter.

I don't speak. Or move.

The pendant lies in my hand like a truth I didn't ask for.

Around us, laughter rises, soft music unfurls from the dais, and the court resumes its dance. Silk sleeves brush jeweled wrists. Perfumed air swells with false joy. But I remain very still and keep my smile steady. My fingers close over the chain, and I tuck the pendant into my palm, concealing it from view.

"You presume a great deal," I say.

"I observe," he replies. "Observation is a skill in Larksbind. One could call it...an art."

A flash of heat rises as my gaze meets his, and I stare into irises the color of summer skies reflected on still water—eyes that are stunning, and too serene to trust. Then his attention slips to the line of my throat and stays, the calm stretched too tight, and a want flickers as he tracks my pulse.

I'm not flattered. Not entirely.

He's too bold. Too poised. Too...certain.

And yet.

And yet.

The pendant bites where my grip hardens.

It's a relief to be chased so openly. To be seen, not as a dangerous or fragile or sacred thing, but as something desirable. Not as a relic to protect or a queen to shape—but as a girl. A woman.

There's power in that.

And danger.

The flicker in my pulse begs me to test the lines of both. Want is easy. But this? This feels like recognition—as if he's named the part of me no one else sees.

I tilt my head. He mirrors me.

"Thank you. Your gifts are...exquisite."

His smile deepens. "They're not gifts. They're intentions."

Warmth pools low in my chest, and I swallow it.

With a regal nod, I turn. But the pendant remains heavy in my hand. I pass it to an attendant with careful composure, though I feel Darian's gaze burning at my back—silent, deliberate. Like a man who's set a game in motion and trusts the board will rearrange itself in his favor.

I step toward the northern dais where Starsfall's council sits like carved obsidian and pearl. Candlelight flutters across their faces. The High Chamberlain raises a thin goblet in greeting, his ivory-and-purple robes echo the heraldic banners behind him—symbols of courage, honor, sacrifice. Of everything my father's kingdom claims to be.

A group of tributes—blue cloaked—wait below.

The pause seems too long. To refuse them would be weakness. To ignore them, cruelty. But to speak...that would be playing the part assigned to me. Tonight, I wear the mask beautifully.

A tall, ash-blond youth bows stiffly, and another smiles too easily, as though he expects to fail anyway. I offer polite nods, ask trivial questions: their quarters, their training. The words taste bitter on my tongue. Their eyes give nothing—no awe, no despair. Just quiet confidence mingled with complacency, as if they already know the outcome.

The crowd's hum swells. My name flickers through the air. Fans flutter; eyes sharpen. The room tightens, thickens.

Then, a light graze on my sleeve. Deliberate.

"I hoped," Darian murmurs, his voice pitched just below hearing, "that I might steal a moment."

The pause hits too hard.

"Very well," I say, careful to keep my voice aloof. "A moment."

Darian draws me to the edge of the chamber.

A quiet recess, lit only by the spill of amber scones and the low draft from the service tunnels that thread beneath the royal kitchens, still warm with the scent of spice and smoke.

He waits until the servants have finished fetching refreshments, their trays clinking faintly as they disappear back into the passageways, leaving behind only the echo of silver and the scent of sugared citrus.

"I had hoped for a...private audience?"

I arch an eyebrow.

"You're very good at this," he says softly, no longer smiling. "The performance. The stillness. The way your silence says more than most speeches."

My silence gives nothing away.

He angles his head. "You wear your role like a veil. Almost translucent. Almost impenetrable."

"What did you expect of Starsfall's heir?"

"That's not all you are," he murmurs, stepping closer. "You're enjoying this."

I glance at him. "What is it you think you're seeing?"

He doesn't answer.

Instead, he lifts a hand—slow, deliberate—and brushes a stray strand of hair from my shoulder. Not possessive. Not tender. Just...curious. Like he's mapping a puzzle. Feeling for a weakness in the grain.

"Some women want to shine like stars," he says slowly, "but I think you want to be the lightning that splits the skies."

The silence that follows is not awkward—it's charged. Measured. A held breath.

"We should rejoin the reception," I say, barely above a whisper.

But my heart stutters behind my ribs, and magic hums beneath my skin—like smoke curling toward flame. I don't know if it's warning or want.

"I will," he says. "If that's your choice."

There's no challenge in it. Just quiet deference. And that makes it worse.

His expression shifts—not smug, not victorious. Recognition, maybe. Or restraint sharpened into reverence. And those eyes—those bright blue eyes—

dazzle with a flicker of something half-wild, half-knowing, like they're frost catching fire and realizing they want to burn.

"We are alike, Princess. Born to a purpose we did not choose. I know that loneliness. I see you."

Then he bows—not courtly, but intimate, deliberate. Like an offering. A secret folded in the palm.

Without another word, he turns toward the golden light of the reception hall—toward the jeweled laughter and the women who wear their interest like perfume. He moves like someone used to being watched, but never truly seen.

I press my back into the alcove for a few breaths more, letting the cold wall ground me. Listening. Thinking. Burning.

By the time I return to the reception, the music has changed. Darker now, slower. A waltz meant for intrigue. The nobles are drifting to the floor in pairs and trios, all satin and suggestion.

And that's when I see Mallen.

He is not at my side.

He stands near one of the pillars at the chamber's edge, half-shadowed by the spill of a jade banner. His arms are crossed, his face carved in stillness. But his eyes are locked on me as I return to the lonely center of the room.

For a moment, the world quiets.

The music slips away like the memory of summer when it's winter. The heat settles low in my chest, and a slow, delicious ache pressing between my ribs. And the slow, silver smile Darian left behind fades, like a ghost settling on my skin.

All I feel is Mallen's gaze. Its heat. Its weight. It's a quiet storm sweeping me away as if I were fallen leaves. This is a maelstrom contained, the calm before the winter's tide carries the shore out to sea. It's not angry, not jealous.

Worse.

It's resigned.

He looks like a man bracing for war, knowing he will not stop it.

My feet take me toward him before reason arrives. Perhaps it's because I want to explain. Or because to be seen differently. Or maybe it's to catch that look again, the one he has worn these past days, as if I mattered more than the orders that bind him.

He watches me approach.

But he doesn't move.

"Were you going to vanish into the walls?" I ask, tone light. Too light. "Or just glare like an old ghost?"

Mallen's voice is low. Rough. "I did not neglect my watch. You didn't need me."

"Don't say that," I say, and it comes out small. "That's not true."

"You walked with him," he says, eyes unreadable. "You let him touch you. Gave him your attention. Your silence. And I've guarded enough nobles to know when they've been dazzled by trinkets."

"You think I can be bought with poems and sparkly things?" I ask, as steadily as I can. "You think I wanted a prince in the Reaping?"

"I think," he cuts in quietly, "you stopped looking for me when you saw something prettier."

That lands. Not because it's true, but because he believes it. And somehow, that is worse.

"I didn't stop looking," I say, voice tight. "You stopped standing where I could see you."

A long breath passes between us.

Then he bows—sharp, fast, too formal.

Not a dismissal. A retreat.

And as he goes, something in me strains toward him, like a thread pulled tight but not yet cut.

CHAPTER SIX

I TOY WITH A SCALLOP ON MY PLATE, BARELY TASTING THE FOOD.

The feast was well underway by the time I'd taken my seat, and now the scent of roasted meats and spiced wine lingers. Music drifts from the dais, dancers swaying in flickers of gold. My shoulders ache beneath the weight of jewelry and expectation. My father is currently conversing with some of the nobles and basking in their regard. When his gaze brushes me, I smooth my face. He saw Darian, and he will count it as a success if I look the part.

The two men who sit beside me have haunted my thoughts for most of the night—and neither of them seems interested in food.

To my right, Darian lounges with the easy arrogance of someone born into power and used to charm doing half his work. His attention lingers on me like a brand, unapologetic and bold. To my left, Mallen is still—a tightly coiled spring—and the tension in his jaw could cleave stone.

The Reaping has begun.

I press my fingers to the stem of my goblet, ignoring the delicate fare in front of me. There's a coil tightening in my stomach that makes it impossible to eat. Harp strings and jewel-toned candlelight can't mask the tension.

"Still not hungry?" Darian asks, his voice pitched low enough that only I hear. There's a smile in it, a private joke I don't understand. "I thought you might have worked up an appetite admiring your gifts."

"I thought they weren't gifts," I sigh. "And I prefer not to eat when I'm being watched."

My gaze slips sideways to meet his.

He grins, unabashed. "You'll get used to my attention."

A muscle ticks in Mallen's cheek.

Darian lifts his goblet and takes a sip, unconcerned. "The Commander doesn't seem to be enjoying my company."

"I wonder why," I say, and this time, it's me who smiles.

Mallen doesn't speak, but his silence is anything but passive. There's a kind of storm to it—contained only by discipline. One elbow rests on the table, the other arm slung behind me, hand braced against the back of my chair. A casual pose, but I know him well enough to feel the promise of violence underneath it.

"I've already explained the seating arrangements to the Prince," he says coldly, addressing no one and both of us at once. "I don't enjoy repeating myself."

"It's almost charming," Darian replies, undeterred. "The way you pretend this is still your decision."

My breath catches, and Mallen's eyes sharpen to ice.

"Mallen," I warn quietly.

The hand behind me doesn't move, but I feel it—like a sharpened blade waiting for instruction. Not touching me—yet. A line of heat against my back that says he's barely holding on.

Darian smiles like he hasn't just taunted a viper. "Relax, Commander. I'm here to win hearts, not start fights. Though if it comes to that…" He lets the words hang, one brow arched as he tips his glass in mock salute. "I don't mind a bit of sport."

"I don't think you understand who you're playing with," Mallen says softly.

He doesn't raise his voice.

He doesn't need to.

Even Darian pauses for a heartbeat.

I draw in a stuttered breath and force my attention forward, toward the dancers and the display of opulence unfolding around us. Sashes move like swallows caught mid-flight, the fabric cascading in jewel-toned ribbons—amber, emerald, wine-dark velvet. They flutter and dip, gliding wherever the music takes them, unbound. I envy that. My limbs stay heavy, carved from stone, while theirs fly free.

The current pulls beneath my skin.

And gods help me, part of me wants the storm.

These men couldn't be more different.

Darian—bold and beautiful, unfiltered, gleaming with the confidence of a man who's never heard the word no. Mallen is cold fire wrapped in duty and control. There's a dark storm contained beneath his skin and a fury that he keeps leashed for me. Where Darian dazzles, Mallen unsettles. Where Darian leads by charm, Mallen commands with gravity. Now, there's no pretending that they aren't circling each other. Or that I'm not the center of the storm.

I reach for a piece of seared fish and force myself to take a bite. It tastes of nothing. The musicians change tempo, and the next course is brought on silver trays. Conversation hums around us—nobles laughing, ladies flirting, courtiers whispering—but our table is a battlefield wreathed in candlelight and good manners.

And then my father leans forward in his chair and flicks two fingers, beckoning Mallen with the kind of imperious gesture that draws no attention but demands obedience. The kind that says he expects to be obeyed.

The kind that comes with consequences if he's disappointed.

Mallen rises, jaw locked, and for a moment—just a moment—his eyes linger on Darian with the quiet intensity of a man memorizing a fault line. Then he steps away from the table with deliberate calm, his sword hanging at his side like a threat left unfinished.

"The Commander of the Royal Guards is a little overbearing, don't you think?"

I glance at Darian. He's draped in the chair like this is a lovers' quarrel and not a political war.

"He's protective," I say. "And rarely wrong."

"I wonder if that makes two of you," Darian murmurs, and his smile turns strange—softer than I expect.

I'm more off balance than ever. I glance at Mallen, looking for reassurance. He's too busy talking to my father. So I speak and let the lie come easily—we've woven its threads with just enough truth to make it gleam. The story unspools. The woods and the thieves. The kidnapping. The too-quiet shadow from Moonrise.

Darian listens with one brow raised, half-amused, half-intrigued.

Everything I say is a deception. Lies, polished and practiced, thread through truth so seamlessly they cannot be untangled.

Darian's hand brushes mine—barely a touch. I freeze but let it linger. His voice drops. "You should have told me sooner."

"Why?"

His fingers glide around the rim of his goblet. "Because I could have helped."

"It's a bit late to stop—"

"I meant tonight, Princess."

There's a flicker of something different in his voice now. A gentler note, almost rueful.

"Between the pageant and the politics, I haven't made it easier for you."

His voice is quiet now, no trace of mockery.

I don't answer. Just breathe in and out. The candlelight flickers. The dancers pirouette in their jeweled blur. And for a moment—we're no longer sparring. We're just tired.

But somewhere behind the smiles and performance, we've stopped playing at opposition. The lines between ally, adversary, and suitor blur with every flicker of his lashes.

Then Mallen returns.

The heat of him reaches me before I see him—the shift in air, the way the tension in my spine draws tight as a bowstring. His palm finds the curve of my back, steady and warm through the chiffon, and I turn toward him. A quiet check, a question without words.

"Are you all right?"

His voice is low, too low for anyone but me. It curls under my skin like a promise, and I nod. The glance we share is brief, but it roots me more than any reassurance could. His eyes are darker than they were when he left—still storm-lit, but quieter now. Focused.

"I told Darian about the attempt a few days ago," I say, keeping my voice level.

Mallen's gaze shifts past me toward Darian.

He wears his restraint like armor, and our lie is his weapon. "This stays between us. For her safety."

A command concealed in velvet.

Darian raises both brows, unoffended. "Naturally. I had no idea she was in danger, or I never would have been so frivolous. I only want to help."

He even leans slightly closer, and now I'm bracketed between them again—heat and shadow, crown and blade. Darian's voice lowers, threading through the air between us.

"If you need anything, Princess, you only have to ask."

The next course arrives in a swirl of citrus and roasted herbs. I manage a few more bites, more out of duty than desire. My stomach knots too tightly to enjoy anything, but I chew, swallow, pretend. Around us, celebration spins—laughter, glass, the clamor of pageantry. Women gaze at Darian like he's divine. The tributes from Larksbind shine with wine and emptiness.

Mallen and I hold steady—quiet islands in a sea of revelry.

And Darian watches us both, calculating.

"This year will be different," he says suddenly. His tone is too light. "You'll gain a husband. And you'll come with me to Larksbind. You'll be safe." He lets his gaze skim me, from crown to collarbone. "It's a beautiful kingdom, you know. Almost as beautiful as you."

I arch an eyebrow. "That's a bold comparison."

"I won't apologize." He smiles. "You deserve boldness."

"It hasn't happened in nine years, Darian."

He laughs, quiet and rich, like the Reaping is a game he's already won. "I wasn't here then."

Before I can answer, he rises—graceful, princely—and drifts to my father's side. They speak in hushes meant to exclude. I don't try to listen, and focus on my breath, on the faint tremor in my hands. On trying to understand why Darian left so abruptly.

Mallen hasn't moved. But I feel him. His stillness, like the weight before a blade falls.

When Darian returns, his emotions are concealed behind a mask he wears well. I wonder what he bartered in that hush: a favor, a rumor, my standing. If my father thinks I misstepped, his disappointment will sharpen into anger. Or is this a move, and I am the piece Darian's playing with?

"Your father agreed you should leave early," Darian says when he returns. "I offered the apology. He offered the solution. Mallen will take you back."

The words don't land right away. I blink, slow, processing.

Another decision made without me.

Another man who's chosen for me.

But I'm not a pawn to be ushered offstage.

A sharpness unfurls beneath my ribs—not gratitude, not deference. Resolve.

I want more. Gods, I deserve more.

"I see," I murmur, and my gaze slides to Mallen.

He doesn't speak. Doesn't urge or direct. He simply rises, gaze on mine, waiting.

Not commanding. Waiting.

I rise—not for them. For the air. For the space to breathe again. To be away from the shift of fabric, the hush of movement around us. The scent of smoke and fruit and wine that never appealed. I step away from the table, and Mallen follows without a word.

Before I go, I turn back.

"Thank you, Darian," I say, and my voice is clear. "For your concern."

His gaze flickers. Just briefly. "Of course."

I don't look back again.

Not until the crowd fades does my breath return. Mallen beside me—no longer a shadow, but an anchor.

We walk in silence, but it's not empty. Not cold.

He doesn't ask what I'm thinking. He already knows.

It's only when we reach my bedroom that he asks the question that's been torturing him all evening.

"Do you like him?"

Mallen's voice is low. Unbothered. The kind of calm that tried to pretend he already knew the answer—and just wanted to hear it from me.

"No."

He steps in, slow and deliberate, until the wall is at my back and he's close enough that I forget how to breathe.

"Then why," he murmurs, lips brushing my cheek, "did it look like you were fawning over him?"

I swallow hard. His hands don't force, they frame. His body is all restraint.

"I was stopping you from starting a war," I say.

His jaw tightens. But he doesn't pull away.

"I thought you trusted me," I add, softer now. "You said you'd give me time."

His eyes are as dark as a forest covered by a midnight shroud. I reach up, my palm resting lightly against his chest. Not to push him away—just to feel his heart stuttering under my touch.

“I need you to keep trusting me,” I whisper. “Even when it’s not easy. Especially then.”

He searches my face, like he’s searching for something to believe in.

“I can’t do this,” he says quietly, “if you don’t let me in.”

“I am. But it has to be when I’m ready.”

And I kiss him.

It’s not impulsive. It’s not delicate.

It’s slow and deliberate, and it’s mine.

My choice.

He doesn’t move for a breathless second, as if he’s stunned I crossed the line first. Then his hand cups the back of my neck. He kisses me back with the quiet devastation of a man who’s waited too long and wanted too much—but still holds himself back, just enough, as if he fears breaking what is sacred.

When we part, I keep my forehead against his, our breaths shared in the silence between us.

His hand slides down to my waist. He doesn’t pull me closer, but he doesn’t let go.

We stay like that for a long moment. The void between us is laden with everything we’ve said and everything we haven’t.

“I’ll be yours,” I say, barely louder than a breath. “But only if you believe I still get to be mine, too.”

He breathes out, almost a laugh, and kisses my neck. It’s a promise, not a claim. There’s no anger in it. No heat. Only patience at its limit as the waiting between us begs to break.

CHAPTER SEVEN

Mallen moves with precision, and I hit the ground again, hard.

We chose a lesser courtyard off the inner colonnade, stone underfoot, and clipped yew along the walls. He sent the other guards away. The archways stay vacant. All that remains are our footsteps, the scrape of steel, and the morning wind.

He doesn't hold back this morning. Not after last night.

This is not the man who cradled my face like it was some fragile sunburst of dawn, trembling beneath the first light. This is the soldier who would see me strong or not see me at all.

"Focus," he says, low and sharp, as he offers his hand.

My fingers tremble a little as they slide into his. Pride has no place between us now. Not when I know what he's trying to teach me.

"I'm sorry," I say.

He doesn't answer. He doesn't need to. In war, apology is useless. He's taught me that—over and over and over—and I haven't forgotten the lesson.

"No." His voice cuts like steel. "You're off balance."

I adjust. Too late.

He surges forward, spins behind me, and raps the back of my head with the flat of his blade. Not hard—but enough to sting. He doesn't finish the move. Doesn't drop me again.

It's not mercy. It's disappointment. And it lands harder than any blow.

"What's gotten into you?" he asks, stepping in close. He doesn't shout. He doesn't have to. The way he looks at me—measured and cold—says everything.

I swallow the heat rising to my face and look away.

"You're hesitating. You're thinking like someone who wants to be liked, not someone who wants to survive."

A pause.

"In a fight, doubt will put a blade through your throat. Or worse—someone else's."

I nod once, sharp. I understand. I do.

We begin again. I strike hard this time, but he turns the blade aside and catches me by the throat lightly—just enough to halt the movement. To end it.

My feet drag across the stone as I walk away. Blood taints my mouth—maybe I bit my tongue—and my pulse hammers with frustration. His fingers curl just tight enough to still me, to force the truth into my lungs.

I am not fast enough. Not sharp enough.

Yet.

"She needs more instruction."

The voice slithers in from behind. We both jerk toward Darian, startled by his interruption.

He's standing against a column as if he's always been there, lazy and amused, surrounded by the other men from Larksbind who lounge behind him like bored wolves. He stares straight at me, bites into an apple, and speaks like he's announcing the weather.

"She'll never learn to defend herself like that. You're training her like she's already a fighter. She's not."

Mallen doesn't move. His entire body shifts, but only inside. I feel my own spine go rigid for entirely different reasons: Larksbind's prince thinks I'm incapable.

Mallen steps forward, frowning. "And you just happened to be strolling through the gardens?"

My fists curl. My face burns—not from shame, but fury. They're talking over me, about me, as if I'm not standing here with a sword in my hand. As if I am nothing more than a girl who is here to smile and bow and do no more.

Darian flashes a grin. "I'll show her."

Mallen scoffs. "Be my guest."

He steps behind me, close enough that his breath grazes my neck. He slides the lighter sword into my hand, turning the hilt just enough for the edge to catch the light.

"He thinks you're weak," Mallen murmurs. "Make him regret that."

His hand adjusts the clasp at my shoulder. A soldier's ritual, not a lover's. Then he looks at me—really looks—and it's not affection that sharpens his gaze. It's expectation. Permission. A quiet command.

Don't hesitate. End it clean.

The small courtyard echoes with laughter as the men from Larksbind strut closer, cocksure and clinking with weapons. Darian selects a weapon and coughs—faintly performative, clearly impatient. He lets the blade catch the light in a lazy flourish, tipping a smile toward his men that says watch and learn.

"Try to keep your feet this time, Princess."

I say nothing.

He points to my back foot. "Too much weight on it."

There isn't.

"Maybe turn your blade. These are blunted, but you'll still cut yourself holding one like that."

I don't move.

His smirk deepens. My silence must read as nerves. Let it.

He lunges.

I barely move, my blade catching his side with the lightest touch. A warning.

The laughter stops.

He spins—faster this time—but I'm already ducking, slipping beneath his reach, striking low. My sword grazes his thigh.

His blade whistles through the air as we turn to face each other. The clash of metal rings out as I parry, twist, and shove—hard enough to disarm him.

His sword hits the stone with a sharp clang. No one speaks.

The silence isn't just surprise. It's appraisal. Measurement. I feel it in the stares that scorch my skin as they rake over my body, and in the way Mallen hasn't moved a muscle behind me.

He's letting them watch. Letting them *see* me.

"Not a beginner," I say, quiet and cool.

Darian retrieves his weapon. This time, he bows. He takes a stance and then it shifts—not in fear, but wariness. His weight settles differently now. He knows what I did. We both do. And so do the other men.

The part of him that wanted to impress his companions begins to vanish, replaced by something colder, more calculating.

Good. I want him angry. I want him to make that error.

"My mistake. It won't happen again."

We circle. This time, no mockery. No corrections. His stance changes again, his weight centered. Serious now.

I feint left. He sees it. Doesn't fall for it. Smart.

"Not merely proficient either," he murmurs.

I smile, just a little.

We move.

Blades flash. The sound of steel striking steel grows louder, drawing attention. Courtiers drift in, whispers rising. Nobles watch from archways, stunned.

We don't stop.

Our swords crash together again, louder this time, the force rattling up through my wrists. He shifts his grip and counters—slick, practiced, fast. A downward arc that slices toward my ribs. I twist, barely dodging it.

Pain flares in my side where his dulled blade bruises skin through my tunic. I don't flinch.

He wants me to hurt. Fine. So long as he hurts more.

Darian presses forward, and I start to notice it—the fatigue, the slowness in my limbs. For a moment, I can't tell if I'm driving this or just surviving it.

Am I keeping up? Or is he holding back?

He's good—agile, ruthless—but I'm faster. Smaller. Sharper. He tries to use his size, and I use the terrain. Let him chase me up the steps, into narrow spaces where his strength means less. He follows and then he drives me back, out of the small courtyard and into the bigger, more imposing main square outside the palace.

I don't care if the whole court watches.

I step back, defending every move I make.

My muscles burn.

Pain is a language I've learned well and speak fluently.

Darian's good, and that isn't a surprise. I won with cheap strikes earlier, and now I have to work. He drives me further back, and I let him. Then I pivot, land a glancing blow on his shoulder, and retreat again before he can trap me.

Our swords lock mid-swing. He bears down, sweat shining on his brow. I hold fast, knees braced, arms screaming. For a second, we're eye to eye.

"Not bad," he mutters.

"Not finished," I growl.

I shove him off, pivot, and drive him back three paces before he recovers.

This is not a game anymore. I aim to hurt, and he feels it, the court mask slipping as the killer steps forward. The crowd's growing. Voices are rising. Somewhere, a man shouts. Guards are coming.

I don't stop.

The guards shout again. A voice calls my name—someone from the nobility, shocked.

Let them yell. Let them panic.

I'm not doing this for their approval; I'm doing it because I can.

This is my moment.

Steel bites air as we break apart, only to clash again with sharper purpose. My blade sings. Darian's grits like teeth.

The main square is roaring now, but it feels distant—like surf against a cliff. My pulse is the only rhythm I hear.

Darian lunges. I slip beneath his arm, twist, and land a shallow strike along his ribs. He hisses and drives me back with a hard downward blow. He presses harder, and I'm forced to yield ground. I rebound and meet him. Sun flashes in his eyes, and I catch it there—real frustration. He is a prince, trained to win, and the set of his jaw says he does not plan to lose. Not to me. Not to anyone.

Mallen's moved to the edge of the square, and his gaze hooks mine, discipline clamped over something louder. Steady. Contained. The look that gives me permission.

End him. Now.

I pivot. Strike. Darian blocks. Hard. The impact rattles down my bones. He twists his blade, and I try to counter, but he's too fast. My sword jerks and then wrenches from my grip. Steel clatters across the stone. My breath catches in my throat. The crowd vanishes. Time lurches. And I dive—low, fast, reckless—but my fingers grasp only dust. My sword's spun further than I thought. Darian laughs, and his boot catches my ankle, yanking my balance out from under me.

I hit the ground hard. Wind knocked from my lungs. Dirt in my mouth, the taste of failure thick on my tongue.

He stands above me, triumphant, his blade poised at my throat.

"Yield," he says. Too sure.

My fingers dig into the earth. I drive my boot into his groin—hard.

He chokes and stumbles.

I roll, leap, and recover the blade I lost earlier. My hands close around its hilt like a prayer answered—and then I move.

One heartbeat. Two. A blur of limbs and silver.

I spin, duck, and drive forward. My foot finds the back of his knee. He drops. I lunge. My sword is at his chest, and I'm on top of him, straddling him like a conquering storm.

His arms fly wide in a show of peace, but I don't lower my blade.

The court is silent. The ladies are breathless. Even the banners hanging above seem to have gone still.

I wait. Without lowering my blade.

"You shouldn't drop your guard," I murmur, voice soft as silk and as sharp as a general's sword. "Unless you want the Reaping to end before it's even begun."

His smirk flickers. Then fades. His chest heaves.

"I yield," he says at last, and this time it lands like defeat.

I rise without help. Take two steps back and breathe him out of my lungs.

Darian lingers a beat longer, face flushed, eyes bright. He bows low, the angle just enough to acknowledge me—but not so much that it stings his pride.

"I'll have to be more careful," he mutters, his smile stretched thin. "Next time."

But the crowd's eyes aren't on him.

They're on me.

Nobles line the courtyard like statues come to life. Ladies glance at Darian with both worry and awe, as if mourning a fallen hero. Finery gleams under the sun, mouths parted in silent disbelief. No one speaks.

The lords stare at me as if seeing me for the first time. My father doesn't speak. He doesn't need to. His posture shifts—just slightly. His long face tightens, and the muscle in his jaw ticks once. A breath leaves him, sharp and measured, like he's just decided exactly how much I've embarrassed him.

I don't look away.

His gaze stays fixed on mine—a weapon honed on silence, folding layers of calculation and venom beneath it. He doesn't shout. He doesn't scowl. He simply stares, as if learning the shape of my defiance so he'll know precisely where to strike when the time comes.

I let my smirk rise anyway.

He's losing a pawn that's easy to control, and he knows it.

Perhaps this is the start of the turn. The Reaping has always kept to its steps, but now it's almost like the rules are changing. Or trying to. This year, the rites don't seem to fit their grooves, and the ceremonies seem off beat. By a breath, no more. Enough.

I walk past Darian without another word. When I reach Mallen, he doesn't speak. Instead, he simply holds out a cloth, eyes locked on mine with a weight that presses beneath the surface. There's no warmth, no consolation—only the quiet command of a man who trusts actions more than words. I take the cloth and clean the blade with measured, deliberate strokes, each movement steadying the storm inside me.

Then he shifts beside me. Barely a breath.

"A skilled display," he says aloud, voice pitched to carry. "Next time, don't waste time toying with your opponent."

The crowd stirs.

Mallen's words do everything he wanted them to. Praise. Unnerve. He's informed the court that I was holding back—and I could have ended it sooner, if I'd wanted to.

I shift my gaze sideways, catching him in the corner of my vision. His arms remain folded, but his eyes flicker—dark, steady. And there it is: a slow, nearly imperceptible tightening at the edge of his mouth. Not quite a smile, and much more dangerous—like pride tempered by quiet satisfaction.

He's claiming this moment, for me, quietly acknowledging what I've done.

He sees me.

Not as a child. Not as a pawn.

As a weapon.

And he likes what he sees.

We turn and ascend the steps together. Behind us, whispers break like waves across the stone. I don't look back. I'm not interested in what they have to say.

"Would you rather I kill him next time?" I murmur, low enough for only Mallen to hear.

His snigger is quiet and rich. "I'd rather you didn't ask permission."

CHAPTER EIGHT

Evie sets the final pin in my hair, admiring the way the moonstone catches the light before placing her hands on my shoulders and smiling at me in the mirror. Silver and jade have always suited me, highlighting my chestnut hair and making my hazel eyes appear greener.

"Beautiful, Highness," she says. "The Prince will be pleased."

Behind us, Mallen sets his cup down with a clink. Not slammed. Not messy. Just...firm. Exact. A full stop.

Evie carries on, oblivious.

"He's so handsome, Princess. The ladies say his eyes remind them of the ocean, and the gods must've—"

"He's waiting." Mallen's voice cuts in—smooth, cool, and unmistakably final. "You have other duties, Evie."

She blinks and then gathers her things quickly. "Of course, Commander. Enjoy your afternoon, Highness."

The door clicks shut.

I cross the room slowly, aware of the quiet weight of Mallen's gaze. I reach him just as he lifts his head to meet me—no hesitation. His hands settle at my waist, firm and familiar, and he pulls me gently to him. He doesn't bury his head in my stomach. He keeps his chin up, his eyes on mine.

"You'll get through this," he says, his voice low and certain. "I'll see to it."

I start to speak, but he beats me to it, a wolfish grin ghosting his mouth. "Darian learned his lesson yesterday."

I arch a brow.

"You should've seen his face when you walked away. And the court." He leans in, brushing a kiss just below my jaw. "You were magnificent. They should know it. You shouldn't doubt it." His fingers flex against my waist. "Magnificent. And mine."

His words settle over me like armor.

I nod.

"Do you regret it?" he asks.

I pause, fingers curling lightly around his wrist as the last few days play through my mind. I do not know which part he means: the prince I humbled before the Court, the kiss I allowed, or the promise I made.

"No."

"You regret something."

The silence hurts. It goes on a beat too long.

"I don't like the way you were last night. It felt like anger."

His gaze holds mine—steady, unflinching.

"I wasn't angry," he murmurs. "I was jealous. It was controlled, measured, and entirely justified."

He kisses my hand once, and then again, slower.

"I'm not asking you to like it," he murmurs. "But you'll never be unsure where I stand. I'll do better, Azhara. But I won't stop protecting what's mine."

He brushes a hand down my cheek and then leans back, as if the conversation is complete.

Because for him, it is.

We step into the corridor. The guards fall in, one to either side. I smooth my face into the one they expect. Wax and steel hang in the air. Our footfall measures the distance. I flex my hands once and let them settle. We reach the stateroom doors, and I taste copper—and then curse under my breath.

My father stands beside Darian, speaking as if they're old friends. His gaze skims me, quick and weighing, then moves on. He's seen enough, and I am here, as he ordered.

"It's good to see you looking well," my father says, every word lacquered with care. "An afternoon with Darian should help you feel even better."

"I thought we could revisit the gardens," Darian offers with an easy smile, holding out his hand.

I hesitate and then take it, careful to school my expression, aware of Mallen's presence behind me.

"Without the fighting this time, Princess."

We walk toward the door. Mallen follows, almost silent.

"I think we can trust a prince to keep Azhara safe," my father says. His words ring loud in the room, and the walls press in.

I go still. My breath snags.

Mallen steps forward, calm and exact. He stops a pace from Darian. "We're all aware of the recent intrusion. Moonsrise reached the inner halls and attempted to remove the Princess. Until that breach is sealed, no movement is routine. Your men will coordinate with mine. If anything touches her, Larksbind will answer."

He gives nothing away. I hear the heat under the ice only because it is for me.

Darian doesn't draw back. He nods once, cool and composed, and steers us away. The guards peel off once we reach an enclosed garden, settling along the outer walls.

"Your guard dog barks loudly," Darian says as he takes a seat. "Is he always this protective?"

I sit beside him—apart. In case Mallen's watching.

"He's always been there," I say.

"He's in love with you."

I laugh, though it doesn't reach my eyes. "He's known me since I was a child. He cares for me. It's not..."

Darian is still watching me. His eyebrows knit.

He shifts closer, his thigh brushing mine, his fingers resting next to mine as he lowers his head. "What was it like, growing up with him always around?"

His tone dares me to answer wrong.

So I don't.

I tell him how the nobles' sons learned where to press, and how they decided to make it a sport one afternoon in the archery yard. How their hands held my arms, and their laughter flooded my ears. Then a torch came too close, and my hair singed while they called it a game. I did not cry. I swallowed smoke and counted breaths, and hid the bruises under my sleeves at supper.

Mallen found me before the light failed. He took off his cloak and set it over my shoulders. He did not ask why I'd let it happen. He asked for their names. I told him. The next morning, those boys arrived for drills with split pride and new respect. No one spoke of why. After that, he began to meet me at dawn. To teach me stance and breath and how to break a grip. How to move when you are smaller. He stood at my back in ceremonies and at my side in corridors. The nobles' sons tried once more. Only once.

"Before Mallen, I had no one. My father called it independence."

Darian doesn't speak at first. Just stares at me like I'd uttered a truth too painful to hear.

"Azhara," he says, and it's not flirtatious or smooth now—it's horrified. "You were a child."

The quiet thickens around us, and I feel it settle over my skin like dust. Like ash.

"I didn't realize it was strange," I murmur. "It's just how it was. My father had to raise me and rule a kingdom. He—"

"Neglected you," Darian finishes, tightening his grip. "You're not a distraction. You're his daughter. His future. He should've protected you."

The words land heavy. Like a cold hand pressed firmly against my chest—not breaking skin, just making sure I couldn't forget it was there.

But he doesn't know what I cost. That I'm the reason my mother died. He thinks I'm a prize, a way to end the Reaping. He doesn't know I'm a monster who could destroy the treaty between our nations.

That my very presence is a wound still bleeding.

He doesn't know about the darkness inside me—the hunger, the pull, the cold rush of power that waits for a crack to slip through. My father has made sure only those in his inner circle know of my gift, and every year that circle grows smaller. Like a snare tightening around its prey. Or a noose.

I look away, gaze fixed on the flowerbeds trembling in the wind.

"Tell me more," he says gently.

I don't want to.

There's something stripped bare in his expression now. He's not a prince. Not a suitor. Just a man trying to understand the shape of me. And maybe it's a game. But maybe, just maybe, it's real.

And sincerity doesn't erase danger. Because in Starsfall, even honey can turn to poison.

"There isn't much." I shrug.

"You're holding back." He waits, and those blue eyes ask me to dive into their depths. "Take a chance, Azhara. I swear I'll tread gently."

I study him. The curve of his shoulders. The way his hands are still. The way he's listening like the answers matter.

I don't owe him anything. Still, the stories rise. Smaller ones. Easier ones. I laugh, and Darian loosens, his smile going golden in the light.

He talks about Larksbind like a boy who loved it. The library stacks he hid in after drill. A tutor with ink on every finger who swore he would sit straight or turn to stone. Dawn runs along the river when he should have been reciting dynasties. A bell tower climbed for the view and the scolding that followed. Honey cakes bribed from the kitchens. A fencing master who counted every breath, every inch of footwork, and expected victory as if it were a birthright. He tells me the mischief and the discipline in the same breath, and it sounds like a map of him.

I offer little pieces back. Roof edges where the wind swallowed my name. Pears stolen from the lower gardens. A book read by a shuttered window until the light gave out. He laughs, and I laugh with him, and for one glorious afternoon, I forget how to hold myself like a princess.

Shadows lengthen and the light softens toward evening. Darian rises too suddenly, and a bitter heat curls in my stomach. Did I say too much? He calls for the guards, and I brace myself until they arrive, confused by the lack of threat.

"The Princess would like dinner here," Darian announces.

My stomach twists. Not *ask*. *Will.* Like it's his right to decide.

And I realize—this is a game to him.

Heat rises up my neck as the guards exchange a glance. One of them tenses, jaw tight. Fetching food isn't in their purview—not for me, and certainly not at the request of a prince from Larksbind.

"Something light," Darian adds, his tone calm but unyielding. "And blankets. She's cold."

The guards trade a look, irritation smoothed into blank courtesy. One clears his throat and waits on me. I give a small nod, heat rising in my cheeks. They bow, clipped and cool, and go, boots a shade louder than necessary.

Darian watches them go, only his narrowed eyes betraying the vicious edge beneath the calm. "They forget themselves. You shouldn't have to flinch when you ask for a meal."

He doesn't realize that it was a choice I made. To let him speak for me. I could've stopped him. Could've spoken first. But I didn't. And I don't know if that was fear...or something uglier.

Something like comfort.

He turns, and I find myself staring. The sunlight filtering through the colonnade lights him like a dream someone once whispered into being. Not just golden, but bright. Warm. Terrifyingly so. It lingers on his hair, softens the harsh lines of his tunic where it clings to his chest. His expression gives no clues about what he's thinking, but there's a gentleness about it now. Less prince. More man.

"Azhara."

My name in his voice. Steady, low. The quiet sound draws me up straighter.

My heart races, and I'm caught staring. "I—I'm fine."

"No, you're not. And I'd like to know why."

He isn't demanding. It's worse than that. He's patient. Sincere.

"You're a princess," he says. "When you ask, others answer. You don't apologize. You do not need to."

I try to look away but he moves closer, not looming—just present. His hand lifts and hesitates at my chin, and when I don't flinch, he tilts my face up. Gently.

"This is not how power works."

I laugh—too quietly to be heard.

This is how majesty works. I've lived in its shadow. My father never raised his voice when a smile would do. He could gut a man with kindness and crown the corpse with roses. Or silence a room with just one look, making you forget everything you knew before your lips started to speak.

And I...I learned to smile while bleeding.

I have no power. Not really. Only the illusion of it, when I stand beside Mallen. Only when he doesn't speak for me. Only when he looks at me like I matter. Without him, I'm just a girl pretending I have a choice.

I should pull back from Darian. I don't.

His thumb grazes the edge of my jaw, featherlight, and when he lets go, I almost miss the contact.

He sits beside me, careful, as if I might flee. "You don't have to say everything now. You don't even have to say anything. But one day, you will tell me all of it. And then you'll decide what you want me to do about it."

His words settle around me like soft cloth, heavy with implication. I hesitate, unsure how to answer, but my hands move on their own. I reach for the blanket, only to find his fingers there first.

Our hands brush. There's a pause.

Then somehow—we're holding hands.

His is warm. Steady. He doesn't grip too tightly. He just lets it sit between us. It's me who's holding onto him.

"I don't know what you're trying to do," I whisper, staring at our joined hands, "but you're good at it."

"I'm not trying to seduce you, Azhara."

My head jerks up, startled.

He smiles faintly. "Not yet. One day I will. But now, I just want to find out who you are when no one's watching. That's all I want."

Attendants arrive before I can reply. One sets down a tray. The other folds blankets with the stiffness of someone suppressing resentment. Darian thanks them. Warmly. Politely. They leave without a word, and the silence they leave behind feels strange.

I exhale slowly, trying not to fidget. My gaze catches on a cluster of white flowers swaying in the breeze as though they've heard what I have not. The sudden movement makes my pulse stutter. Even beauty feels dangerous today. The wind shifts again, brushing petals like secrets spoken too loud, threatening to expose what should stay hidden.

I fold the blanket tighter around myself. My hands won't stop trembling.

"You've spent your whole life being careful," Darian murmurs. "That's not the same as being safe."

I glance at him, caught between wanting to retreat and wanting to be near him. His hand is still there, not demanding, not pressing, just...there. I cover it with my own. A choice. A risk. Maybe a betrayal.

"I know what I'm doing," I say, half to him, half to myself.

"I believe you."

I shiver, not from cold. There's no urgency in him. No heat that scorches. Just a steady fire, coaxing me closer. The air between us hums with necessity and want, with wishes that remain as unspoken and unknown as dreams. It unnerves me more than any flirtation could. It's not hunger. It's attention. Like he's listening to the part of me I've spent years silencing.

"You always get this quiet when someone sees you?" he asks gently.

My silence burns as it doesn't answer his question.

"I won't push," he says. "But if I were to kiss you—just your cheek—I'd ask first."

I blink, startled. Then nod. Just once.

He leans in, his breath warm, his movement slow and deliberate. When his lips graze my skin, it's like the brush of a promise. Nothing more. Nothing less.

I don't stop him. Or look away.

And still—

Guilt tears through my chest like a blade unsheathed.

Because I knew what I was doing and waited for it. A part of me wanted Mallen to see. And that part? That part was cruel. This wasn't innocence. This was betrayal. And no matter how gently Darian touched me—I let it happen.

I let it *mean* something.

Darian says nothing, only passes me a plate. I eat slowly, picking at the bread and cheese. He makes me smile without trying—makes me forget, for a moment, everything I'm supposed to be afraid of. He teases, soft and wry, and I tease him back. It's easy. Too easy.

"You nibble like a bird," he laughs.

"I'm not hungry."

His grin tugs at one side of his mouth. "Or maybe the kiss was that good."

I roll my eyes and stuff a canapé into my mouth just to shut him up. He laughs again, genuinely delighted, and somehow it makes everything more treacherous. Because this—this comfort, this warmth—shouldn't exist between us.

The sun sinks low, draping shadows across the flagstones. When I shiver, Darian rises without comment and offers me his arm. I take it. We walk slowly through the garden paths, twilight spilling around us.

At the foot of the stairs leading to the royal suites, we stop. He turns, but I step back. A boundary, clearly drawn. Not because I fear him. Because I fear myself.

"Thank you," I say, softly. "For...today."

He nods, as though he understands exactly what I mean and has guessed what it is I haven't said. He doesn't try to kiss me again. Every time I glance at him, he's tracking me with a gaze that might be longing. Maybe it's hope.

Whatever it is, it's enthralling. New. Different.

My chest tightens with every step I climb.

Because this—*this*—wasn't harmless.

And if Mallen knew—if he even glimpsed the truth behind my silence—I fear it would shatter the brittle edges of him, those fragile shards barely holding together beneath his calm.

And I don't know if I'd be able to forgive myself.

CHAPTER NINE

"Azhara."

My name drifts down the corridor like a warning cry long buried and remembered like a prayer to a cursed god. The dream of this afternoon shatters, and I freeze. My father isn't furious that often—at least not loudly. But when he is, it's the kind of anger that calcifies in the air, invisible and choking. I turn toward him, each step sinking heavier, as though I'm walking toward my own execution.

"A word, Daughter."

He disappears into his study, and I follow, swallowing the taste of iron. The room is lined with bookcases, cluttered with papers, harmless by design. But when my father stands at its center, the space becomes a cell dressed in civility. A cage with gold trim.

I remember the first time he bruised my wrist—how he kissed my forehead afterward and said it was my fault for flinching. I remember the lashes painted like medals across my ribs. The days I spent locked in this very room with no food, no light, only silence sharp enough to cut. He called it discipline. It was really a lesson in how to disappear.

"How was this afternoon?" he asks, voice smooth and glinting.

"Fine."

"Do you like him?"

I stare at the rug, tracing its patterns like a prayer. I don't need to look up to know what his face will be—serrated and shadowed, the weight of fury carved into every angle. Age has not softened him. The years only scorched him hollow. His hair, once reddish like mine, is veined now with gray, as though the fire in it is slowly burning itself out.

He taps his foot once. It's not loud, but the room still flinches.

"Enough. We will not waste time. Does he intend to marry you?"

"Darian didn't ask."

His fist hits the desk. The sound is not loud, but I jolt anyway. It never is loud—not with him. He never needed volume to terrify. Just certainty. Just the cold inevitability that pain will follow. Once, he didn't raise his voice for three months straight. I still bled.

The chair groans beneath him as he sits, eyes dark and narrowing. He jabs a finger toward the opposite chair.

"Of course not. He's a prince. Will he or won't he?"

I sink into the chair, nodding numbly.

"You seem uncertain."

I clasp my hands together, pressing my thumbs into each other until the pain helps me breathe. I imagine what it would be like to speak with him without fear. Without raised voices. Without broken things or bruises. Without blood.

He snaps my name like a whip, and my eyes lift, even though I don't want them to.

"I thought you despised Larksbind," I mumble.

He leans forward and lifts the letter opener from the desk. It's shaped like a ceremonial dagger, its hilt adorned with dull rubies. My father loves that blade. Not for its elegance, but for the blood it's tasted.

I've seen it at too many throats.

And known it at mine.

"Azhara," he says, almost gently, "Larksbind is weakness dressed in silk. And you—" his mouth curls, "—you were the gods' cruelest jest."

He turns the dagger in his hand like he's rolling a coin, slow and deliberate.

"I need an end to the disgrace you brought on this house the moment you breathed. If he marries you, the curse breaks. And I can finally be done with you."

This is not the moment to speak. This is the time to disappear into myself and hope he loses interest.

He returns to the treaty—his favorite complaint. The one that chained his hands and barred him from the conquest he believes is his divine right. The Reaping, with its annual parade of suffering, is less about alliance and more about punishment. He doesn't care about peace. He cares about being seen as a man who is not wrong.

"Even I couldn't stop you from killing your mother."

The words crack through me. My breath goes thin, sharp-edged. I stare at the floor until it steadies.

He wears martyrdom like armor, as if surrendering his magic to cage the power that lives in me was noble. That magic became daemons—half-beast, half-curse. He calls the creatures necessary. Most call them barbaric.

He always circles back here—to the death he couldn't prevent, the strength he sacrificed, the kingdom that would be complete if it wasn't for me.

I curl behind the walls I've learned to raise when his voice turns to venom. I push my feelings into the deep, dark places where even he can't reach.

"I am sorry, Father."

"That doesn't change what you are. Or raise the dead."

I nod again. Not in agreement. In survival.

He paces. His breath turns harsh. I feel him thinking, scheming. Trying to fit Darian into his vision of control.

"Heirs with Larksbind blood," I murmur, thinking aloud.

"That's the point," he says, and the derision in his tone makes me feel like a child again. "There's a distinct possibility he'll survive the Reaping. He is trained, after all, and I've wondered when Larksbind would stop sending boys to die. I prepared for it. If he wins, the Reaping returns our sorcery—*mine*—to the gods and Larksbind becomes our equal. I won't allow it. Now, if he marries you, I own his appetite. If he wants you, he kneels. Through you, I hold him. Through him, I get Larksbind. No blood required."

He pauses.

"But only if you play your part."

There it is. The truth in all its simplicity. Not peace. Not redemption. Just control. Just power. My father always has a plan. One that closes every door before I even dream of opening it. That's how he nearly won the war—

through anticipation, through cruelty, through fire. The stories he tells of that time are his lullabies. Bloodshed as legacy.

I've heard them all before. Today, they slide off me like oil, and my thoughts drift to the afternoon. To Darian. To the danger. The way it made me feel alive again.

Then back to Mallen. To the steady darkness of him, the way his eyes linger like he sees through every lie I wear. I want him. Gods, I want him. I shouldn't. Not if choosing him wakes Starsfall and lets my power bleed through. I have always believed it is not a gift but a hunger. If I loose it, it will take. That is where I hesitate, and it's the same place that left a door ajar for Darian.

The dagger taps against his nails. A rhythm like a countdown. He watches my hands, the lift of my breath, and reads what I do not say.

"You thought this would end with marriage to a man from Larksbind?"

I don't flinch. Not this time.

"I thought the curse would break," I say. "That you'd finally be done with me."

His eyes widen. For a moment, silence stretches between us like a blade. I've spoken out of turn—and he's shocked I dared.

There's a reason I rarely do. I've learned caution the hard way. Learned that silence survives longer than defiance. And I've been reckless.

His teeth stop grinding. A slow smile curves his mouth—not amused, but cruel. Something in me goes still.

"You know," he murmurs, voice like ice over stone, "I might have loved you, had your curse not killed my wife."

I refused to flinch for a second time. "What if I choose Starsfall?"

He gives a soft, delighted hum, as if I've handed him a favorite weapon.

"Then Larksbind loses," he says. "Their kingdom drowns under the dark magic you unleash. I win without lifting a finger. Their sun fades, their crops wither, their children are born cursed—and I reclaim what was stolen from me. Breaking the curse doesn't mean freedom—for me or you. It means power shifting hands, the leash never truly loosening."

He lies so clean I almost believe him. The rites I was taught say the gods bound the curse to keep our countries from men like him. He folds truth around a blade and offers it as mercy. Maybe he knows something I do not.

Maybe he only wants me to think he does. With him, the ground is always moving.

His fingers toy with the blade beside him. *Tap. Tap.* A sound too measured to be idle. "And don't think of turning your gifts on me. You know better."

I nod once. Eyes to the floor. The choice he lays out is a noose, no matter which way I turn. Marry Darian, and the curse breaks—only for my father to tether me to a throne and wield me like a weapon pressed to a king's throat. Or choose Mallen, and the curse returns magic to Starsfall, letting Larksbind fall to ruin while my power feeds his conquest like carrion feeds the crows.

"You know I'll lose my powers if I marry Darian."

I blink. Too rapidly. Because my father will lose his powers too, and he's sworn he'd never let that happen.

"You think I'd give up power so easily?" he says, almost laughing. "I've taken precautions. Old rites. Dark ones. The curse is only the first leash. I have others. You will still serve, even if the prince thinks he's won you."

My stomach knots. He's bound me deeper than I knew. And now, even escape tastes like chains.

He's changed the story again. Rewritten the rules. That's how he works—truth laced with lies until even your memories rot beneath them. The story twists and folds like the shifting labyrinth beneath Threnos, walls sliding, paths vanishing, leaving you trapped in a maze that never stays the same.

You're left doubting the sky, the stars, and even the blood in your own veins.

"You understand what breaks the curse?" he asks.

"Yes."

"Then make it right." He leans back in his chair, drawing the dagger with him as if it belongs in his hand. "Seduce the prince. You can manage that, can't you?"

This isn't how the Reaping is meant to work. Marriage has always been the lever. He's pressing for a bed now, shifting the ground so I cannot find my footing.

"I don't think—"

He slams his fist into the table. The sound is thunderous. I startle as the papers on his desk scatter like frightened birds. My pulse stumbles.

"Don't try my patience!" he bellows. "Just do."

Careful now. Measured steps across a tightrope that stretches over knives.

"What I meant," I say softly, "is I don't think Darian wants a meek bride."

His eyes narrow. A twitch of his jaw. The weight of violence barely held back.

"He wants the girl who bloodied him in a duel," I go on. "That's why he noticed me. He wants a conquest."

A slow, contemptuous laugh curls from my father's throat.

"He'll be disappointed," he says. "When he sees what you are."

I say nothing. I don't look at him. If I let myself cry, he wins.

"Do whatever it takes to make him fall," he says. "But don't bed him before he's bound to you. No man marries what he's already taken. No king crowns what's already claimed."

This is a rule I have never heard from my father. The Reaping has always meant marriage, seal the bargain, let the rite decide. Now he wants a pursuit that stops at the cliff. Make him fall, stay untouched. It is contradiction dressed as strategy. A test and a leash at once. Keep me valuable. Keep him hungry. Keep every door half open. Either he knows more than he has taught me, or he is bending the truth to fit a snare. He rewrites the rite in whispers, and I cannot yet see the pattern.

This Reaping is different. The rules are changing. I just don't understand how. Or why.

My father's gaze flicks to the door. A dismissal. I rise, bow low, and begin to back away.

Then—tap. Tap. Tap.

The dagger again. My blood chills.

"You are still untouched, aren't you?"

"Yes, Father."

"Good," he says, and smiles like a knife. "Mallen will ensure it stays that way."

Shame burns under my skin. He's too good at making me doubt my own pulse. He stacks truth beside threat until I cannot tell them apart. Control becomes protection, and refusal ingratitude. If I stay, I drown. If I argue, he'll drag me under. I get out before I mistake his plan for mine.

I make it only halfway down the corridor before the tears come hot and fast. I don't want to cry—not here—but the ache is too sharp, too deep.

I throw open my door and—

Arms catch me before I fall.

"What did Darian do?"

Mallen's voice is quiet. Too quiet.

I don't answer right away. I only fold into him, my arms around his neck, seeking refuge in the heat and the shape of him. He holds me tightly. No questions. Just presence. He lowers me onto his lap like I deserve all this and more.

"Did he hurt you?" he asks, and this time his voice could flay flesh from bone.

He's wrong. He thinks Darian hurt me.

And part of me wants to let him believe it—because the fury in his voice feels like protection, and I've never needed it more.

He's already made up his mind about who to blame. He hasn't realized that it wasn't Darian who caused this—and though some part of me is soothed by the fury in his voice, I can't let him wage war on the wrong enemy.

"It wasn't him," I whisper. "He took my hand. Once. For show."

Mallen doesn't flinch. Doesn't growl. Doesn't rage.

He just exhales slowly, the tension in his shoulders easing.

"Good," he says simply. "Because if he had touched you, I would've buried him before the Reaping and let the gods howl about it after."

There's no boast in it. No fire. Just steel.

I sink against him, and through the haze of tears, start to explain. The encounter with my father. His voice. The way it hollowed me out. Mallen doesn't interrupt. He listens. Every muscle in his body stays coiled, but his hand doesn't stop moving—stroking my hair, steady and warm.

His touch isn't soft. It isn't like Darian's. It's harder. More certain. Like armor with breath behind it. Like safety with edges.

"I won't let him hurt you," he says, voice low. "You are mine, Azhara. As I am yours. And I'll deal with your father."

"Mallen..."

"I'll deal with him." His tone sharpens. "He's only kept his grip because I wasn't strong enough to stop him. But I can now. I will."

Sound catches in my throat as air leaves my lungs.

Mallen doesn't make promises he can't keep. And this one sounds like a vow.

I rest my forehead against his and whisper, "What now?"

"You fight," he says, softer now. "Because you can. You just haven't seen it yet."

My head finds his shoulder, and I close my eyes. I don't know if he means my father, or the fear, or the legacy carved into my bones. Maybe all of it. Maybe none.

But I believe him.

And for the first time in years, I let myself wonder what life might look like if I fought to keep it.

The tears fall like torrents carving rivers through stone, finally etching themselves into something that's been buried for too long.

I am not safe. Not alone.

Now I have a choice. One that will cost me.

Darian or Mallen. Light or shadow.

Neither path is without pain.

Both roads end in fire.

I just have to decide which one I'm willing to burn for.

CHAPTER TEN

The gods require royal blood in the week before the Reaping.

Not much. Just a drop. A whisper of devotion to prove we remember who we belong to. A symbol, nothing more—unless you believe the stories that say it binds our will to theirs. And even then, you'd have to believe the gods are listening.

I don't.

My father derides this rite as superstition and refuses to attend because even he cannot make standing at my side when my blood is taken look like strength. So this morning I follow Mallen through Threnos's streets before dawn, our boots crunching through the splintered remnants of yesterday's celebration—trampled garlands, wine-stained ribbons, crushed wax from guttering lanterns. The scent of char and old flowers clings to the air like a warning. The capital is still asleep. Everything is hushed, bruised violet in the half-light.

The shrine at the labyrinth's entrance must be visited at first light. That's when the dark is thinnest. That's when the gods remember.

"You're quiet," he says.

I glance sideways. His cloak is dusted in pale ash, the hem dark with dew. The man is nearly a shadow beside me, all stillness and steel. But his eyes don't match his body. They're restless, flickering toward me like he's scanning for wounds he isn't allowed to dress.

"I don't have anything to say," I murmur.

He nods once. Accepts it without flinching. And that's the worst of it—how easy it is to be angry near him. How he gives me space to bleed and doesn't demand I sew myself back together. I hate how grateful that makes me.

The sun is rising when we reach the steps, its midnight paling into pinks and golds.

The entrance to the labyrinth is older than the palace, older than the city itself. A circle of worn stone descends like an amphitheater into the earth, each ring lower than the last, until it meets the iron gates that seal off the labyrinth mouth. And above those gates stands the statue.

She's twice my height, cloaked and hooded, one arm raised in warning. The other holds a curved blade, rusted at the tip where generations of offerings have dripped. Her face is lost beneath the cowl, only the faint suggestion of features beneath the veil of weathered stone.

The gods have no faces. Only hungers.

I step forward, pulling off my glove. My palm is already marked—my father made sure of that, slicing it open in front of the court like the ceremony had meaning. I press the cut against the rusted blade and feel the sting as fresh blood joins the stains of centuries.

It's always cold here. Even in summer, even when the festival fires are still smoldering in the streets behind us. This place belongs to something older. Something that doesn't care for the sun. And this year, it seems darker than before. Less stable. Like it too is changing.

Mallen waits beside me, silent. Watching.

"I thought you didn't believe," he says softly.

"I don't," I say. "I know how to follow orders."

He hums low in his throat. Not quite agreement. Not mockery either.

We linger.

The gates are sealed shut by thick iron vines—interlocking curves like thorns or talons, impossible to bend by mortal hands. A faint shimmer pulses behind them. The magic of the Reaping hasn't awakened yet. But it will.

This is the tenth Reaping I've endured.

I know its rules and rituals—or what they've always been until now. I know what waits beyond those gates. And I know what they say about the monster in the labyrinth.

Mallen shifts, not touching me, but close enough that I feel it. That low hum beneath his skin. The restless containment. It radiates off him like heat from a furnace its keeper forgot to extinguish. There's always been an unnamed pull contained within him—a darkness that's luminous, like a night lit by too many stars. I've spent years not letting myself look too closely. But here, near the labyrinth, it dazzles. And I look.

Heavens, I look.

Darkness stirs beneath my skin—burning, silent, restrained. My magic. It shouldn't be surfacing, not yet, not until the Reaping begins in earnest. But here, at the threshold, it coils like smoke in my veins. A presence more felt than seen, pressing up against the wards that bind it, the way water presses against glass. It doesn't burn. It hums. Not in pain. In anticipation. It remembers this place and the people who perished. It remembers the gates and the gods that bound it. And though it's leashed, it wants out.

We look at the iron bars too long. Like they're a nightmare that will not let us wake.

"Have you ever gone in?" I ask.

He doesn't answer at first. His jaw tenses. "You know I have."

"Will the gates open?"

He finally looks at me, and shadows twist through his sharp features. Not cruel. Not tender. Just dark. Old. There.

"If you ask them to."

I pull my glove back on, fingers tight, throat tighter. The stillness between us isn't still at all. Not really. It's laden with what we do not say but both feel. It's stirring, disturbed, as if it's an ocean whose smooth surface conceals turbulent currents in its depths. My heart beats not from habit, nor of its own accord. My father's words still echo behind my ribs, bitter and poisonous. You are a girl with no choice left but one. You belong to your bloodline. To the court. To me.

You owe me.

But standing here, with Mallen, I don't feel small. I feel dangerous. Not because the chains are gone. The Reaping still waits and the gods still count, yet I can place my next step where I choose and watch the pattern change. Even the possibility is new, and I intend to see how far it carries me.

The wind shifts—barely a breath—but it lifts a lock of hair across my cheek, and I don't brush it away. The moment is balanced on a blade's edge. One move could break it. Or change everything.

"Thank you," I say.

He frowns. "For what?"

"For not trying to fix it."

He nods. So simple.

"I'm not here to mend you, Azhara." His voice is steady. Constant. "I'm here to make sure no one else breaks you."

The way he says it is tender and terrifying. Not a promise. A certainty. A warning.

A shadow moves at the top of the steps, and I glance up just in time to see the priestess who oversees the shrine as she turns away. She's always here for the blood. For the prayers. But she leaves us alone now, her white robes catching the wind as she slips back toward the palace walls.

The gods have no faces. But their servants know when not to interfere.

We are alone at the labyrinth's entrance.

I should walk away. The offering is done. Dawn has broken. There's nothing left to say. But I don't move. And neither does he.

Mallen watches me with that impossible patience. The kind that isn't passive at all—it's feral, coiled, waiting for permission. It burns through his stare, in every little glance he gives me. Not lust. Something hungrier.

"I hate this," I say at last.

He nods.

"I hate the Reaping."

He nods again.

I take a breath, and it comes out crooked. "But I hate being afraid more."

He exhales. And inclines his head.

The silence stretches. I let it.

The cold sinks deeper now that the ritual is over. My blood still stains the shrine blade. A single droplet trails from my wrist, winding down the curve of my palm, catching at the edge of my dress. I don't wipe it away. The gods are greedy. Let them take what they want.

A gull cries high above the palace walls, ragged and sharp. In the clearing below the statue, the wind shifts, drawing through the iron bars of the labyrinth gate. It makes a low sound—half breath, half sigh.

"I used to fear this place," I say.

Mallen doesn't look at me. "You still should."

"I don't."

He glances down, eyes unreadable. "Then you've forgotten what waits inside."

"No," I murmur. "I learned to bleed slower."

His eyes narrow, barely. His jaw ticks, just. The flicker of understanding that flashes over his face is not gentle, nor comforting, but it is real. He sees me—as he's always seen me. A girl gifted violence for a spine, who has the discipline to hold it back. A woman who could become ruin, if I chose to stop pretending. The princess who beat Darian without blinking, not the daughter my father kept in velvet cages.

I am not soft. I am not tame. I am not afraid of monsters.

The rusted gate looms in front of us, every bar twisted into a shape that suggests movement—like barbs mid-thrash, like teeth about to bite. The shimmer of the royal seal is barely visible now, but its presence pulses behind my eyes, crawling down my spine like a thought I didn't choose. It's old magic. Labyrinth magic. And it's waking. Maybe it's changing.

I step closer, until the iron is only inches from my skin.

"Azhara," Mallen says behind me, a warning curling through my name.

"I'm not touching it," I say.

But I could.

I could press my fingers to the lock and know if it pulses for me.

I could speak the names they gave me at my first Reaping and see if the gates answer.

I could offer more than blood.

But I don't.

The power is in the restraint.

The clearing is still empty but for us. The priestess has retreated. The guards won't come until midday. No one is meant to witness this hour. This half-light. This soft shift between sleep and memory.

The wind cuts colder now, curling around my bare wrist, biting through the fabric at my throat. The amphitheater clearing is still steeped in the dawn, but the line of sun is creeping up over the palace behind us, gilding the edges of the highest stones. Soon, the labyrinth will be fully awake. Soon, the Reaping will begin.

I remember my first one. I was ten. The first trial drowned in blood. The next year, the screams lasted longer than the fire. They told me not to look away.

I didn't.

I watched. I learned.

No one ever survives the labyrinth.

"I dreamed about this place last night," I say. "I've never dreamed of the labyrinth before."

His shoulders shift almost imperceptibly. "What did you see?"

"Nothing. I was alone."

"That's not nothing."

I shake my head. "It was dark. I knew I was inside, though I could barely see anything. I stayed still and something moved. Something came."

Mallen doesn't respond right away. Doesn't try to soften it.

Finally, he says, "You stayed still?"

"Yes."

"That's how it finds you."

I nod. "I know."

The wind picks up again, funneling through the circular steps and catching the edge of my cloak. I don't reach to fix it. I let the cold bite. I let the gods see I'm not afraid of a little pain. I've lived with worse.

Mallen shifts beside me, his voice quiet now. "That dream wasn't just a dream."

"I know."

"Something's changing."

I don't ask how he knows. I can feel it too. The labyrinth's breath is heavier this year. It's hunger more awake. The seal on the gate pulses once, faint but real, like the monster caged inside just turned in its sleep.

"No one's ever made it to the final trial," I murmur. "Everyone else died in an arena before they went into the labyrinth."

Mallen's expression doesn't change. But I see his dark eyes darken further. "They won't make it through this year either."

He says it like a fact. Like a warning. Like the Reaping is already rigged, and the ten men from Larksbind have no hope. Like their prince is leading them to certain death.

A glint of rose-gold catches on the statue's blade, and I pause. It's the dawn—it must be—but for a moment, the edge gleams wet, like fresh blood rather than rust. I blink, and it's gone. Just morning light on old iron. Still, an unpleasant cold slides down my spine.

"We should go," I say, my voice quieter than I intended.

He inclines his head. He doesn't look back at the statue, doesn't ask what I saw. He knows better. We scale the stone steps together, side by side, and the wind does not follow. It stays behind us, caught in the ribs of the labyrinth, as if reluctant to let us leave.

The streets are still empty when we reach them. No carriages yet. No bells. Just the abandoned aftermath of celebration, scattered like bones across the flagstones. I sidestep a broken wine cup, its lip stained red, and brush my fingers against the wall beside me for balance.

Mallen doesn't speak, but his nearness speaks for him. Every step he takes is perfectly matched to mine. Not dominating. Not deferent. Just...aligned.

I feel him look at me, once. I don't return it. I don't need to. His gaze is a gravity I've already surrendered to—and it steadies me more than any wall beneath my hand.

"Why do you come with me? Every year?" I ask, finally turning to him. "You could send your guards instead. I don't understand why you insist on this."

"I don't take orders from your father," he says simply.

"Everyone takes orders from my father."

His gaze settles on mine. His eyes are so dark in the shadow of his hood that they look like they're brown or black or a color far colder than the green I know them to be.

"Because you are here," he says. "That's why I come."

He says it like it's a truth he doesn't need to defend. Like it's reason enough.

And maybe it should be. But I've heard too many pretty lies dressed up as loyalty. I've seen too many promises rot before they bloomed.

"Do you make a habit of following girls into holy places at dawn?" I ask, a brittle edge to the words.

His mouth curves—barely.

"Only the dangerous ones."

We don't speak again until the palace rises into view, its pale towers catching the dawn like spears of light. The silence is no longer quiet. It hums with a different tune—one that's low and rising and refuses to be suppressed.

I stop. So does he. His face is inches from mine, the hood shadowing his sharp cheekbones. Tension knots his jaw; I see the effort it takes not to move.

Not to reach.

Not to claim.

"Your father wouldn't approve of more," Mallen says at last.

"No," I reply. "He wouldn't."

Another pause passes.

"That's not a no." He presses his lips together.

"Maybe it should be," I whisper.

His eyes search mine, his green and gleaming in the shifting light. "If that's what you want, why don't you run?"

I shouldn't answer. I shouldn't say anything. But I do.

"Because I've already been caught."

It happens slowly. Deliberately. His hand brushes mine—just enough to ground me, not enough to risk being seen. His fingers curl, faintly, as if asking permission.

I don't pull away.

We walk the rest of the distance like that—never looking at each other, never touching fully, but tethered all the same.

When we reach the back gate of the palace, he lets go first.

He doesn't speak. Neither do I.

We say nothing, but in the silence, I hear myself making a choice.

CHAPTER ELEVEN

The golden bracelet twirls on my wrist, the cool kiss of its sapphires against my skin. Like everything I wear tonight, it wasn't chosen by me. The dress, the jewels, the braided hair with waterfall tresses—all chosen for a single purpose: to attract Darian's attention.

Mallen watches from across the salon, motionless save for the slow curl of his fingers at his side. There's a stillness to him that always comes before violence. He doesn't hate the dress, or its sweep of pale fabric that clings to my figure, or the way the cobalt embroidery glints with every breath I take. He hates the eyes it draws. The message it sends. That tonight, my beauty has been weaponized for someone else.

My father's gaze is colder still. The kind of cold that kills crops, freezes rivers, and starves cities. He taps one knuckle against his palm, over and over, each beat a warning. He doesn't like me being noticed. Doesn't want me wanted.

And yet here I am—gilded, poised, no longer his.

At the far end of the salon, a low platform rims the windows, two shallow steps above the floor, made for musicians rather than display. I wait there with my hands light on the rail while the room eddies below in ribbons of silk and talk. Courtiers drift close, offer a bow or a safe word, then peel away when I do not draw them in. The space is public, but high enough that anyone who joins me will be seen.

Darian ascends the steps like he was born to them, smiling as he offers his hand. I place mine in his without hesitation, though the heat of Mallen's fury burns like a brand against my back. Darian's grip is gentle—deferential—but he walks as if I belong to him. Through the crowd, past the watching eyes and the women who lower their lashes and tilt their throats, offering softness like a promise.

As though he's used to walking into danger and expecting it to yield.

There will be more drinking tonight. More dancing. Revelry beneath a sword. The first challenge begins tomorrow, but the men from Larksbind laugh freely, as if they aren't marching toward their graves. They speak with the nobles my father courts, manipulates, and tolerates. Maybe they don't see the teeth behind the smiles. Maybe they think they're the wolves.

"Princess?" Darian leans in, brushing his shoulder lightly against mine. "You seem far away."

"I was thinking," I murmur. His eyes catch the sapphire light of my necklace, and the blue of his irises is tinted with a depth that pulls, like tides under the moon.

"About tomorrow?" he asks.

I nod. He smiles.

"You needn't worry. I don't plan to die."

I press my lips together.

He leans closer, voice low, meant only for us. "You're afraid for me."

I turn my head away, cheeks hot. He laughs, soft and low, and my protest dies on my tongue. I focus instead on the banners lining the columns, tracing the patterns stitched in gold thread.

"I didn't think you cared," he adds, and I don't miss the way he watches me.

Hungry, but for more than power.

"I barely know you."

"The lies we tell for comfort are cages too, Princess."

I turn sharply, but he's still smiling. As if the game's already won. As if I'm another prize he's claimed.

"I dislike men dying for entertainment." My tone is cool. "That does not mean I care for you, specifically."

He studies me then, his smile fading a little. Arms crossed. His muscles flexed enough for them to catch the candlelight. He's not angry—just curious. Calculating. The space between us narrows, though neither of us moves. People pause around us, pulled into our orbit, as though they cannot escape until they know which one of us moves next.

He steps back without a word, bows, and turns, rejoining the men from Larksbind. The crowd shifts to fill the space he leaves behind. But the whispers remain. A pointed, poisonous hum.

"Did you see that?" someone hisses behind a jeweled fan.

"She turned him down. In front of everyone."

"No fear at all," another whispers. "Just ice. Just like her mother."

"Gods help the man that survives the labyrinth to reach her. I've never seen her smile."

I'm alone, and no one dares to join me.

No woman here knows me well enough to side with me. Not yet.

I lift my chin, take a glass of wine from a passing attendant, and smile at the nearest noble. I force myself into conversation. The man drones on about his painting collection with exhausting pride. I nod, sip, nod again—my magic restless under my skin, pushing for release.

But I don't retreat. I let the crowd circle me.

Tonight, I'm not the hidden daughter, neither a veiled threat nor a weakness. I'm visible. Valuable. And they know it.

Mallen hasn't looked away once. He stands near the throne, but his presence is a shadow on my shoulder. Each time a man draws too close, his fingers tighten around the hilt at his side.

He doesn't move. Doesn't speak. But he watches.

He's not my shield. He's the blade held to the throat of anyone who might harm me.

And yet, despite the darkness in him, I trust him more than any man here.

A hand brushes my wrist.

I spin. My magic flares to the surface, snapping against its leash. My breath catches.

Darian steps back, eyebrows lifting slightly.

"I didn't mean to startle you," he says smoothly. "I only came to ask for a dance."

"You didn't," I lie.

He smiles again, slow and knowing.

"May I?"

He holds his hand out. I glance down.

He waits. Patient. Poised. "I'll tread carefully."

"I don't dance."

He leans in, voice softer now. "Then let me walk with you."

"I said I don't dance," I repeat. "Not that I can't."

"Ah," he says, smile widening. "So it's a choice."

Darian smells like wild air, like salt and moss and wind in high places. Like freedom.

"I don't dance either," he says, and his fingers brush mine again. "We'll improvise."

He takes my hand, before I can protest, and pulls me toward the center of the hall. The court watches, sharp-eyed. A foreign prince should not be leading me to the dance floor. Especially one from Larksbind. This could read as more than a claim. But no one moves to stop him.

The music shifts.

Soft. Slow. Something old and ceremonial. A lullaby for ghosts.

He turns and steps into me, his arm slipping around my waist. His other hand lifts mine with careful grace, and I let him guide me, my body stiff at first and then fluid. It's a simple pattern. Intentional. Familiar.

"Is this walking, then?" I murmur.

He laughs, low and velvet. "No, Princess."

"You lied."

"Only because of you." His hand tightens at my waist. "You're impossible not to follow. Spin."

I blink, startled by the shift in tempo as Darian spins me away from him, releasing my hand so I pivot alone. The silk of my gown arcs like water, catching the light as I twirl back and reach for him again. Our hands meet. The music bends. And he pulls me into him with perfect ease, the movement smooth as breath—too practiced to be chance.

"You dance like you were born to it," Darian murmurs, smiling without arrogance as we sweep into the next movement. "I suspected as much when I saw you fight. The way you move—" his fingers flex around mine, just enough to remind me of his strength "—it's like watching fire move with a breeze."

I arch as he turns me again, head tilting back to stretch the line of my body. We hold at the apex of the movement, breathless and still. The room blurs at the edges, like a painting smeared by rain. The strings climb and slip into our breathing. His hand finds my waist, and my body answers without thought, step answering step, the music threading us closer.

We are not prince and princess. Not pawns.

Only two bodies suspended in a truth too fragile to name.

A sharp inhale ripples through the crowd. We haven't broken the rhythm, only suspended it—and for that single beat, we're untouchable. The still point around which the court turns. Darian lingers, his palm pressed to my spine, then draws me into motion once more. A sigh follows us like a tide. The women watch as if, just for a breath, I've stepped into the life they wish they were promised.

"It's a shame," he says, leaning closer. "That you only let yourself move like this when it can be mistaken for duty."

We drift, circling each other in tense silence. His gaze never leaves mine. A step. A turn. Our fingers brush, hold, release. He mirrors me. Or I mirror him. The world falls away, and only the rhythm remains.

"You loathe the Reaping," he says softly.

I nod in time with the music.

"Not dislike. Not tolerate. You hate it. And nothing they've told you has ever made it make sense."

Another turn. My skirts flare as he leads us into another sweeping step, the spin tighter, quicker than before. He shows me off, not as a trophy, but as a blade in motion. Something honed. Something dangerous. My head swims with it.

"Maybe," I whisper.

His hand shifts lower, settling with intention just above my hip, and he draws me closer—less than a breath between us now. I feel the tremor beneath his skin.

"What were you told?"

My heart scrapes against its prison, frantic and wild.

This feels dangerous.

Risky.

And I make a choice.

"It preserves peace. Ten men are offered the chance to win my hand in three trials set by both kings. If Larksbind wins my hand, Starsfall loses its magic."

He exhales sharply and spins me again, this time counter to the last.

A flash of temper beneath the grace.

"Those aren't the terms," he growls. "My father has no say in the challenges. Men don't volunteer, Azhara. They train knowing they'll die. They do it anyway, praying one of them will sever the treaty and save Larksbind."

"Why would they die for that?"

"Because once you reach twenty-five, your father inherits every inch of Larksbind. And he won't preserve it. He'll consume it."

Our eyes lock mid-step. The room might as well have vanished.

My breath stutters. My thoughts snag on what he's saying—but it isn't just his words. It's the quiet urgency of them. The way he doesn't flinch as I search his face.

I knew my father made another bargain. One that let him reclaim his magic bound by the Reaping. And I've always known he hated Larksbind—but I never thought he'd try to destroy it. Not when it's the counterpoint to our magic and stops it from spreading like a plague. Still, the change fits too neatly to ignore. The sudden press toward seduction, the rule that keeps me valuable but withheld, the way he spoke of Larksbind answering. He has never said break it, but every plan of his cuts toward ownership. Maybe I believe it because it is the pattern I have dreaded. Maybe because giving my fear a shape is easier than waiting for it to find one.

If Larksbind falls, there'll be no leash. No lines. No balance.

Only chaos. Only carnage. Only *him*.

My father is ruthless. He protects what's his. He speaks of Larksbind as if it belongs to him, yes, but he's never spoken of breaking it. Not to me. Not out loud.

But this.

This isn't conquest. It's collapse.

The gods forged the Reaping to prevent this madness.

To defy it is to spit in their faces—and dare them to strike back.

"He's raised you to live a lie," Darian says, slower now, adjusting his pace to steady me.

I shake my head. The music thins. This dance nears its end.

"I don't believe you."

"You should." His voice is gentler now. "I gain nothing by lying."

"You're from Larksbind," I whisper as he spins me into the final pose, bodies folding back together.

"That doesn't make me a liar."

My lips part, but before I can respond, Darian sweeps me into the closing step and dips me low. My body arches, arms outstretched, hair trailing behind me like spilled ink across the marble. His hand steadies my back. The court is silent but for the final notes of the music.

We rise together.

The applause comes fast—thunderous. We look like lovers. Like a fairy tale that men will tell in hushed tones for generations. They didn't hear a single word. They saw only a prince who danced with his enemy's daughter like she were made of flame and silk.

I feel the gazes locked on me, hungry for romance, blind to rebellion.

They cheer for a performance.

They don't know they've just watched the match strike the powder.

"I thought you'd be *his* daughter," Darian says. "But you're...unexpected. You're not a piece. You're the move itself. The one the board was waiting for. And when the game comes to an end, it'll be because of you."

I blink. Step back. Bow.

He closes the distance.

"It's already happening. You've decided it's ending, whether you know it or not, and here we are. This will be the last Reaping."

I draw a breath. It snags like a thorn in my throat. "The gods aren't watching this."

A smile threatens his lips. "They don't need to. You're writing the story for them."

I want to believe him.

But then his eyes still—just for a breath—and the warmth in them goes glassy, like a mask settling back into place. Too calm. Too careful. As if he's been waiting to deliver this line, practicing it in the dark.

Darian isn't lying. But he isn't telling me everything either.

He wears truth like armor and misdirection like silk. And right now, I can't tell which one is meant for me.

So I let the silence stretch. Let him see the weight in my eyes. The fear. The fire.

"Then we'd best hope we'll both live to see the ending," I say.

He inclines his head, not quite a bow. Not a surrender, either.

I walk away with my spine straight and my pulse thrashing.

Mallen doesn't move until I reach him. Doesn't speak until we are alone. But his breath growls in his throat. He saw enough. It coils between us like smoke off a fire not yet stoked, waiting to consume.

When I open my mouth to tell him I despised the dance—

I can't.

And worse, I can't tell him what Darian said.

And that—that *can't*—lodges like a blade between my ribs.

Because silence is power.

Silence is a choice.

And I'm done letting the men around me make mine for me.

CHAPTER TWELVE

The two nobles flanking my father are pressing their luck. They've mistaken his silence for grief, not fury. His compliance with the Reaping for contrition. They flatter him with words like *magnificent*, congratulating him for shaping me into the perfect ornament. They think they'll soften his mood by praising my display yesterday. They're fools. He's deciding how best to unmake them, and if I were a crueler woman, I'd smile at the thought of how little time they have left.

Mallen stands beside me on the royal balcony, his palm resting low on my spine. The pressure is possessive and a little too firm. A reminder. He hasn't forgiven me for yesterday—not for the way I looked at Darian, nor for what I said when we reached my rooms. Larksbind's prince came between us like a blade, and I refused to look away. Our last words before sleep had burned between us.

And I cannot take them back.

Below us, the tributes wait.

The sight of them makes my stomach clench like a fist around fire. My hands tremble. Color bleeds from my skin and my knees threaten to fold. Mallen catches my arm, steadying me before I stumble. His grip leaves no room for refusal. No one can know I'm breaking.

Especially not my father.

The royal balcony is a cage of opulence—gilded and cruel. A stage from which Starsfall's king can oversee the slaughter below, close enough that we can hear and taste the carnage, yet high enough that his silhouette casts long over the tributes from Larksbind. Everything here was designed to remind the world who rules. Every inch of it reeks of blood.

The amphitheater curves around the pit like a holy wound carved into the earth, tier upon tier of alabaster stone stained by centuries of blood. Velvet-cloaked nobles fill the highest rings, sipping wine while they wait for violence to entertain them. Below them, merchants, soldiers, and children jostle for space, eager to watch strangers die. A sea of faces turned toward death like it's divine. I used to think I hated this because it was cruel. Now I wonder if I hate it because it's familiar. Maybe I'm not disgusted by death—I'm disgusted by how easily I've learned to stomach it.

"I know you despise this," Mallen murmurs, low enough that only I hear. "But it will be quick. That's mercy, of a kind."

"It's not mercy," I say through gritted teeth.

"Compared to me, it is," he answers, tone flat as cold steel, and just as sharp.

In the pit, Darian swings his sword through a slow arc, letting the silver catch the sunlight. There is a grace to him that borders on insolent. He's not afraid. He doesn't even seem tense. But when he sees Mallen's hand on me, he goes still. His jaw tightens.

Others move behind him—men with spears, shields, swords—but it hardly matters. Their weapons are sharp but usually ceremonial, their deaths preordained. I remember only two men surviving the Reaping's first trial, and neither lived long afterward.

My father steps forward, sweeping the sycophants aside with a rustle of silk and steel. He lifts his arms. The crowd erupts. This is what they came for—velvet gowns and crimson gore.

This is Starsfall's idea of theater.

Even Mallen seems hungry for death.

Once, I believed I wasn't alone in hating it. Once, Mallen's disgust matched mine. There had been solace in that shared revulsion. But not this year. This year, he wants blood. This year, he needs it.

My father begins his speech, thanking the gods for this abomination. I bow my head out of necessity, not reverence, my teeth clenching as I mouth their names. If this is divine will, then their thrones should be overturned and set to fire. I would rather burn than worship what they are. I would rather let Larksbind swallow all Starsfall's magic than endure this again.

"Azhara," my father says, and my name becomes a weapon.

I step toward him, still shaking. I cling to Mallen's arm until the last possible second. My father watches the weakness with thinly veiled contempt.

He walks to me and takes my hands, all fatherly grace and cruel affection. His smile is for the audience. His voice is for me alone.

"He wants a challenge, not a fragile disappointment," he murmurs, his voice silk-wrapped venom. He kisses my cheek. "You managed to be bold last night. Don't shame me now."

I lift my chin. I do not flinch. Then I turn and step to the edge of the platform, fingers dipping into the silver bowl. The petals are soft as breath, crimson and gold. I cast them over the tributes, and the breeze takes them like ashes. There is no joy in this. No celebration. No triumph.

The crowd cheers. Darian steps forward and lifts his sword in salute. He is playing the part they want from him—the golden prince, bold and brazen—but his eyes are on me.

He kneels, picks up a fallen petal, and raises it to the sky before sliding it beneath his breastplate. The gesture is pure theater. The court sighs and claps. The women swoon. They still think it's a love story.

They still believe.

His gaze never leaves mine. And despite myself, I flush.

My father notices.

"You'd almost think you cared for him," he hisses through clenched teeth. "Do you?"

"No," I say, the word shaped like poison.

He isn't just another man about to die. His isn't a name to be forgotten or a body to be buried. I don't know what Darian is to me—but I know he's not nothing.

Darian smiles again, slow and knowing, and the court devours it. I clench my hands until my nails bite flesh. Too late. They've seen it. It doesn't even have to be true. The story writes itself.

"Can we get this over with?" I snap before I can stop myself.

"I thought you'd never ask, Highness," Mallen says, stepping forward with grim elegance. He raises his hand, and the roar of thousands falls into silence. Even the wind obeys. Starsfall holds its breath. Darian bows once more and strides into the arena's heart. The sand waits. The gods wait. The gates groan.

Three daemons. That is the usual offering. Creatures torn from nightmare, caged beneath the arena. Mallen traps them himself, ensuring the quota is met. What we were, what we are, and what we might yet become. Their hunger is the same as mine, their darkness born from the same night.

Blood buys us peace.

And they are the price of containing my magic.

Mallen lowers his arm, and the trial begins. Trumpets tear the hush. Winches catch, and the iron gates grind upward, chains screaming under the tiers. Sand whispers as the crowd stills. The ward sigils along the rim flare cold and then steady. But this year, something's different.

The first daemon bursts into the arena on two legs, towering three times Darian's height, its shoulders scraping the lifted gate. Its hide is oil-black stone, ridged and scarred beneath the ward light. Ram horns curl from its skull, and its jaw unhinges too wide, rows upon rows of jagged teeth. Spittle hits the sand and smokes. Its arms hang to the knees, fingers hooked into sickles, and jointed legs end in split talons that bite the ground. A barbed tail lashes, carving furrows. It roars, and the sound shudders through the tiers.

The tributes don't scatter. They form a line—shoulder to shoulder—at the heart of the arena, boots set in the churned sand. Blades lift. Helmets turn as one, like a dare thrown at the dark. Not frightened boys. Not desperate conscripts.

A unit.

Darian barks commands. Two clipped words. His hand cuts left, steadies, and the line shifts with him. They move like water, fluid and precise. Gone is the charming rogue with the devil's smile. What remains is colder. Sharper. A commander born of blood and battlefield.

These men aren't carpenters. Not merchants or dockhands dragged into sacrifice. They are trained. Drilled. Ready. They hold the ground and make it theirs.

I step to the railing, heart hammering. I dare to ask, for the first time, could they survive this?

My father watches with a predator's stillness, his fury like heat on my skin.

He had not foreseen this. I glance at Mallen—his features carved from shadow and ice, his expression a sculpted mask of bored detachment that only highlights the glint of fury beneath.

"They're working together," I whisper, just as the gates open wider.

"Yes," Mallen snarls back. "Darian has a plan. This will be interesting."

The men from Larksbind still don't run. They turn in sync, shields locking, bodies bracing. It's a soldier's wall—disciplined, fearless—but this isn't a man they're facing. It's a nightmare made flesh, the kind of horror that lives between a heartbeat and a scream.

The daemon lowers its horned head and bunches to charge, claws gouging trenches in the sand. The Larksbind line doesn't waver. Shields stay locked. Feet stand set. Darian takes the point, blade lifted, voice low, calm and defiant.

They're not going to break. They're going to die.

My fingers clamp the rail, breath catching in my throat. I squeeze my eyes shut.

A scream splits the air—high, violent, inhuman. It tears through the crowd and lodges in my chest, a sound born from pure pain. I nearly drop where I stand.

My body rebels—quaking, breath ragged, skin damp with sweat. But beneath the panic, something deeper unspools. A terrible knowing.

This isn't sport. It's sacrifice.

Shouts echo from the arena. Panic. Orders. Footfalls pounding earth. A crash like thunder. Then another.

And then—stillness.

I force my eyes open, expecting ruin. But the daemon lies severed and steaming, black blood pouring into the sand.

Darian stands beside it, sword raised and dripping.

The crowd erupts, wild with disbelief and glee. Their cheers shake the stadium as if the earth itself is celebrating.

He bows—not for vanity, but control. Command. He's working them like a maestro works a symphony. The soldiers split on cue, dividing formation and anticipating more.

He knew it wouldn't end with one.

"One down," I whisper.

Vapor curls from his bloodied blade as the cheers build to a roar.

Two more daemons charge into the arena. This time, silence grips the crowd.

They're bigger. Smarter. They're bigger than the first—low-slung and four-legged, all coil and claw, horns swept back and a ridge of quills along the spine, eyes slit and calculating. Shrieking like banshees, their cries knife-thin and piercing, circling the soldiers with twitching muscle and gleaming fangs. Their fur shimmers—black laced with violet and blue like oil slicks under a full moon. They move like shadows, like beasts tasting fear.

The daemons shriek louder and circle the men, their footfalls unnervingly soft for creatures so massive. They pace like panthers, but there's too much rage in their movements—too much hunger. Saliva ropes between their jaws, thick and steaming. Their eyes glow molten red as they snarl and snap, baiting a misstep.

The audience doesn't flinch. They've already watched Darian fell one daemon. That bloodlust has only whetted their appetite.

Darian doesn't blink. His stance is loose but ready, shoulders low, every movement controlled. There's fury in his eyes, but deeper than that—calculation. He's watching the beasts, reading their rhythm.

"Fan out," his voice cuts through the chaos like it deserves to be there. "Five on either side."

A daemon lunges.

Darian sidesteps the soldier beside him. A blur. A streak of muscle and teeth. A shield slams up to meet it, but it's Darian's blade that rips through the daemon's chest, sinking deep. It shrieks—an unholy, piercing sound—and the soldiers move in unison, carving into it like a practiced machine.

Its body convulses. Blood, thick and black, sprays in wide arcs as one soldier drives his spear through its throat. Another goes low, severing tendons with clean strikes. The daemon drops, twitching. A final blow cleaves its head from its neck with a wet crack.

But the third daemon isn't idle. It slinks along the outer edge of the fight, eyes fixed on the one group of soldiers. It's cautious now. Clever. And it's learning.

Darian sees it. His hand slices left in signal. "Unit Two, peel wide—take its flank. Center, hold. Shields high. Spears low." The second unit slides out, skirting the arc to cut behind it.

They're readying to strike—when a fourth daemon explodes into the arena.

The crowd screams, ecstatic.

My stomach drops.

It's grotesque. Bloated with muscle, its legs are bent backward, as though broken and reset wrong, but it moves with horrifying speed. Horns curl from its skull, slick with gore. One eye is missing. In its place, a cavernous socket weeps black ichor.

It tears into the second unit before they can react.

Steel scrapes bone. A man screams as claws punch through his chest, lifting him clean off the ground before hurling him like a ragdoll. He slams against the arena wall with a crunch.

Nine men remain. Two daemons.

This isn't a fight. It's a slaughter.

Darian roars—as violent and visceral as it is wordless—and his men charge to reinforce, coming at the daemons from behind.

They crash together in a storm of steel and teeth.

The air explodes with noise. Screams. Howls. Bones breaking. One daemon lashes out, carving its claws across a man's face. His helmet splits. Blood sprays. He crumples, gurgling.

Darian ducks under a swing of jagged claws, rolling into a thrust that punches his sword deep into a daemon's side. It howls. Its tail snaps like a whip, catching a soldier and flinging him into another.

A soldier in a battered breastplate cleaves through the daemon's front leg with a two-handed strike, spraying blood in a dark geyser. The creature collapses with a deafening thud.

They converge. Darian presses the open wound, driving forward with sheer fury. The daemon twists, snapping its jaws, and Darian hits the sand hard, teeth gritted as he rolls to avoid being shredded.

He's not fast enough.

The creature's claws rake across his side—the plate deflects, then fails, and the points get under and open him up. He grunts, blood christening his chest. A soldier lunges to cover him.

Too slow.

A claw rips across the soldier's back, shredding leather and flesh in one devastating swipe. He falls screaming, blood pooling beneath him as he twitches in the dirt.

The daemon rounds again. The other is charging.

They're going to die.

They're going to *die.*

And still Darian rises, sword in hand, face pale and blood-soaked, lips pulled into a snarl. Not backing down. Not breaking.

Gods help us.

Blood bursts across the arena floor. Darian drags the wounded man beneath him, shielding him with his own body as he lunges forward. Around them, the others attack with savage determination, flanking the daemon like wolves.

It bellows and whips around, but Darian's already inside its guard. His sword punches past its gaping jaws and into the roof of its skull. The daemon screams—a raw, bone-splitting sound—but it doesn't fall.

It thrashes. Flails. Claws rake the air, nearly catching one of the men in the throat. The men from Larksbind duck, their movements sharpened by exhaustion and desperation. Blades flash. Limbs are severed. One soldier gets in close enough to hack at the neck, again and again, as hot blood spurts in violent jets.

The head doesn't come off clean. It takes several brutal blows, each one sickening, each one splashing the sand with black blood. Finally the thing collapses, shuddering, twitching. Dead.

But there's no time to rest.

They sprint toward the final daemon.

It's still alive—and still deadly.

Its flanks are shredded, one eye hanging from its socket, but it crouches in a pool of its own blood, snarling. Saliva froths around its broken teeth. It lunges and the men from Larksbind close in, forming a ring around it like a trap snapping shut.

The beast fights back. Its claws sweep low and catch one man's leg, ripping it open to the bone. He collapses, screaming. Darian moves in to cover him. Another soldier thrusts a spear into the daemon's ribs—deep—but the creature doesn't falter. It sinks its teeth into the shaft and snaps the weapon in half.

Still, they press it. Surround it. Bleed it.

The daemon's roars go hoarse as it weakens. Cuts crisscross its entire body. Blood drips in thick lines onto the floor. It tries to leap away—tries to flee—but it's too late.

Darian slams his sword through its chest.

It stumbles. A second later, a spear pins it to the ground like an insect beneath glass. The creature screams, an agonizing, gurgling howl that makes my skin crawl.

It writhes. Fails. And then—

The soldiers charge.

They tear it apart.

One last decapitation. One final spray of blood. The arena floor is a butcher's yard, soaked with gore and littered with twitching daemon limbs. Of the ten men, three are dead and one might never use his leg again. Darian stands, panting, blood running down his side. His sword drips. Behind him, one of the soldiers hauls up the daemon's severed head in triumph—but he can barely stand. Another man loops his arm around his waist and half-carries him toward the podium, where my father waits to deliver his approval.

He steps forward, beaming, raising his arms to the crowd like a benevolent god. The audience screams his name.

"Starsfall salutes the valor of Larksbind," my father says, voice warm as wine. "It is good to see they send soldiers who can stand." He lifts a hand to the sky. "We thank the gods for their discernment; they have kept alive those worth keeping. May tomorrow prove today was skill, not fortune."

I press my hands together, a silent offering to Darian. He sees me. And smirks.

"Daughter," my father calls, his voice cutting through the crowd. "Have you anything to say?"

I step beside him, eyes on Darian, and echo his words. Praise, thanks, reverence. Darian bows and then slowly reaches beneath his breastplate and pulls out the bloodstained rose petal he kept hidden there.

He lifts it to me. A tribute. A symbol.

The arena falls still.

Everyone is watching.

"For Gods' sake," I shout, "get those men to a healer."

Mallen's voice cuts through the silence. "We don't help during the

Reaping." He doesn't even look at the wounded soldier. "Not even when they're dying."

Bitterness drips from every word.

I step forward. "Get. A. Healer."

My father turns.

His gaze meets mine. He's standing tall, looming—trying to intimidate me with his presence like he always does.

But I don't flinch.

If Darian can defeat four daemons, I can stand my ground.

"Why am I repeating myself?" I ask. Softly. Deliberately.

And that's when it shifts.

His eyes flash with something primal. Not anger. Not even fury. A hatred so violent it almost knocks the breath from my lungs. It tears through him in an instant—and then it vanishes. Replaced by something even worse: a cold, calculated stillness. An evil that doesn't scream, that doesn't lash out. It waits. It plans. It kills without blinking.

My father's eyes narrow. Barely. Almost imperceptibly.

Mallen moves instantly.

He steps between us, fast and silent, and grabs my wrist—firm, not painful, but unyielding. A barrier. A wall. A message.

Don't provoke him. Not here. Not now.

His eyes lock on mine, and I see what he wants me to see: *this* is protection. *This* is safety. I am *his* to shield.

But it's not just that.

It's a claim.

"Of course, Azhara," he says smoothly, venom sweetening his voice. "How could I refuse anything you ask of me?"

He flicks his fingers. Healer. Immediately.

And then he turns, his face twisting into a smile that doesn't reach his eyes. Mallen half-leads, half-drags me from the royal balcony, his fingers tight on my wrist now as his gaze flicks back to my father like a man who's just won a prize.

His grip doesn't ease until we're out of view.

Only then does his body relax—just barely. Like some essential part of him has unclenched now that I'm away from my father.

But I sense the possessiveness that coils beneath Mallen's skin.

Silent. Burning.
He doesn't say a word as we walk. Doesn't let go.
And I don't stumble or resist.
I don't thank him either.
Because he protected me.
But I didn't ask him to.
And we both know this wasn't just about safety.
It never is.

CHAPTER THIRTEEN

The door swings shut behind us with a quiet thud, and the silence that follows is sharper than any shout. I stand motionless, my breath ragged, my skin still thrumming with echoes I haven't outrun—the flowers, the eyes, the cheers for Darian that sound like both ruin and salvation.

I wanted to hate it. That part of me wanted to smile back. The fragment of me that had reached for the light in Darian's eyes—not because I trusted him, but because I was drowning and it looked like shore. And beneath a sky of painted lies, in a hollow arena full of false pageantry, I faltered.

And I hated that Mallen saw it.

He crosses the room slowly. His boots echo against the stone as he stops in front of the mural. He doesn't look at me—only at the paint. His hand rises and lays his fingers on the painted sky. Then he applies pressure, then more, steady and deliberate. The plaster answers with a thin crack. A hairline seam runs through the clouds, cleaving a flock of doves mid-flight, severing wings and turning grace to ruin. He breathes once, twice, and presses harder until the wall yields with a low groan and the mural crumbles further.

"I watched him hold petals up to you," he says quietly. "You smiled."

His voice is level. Too level. I step closer, but he still won't look at me.

"Mallen," I say. "You can't—"

"Can't what?" He turns now, slowly, like a winter tide deciding to come in. His eyes are the color of storm-drenched pine, dark with unspoken thoughts. "You would've let him kiss you."

"No. I wouldn't have."

"You didn't stop him."

I lift my chin. "I didn't need to."

That gets a reaction—a flicker of surprise. A beat of blistering heat, banked but alive, seems to curl through the hollow of his chest.

"I would've faced my father, though," I continue. "I would've stood in front of the entire court, declared myself, and taken the punishment. You weren't ready to face him."

"You don't understand what that would have meant."

"I understand." My voice is quiet, but steady. "You're not the only one who's bled for Starsfall. I know the price of crossing my father. I have paid it in skin and in nights without breath."

His jaw flexes. His hands curl at his sides, not into fists, but something more dangerous—the kind of tension a soldier holds before the battle starts. Still restrained. Still silent.

And still not meeting my eyes.

"I loved you before he even knew your name," he murmurs. "And now the crowd sings for him like he's some savior come to claim you."

I say nothing.

"Tell me what you see when you look at him."

My answer doesn't come quickly enough. He moves past me, slow and deliberate, the air around him tightening. "Azhara," he says, and his voice cuts sharper than steel. "Do you want him?"

"I want to survive this," I whisper. "I want to live through this. Gods, I want a life I have to lie to live. Most of all, I want you to stop treating me like I'll break if you love me aloud."

That lands a hit, clean and deep.

He staggers back a step, and this time, it doesn't look rehearsed. He looks gutted.

It's just one step—barely more than a shift of weight—but the crack has formed. His eyes glint, too bright for the dim room, and his hands flex like he's seconds from either pulling me into his arms or punching through the wall.

His voice lowers, fraying at the edges. "I've waited years, living on scraps. A glance. A smile. I stayed silent while your father paraded suitors past you like you were a prize in a glass cage. I fought for you while pretending I didn't care. And now, when I finally come close—he's there. Always there."

Jealousy creeps in, slow and cold. But still, he holds the line.

"I didn't ask Darian to flirt," I say. "But you would not name what you wanted us to be. Not before them."

His eyes finally rise to meet mine. "Because if I named it, I would not have stopped."

I take a shaky breath.

His voice softens, but the tension only coils tighter. "He doesn't love you, Azhara. He wants the crown. He wants to win. You're a symbol to him. Tell me you know I'm right."

"And what am I to you?"

For a moment, everything halts. Even the clock waits.

Then—

"You're everything. You're the only thing I can't survive losing," he says, almost broken. "Azhara—"

My name slips from his lips again, softer this time. Not a plea. Not a command. Just a sound full of ache, like it's the only word he remembers how to say. His eyes glint with something I can't describe, and for a heartbeat, I think he might fall apart. From grief. From loss. From failing to protect the only thing he ever wanted. There's a question in his eyes, and his body screams that the answer's already killing him.

He crosses the distance between us in two strides, his hands braced against the wall on either side of me. Still not touching me. Still in control. But barely.

"I see the way you look at him," he breathes. "And I'm trying not to come undone."

"You already are."

He shuts his eyes. His voice is hoarse. "Do you love him?"

"No."

"Then say it."

"I don't love him."

His breath shudders out.

I want to feel relief—but I don't. The sunlight is too hot on my skin. Too bright. My body is too full, as if it can't contain what's rising inside me. Not rage. Not grief. *Power.* The kind that rattles the gods. The kind that undoes things.

The magic in me uncoils. Uncaged. Uncontrolled.

The darkness flickers again—then catches, a spark on dry leaves. It crawls higher, clawing its way through my ribs, like it's prying them apart and trying to get out. Every breath is a wound. Every heartbeat rings too loud, too fast. There's no space inside me for this much wanting, this much terror.

The magic of death bound in me stirs.

It moves, but not outside. It's inside. Inside me—building like a storm gathering on the horizon, licking at the edges of my soul with fingers made of shadow and inevitability. My veins thrum like wires strung too tight. My hands tremble. I can't keep it down. I can't hold the edges in.

"I can't—" My chest contracts. "I can't breathe."

Dread descends like a curtain. I claw at my ribs, my arms, the walls—anywhere to anchor myself. My vision smears. The floor tilts. Light fractures. The thundering in my head drowns out the world, and still it rises—*still it wants out.*

Mallen freezes. Just for a second. But it's enough. The shift is seismic. His pain shatters beneath my panic, and he's reaching toward me. Whatever storm was in him gets bottled, corked, sealed.

He grabs my wrists, not rough, not harsh—just anchoring. Grounding. His eyes are wide and terrified.

"Don't you dare leave me," he says hoarsely. "I need you to calm down. Stay with me."

But I'm already gone.

I'm not in this room. I'm not in this body. I'm trying to claw my way out of everything all at once. My skin feels wrong. My throat's closing in. I kick, I flail, I thrash against him. My fists pound at his chest and my screams pierce the air. I'm suffocating—not on air but on pressure, on history, on the mess of my life that never stops compounding.

He wraps himself around me like a shield. Like a cage. Like a prayer.

"Azhara...let me keep you safe. Please—"

But his voice is distant now, like it's traveling through water. Like it doesn't belong to this moment. The panic is too loud. My pulse is a roar in my ears. There's a tearing sensation deep inside me, like something sacred is splintering apart.

"Let me keep you safe, Azhara. Please."

"No," I shriek, fighting like a wild animal. "Let me go. I can't do this. I can't breathe. I need to—"

"What the hell?"

The voice cuts through everything.

We both freeze.

Mallen goes rigid beside me. His limbs lock, his breath sharpens, and the sudden coil of violence simmers beneath his skin.

I twist in his grip, and he doesn't stop me.

Darian stands in the doorway, eyes wild, chest heaving, his tunic half undone and his fists clenched like he's holding himself back from running—or striking. His gaze darts from me, to Mallen, to the shattered wall—and back again.

He doesn't understand. Of course he doesn't.

He sees a man gripping a woman who's screaming.

He sees darkness in a place where light died long ago.

He doesn't see the panic in my lungs. The terror threatening to tear me apart.

The fury on his face is cold, calculated, and devastating.

"Let her go," Darian growls, "or I will end you."

"Darian—"

Too late. He's already in motion.

Mallen spins, releasing me just in time to meet Darian's charge head-on. The crack of a fist meeting a jaw echoes in the room. Mallen staggers. Recovers. Responds with a brutal punch that sends Darian reeling into the wall.

They collide like gods in a ruin.

I scream, scrambling backward into a corner, my heart still racing from the panic attack, now layered with a fresh wave of horror.

They don't stop. Darian's fists fly, precision and fury blended into each strike. Mallen counters with brute force and frightening speed. He's not holding back. Neither is Darian. Every hit lands like thunder.

Darian is protecting me. Mallen is fighting for me. And neither of them is listening to the person they're trying to save.

I scream again, louder this time. My voice is raw and ragged. "Stop it!"

No one hears.

They crash into the dresser. Wood splinters. They tear through my chamber like beasts with no logic. A chair flies. A vase shatters. My room is wreckage and war.

"GUARDS!" I scream, shrill and commanding.

The door slams open and palace guards flood in, weapons drawn, confusion on their faces as they try to untangle the fight. They charge, far too late. Mallen has Darian by the throat, and Darian's driving an elbow into Mallen's ribs.

I'm done screaming.

I grab the nearest thing I can—a porcelain vase—and hurl it. It shatters against the head of a guard trying to restrain Mallen.

Everything halts.

Eyes whip to me. Shocked. Silent.

"Now that I have your attention..." I snarl. "You can all just stop."

The guard clutches his bleeding head, too stunned to speak. Mallen and Darian breathe like creatures dragged from opposite ends of the same storm, sides heaving, bruises already blooming across their skin.

The silence between them isn't peace—it's a powder keg.

Every breath is a fuse waiting to be lit.

"Take him to the dungeons," Mallen snarls, pointing at Darian.

"He attacked the princess," Darian snaps, teeth bared.

Two guards close in on him anyway.

One grabs Darian's arm. The other reaches for his sword.

It's all happening too fast, and no one's thinking. They're still fighting, still ignoring me.

"Stop," I command.

Everything stops. The room goes silent. Even Darian stops. Mallen too.

My voice cuts like steel. I've never used it like that. I wasn't sure I had it in me. Maybe they have heard it before, buried under doubt, waiting for me to use it.

"I'm fine. Your concern is noted, Darian. You will apologize."

He bristles. "I know what I saw. You don't have to defend him—"

"I'm not," I interrupt. "I wasn't in danger."

Darian exhales. "He attacked you."

"I will not repeat myself. Apologize, or leave."

Silence cleaves the room. The Guard salutes. "Your Highness." He takes Darian by the arm.

"You cannot be serious. I am the prince of Larksbind."

"You are a guest in my chambers."

Mallen stays silent. His fists are still clenched. He's poised. Ready to move. But he's watching me with an expression I don't understand. It's not just surprise. It isn't just awe. It's complicated, fiercer too—pride maybe, or hunger—for the girl I've stopped pretending to be. It's like he hates that I defended Darian, but he's seeing me now.

All of me.

And he likes it.

"Princess—" Darian starts again.

I slice his words with a finger, held up in the air. That's all it takes.

"Darian, if the next words out of your mouth are not an apology for your behavior, I will have you and your men removed from the palace until you remember your manners."

I notice the subtle smirk lighting up Mallen's face.

I know that look.

It's the glint of a serpent coiled, not yet striking—patient, watchful, every muscle taut with quiet menace, waiting for the opportunity to be dangerous again.

I arch my eyebrow.

Darian flinches. Grits his teeth.

I wait.

His shoulders fall. "I'm sorry."

I nod and then glance at the wreckage around me. Smashed ornaments. Crushed furniture. My sanctuary has been reduced to a battlefield. Curtains torn from their hooks, shards of porcelain glittering like ice across the rug. The chair my mother once sat in, broken at the leg. I want to scream again. Or fall to my knees. Or gather every shattered piece and pretend I can fix what's already gone. But I just stand there, rigid, at the center of a mess that mirrors the turmoil inside me.

Because I will not shatter.

"What was it you wanted, Darian?" I ask.

"To thank you for sending a healer. It's more than we expected. Your father gave me leave to come to your rooms and..."

His voice trails off, but I'm barely listening. My pulse hasn't slowed. My throat still burns. The air tastes of ruin. Mallen's gaze keeps flicking to me like he's counting every breath. And Darian—his bruised face is too open, too human. He meant well. He always does. That doesn't mean I forgive him.

"I want everyone out," I say. "Escort Darian back to his quarters."

For a moment, he looks like he might protest. Then he thinks better of it. He nods and leaves without another word.

The guards file out too. Only Mallen remains.

"Azhara, I—"

"Don't. I can't bear to talk."

He bends to start picking up broken pieces, as if that can repair what just happened.

He doesn't look at me. He doesn't need to.

The guilt is eating at him, but that doesn't undo the wreckage. Doesn't silence the jealousy that still coils beneath his ribs. Doesn't fix the fact that I'm suffocating in this palace with one man trying to protect me like a secret, and another trying to save me like a prize. And underneath it all, the magic of death bound in me is growing hungrier, more sentient, more desperate to devour everything I love.

Everything is shifting, and nothing sits right. I cannot say how, only that the Reaping is wrong this year. This was not meant to happen. More is hidden from me than I dared believe, and the truth presses close with no way out.

I walk away and lean against the archway leading onto the balcony. I stare out at Threnos, at the marble towers burning gold in the daylight, the silken banners drooping as another afternoon passes, the thousand windows watching like eyes I can't escape.

Starsfall gleams like a dream, but I know the rot beneath.

I know that beauty can be a prison.

I cry. It rips out of me, its pain violent and loud and soul-deep. An agony so sharp it won't let me sleep tonight. Won't let me breathe. My chest caves in and I know—without doubt—what this hurt is.

My heart's breaking.

It burns. It scorches. And I realize why too late.

A heart can't break unless it loves.

And I do.

But Mallen loves like a wound, not like a cure. He is the storm I keep walking toward, praying it won't devastate me. He was never going to save me.

Because the terrible, inescapable truth is that the only shield strong enough to face what's coming is the one I build myself.

CHAPTER FOURTEEN

My hands shake as I read my father's note for the third time. The ink has bled through the parchment. His fury can't be contained by the page which has been tortured where the quill caught and dragged. He's livid I missed the banquet last night. Furious about yesterday. Anxious that Darian might have lost interest.

The servant who brought the message is pale, trembling, eyes flickering between the note and me as though he expects my rage too.

"Tell my father," I say, folding the letter, "that Darian wants a chase, so I'm giving him one. I'll meet the prince this afternoon. No sooner."

The boy bows and leaves like he's been unshackled. Mallen closes the door behind him with a soft thud that sounds heavier than it should.

The silence isn't peaceful—it's taut.

It's the quiet before the first drop of rain falls.

I reach for a book, hoping he'll give me space, but his presence is like a night that summons the tide toward the shore. Heavy. Measured. I can feel him across the room—every inch of him—like heat from a fire I don't dare get too close to.

I feel him watching. Too contained. Wanting.

I want him too.

I ache to let his arms wrap around me, to know the strength of his body as he closes off the world. There's comfort in his control, in how completely he commands danger away. But yesterday, that control slipped. I saw what he keeps beneath the surface—jealousy so sharp it cut through the room—and it shook me.

It wasn't the aftermath. It was the hunger in his voice, the shadow in his eyes when he thought Darian might take me from him. I know the heat of that possessiveness. The lengths men will go to when it consumes them. The terrifying certainty of it. And I've seen what that kind of obsession becomes if no one stops it.

"We should talk about yesterday," he says, voice lower than usual. Too careful.

My eyes stay on the page.

He walks closer, slow enough that tremors roll up the base of my spine. One hand slides over mine, light as breath, and only when I don't pull away does he gently press the book shut. I don't flinch, but I don't look at him either.

"I made a mistake," he murmurs. "You did too."

My gaze lifts. Slowly.

"I promised to give you time. To win your affection—and to let you breathe. To let you feel whatever this is. I meant it." His jaw tenses. "But I didn't know how much it would cost me."

"You broke your word. Gods, that fight...my room...my mother's chair..."

He flinches. Just a flicker of pain in his eyes, so raw and human that I almost forget how furious I am. But he doesn't defend himself.

"It shouldn't have happened," he says. "None of it. You have every right to be angry."

I set the book down with care. "You think I'm angry?"

He breathes in like he's bracing himself for impact.

"I'm not angry. I'm afraid."

That gets his full attention. The heat drains from his face.

"I won't live like this," I add, voice flat.

There it is. So simple. So ordinary. But it breaks something between us.

"I would never hurt you," he says quietly. "Not now. Not ever. But I know how it looked. I know what I sounded like. That wasn't the man I want to be for you."

I don't speak. I can't.

"I am not my jealousy," he adds. "But I carry it. I carry it every time he looks at you like you're already his. Every time he dances with you, while I stand in the shadows. Every time he makes you laugh like I don't exist."

His control is starting to fray. He takes a breath and his shoulders tighten, as though physically restraining the urge to reach for me.

"Don't run from me because I failed once," he says. "Don't throw yourself at Darian because I lost control. That boy will use this. I know his kind. I've seen it before. He'll smile at you while he locks you in chains and takes what he wants while pretending it was always yours to give."

There's no venom in his tone. Only knowing. And something like fear.

"I'm not throwing myself at anyone," I say.

He exhales sharply. Relief.

"Least of all you."

His knuckles whiten as they grip the edge of a table that survived the carnage like he's grounding himself in the wood.

Evie arrives before either of us can say another word. She gives me a knowing look and helps me dress, her movements brisk but gentle. Mallen doesn't speak and doesn't watch as I dress, but his gaze burns anyway—like a low flame flickering through the quiet hours of the night—especially when Evie chooses the emerald green gown.

It matches his eyes. But it's not for him.

"Darian will like this," Evie murmurs as she fastens the gold bangle around my wrist. It sits too tight, and I wince, and Mallen shifts, his attention fixed on me.

The heat of his gaze is unmistakable, but he doesn't move. Doesn't speak. Doesn't explode. He looks like a man teetering on the edge of reason, as if it's taking every ounce of restraint he has not to act on the fire burning beneath his skin. His fingers cling to the table, and he stays there, immobile, while I glide to the door.

I stop and turn.

"Are you coming?"

He looks up. The air is still. His nod is a single movement, tight and wordless. He follows me two steps behind, silent until we reach the edge of the garden path.

Then, just before the gate, he catches my wrist.

"Please," he says. "Don't give him ground because I lost mine."

I lift my brows slowly and then glance down at his fingers still curled around my arm.

"I'm not giving anyone anything."

I shake his hand off and step into the light, toward the prince waiting among the flowers. He's waiting in a patch of pale light, bathed in gold and the faint perfume of roses. Up close I see the stiffness in his right shoulder, linen peeking under his collar where a bandage sits, and the purple bloom along his throat. He still looks almost too perfect to be real—like someone conjured him from a dream I once had and barely remember. Not like the man who was shouting yesterday. Not like someone who stormed into my room, hands clenched and voice shaking.

"Azhara," he says, soft as silk.

"Darian," I reply, holding his gaze but not stepping any closer.

His smile falters. "You're not alright."

"I didn't say I was."

He nods, hearing the edge in my voice without flinching. "I owe you an apology. For yesterday. For how I acted when I thought—" He breaks off, lips pressing tight. "I thought he was hurting you. And I snapped."

His voice cracks, just faintly. He shifts his stance as if he's suddenly uncertain. I don't feel like I'm standing in the shadow of royalty anymore. Just that of a man who made a mistake and regrets it.

There's a flicker of boyish charm in the way his weight alters—uncertainty or shame or both—but it makes him real. Fallible. Not a prince out of reach, but a person I might be able to trust, one careful step at a time.

"I'll never forgive myself for it—but I will make it right. If you let me."

His tone is even.

His words are what I needed to hear.

It sounds so easy. And tempting.

I nod, but I don't say anything. My silence is an answer.

Darian watches me for a long moment before asking, quieter this time, "Did he hurt you? Last night. After I left?"

"No," I say quickly, maybe too quickly.

His eyes narrow slightly, not in suspicion but in sorrow.

He steps closer, slow enough to make sure I'll allow it.

"You don't have to protect him. Or explain him."

"I'm not."

"Alright." He dips his head, brushing a hand through his hair. "But I saw your face. You were scared. Not startled. Not overwhelmed. Frightened. And you were asking him to let you go."

I close my eyes, and the image of the shattered mural returns.

"I'm not here to turn you against him. I'm not going to paint him as a monster. Maybe he's not. Maybe he's just...dangerous in ways he doesn't see yet."

I open my eyes and immediately look away. He doesn't push.

"And maybe," he adds gently, "you're not ready to walk away from him."

My gaze snaps back. "I don't belong to anyone."

A flicker of amusement crosses his lips. "Good. Keep it that way."

I almost laugh, but I don't. Instead, I drift toward a tall stem of midnight-purple blossoms nestled between some white roses and let my fingers trail their petals. They're cool against my skin. Velvety. Fragile.

"Did you want me to pick them for you?"

I shake my head. "My father dislikes it if the garden looks untidy."

Darian steps beside me. "Then we won't pick them. Just admire."

A pause.

Then, quieter, "You don't have to stay here, Azhara. Whatever he says, whatever your father insists—this doesn't have to be your life. I know how tightly they've wound you into this cage, but cages can be broken."

"You think it's that easy?"

"No," he says simply. "I think it'll be hell. But I also think it'll be worth it."

My heart lurches.

He turns toward me, eyes open and honest. "I'm not asking for anything now. I'm not expecting a decision. But when you're ready—when *you* decide—Larksbind is yours. You'd be free there. Not hidden. Not claimed. Protected, yes. But never controlled. Not by me. Not by anyone."

"Even if I never...?"

"If you never love me?" He smiles faintly. "Then I'll still be proud to stand beside you."

Tears sting the backs of my eyes. I blink them away, stunned by the gentleness in his voice. I didn't know how much I needed that softness until he gave it without asking. It slides into a part of me still raw, still trying to mend itself beneath old wounds I no longer bother naming.

"I'll wait," he says. "Not because I expect anything from you, but because

I believe in you. I've seen the woman that you are, and the one you're trying to become. She's there. Still fighting. Even when they try to bury her beneath obedience and silence."

My throat tightens. I think of my father's hand on my shoulder. Mallen's voice rasping my name like a possession. The loneliness left by my mother's death.

"Why?" I ask. "Why would you wait?"

"Because you're worth it."

I stare at him, stunned by the calm certainty of it. There's no hunger in his gaze, no claiming. Just truth. Just light.

It's so simple. So disarming.

And gods help me, I want to believe him.

His fingers brush mine—not pressing, just there. Offering.

"I won't crowd you," he adds. "I won't push. You've had too much of that already. I know what men like your father do. What men like *him* can become. But I'm not your jailer. And I'm not in competition."

He nods toward the far side of the garden. I don't have to look to know who he means.

"I'm just here," he finishes. "If you want me."

My breath catches.

He doesn't lean in. Doesn't even try to kiss me.

He just waits.

After a long moment, I let my hand curl around his.

Not a promise. Not a choice. Just a thread of connection in a life where most have snapped. His touch lingers like he doesn't want to let go. Like he wants me to know that there's a shoreline in the distance, even if I can't see it yet.

His expression softens. He squeezes gently and then lets go.

We stand like that for a while—side by side, not touching, just breathing in the scent of the flowers and the coming dusk. The wind brushes past like a memory half-remembered. Somewhere, a bird calls, and it sounds like hope.

And for once, I'm not watched. I'm not judged. I'm not afraid.

The shadows stretch longer across the stones.

A guard's voice cuts the silence. "Princess. It's time."

Darian turns toward the sound and then glances at me. "May I walk you back?"

I hesitate. Then nod.

He rests his hand in the small of my back, just warm and steady.

I walk beside him, step for step, wondering if it's possible—really possible—to begin again.

To choose something different. *Someone* different.

Not because he's perfect. But because he's kind. Because he waits. Because he doesn't ask me to be anything except myself.

And for the first time, I wonder if that might be enough.

CHAPTER FIFTEEN

Starsfall was never empty. I've heard the stories. Once, it thrummed beneath your feet. Magic clung to the wind, heavy and sweet, humming in the marrow of your bones as it sang songs of birthrights and endings. Its clay pulsed with power drawn toward the heart of the world, its rhythm in harmony with the stars. Its breath was as steady as the constant waves that crashed against our cliffs. It shaped the beasts we lived beside, seasoned the grain we ate, and shimmered in the water we drank. You didn't question the wonder—it simply was.

Then it was gone. The land stilled. The air turned hollow. The only magic left now is the rot I spill into it. The daemon-breeding corruption that arose when my father held back my magic as I took my first breaths.

It didn't have to be this way.

Starsfall's magic was never meant to be spent, only guided. Balanced.

We had Larksbind. Their power was quiet. Enduring. The slow, incorruptible tether my father wanted to control, not break.

The gods grew weary of his lust for power, so they created an instrument of ruin. A weapon made from flesh. A curse my father says my birth brought into the world.

He claims I should never have been born. That the gods themselves realized their error and tried to snuff me out before I even drew breath. That I clung to my mother's life like a parasite and bled her dry from the inside.

I was stubborn. Unyielding. Unrepentant.

And with every day, I came closer to life while she drew nearer to death.

My father rarely speaks of how he fought to save us both. His fire burned brighter than any man's, bright enough to scorch the gods themselves. But my darkness eclipsed even that. In the end, he made the only bargain he could: all of Starsfall's magic, drained in a single moment, to cage what I was becoming. My mother's life traded for mine. One soul for another. The gods like things even.

Balanced.

He gave up more than magic that day. He gave up Larksbind.

Everyone knows Larksbind isn't a source of power—it's the brake. The binding stone. It absorbs magic, holds the excess, and tempers the wild. It's the dam keeping Starsfall from drowning itself. That's why he wants it. To move the balance. To become untouchable.

I always knew that. We all did. My father went to war not because he feared Larksbind, but because he feared what it kept from him.

But maybe even this is a lie.

Darian told me, plainly. If Larksbind falls, no one will be left to hold back the tide. Not him. Not me. Not anyone. The magic will rush in and raze everything. And my father will be free to wield it all. To twist the storm into a menace worse than darkness.

My curse is tied to that balance. While I remain unclaimed, my power sleeps. If someone from Larksbind takes me, their blood binds the chains tighter. Unknowingly, unwillingly, they'll keep me from tearing our kingdoms apart. My father claims he's found a way to keep his power despite the Reaping's terms, but at least the world would stand a chance.

But if they're from Starfall—if I choose a man and a future without Larksbind's control—my magic will detonate like a star dying. Beautiful. Enthralling. Catastrophic.

That's the real prison.

It's not the gilded cage my father keeps me in. Or the two men pulling me in separate directions. It's the choice. The consequences. The slow, devouring spiral of the hell I'll unleash just by choosing wrong.

Choose Darian, and I choose one war.

Choose Mallen, and I face another.

"The Reaping isn't your fault," Mallen says, voice low, the usual steadiness strained. His eyes are fixed on me, green storm clouds flickering. "Not all truths are absolute."

I don't answer. His words don't comfort. They're an anchor being thrown too late.

He's reading my silence, as always. A muscle ticks in his jaw. "Tell me how to fix this, Azhara. Anything. Just say it."

I turn slowly and lean against the cracked wall, placing cold stone at my spine. He mirrors me across the room, rigid and still, but I see it—the crack in the mask. The faint tremor in his hands. The coil of envy unraveling in his eyes.

He's always been control incarnate. Steel sheathed in calm. But now that calm is fraying. I can see it in the line of his shoulders, in the way his fingers keep curling into fists and then flexing open again.

Mallen is not a boy. He is a blade—and blades do not bend, they break.

"You swore you wouldn't keep me in the dark," I say quieter than I mean to. "Once. When I was foolish and believed in hope."

His expression doesn't change. He looks haunted. "I never hid what would take your choice."

"Just the names you erased and the warnings you kept."

He looks away, jaw tight. His composure wavers again before he reins it back in. "You think I wanted this? You think I wanted to see him—with you, the way they cheered him, the way you smiled? I've spent my life restraining myself—for your sake and for Starsfall. Do you know what it cost me not to tear him apart in front of them all?"

There it is. Not boyish jealousy. Something older. Fiercer. Less about wanting and more about keeping.

I should be afraid of that, but I'm not.

"We can't fix this," I say. "Not unless you tell me everything that's going on. I know this Reaping is different. The rules aren't the same. What else is my father changing? What are you keeping from me?"

He flinches. Just once. But he hides it well. "You asked for my help once," he says softly. "Ask again. Let me keep you safe. Let me make things right."

The offer stings. Because I want to believe it. Because a part of me still hopes he might. That's the most dangerous part of all.

"I cannot trust you unless you trust me, Mallen. I cannot breathe."

He exhales, ragged, and his hands go to his hair like he's about to rip it out. He catches himself, but barely. His body is taut with restraint. As though there's a fault line running through him, and he's terrified of what happens if it cracks.

When he speaks again, his voice is hoarse. "Then let me give you what I can."

I don't answer. I won't give him that. Not now.

He stares at me a moment longer, as if memorizing the last light before the sun goes down.

Then he turns. "Wait here."

He's gone before I can stop him.

A moment later, four palace guards file into the room. None meet my eye. One clears his throat and gestures toward the window with forced politeness.

"If you'd kindly...step away."

I comply, slowly. Not for them, but because I know Mallen sent them. And I want to see what price he's paying to keep hold of me.

I pick up a book, letting my eyes scan the lines without absorbing a word. My mind is elsewhere. On what Darian said. On what he didn't. On the possibilities he offers, and the flaws he's trying to hide in his perfection.

When Mallen returns, he's breathless and holding out my cloak like a peace offering.

"We're going out," he says.

I blink. "We're what?"

His grin is too tight. "Your father agreed. Eventually."

"My father doesn't agree to anything."

"I lied," Mallen admits. "Told him it would make you seem more appealing to Darian. He liked my idea." His smile falters. "Don't ask what else I said. I'd rather not think about it."

He steps forward and catches my hand before I can withdraw. His grip is too firm, as if he's afraid I might vanish. I should ask him what he offered my father to persuade him to grant me this rare indulgence—one of the few times I'm permitted beyond these walls. I'm not allowed to roam Threnos freely. Not unless it's for ceremony, or the Reaping, or the bloodsport Mallen calls training.

"You used to smile on our walks," he says. "You were free. With me."

I almost believe him.

But when I say, "This doesn't fix anything," I mean every word.

He nods, slowly. "I know."

We leave my chambers in silence. Guards shadow our steps through the gilt-marble halls, past the colonnades veined with ivy and ashstone, past the paintings of heroes from Starsfall's past; the ones even kings bowed before. The palace feels colder than it should, like it knows we don't belong to this moment. Outside, the wind bites against my skin, crisp with late-autumn frost. We stop at the top of the palace steps. The city sprawls below, dim and restless, silver torchlight flickering in the bones of its avenues. A hush gathers around us, heavy and expectant.

His voice is quieter now. "This is what today costs."

The flick of Mallen's eyes tells me to glance left, and when I do, I meet Darian's gaze across the palace courtyard. A breath catches in my chest as the look between us lingers longer than it should. Mallen's hand moves, brushing at my cloak with more force than necessary, his fingers tight against the fabric.

"I don't coat my flaws in gold," Mallen says quietly, brushing my hair back. "I've shown you the truth of me. Even when it cost me."

Darian's jaw tightens. He looks away.

"This isn't helping."

My voice lacks conviction. The heat of being wanted burns up my neck and spreads over my cheeks, and it's not because they're fighting. It's because it's over me. I've rarely been the center of anyone's gravity before. I've never had anyone want me like this. Now, there are two of them, and I'm standing too close to lightning to know if I'm burning or becoming the fire myself.

A curve threatens Mallen's lips. "Your father insisted on teasing Darian. Forgive me for taking a little pleasure in having you be mine for the day."

He doesn't sound smug. Just like a man trying to convince himself it's true.

Darian watches everything. There's no weapon on him now, but I doubt he needs one. He's already bled for me. Already killed. He's gauging Mallen's every movement, not with suspicion but readiness.

Mallen turns, offering his arm. "Shall we?"

I take it.

The gates shut behind us with a shudder of iron, and Mallen exhales like he's shed a weight—not the tension, but the audience. He doesn't apologize.

He doesn't ask me how I am.

He knows me well enough to know the answer.

"Glad that's done with."

I don't ask what he means. The moment is brittle, and we both know it won't take much to crack.

"Where do you want to go?" he asks.

I hesitate.

I don't know all of Starsfall's capital, and Threnos feels like a stranger. Like a crown made of thorns and glass—dazzling but meant to cut. I haven't been allowed to touch. I know it by outlines and warnings, not by affection. Not in the way the heir to the throne should know it.

I fumble for an answer.

Mallen offers me his arm. "We'll walk. Tell me if anything catches your eye."

So, we walk.

The city streets are wide and restless, light spilling in golden bands across worn stone. Mallen keeps to my side, guards forming a loose circle behind us, but he's the one people watch. Not because he demands it—but because he doesn't have to. His silence commands more than any threat.

I pause now and then to glance at a market stall or let my fingers drift over a fabric bolt. I'm not used to browsing. Not used to time that belongs to me. The unfamiliarity of choice makes me slow.

Pastry smoke hangs thick in the air. Wine vendors call out blessings in a dozen tongues. Somewhere, a harp plays notes that remind me of dusk. It's almost too soft. Almost too perfect to be real.

There's a tension stitched into the seams of the city. An ache in the air, subtle but insistent, like bruises blooming beneath silk. Below the golden stones and perfumed air, Starsfall's capital has a pulse I don't trust. Like the essence that flows through its veins is snarling in sleep. The labyrinth under Threnos feels alive, its teeth beginning to ache with hunger.

In the merchant's quarter, the streets widen again, the river carving silver through the city. Men shout orders from moored boats. Coins clatter. I walk and let the noise wash over me while my thoughts pick at the seams. My father said a bed, not a vow, moves the magic. If that is true, then every glance is strategy, every touch a lever. The first trial spat men back alive when it never used to. Hope is being fed to Larksbind on purpose or starved in a new way.

The rules are shifting under my feet, and I do not yet see whose hand is on the floorboards.

Face tracks us as we walk. Mallen feels like a possibility that did not exist before, a choice that thrills and terrifies in equal measure. To choose him would be to step into a vow that looks like freedom and might be another cage, and my pulse rises at both possibilities. Darian is another calculus: a prince where Larksbind sent only the condemned, polished grace and quick smiles, truths offered like gifts that are too neat to trust. I want to choose, but first I need to know which parts are real and which are theater.

Mallen angles me toward a jeweler's window. Glass holds my reflection between his and the street. He does not posture. He places us where eyes soften and heat drains off danger. I could ask what bargain he just made with the world, but the light is gentle here, and I want the quiet of it for one breath. I let my fingers hover over the gilt in the case and keep my questions in my mouth.

He turns toward me, his voice quieter. "You may not always like the things I do. But everything I do is for you."

That should unsettle me. Maybe it does. But there's a brightness in his eyes now—not hunger, not heat, but strain. A breaking point held in check by discipline alone. He's been unraveling, quietly, and I'm only just starting to see the edges fray.

He gestures at the window. "Choose something."

I let my hand drift along the glass. The jewels catch the afternoon light, scattering it like shards of a broken promise. They're beautiful. I don't ask the price.

"I don't want to owe anyone anything," I say.

He watches me a moment longer. "Not all debts are counted in gold."

I leave the window before he can explain what he means. We walk. The river winds alongside us like a spine through the city. A stone bridge curves into the older districts, where buildings lean like they're whispering secrets.

"I saw a map once," I say, watching the architecture change, "of Threnos before Starsfall was built on top of itself."

Mallen nods.

I remember how he once told me the bones of old cities never sleep—that magic seeps down into cracks and what festers there learns to survive. To adapt. To hunger.

"The labyrinth still exists." I pause. "Does the monster?"

He nods. Just once.

"What is it?"

He hesitates. "A mistake."

"That's not an answer."

"No," he says, quiet.

His hand remains on my back, and I wonder if he even realizes it.

The light softens as the day turns to evening, and time passes with a hush. Too easily, perhaps. I walk beside a man whose attention is constant, in a city ruled by one monster while another waits in the dark beneath it. And I wonder, not for the first time, if I've mistaken control for care. Or if I've survived by believing that one day I'll solve the maze of lies that only deepens its hold every time I try to escape its clutches.

CHAPTER SIXTEEN

I WAKE BEFORE DAWN. PALE LIGHT SPILLS ACROSS THE FLOOR, gilding the velvet rug in shades of gold and ash.

Mallen is asleep on a new chaise he's brought to replace the one that was destroyed, boots off, jacket folded across the arm. His sword rests within reach. His body does not.

He looks uncomfortable, as if even in sleep he doesn't quite believe he belongs here.

I shift beneath the sheets, and his eyes open instantly—clear, alert. That familiar stillness settles over him like armor.

"I didn't mean to wake you," I murmur.

"You didn't," he says, sitting up slowly. "I was just resting my eyes."

He doesn't comment on the absurdity of the lie. Just scrubs a hand down his face and stands, stretching the stiffness from his shoulders.

My father's orders were explicit. I'm to be guarded at all times. When I sleep. When I eat. When I breathe. Mallen's refusing to let anyone stand post. He'd rather swallow his own sword than leave me with one of the palace guards, one of those soulless watchers who obey without thought or care. Mallen watches, but he *thinks*. *Feels*. That's the danger.

He's been here every night. Quiet and precise. Folding blankets, tending the fire, standing sentinel with a vigilance that would be touching if it didn't feel like a wall between us.

He never looks at me when I'm dressing. Never intrudes more than necessary. It would be chivalrous if it weren't so complicated. It's the fleeting glances. The longing. The restraint. And the jealous edge that threatens to cut through.

I rise and stare out the window, turning away from the ruins of my room that are being reconstructed around me. I think of yesterday. Of Mallen beside me in the half-empty streets, his silence heavy but not cruel. He pointed out a bookshop rebuilt from ash, lingered by the fountain where children once played. There was no apology, not really. Just his presence, offered like a balm I couldn't yet accept. I almost laughed. Almost threaded my fingers through his.

But the things left unsaid were too loud, and the wounds we carried had barely begun to heal.

"The streets are quiet this morning," I say, peering through the veil of fog beyond the glass.

Mallen crosses the room silently and pours water into the basin, laying out a cloth with the same care he gives to drawing his sword.

"They've increased patrols since the attempted kidnapping," he says. "No one's taking chances."

"We both know that wasn't what happened."

"That doesn't matter. If we change the story now, someone bleeds," he says without looking at me. "Not all lies harm. Some aren't worth the cost of correction."

His hands still. He doesn't ask what I mean. He just wrings out the cloth and offers it to me with eyes that say he's heard more than he should.

I take it anyway. Our fingers brush. Lightning sparks in the space between them.

"You should eat," he says, his voice gruff.

I dab at my face and watch him from the corner of my eye. "Do you always order people around this early in the morning?"

"Only those I care about."

That lands heavier than it should. I don't thank him. I can't.

Instead, I nod toward the corner where he's made his strange little camp—books, maps, an untouched tray from the kitchens. "How long are you planning to stay?"

"As long as it takes," he says simply.

To keep you safe, is what he means.

From what, he doesn't say.

From Darian, is what I hear.

We stay like—hands touching, legs pressed together—until time slips from us, quiet as breath. The second challenge is tomorrow, and my father has arranged another meeting with Darian. Neither of us wants to speak of it.

Mallen waits until I'm dressed before breaking the silence.

"Azhara?"

When I don't answer, he takes my wrist—not roughly, not cruelly, but enough to make me look up and see the storm in his eyes.

"He is unlikely to survive the next challenge, but if he does and so much as lays a finger on you, I'll kill him myself."

"You said that last time," I reply, sharper than I mean to.

Mallen scoffs, the sound brittle. "They performed better than expected. But no amount of strength will see them through the second trial."

I don't ask what my father has planned. Mallen wouldn't tell me, and I'm not sure I want to know. Another jealous outburst could burn the whole room down, and neither of us is ready for that.

"The pink suits you, by the way," he says, just as I reach for the door.

He means it as a compliment. But this gown is another costume I can't take off.

I glance down. The dress is a confection of flowers and silk—soft, sweet, utterly unlike me. I loathe it. I told him so ten minutes ago.

"I look like the spring equinox spat me out," I mutter.

His smirk is infuriating. But the way he opens the reception room door—quiet, controlled, bracing himself like he's sending me into battle—sends a sliver of warmth through me.

On the other side, Darian is already waiting.

He stands the moment he sees me. And then he sees Mallen.

Neither speaks.

Their eyes lock in a quiet clash of history and warning—like swords sheathed but still drawn beneath the skin. Darian refuses to move aside. Mallen's growl is low, guttural. It vibrates through my bones.

"I'll be just outside," Mallen says, gaze never leaving Darian. "One word, Azhara."

He doesn't say what he'll do with that word. He doesn't need to.

Darian watches him go, only relaxing once the door clicks shut. He sits, as if nothing happened.

"You decided to bring the garden with you, Princess?" he says, eyes flicking down my dress with a bemused smile.

"I hate this dress," I sigh, sinking into the chair opposite him.

His head tilts. "Your father picked it, then. He did better yesterday, if he wants to provoke me."

The way he says it is too casual. As though he's laying out pieces on a board only he understands.

"How was your day outside the palace?"

I blink.

He smiles faintly, almost to himself. "Ah. So he didn't tell me the truth. How surprising."

My pulse stutters. "You knew he was lying?"

"I suspected," Darian says, folding his hands. "There's no point pretending Mallen doesn't care for you. He's made sure I know."

I don't know what to say. My cheeks burn.

"He was told to make you jealous," I say finally, the words flat and defensive. "That's all."

Darian leans forward, voice soft. "Was he told to sleep beside your bed? To watch you like he'd kill the air for brushing your skin?"

I flinch. He sees too much.

"Why would your father want me to be jealous of Mallen?" he asks, but it isn't a challenge. It's a puzzle, laid gently in my lap.

I meet his eyes and find no anger there. No bruised pride. He's calm. Waiting for my answer.

"To distract you from tomorrow's challenge," I whisper, each word a tiny betrayal. "He won't let me you claim me without a fight, Darian. He'll take any advantage he can, even if I pay the price."

Darian nods, his hand brushing mine. He squeezes gently.

"The Reaping isn't the only game being played," he murmurs.

My gaze drifts around the room. The decor is subdued, almost forgettable. No gilded mirrors, no grand tapestries. The paintings are old—still water, winter trees, the gods giving gifts. One even shows the first King of Starsfall kneeling to offer the Bow of Honor to a commoner who saved his life. A symbol of humility. Of the crown's debt to the brave, now all but forgotten.

My father despises this room.

So why bring Darian here?

"What is it?" he asks.

I reach for his tunic and smooth a non-existent crease. "The room doesn't make sense."

"Oh, I don't know." Darian's gaze shifts to the painting that dominates the east wall. "It has some appeal." He leans close and puts his lips against my ear. "If you know what to look for."

He straightens and rubs his earlobe once and again glances at the painting. As understanding arrives, my knees almost give out. We are being watched. My father is listening.

I force my breath to steady. My stomach knots. I want to be wrong. I want to believe I've misunderstood. But of course I haven't. There's no garden meeting today. This room was chosen because it serves him.

Darian tilts his head and smiles. "It's my turn to make Mallen jealous."

He shifts closer, his gaze heavy on mine.

I don't move.

He leans in and stops. A breath away.

Our lips don't meet.

"You're changing," he murmurs, his voice a thread of velvet. "You won't let yourself be used anymore. Not even by me."

"I'm tired of all these games," I whisper.

His smile fades. Not fully, but enough.

"I'm not playing," he says.

I close my eyes for half a breath. I want to believe him. I want to believe anyone. But trust has become a trick mirror—showing me only what I wish to see, never what's true.

"I will survive the Reaping and win your affection, and not because you're a prize to claim," Darian replies, quieter now. "You're remarkable, Azhara. And you're finally beginning to realize it."

I don't respond. I don't need to. The silence does what words cannot—it admits he's right.

We drift into small talk, the kind that's dull enough to bore anyone listening. It's all smoke—scattered phrases and idle nostalgia, chosen carefully to hide the deeper pulse beneath them. He leads, weaving a picture of Larksbind like it's a lullaby meant to seduce the restless part of me. The capital built high on the clifftops, white stone gleaming above the raging sea. Fishermen pulling nets through the surf. Lanterns bobbing like fireflies as ships return to harbor. He speaks of the forest and the salt-thick wind, the hunt and the feasts, and a kind of joy that feels unfamiliar to me—quiet, wild, unburdened.

It sounds like freedom.

It sounds like peace.

But it also sounds like danger.

Because I know what magic costs, and I know what my father took from them. Larksbind has already bled for its safety, and that may not be enough. If I leave with Darian, if the curse breaks and my father comes for us, the price of safety will rise. And it won't be paid in coin.

He taps my hand, drawing me back. I blink once and smile. He softens in relief.

If he knew what I was thinking, he'd stiffen instead.

"How are the injured men?" I ask, voice low.

His composure falters—just for a beat—as if the truth touched a raw nerve, and the mask slips a little. "The healer's done what he can. But one won't last another trial like the last."

No one will, I think. Not if my father wants blood this time.

Outside, the sky is bruising with night. Time's run out.

Darian shifts closer, head tilting. I can see the intent in his eyes a moment before he leans in—slow, deliberate. A kiss. For the watchers. For my father. Maybe even for himself.

I turn my head, and he pauses mid-motion, his breath touching my cheek.

"The next trial isn't physical," I whisper, quiet as a prayer.

He's still for half a second. Then his fingers twitch once against the chair, and his expression smooths into studied elegance, like a man already imagining the next move. He gazes at a painting on the far wall like it's suddenly caught his interest, and then turns back to me and reaches up. As if there's another strand of hair that needs brushing from my face, even though we both know there isn't.

Just like he did earlier.

Just like Mallen did yesterday.

It's deliberate. And it's enough. A perfect performance, for whoever's watching. My father will be pleased Darian's still in pursuit. If it's Mallen, he'll be jealous—but not as jealous as he would have been if I'd let Darian kiss me. That line I won't cross.

Not tonight.

Maybe not ever.

Darian's mouth tightens slightly, and I see the confusion he quickly disguises with a half-smile. He doesn't look like he understands. He thinks I'm worried he won't survive the next trial. He thinks I'm beginning to fall.

And, heavens help me, maybe I am.

And what terrifies me is how easy it would be.

To believe.

To trust.

To hope.

"I'm not dying," he says softly. "Not yet."

I nod anyway and let the silence return, because I don't want to explain what I'm really feeling—the twist in my gut, the quiet ache I don't have a name for. I don't like how much Mallen's silence is beginning to mean to me. I don't like how wrong it feels to keep walking this knife's edge between two men who've both risked everything for me.

I've been used all my life; shaped into a weapon, molded into a daughter who can serve a king's purpose. But this guilt is new. This dread is mine.

Eventually, Mallen comes for me. He's quiet on the walk back to my room, one hand always close to his blade, the other near my spine like a ghost of a touch. The palace is too quiet. The stone hallways echo in ways they shouldn't.

Inside, I undress slowly. Mallen stands with his back turned at first, but when I slip into bed, he moves to my side and crouches low. His face is darkness without light, carved from shadow and restraint, and his eyes lock to mine with fierce precision.

"What did you whisper to him?" he asks.

I don't flinch. I lean into the lie like it's armor. "Nothing of any importance."

Mallen studies me for a moment and then tilts his head in that familiar way—like he's watching me from a place I'll never quite reach.

There isn't any doubt in his expression.

He knows I've lied.

And he's choosing not to challenge me.

And that hurts more than if he'd lied.

He brushes a finger against my wrist, tracing the spot where Darian's hand held mine. Darian clings like fire—bright, consuming, dangerous. But Mallen lingers like shadow—patient, watching, always waiting to be chosen.

Mallen's voice is gentle when he speaks, deep and full of quiet conviction.

"So it's a lie that comes between us," he says.

CHAPTER SEVENTEEN

A HEAVY GOLD NECKLACE HANGS AROUND MY THROAT, BRIGHT AS a sunlit serpent coiled to strike. When the light hits it, fractured beams scatter across the walls like splintered glass. It gleams like something sacred. But it feels like a shackle. Mallen notices, eyes flicking down, jaw tightening.

"You'll never wear another chain, even if it is gilded in gold," he says, quietly. A promise, not a question.

My shoulders ease, but he doesn't reach for me. Doesn't offer comfort.

"Shall we go?" he asks, cool and clipped.

We walk in silence. His hand hovers near mine, never touching. His jaw is set hard enough to crack and it's not the trial making him rigid. It's me. It's last night. The lie he recognized for what it was—and who it was for. He doesn't speak of it. Doesn't rage. He just withdraws, leaving silence in his wake like a blade left hanging in the air.

Guilt churns in my stomach. He's hurting. And I want to reach through the wall he's built. I want to say I'm sorry. But I can't say it aloud. Not when I'm not sure I am.

We stop outside the arena. Mallen turns. His face is granite. His eyes storm. There's something in the way he's holding himself—as if his own skin is too tight.

"It will be fast," he says. Low, gritted. "I'll be close if you need me."

I hesitate, reaching for him. A small gesture. A plea.

He steps back. Almost imperceptibly. A slight shake of the head. He nods toward the doors instead. Dismissal cloaked as direction.

I walk forward, spine straightening. Each step is a refusal to be diminished. The arena opens before me like a wound.

My father smiles.

It isn't warmth. It's a grin carved from bone and ice, honed on the edge of cruelty. He welcomes me with that hollow, rehearsed benevolence he wears like a second skin. I move to my place beside him, slipping into the role he cast for me—princess, prize, ornament. The sovereign daughter groomed for auction.

Below, the tributes stand in formation, prepared for whatever torment comes next. All of them follow Darian as he steps forward and bows. He stands tall as the others echo his movement. One of them sways, limping.

"Can't we spare the injured one?" I murmur.

My father's lip curls. "Rules are rules, Azhara. You've broken enough of them already."

I don't respond. The crowd roars, free from the burden of his malice. The stone of the arena gleams white under the sun, too pure for what's about to happen. Arches rise like cathedral bones, and the people give thanks to their gods, blind to the blood being poured in their name. A child balances on the railing with a fistful of sugared figs, giggling as a blood-stained banner dances in the breeze beneath them.

Darian's gaze stays locked on mine. Clear, unflinching. Sky blue and sunlit gold. There's a steadiness in him, a grounding. He's unafraid. Or he hides it better than most. He turns slightly, directing the others with a single hand.

The arena is unchanged—sand underfoot, walls too sheer to climb, flags whispering in the breeze. But something is wrong. The crates along the edges are too large, too still. Five of them. And the servants waiting by the ropes look like they'd rather flee than follow orders.

I glance at Mallen.

He sees me. But he doesn't move.

His stillness cuts deeper than a thousand outbursts. He's showing me how often he's come to my aid. And how he won't do it this time. Not when I reached for another man.

It hurts. But I understand.

I've hurt him too.

And actions come at a price. In Starsfall. In life.

My father leans forward. His glee is starting to surface.

Whatever he's planned—this isn't strategy. It's cruelty.

I go cold.

Sweat beads on my upper lip. My stomach twists. But I force my chin up.

"Perhaps the princess should begin the proceedings?" my father calls, loud enough to draw cheers from the crowd.

It's not a request. It's a challenge. Submission or strength. Let him humiliate me or let him turn my defiance into a spectacle.

My eyes flick to Darian. He nods. No theatrics. Just understanding. We are both pawns. But I still have hands. And I move them.

I draw breath and step forward. I make sure to meet my father's eyes and raise my voice to carry to the crowd. "By my words, and by my will," I pause to let the implications land, "let the next trial begin."

The slaves open the crates and flee. Ropes pull them out of danger. The tributes form ranks, shields raised, knees bent. Braced for what they cannot see.

Silence falls.

Not the hush of reverence, but a void. A vacuum that devours even thought.

Something is coming.

The stillness presses down like a held breath, like a scream waiting to tear loose. The tributes shift, uneasy, as if the air itself could wound. Outside the stands, even the animals are silent. No birds. No wind. No gods.

Just the sound of a man vomiting in one of the stands, retching onto the arena's stone because he already knows.

Then—smoke.

It spills from the crates. Thin tendrils at first, brushing across the sand like fingertips. Then thickening. Crawling. Shuddering. Growing darker with every breath it takes.

The air changes. The light bends. The smoke isn't smoke. It moves like water, but it's not water either. It pulses. It thinks. It seems alive, evil. And it hates.

A pressure builds in my chest. Not fear. Not entirely.

Recognition.

The smoke deepens—gray to black to a shade beyond midnight. A shade that swallows all light. A magic that devours instead of radiates. I know its name, though no one taught it to me.

Obcasus.

Not a spell. Not a force. *A hunger.*

Death made manifest.

Once, it was sealed beneath the deserts of the dead, locked in runes of salt and bone. Before the first gods fell. Before men grew bold enough to think they could tame what was never meant to serve.

Obcasus is the oldest wrong. A hunger that learned to wear magic like skin.

I stagger. My hands tremble. My skin prickles.

And in my marrow, a pressure begins to mount—coiled and blistering. There's a thrum in my blood like a locked door remembering it has hinges. Like a breath drawn too deep in a place that forbids air.

The darkness inside me—still bound, still waiting—shift with want. With memory. With *need*. It presses against my ribs like it's testing them for give. As if my body is no longer enough to hold the magic.

"What have you done?" I whisper, staring at the dark tide slithering toward the men.

My father laughs. Quiet. Cruel. "By your own hand, indeed. Don't tell me you fear your own nature, Daughter."

My magic coils tighter in the pit of my gut. I clench my fists, breathing shallow.

It pushes harder now, as if the veil between us thins—between me and the thing stitched into my blood. As if the darkness before me isn't a threat, but a summons, and the magic buried deep beneath bone and rite and silence lifts its head. Not to run. To seek.

Its pulse beats in tandem with mine, not foreign, not separate—only divided. A mirror, unfinished. And I feel it lean into me, not as an invader, but as a part returning to the whole. The silence between us collapses. And for one breathless moment, I'm not alone in my skin.

Mallen shifts. Alert. Ready. His gaze is on me. But I don't look at him directly. I let him feel it. Let him know: I don't need saving.

I look to Darian instead. And he looks back. Steady. Unmoving. Already waving his men back. He's going to face it. With nothing but a sword and the will to survive. He sees what's coming, what it is—and he doesn't flinch. Doesn't run. His stance lowers, breath steady, sword held like it's part of his body. He's already calculating how he'll die.

And he's choosing to do it standing.

All of Starsfall sees the decision settle in him like stone. If this is how the world ends, then it will end with his spine unbroken.

"It will kill everyone here," I say. My voice is steel.

My father only smiles.

"Breathe," my father says, and his voice is too calm. Too amused. "A sorcerer has ensured it will stay within arena walls. The tributes are the only ones who'll die. The Obcasus will be recalled at the end of the trial. It can't escape or set your blight free."

I grind my teeth.

My cheeks burn hot. With shame. With anger too.

"Unless Darian defeats it," I whisper.

Below, Darian steps forward, his shield discarded. His sword gleams in the torchlight as the black smoke coils toward him like a living thing. His spine is a line of tension. He watches the Obcasus, and it watches him.

He's not just reacting. He's baiting it.

The Obcasus spirals—slow at first, searching. Then faster, narrowing, hunting. The tendrils split and stretch across the arena, severing the space around the tributes like they're being penned in for slaughter.

He moves again. A sudden pivot. A calculated lure.

The Obcasus lunges—and misses.

It crashes into the ground, a dense, writhing wave of black. Not smoke. Not shadow. It's heavier than that. Like oil and bone and the air between heartbeats. It rises again, impossibly fluid, reshaping itself with every strike.

It should be beautiful. It almost is. But the cold crawling up my spine says otherwise.

"They don't stand a chance," I murmur. "The trials are meant to be fair."

"They are meant to be decisive," Mallen says, and his tone scrapes like flint. "Your father wants proof Darian can contain you."

I don't turn to look at him. "Would you set the same test? Or pass it?"

Silence.

No denial. No argument.

Just the iron stillness of a man too controlled to lash out but too possessive to like the questions. His fingers flex ever so slightly beside me. The heat of his attention licks through me, as if my body is a territory he's already claimed.

Below us, Darian crouches, one knee to the ground, tracking the Obcasus. The creature hovers, shifting its weight from one spiral to the next. It's testing him now. Learning.

"You said this wasn't about strength," I say softly.

"It's not," Mallen replies, his voice low. "Either he withstands death, or he doesn't."

The Obcasus slams down again, this time with devastating force. The entire arena vibrates. The air trembles with a pressure that spreads through my bones.

Darian rolls. Fast. Fluid. Controlled. When he lands, he lashes out, sword cutting through the thick body of the thing—and it splits. Not a graze. Not a surface wound. A true division.

The Obcasus obeyed him.

Mallen stiffens.

Darian turns and moves again. Every step is intentional. Every swing carves the air like music—deadly, elegant, precise. His blade arcs, and the Obcasus divides again. Then again. It's fragmenting before him, unraveling as he presses on, forcing it to fracture to survive.

My breath catches. This isn't just defense. He's dominating it.

The Obcasus circles behind, striking from two sides now. He turns, fast enough to parry. A blur of motion. He moves like he's been trained by fire and made for this moment.

And still it comes. Fiercer. Hungrier.

The air darkens. The black smoke thickens until it gleams, tar-like, in the light. It rears and collapses. A hundred strikes. A hundred evasions. Darian weaves through them like a man dancing with his own death.

But even he begins to slow.

His movements are less sharp as the effort takes its toll.

I see it in his shoulders. His breath. The tremble in his thighs as he pushes forward. Sweat shines on his skin and still he moves. Still he fights.

The Obcasus breaks toward the other tributes, flowing like a breached dam. The crowd gasps. The men below freeze.

Darian moves.

He surges after it, reckless and too fast, his boots pounding the blood-soaked sand. He throws himself into its path, sword raised—and brings it down.

The blade punches into the heart of the Obcasus, and the world freezes.

A perfect, impossible stillness.

Then—

Collapse.

The blackness recoils around him, spiraling up, devouring itself as it tries to consume him whole. Darian is swallowed, completely encased in a cocoon of churning smoke and dark light.

I jolt forward.

Mallen's hand grips my arm, steadying me before I fall. But his jaw is clenched, and his breath has gone silent. His restraint is absolute—but only barely. His pulse throbs beneath the thin leather of his gloves.

"He's—" I choke on the words.

I can't look. Can't breathe. Can't think.

He's dying.

I know it the way prey knows the instant before jaws close around its throat. The Obcasus is devouring him from the inside out, a living storm of death magic, and I am certain of this because its magic belongs to me. It's not just smoke or shadow—it's hunger.

It's feeding on him.

And it's fueling the darkness locked in me.

Then I see him.

Darian.

Still inside the storm. Still standing.

His back is arched, his body taut with agony. His hands shake around the hilt of his sword, still buried in the Obcasus. His face tips to the sky. His mouth opens in a soundless roar as the shadows tear at him.

But he does not fall.

He endures.

He breaks the storm open with nothing but his will.

He roars—not in pain, but defiance—and the gale answers him. It flares, shrieks, trembles on the edge of unraveling. Then, piece by piece, it yields. The darkness recoils from his skin, shattering around his form like a mirror struck by lightning. He doesn't destroy it with brute force. He refuses it. Commands it. Bends it until it breaks.

The Obcasus fractures.

Splits into a thousand shards of shadow and disappears, as if it had never been there. As if death itself bowed its head and retreated.

The crowd erupts.

Darian crumples.

He sinks to his knees, his sword falling beside him. The remaining tributes rush forward—some to help, some just to touch him. His chest rises and falls like he's been dragged from the edge of a cliff. One tries to steady him, but Darian flinches like he's been burned—like whatever just touched him was worse than the Obcasus.

I sway.

Mallen catches me. His arm bands across my back like steel.

Too steady. Too possessive.

"You saw it too," I whisper, my voice trembling. "He mastered the Obcasus."

"It's the labyrinth, then," Mallen replies.

He doesn't sound disappointed that there will be a third trial. Or concerned. He's not blinking. Not breathing. His gaze is locked on Darian like a man watching a funeral procession. And when he speaks, it's not with fear or doubt—it's with a calm that fractures at the edges. As if every word is threaded with rust. Or something long buried in him is clawing its way back to the surface.

"Let's see how he fares against what waits inside."

His fingers flex against my spine, not with comfort but control.

He's unraveling. Not openly, but it's there. In the grip that holds me too long, and the fingers that cling a little too tight. In the way his gaze lingers on Darian with a look that holds no respect.

I should pull away, but, right now, I need him.

I look down at the place where the Obcasus vanished.

The ground still pulses faintly. And I feel it.

Not just beneath my feet.

Inside me.

Cold. Familiar. Insatiable.

undercurrents of greed and ambition. Or perhaps he isn't affected by them because they're so similar to his own.

Mallen sits to my left, his posture rigid, eyes scanning the room with calculated precision. "He wants to provoke you," he murmurs. "Don't let him."

Another dance begins, faster than the last. The remaining tributes watch with newfound vigor, their near-death experience igniting a lust for life, while the ladies of the court fawn over them. Darian catches my eye, a flicker of understanding passing between us. We look away simultaneously.

I turn back to Mallen.

"I thought you'd discovered the trial was Obcasus and warned him," Mallen says, leaning closer. "But your reaction was genuine. Shock, then horror. You didn't know." He swirls his wine, contemplating. "Are you going to stop lying to me, Azhara?"

"What do you want, Mallen?"

"Your honesty. Your respect. For you to honor our agreement."

The dance ends, applause erupting. I clap, smiling at Mallen, noting the jealousy simmering in his eyes.

"I can't talk to you like this," I murmur.

"Like what?" he growls.

"There are too many people, too many interruptions." I let my hand graze his thigh. Subtle. A provocation. A dangerous one.

Mallen stiffens, his gaze fixed on the dancers. He exhales and waits for the dance to end before setting down his goblet. His hand brushes my arm, a touch that sends a shiver through my core.

The music changes.

He signals for more drink.

And the servant spills wine into my lap.

I gasp, jumping to my feet—and the hall falls silent. My cheeks burn as I attempt to brush off the red stain. Darian's on his feet. My father wears a grin that curves with both delight and irritation.

"What are you doing?" Mallen's voice is a controlled snarl, directed at the servant.

"I'm soaked."

Mallen stares at me, and I can't understand the emotion swirling through those green irises. It's too intense. Too raw. He offers me his hand as he announces he'll be escorting me to my rooms.

My cheeks burn hotter as we leave.

Mallen thanks him, then turns to me. "You wanted to talk."

I stare at him, drenched and humiliated. "You had that planned?"

He smirks, stepping closer. "A contingency."

"For what?" I remove my bracelets, tossing them onto the table. "Public humiliation? You could've just asked me to leave."

Mallen's eyes go still. No flicker. No flash. Just a slow darkening, like dusk bleeding into midnight. "Would you have come?"

I pause. He knows the answer.

"Exactly." His voice is quiet, but not unkind. "You've been avoiding talking to me. So I made sure we had this chance."

"You could've waited." I untie the wet sash at my waist, letting it fall. "You always do."

"That's the problem, isn't it?" He closes the distance between us, slow and deliberate. "I wait. And wait. And now you're circling Darian."

I stiffen, fingers hovering at the first clasp of my gown. "You want to chastise me now?"

"I want to listen," he says. "You're not making it easy."

I turn away from him, cross to the fireplace, and press my hands to the marble. My dress clings to me, soaked and heavy against my skin. I want to be out of it. I want to be out of all of this—my father's games, the court's eyes, Mallen's relentless scrutiny. But most of all, I want to be understood.

"You think I've been lying to you," I say.

"I know you have."

The silence between us stretches long and thin. I close my eyes. "Fine. You want truth? I didn't know about the second trial. If I had, I would've warned Darian."

"Because you want him to win?"

"Because I don't want him to die."

Mallen exhales behind me, a sound half-sigh, half-snarl. "That's not an answer."

"It's the only one I have."

His footsteps are quiet on the stone floor. He's near again. Close. I can feel the weight of his presence behind me.

"You made me a promise," he says. "No others."

"Don't," I whisper. "Not tonight."

"Why not?"

"Because I'm soaked in wine and court politics, and I can't think. I'm barely standing. I can't stop flinching at my own shadow."

I hear the hitch in his breath. "You think I'd hurt you?"

"No," I say, turning to face him. "I think you could."

The words land heavy between us. His jaw tightens. He looks at me like he's searching for something in my expression—for certainty, for choice, for everything that's in between. I don't know which he wants more.

"You're not the same anymore," I say, gentler now. "You used to be my friend. Now, you're not. You're more."

"That bothers you?"

"Yes."

He lifts a brow. "Why?"

"Because you were the only one I had."

The admission makes my throat tighten. I didn't mean to say it. But now that it's out, I can't take it back.

Mallen's expression shifts—barely—but enough. Not with pity. It's quieter than that.

A kind of ache held too long behind the ribs. Something patient. And ruinous. Understanding, maybe. Or restraint.

"You didn't lose me, Azhara," he says quietly. "I haven't gone. I'm not standing where I used to, but I've not stopped being yours. I've always been yours. You're just starting to see how things have always been."

My breath hitches.

"I don't know what we are anymore," I whisper.

"We don't have to name it," he replies. "Not until you're ready. But don't pretend it's nothing. Not after everything. Not after the way you look at me when you think I won't notice."

"I'm afraid," I admit. "That if I let myself believe you mean it, I'll fall. And this time, no one will catch me."

He nods, slow and solemn. "Then fall," he says. "I haven't dropped you yet."

He steps closer, close enough that I can feel the warmth of him against my damp skin. His gaze drags down my body—nothing indecent, just observant, like he's cataloging every bruise and frayed edge I'm trying to hide.

"Take it off," he murmurs, nodding to my gown. "You'll catch a chill."

I hesitate.

"I won't touch you," he says.

"I didn't ask you to."

He lifts a brow. "Didn't say you did."

For a long moment, we just stare at each other. Then I reach behind my neck and slowly undo the clasps of my gown. I let it fall in a sodden heap, standing in the shift beneath. He doesn't look away. But he doesn't move either.

"Do you want me to leave?" he asks.

I don't answer right away. I cross the room—deliberately—to the hook where a fresh robe waits. I slip it on, relishing the dry silk against my skin, and cinch it tight at the waist.

"No," I say at last. "I want you to stop treating me like I'm broken."

He tilts his head. "I don't think that."

"You act like I might shatter."

"I act like you've been made to believe you should."

I blink.

He sits down on the edge of the low couch, bracing his forearms on his knees. "I know you. I've seen you lie, manipulate, scheme, and survive. You don't see yourself doing it, but you do. And I've seen you choose mercy when no one else would. You think no one sees that either. But I do."

"I'm not the girl you first met, Mallen."

"I know," he says again. "Nor am I the man you thought I was."

I cross the room, barefoot and slow. "Then who are you?"

He meets my gaze, and for the first time in months, he doesn't look angry. He looks tired. And sad. And real.

"The man who's tried to protect you for years without ever touching you," he says. "One who doesn't know how much longer I can keep doing that. I gave up everything that did not serve your safety. I called it honor and I believed it. Now, I have nothing left to trade but the truth that I want you and the fact that I am breaking on the edge of it."

The breath leaves me.

I sit across from him, drawing my knees to my chest on the cushions.

I study him in the firelight—this man who has haunted the edges of every choice I've made. Who's waited in the shadows, not to punish, but to protect. And now he's here, close enough to touch, and I don't know how to want that without hurting.

My pulse thrums, aching with a truth I've kept buried.

I've always wanted to be chosen.

Not out of duty. Not out of pity. Not because of some wicked game the gods set in motion long ago. But because I am worth being chosen, even after everything I've been through. After everything I've become.

I used to believe survival was enough. Now, I'm not so sure.

He watches me for a long time. "Darian isn't just a threat to your father. He's a threat to you."

I frown. "Because he's strong?"

"Because he believes he's right." He leans forward. "He's not afraid of you. And you're not afraid of him. That makes him dangerous."

"Not every man who doesn't fear me is dangerous, Mallen."

"No," he agrees. "But every man who wants to use you is."

"You think he's using me?"

"I think he wants to win," Mallen says. "And I think you've convinced yourself that letting him would be the easiest way out."

"Out of what?"

"This," he says. "This prison. This power. This throne. This version of yourself that you hate so much you'd rather die than claim."

The words split me open.

"I don't want to die," I say.

"I know," he replies. "But you don't want to live like this either."

We stay silent. There is no defense I can make that doesn't sound hollow. No retort sharp enough to wound him without also drawing my own blood.

"You could've let me fall a dozen times," I say at last. "But you never did."

"No," he agrees. "I let you run."

I glance at him. His posture has relaxed slightly, though his hands are still clenched between his knees.

"I didn't want to be caught," I whisper.

"Is that so?" he says softly. "Or did you want someone to chase you? Maybe you just didn't think it would be me."

My heart trips over itself. I hate how easily he sees me. Hate it and crave it.

"I thought I'd be safer with someone who couldn't read me," I admit.

"And now?"

I look at him. "Now I don't know what's worse—being read or being wrong."

The air between us shifts. Heavy, but not stifling. A quiet understanding, old and tender, rises between our words.

Mallen straightens slowly. "Come here."

I hesitate. "Why?"

"So I can kiss you," he says. "And then put you to bed before I do something more foolish."

My pulse stumbles.

I rise, and he meets me halfway. We stop a breath apart, our shadows flickering in the firelight. His hand lifts, brushing my jaw, calloused thumb grazing the hollow beneath my cheekbone.

"You're not broken," he murmurs again.

"I know."

His mouth finds mine—not greedy, not bruising. Just...patient. Starved. Reverent. I lean into him, fingers tangling in the fabric at his chest. For a moment, we're nothing but the press of mouths and memory. The ache of what's always gone unsaid.

He pulls back first. But his hand lingers on my face.

"When this is over," he says, "when you choose—really choose—I'll still be here."

I don't answer. I don't know how.

Because some part of me still wants to ask *what if I don't choose you?*

Some part of me is afraid he already knows the answer.

But the rest of me—the tired, fractured, wholly human part—just wants this.

His mouth brushes mine again, softer this time. A question. An anchor. I kiss him back like I mean it. Like I haven't spent years building walls just to keep these feelings out.

He makes a sound, quiet and rough, as his arms come around me and he draws me into the heat of his chest. I melt into him, into the quiet hush of firelight and shadows and the steadiness of his breath. My cheek rests against his shoulder. His pulse flutters just beneath my mouth.

I don't know how long we stand there. Long enough for the questions to fade, for my doubts to hush. Long enough for me to forget I was ever afraid.

Still, when I finally speak, my voice is quieter than before.

"Tell me something true."

He's silent. For a beat too long.

"You've never left my thoughts. Not once."

It's a good answer. The kind you want to believe. One that fits too neatly into your ribs if you stop thinking.

"You're mine, Azhara," he murmured, voice low and certain. "But only if you choose me."

I nod. Slowly, finally, I nod.

And Mallen, my warrior, my storm, simply holds me tighter.

He kisses me once more—slow, deep, like a promise. When he finally leads me toward the bed, I let him.

CHAPTER NINETEEN

I WAKE TO WARMTH. A WEIGHT ACROSS MY WAIST, A STEADY rhythm of breath at my back. Not a trap—an anchor.

"Morning, Princess," Mallen murmurs against my neck, his voice rough with sleep.

"Did you sleep in my bed?"

He goes still. A breath, tight and slow. "You asked me to stay. I did."

He draws away before I see his face. By the time I roll to look at him, he's sitting upright at the edge of the bed, muscles tense, spine drawn like a bow.

"I just meant—" I reach out, my fingers brushing the ridges of his back. "I was worried we'd be seen."

He glances over his shoulder, wary, reading me. Then he sinks back down beside me, careful. We lie facing each other, breathing the same hush.

He's unconcerned.

Of course he is.

My father made him Commander of the Royal Guard for a reason. Those guards answer to Mallen now. There was never any risk. I trace a line down his chest, watching him watch me. His jaw ticks, but he doesn't stop me.

"You're warm," I whisper.

He catches my hand, pressing it flat over his heart. It beats hard beneath my palm. "This will be over soon. I promise."

"How will you deal with my father?" I ask.

His gaze sharpens, forest green and flint-edge. "I taught you better than this."

He's not angry. He's reminding me—who he is, what he's capable of. His restraint is terrifying. Cunning threaded through every breath. There's little cruelty in him, but there's little mercy, either. None for a man like my father.

"Does it upset you?" he asks.

"Would it change anything if it did?"

"Maybe." His eyes hold mine, unreadable. Then he brushes his knuckles down my cheek. "Your father deserves to be erased."

The words aren't snarled. They're cool, quiet, steady. That makes them worse.

But he isn't looking at my father. He's looking at me like I'm his whole world, or the war worth waging and the ruin he welcomes. Maybe I'm the reckoning he's waited for, and the altar he'd burn the world to reach.

It feels like gravity. Like drowning.

I bury my face against his chest and let him hold me.

"I don't care how many men fall," he says softly. "You've been trapped long enough. Let me break the walls."

"And my magic?" My teeth grate over my bottom lip. "What if it's too much? What if he's right?"

Mallen huffs a bitter breath. "You're stronger than that. Than him. Stop giving him power he doesn't deserve."

I want to believe him. I want to be that girl.

I don't remember blood on the marble. I don't remember my mother's scream as it tore from her throat. Or the way the light went out in Starsfall, as if the land itself recoiled from what I'd done. My magic's been waiting. Hungering. Sealed in shadow for twenty years. One wrong move and the darkness inside me will rise and devour everything.

It stirred yesterday—called to the Obcasus like a temptress beckoning ruin.

If it hadn't been for the binding woven by the gods themselves, I'd have killed everyone in Starsfall. My father, as he basked in his glory. The nobles, busy indulging him and vying for his attention. The children, playing games while blood drips onto the arena floor beneath them.

I turn my face away.

Mallen shifts closer. His hand smooths down my spine with aching care.

"Wherever you just went—don't. Not now." He tilts my face to his. "You're not weak, Azhara."

His thumb grazes my lip. To remind himself I'm real. Then he kisses me—not to claim, but to quiet the storm. My pulse jumps, but he doesn't press. Just lets his mouth linger like a promise I haven't decided to keep.

We lie tangled together, sharing breaths and quiet laughter. For a while, we forget. It's easy with him—too easy. Like nothing outside this room exists. And I let myself believe that nothing can touch us. Not now, not ever.

But the summons comes anyway.

He's silent while I dress, pacing behind me, a tension radiating off him like storm heat. When he catches my wrist to steady me, his hand shakes. Just once. He hides it fast.

He walks beside me to the doors of my father's chambers. A sentinel. A sword held back by sheer will.

"You don't have to meet with your father."

I stop.

"This is reckless," he says, low. "Let me find a way to hold him back. To delay."

I shake my head. "Maybe. But I'll never be free if I keep hiding behind someone else's strength."

His mouth opens. Closes. Then he nods, barely. "Then don't flinch, Azhara. Not once. He'll see blood in the water." His eyes close for a moment too long. "You don't have to beat him. Just don't let him make you small."

I pause. His words settle in my chest like flint. This time, I don't curl in on myself.

This time, I knock.

The door opens. My father doesn't rise. He just stares. The chill in his eyes is absolute.

"Darian passed the second trial," he says flatly.

I close the door behind me.

The click of the latch is too loud. The silence after, worse.

Alone, the courage I carried starts to fracture. The air feels stripped of warmth—emptied of the quiet I didn't realize I leaned on. Mallen was the stillness I trusted to catch me.

Without him, the cold bleeds in, an old fear that creeps like frostbite.

I breathe deep. Straighten my spine.

I've seen monsters. Seen men bleed for this kingdom.

I will not be a child cowering in her father's shadow. Not anymore.

I lift my chin and I look him in the eye.

"He did." I fold my hands in front of me. "They say Obcasus is difficult. Even for seasoned mages."

It's not just difficult. It's notorious. My father raised me on tales of how dangerous the magic of death could be. He did it to terrify me. To put me in my place. But he taught me another lesson too—that he feared what he could not control. And even he couldn't silence the stories that told how he struggled to master Obcasus.

The corner of his mouth twitches, not a smile. An edge. He rises slowly, fingers dragging over the polished hilt of the ruby dagger on the desk.

"He's more dangerous than you think," he says. "The Obcasus didn't touch him."

He lifts the dagger, turning it in his hands.

A flicker lights his eyes—something memory-shaped. Shame, maybe. Or fear.

"He will break you," he says. A deliberate beat of silence passes. "Piece by piece."

I don't move.

He starts toward me, each step deliberate. Measured. The light glints off the blade. "You think you're ready for him, but you've never had to submit. Not truly."

"I haven't chosen him," I say quietly.

He stops in front of me. His breath touches my skin. "That doesn't matter. He has the crowd. The favor of the gods. The scent of victory all over him. All he has to do is pass the final trial."

My father lifts a petal from the desk—a single, dried remnant from the first trial. "He gave this to you. Declared it to the crowd." He drops it at my feet. "He's in love."

I step forward and crush the petal beneath my boot.

"Then let him prove it."

His fingers tap the dagger against his palm. I meet his eyes and say nothing.

"You're bold today," he murmurs.

"I don't want to waste your time with small talk."

His smile sharpens, edges drawn in hunger, and turns the dagger in his fingers, lowering it to the map spread across his desk. Slowly, almost gently, he drags the point through the inked borders of the Northern Reach. The blade cuts a jagged line through the territory like he's already carving out blood.

His gaze never leaves mine.

But I feel it—his power, his fury—coiled like a whip waiting to strike.

And I don't flinch.

My father grabs my throat before I can react. His fingers press in—not wild, not frenzied, but deliberate, methodical. I claw at his skin, eyes wide, lungs burning, but there's no fury in his face. Just the same patient, practiced calm of a man who's done this before.

"Stop," I rasp.

I lash out blindly, land a punch—but pain explodes in my cheek. His strike is fast, sharp, a flash of heat that blinds me with tears. He lets go just long enough for me to gasp air before wrenching my arm behind my back. His grip coils in my hair, steering me like a puppet as he marches me toward the balcony.

My chest hits stone. The cold marble bites through silk and skin alike as he forces me forward. His weight settles behind me—not lecherous, just heavy, immovable. I twist, but there's no leverage. No escape. My scalp burns as he yanks my head back.

"You forget yourself," he says softly. "You breathe because I let you."

Below us, a prisoner is dragged into position. Her hands are bound tight. Her back is bared, hair wrenched up and out of the way. Relief flickers because it is not Evie, and shame follows in the same breath. It gutters at once. It is still a woman with her hands bound. Dread fills the space relief left, and my stomach knots.

The guard approaches with a coiled whip.

"This is because of you." My father's voice stays low, even. "Your defiance costs blood. That blood stains you."

He doesn't need to shout. The silence is heavier. Crueler. My limbs go still. He wants me to see. Wants me to understand.

He wants me to watch.

The whip cracks.

The sound alone sends a jolt through me—before the scream even starts.

The second lash cuts deeper. The girl jerks against her bonds, and the smell of copper rises into my throat.

I can't look away. I try. My eyes don't obey.

Don't flinch.

Crack.

Another scream. The whip slices across her back, ribboning skin into ruin. My nails dig into the stone wall. A scream builds in my throat but doesn't escape. Not yet.

"If Darian survives the labyrinth, he'll have to marry you," my father murmurs. "I can't allow that—not while you think your spine's intact. Not when you believe you're stronger than you are."

The whip cracks.

"I wonder if she was a mother," he says.

I recoil. My body lurches with the force of my horror, and still his hands hold me fast.

A sound rises from my throat—a cry I didn't intend. I don't know whether it's grief or rage. But he hears it. And he smiles.

"I thought a child would tame you," he continues. "But if Darian gives you one, you'll fight harder. You'll have something to protect."

The lash lands again. The slave doesn't scream this time. Her body twitches, but her voice is gone. I shut my eyes, but it's worse in the dark. The sounds keep coming. The smell of blood won't let me forget.

I open my eyes to the world below. Her blood pools in the sand, soaking the earth that bore it. I cannot breathe. I cannot move.

He wanted to make me small. Instead, he made me sharper. And something inside me begins to shift. My fingers curl into fists. The stone cuts into my skin, but I don't release it. I *want* to bleed. I want the sting to tether me to now—because what's moving inside me isn't slow. It's rising.

Not horror. Not helplessness. Fury.

A rage older than me, older than him, born from every time I was silenced, every time I was told to smile while part of me died inside. He wants me passive. He wants me docile. But he wouldn't go this far if he thought I was already broken.

This is a show of control, a cruel display of power.

And it's all an act.

Don't flinch.

"By the way," he says, too casually. "You won't be leaving Starsfall if Darian survives the Reaping. You only have to marry him. What happens beyond that is out of the gods' control."

My spine locks. Heat surges through me, wild and wrong and electric—my magic, lashing out, trying to protect me. It isn't obedient anymore. It writhes beneath my skin like a living thing, striking against my ribs, clawing at my throat. My breath catches. The stone beneath me vibrates faintly, as though the whole balcony is waiting to split.

My father doesn't move. But he notices. His gaze sharpens.

"It was Mallen's idea."

I don't believe him. I do. I don't want to.

But it fits.

Mallen, who watched, who smiled, and said nothing. Mallen, who would not stand in the open and say my name, though his gaze devoured me.

If Darian survives, he'll stay. And Mallen will end him.

"I'll get my magic back," my father says. "And you'll lose yours. No more games. Or fighting. Only obedience."

I'm not sure when I collapsed, only that I'm no longer upright. My body has gone slack against the floor of the balcony. I shake with a cold that's deeper than fear. It's luminous and final. It's ending.

This isn't a fairy tale. There is no hero. No rescue.

There's only me.

And the choice I make: to face what I fear or run from it.

The yard below is silent as a crypt. No cheering crowds. No laughter. No music drifting from the feasting halls. Even the single golden leaf that had been spinning in the air, caught in a lazy current, falls straight down, with no grace left in it. No resistance.

Like a body that's finally stopped fighting.

My father inhales, as if enjoying the scent.

"This is what you bring, Azhara."

His grip shifts. Not brutal, just necessary. He drags me from the balcony with the efficiency of a man discarding a piece of himself he no longer intends to acknowledge.

He hurls me into the corridor.

My knees buckle. I slide against the wall, cheek pressed to cool stone. The door slams shut behind me.

I don't cry. I can't.

But I breathe.

Light glints on the door handle. I stare at it. My heart's still racing, my body wrecked, but a single thought roots itself in the center of my mind, cold, absolute, and inescapable.

He's afraid of me.

He wouldn't do this if he weren't. Wouldn't bind me tighter unless I'd started to slip the leash. Wouldn't strike unless he feared I could strike back. He thinks he's won—but he just showed me where to aim.

CHAPTER TWENTY

I WANTED TO BELIEVE MY FATHER WAS LYING. THAT HE'D TWISTED the truth in the horror of his stifling study and what happened beyond it—twisted it because he knew it would cut deepest. But when I asked Mallen—when I pressed him about the idea of keeping me here in Starsfall, even after the Reaping ends—he didn't deny it.

He looked me straight in the eye and said yes.

He told me it was necessary. That it would protect me. That he couldn't let me go.

The days since then have been quieter. Measured. Distant. But underneath that stillness is a slow, suffocating burn. I keep turning his words over in my head, trying to parse what was strategy and what was truth. Wondering if the man I've begun to trust has been playing a longer, darker game all along. Wondering if I should be afraid of the answer.

Mallen doesn't push. He lingers like a shadow, always near, always watching. He touches nothing, says little. Just tracks my movements with eyes that give away too much. He's controlled. But it's the kind of control that feels like a dam in spring—cracked at the edges, holding back a flood that's already begun to rise.

And it makes me wonder—who is he holding back for? Me? Or himself?

I don't trust myself to ask. Not yet.

I've barely left my rooms in days, attending the formalities demanded by the Reaping—the ritual blessings and carefully choreographed appearances meant to signal strength. At first, it was easier to hide inside them. To retreat behind protocol. And Mallen agreed. After what my father did, he insisted I stay close—where he could protect me. But now the walls feel tighter. The ceremonies louder. I need air. I need quiet that doesn't feel like confinement.

So, I ask for the one thing that might help. "May I visit the library?"

He pauses.

That's all—one beat too long.

"No."

A simple word, but final.

His gaze lingers on my face, the emerald of his eyes scanning me like a threat he hadn't decided how to neutralize yet. He doesn't shout. Doesn't touch me. Just refuses.

It's the first time he ever has.

I could press him. Maybe I should. But I catch a flicker before he turns away—a raw twist of jealousy, taut and ugly, like an old wound rubbed open. That's what gives him away. He's not afraid of what I'll find in the library. He's afraid of what it might confirm.

I let him go. I let the moment pass. But I won't forget.

Now, I'm left unraveling everything on my own—half-truths knotted through with careful silence. My father spins stories in broad daylight and smiles as he does it. But Mallen's lies are quieter. He lies by omission and hides falsehood in truth. He carefully constructs timing. He never quite answers what I haven't fully asked.

The festivities of the Reaping drag on.

No one expected seven men to survive the second trial—least of all my father. The court grows tense under the weight of too much celebration, and too little certainty. The men are paraded, applauded, posed for effect. Even Darian looks wearied by it. The cracks in his perfect composure are small but real—his hair always pushed back, his smile a little too quick. He hides it well. But I see it. I think he knows I do.

We find each other in those brief, carefully guarded moments during events. A few breaths snatched behind rose-draped walls or between spiraling stairs. He doesn't touch me—he can't—but when our fingers almost graze, my pulse trips like it's leaping from a cliff.

It's stupid. Dangerous. I shouldn't want it. Not with Mallen watching.

Darian's voice is low against my ear, and no one's looking. "I can't keep pretending. I want more with you."

"We have this," I whisper, the words brittle in my mouth.

His expression falters, just for a heartbeat. That shine in his eyes dulls. "It's not alone."

He leaves before I can say anything else, slipping into the crowd with effortless grace. He knows how to move through this world—knows how to charm, how to win people over. Even the nobles who once sneered at him now tilt their heads to listen. He's collecting women without even trying—earning glances, curling smiles, the kind of attention that opens doors and silences doubt. They follow him like moths toward heat, not realizing the fire isn't meant for them.

It's impressive. It's calculated.

He's everything Mallen is not.

Mallen is beside me before I notice him. His hand grazes the small of my back, not possessive, just present. "He's playing a long game. Men like that don't offer affection freely. Be careful where you step."

I study Darian as he charms a pair of councilwomen. He's golden, effortless, too practiced. A man who could love you while planning your downfall.

Mallen's words lodge behind my ribs and twist—tight, instinctive, protective. Because he's not wrong. And yet—he is.

"You're leaving," I say, my voice too soft.

Mallen hums, low and sardonic. "Your father's requested that I deal with a problem in the west. The labyrinth needs preparation. It'll be two days, maybe less."

"You think he's trying something."

"I think he's always plotting. But this time, it's about you." Mallen pauses. "Don't be surprised if he uses my absence to...test you."

The silence between us is thick. His gaze drifts to my mouth and then back to my eyes. There's a coil beneath his expression—tight, sparking, volatile. Not just want. Control held by a thread. Something that won't be named unless I ask for it.

"Will you miss me?" he says lightly.

"I'll manage."

His mouth twitches. "But you'll miss me."

I should tell him what I'm really thinking. That trust is built, not demanded. But keeping things from me isn't protection—it's constraint. And if he wants to keep me safe, he should start by being honest. By telling me everything that is happening and why everything is changing this year.

But then he smiles—soft, dangerous, hungry—and for a moment, I forget every word I rehearsed. Because he looks at me like I'm the last thing tethering him to humanity. Like if I pulled away, he'd stop trying to be good at all.

And I don't want to lose this. Or damage it. Whatever this is, however dangerous it might be, it's mine to navigate. I'm not ready to tear it apart. Not yet. I won't ask for honesty with a blade at his throat. I'll wait—watch—decide for myself what parts of him are armor and what parts are weapon. For now, I choose silence. Not because I'm afraid—but because I'm not done learning him.

I don't say anything. His fingers linger just a little too long, and then he's gone. A whisper of black disappearing between columns of silver stone.

I hate that I miss him already.

Darian is there before I can even exhale. "Thank the gods. I thought he'd never leave." He hands me a glass.

"He'll be back soon."

"I don't like him," Darian says, smiling with his mouth and not his eyes. "You're not safe near him."

"Mallen wouldn't hurt me," I whisper, but the words taste like rust.

Darian leans in, voice low. "There are many ways to wound, Azhara."

My throat tightens.

The way he says it—measured, quiet—sounds rehearsed. Not a warning. A verdict. I glance around, but the room and its decorations offer no comfort. The sunlight is too bright. The shadows too sharp.

"There's a hunt tomorrow," he adds. "Ride with me."

"No."

His smile falters. "You're refusing to accompany me?"

"Yes."

He moves from my side and stands directly in front of me. His stance is casual, but my eye is drawn to the angle of his shoulders—it's too perfect, too easy, like he's practiced this a thousand times. The tilt of his head sends golden hair sliding forward to frame his face, and when his lips curve into a slow, confident smile, the crowd fades. It's just him and me and the warm pressure of his presence.

And heaven help me, he's beautiful.

"Charm won't work on me, Darian."

"No?" he asks softly, voice wrapped in velvet.

My fingers tighten on my glass. He catches the movement, and his smile stretches, not cocky, but knowing.

"I have competition," he says, sipping his wine. I open my mouth, but he keeps going. "You truly care for Mallen."

"He's protected me for as long as I can remember," I reply, and we begin a slow path through the garden. My smile is practiced, dutiful, for the nobles we pass, but I keep my eyes ahead.

"I know," Darian murmurs. "Which is why we need to talk when no one else can overhear. Ride with me tomorrow."

His words hang like smoke between us. I wait until we're safely out of earshot before turning to him.

"So you can insult him?"

Darian's gaze sharpens, but he steps closer, careless of the audience behind us. His voice is barely a breath, a seduction of sound. "So you can decide for yourself what's real and what's not."

There's a charge in the way he watches me—reckless, deliberate, brimming with the kind of danger that doesn't announce itself. Not forceful. Not cruel. But willing. To take the risk. To step over lines.

"Do you love him?" Darian whispers, his breath brushing my skin, making me shiver.

I shake my head, too fast.

He lifts my chin. "I care for you too much to let anyone hurt you. I know I'm not perfect, but I swear this—you won't be a pawn in my house. You'll be honored. Protected. Worshipped."

The word startles me.

My eyes flick toward the door, toward the memory of Mallen's touch—possessive, secretive, aching—and the way my father's voice trembled with fury when he told me that it was Mallen's idea to keep me in Starsfall, no matter what the Reaping decided. I hadn't believed him. But Mallen admitted it.

"Gods, you're magnificent," Darian murmurs, and there's real hunger in it now. "I know it's too soon. I won't rush you. But it's getting harder to pretend I don't want you."

Heat creeps up my neck and Darian's eyes flare with delight. He sees it —my hesitation, my reaction—and he doesn't gloat. He just watches, hopeful.

"Do you like this?" he asks, and I don't answer. "Is it me, or is it the freedom? The danger? The secret?"

I glance down, caught off guard by how badly I want to say yes to all of it.

His voice lowers, coaxing. "Or maybe you just want to be chosen. For yourself. Not because of what you are, or what you can do, but because someone sees you. All of you."

It's too much. Too intimate. But he doesn't touch me—he just waits.

"You don't know me."

The blue in his eyes brightens. "Then let me. Let me learn who you are when no one's watching. What you crave. What you fear. What you would be, if you weren't always choosing who to please."

"I don't know what I want," I whisper, and the truth of it catches in my throat.

"I do," he says, finally touching me—his hand a warm weight at my waist, carefully hidden from view. It's not possessive. It's reverent. And it leaves me breathless.

"You're riding with me tomorrow, Princess." His smile returns, soft and certain. "I won't push. But I won't give up."

My head nods before my mind can stop it.

A habit. One I need to break.

"Good," Darian breathes. "We'll talk properly. About everything."

He releases me slowly, fingers sliding away, and guides me back toward the gathering. A few women glance up as we approach, and Darian slips easily into conversation, charming them with effortless grace. I try to match his ease, but I can't settle. I can't stop thinking.

My father's words. Mallen's silence. The way Mallen watched me with Darian earlier—stone-faced, still, every line of him taut with control. He didn't interrupt. He didn't lash out. But his eyes followed every movement.

Darian, meanwhile, laughs at some remark, and I feel the ache of possibility in my chest. There's a version of my life where this moment becomes normal. Where I choose a future that isn't trapped in shadows and secrets. Darian's right—I don't need to fear him. He's offering freedom, and the fact that I'm thinking about it means something.

The party draws to a close, and the guards appear at my side. I murmur polite farewells and allow them to escort me through the winding halls and back into solitude.

Once, I would have relished the quiet. Now, it feels like exile.

I sit on the edge of my bed, staring at the door. Trying to understand what's happening. Trying to solve the puzzle of this year's Reaping. Waiting for someone who doesn't come.

Not Darian.

Not Mallen.

Only silence.

And the weight of choices I don't yet know how to make.

CHAPTER TWENTY-ONE

My horse spins, dancing beneath me with more spirit than sense. She isn't my usual mount, and after an hour's ride, she's still barely winded, too full of nerves and fire. I tighten the reins, thighs clenched as I work to keep her from bolting. My father watches, feigning concern with a smile I know too well. He's enjoying this.

Darian shifts forward in his saddle, eyes flicking between me and the mare. She kicks out when he approaches, ears pinned, breath flaring hot.

"Want to trade?" he calls, easy and amused.

I shake my head just before the mare rears. I manage to stay in the saddle, keeping my voice calm as I assure him I've got it.

"You don't look like it," he says, watching the horse's sweat-flecked flanks. "She's running hot."

The hounds give tongue, and the rest of the riders take off after them. I try to urge my horse to follow, but she twists and stamps in protest. A guard rides up, strikes her flank, but it doesn't work. She bolts.

Wind tears the breath from my throat. She's not galloping—she's fleeing. I lean forward instinctively, trying not to fight her too hard, but we're off the path, barreling through undergrowth, hooves scraping stones. My fingers are numb around the reins. I shout once, a command she ignores.

Hoofbeats. Behind me. Gaining.

"Let her run!" Darian shouts.

He's chasing.

The guards fall behind. Darian's the only one riding fast enough. He rides low, reckless and swift, cutting through the trees, angling closer.

"We'll lead them off!" he yells.

The mare screams beneath me, biting the air, and I don't have time to argue.

We break through the trees toward the outer wood, her pace barely slowing. I catch a glimpse of the guards dropping behind us as Darian pulls ahead and slams his horse's shoulder into mine, forcing the route. He points toward a narrow path that's half-overgrown.

"This way!"

We vanish into the underbrush, thick branches clawing at my arms. Darian pushes through first, carving a route through the narrow path. My mare follows his gelding by instinct. Her ears twitch—still alert, but not furious now. She's tired. Slowing.

I pull harder on the reins and finally get her under control. We reach a clearing and stop, both working hard to breathe. I slide off, legs shaking, hands slick with sweat.

Darian dismounts smoothly, tossing the reins over a low branch. He moves toward my horse, and she snorts, warning him. He murmurs something low. Calming. Then crouches.

"Hold her," he says.

I do. She shifts under my hands, edgy but no longer wild.

Darian reaches under the saddle, feeling carefully. His fingers go still. Then he pulls out a narrow, wicked shard of metal. Blood stains the leather.

He doesn't say anything at first. Just stands slowly, the blade cradled in his palm like an accusation.

"I should've checked her myself," he mutters. "That's not an accident."

I look away. My skin crawls.

"You know who did this."

"My father," I breathe.

Darian exhales. "He meant for you to fall. Injure you enough to bring you into line."

I nod.

Darian watches me. His eyes are too sharp for his easy smile. There's a stillness in him now—precise and calculating, like a scalpel deciding where to cut.

"It's more than that."

I don't answer. I don't need to. This morning's mount wasn't a mistake. The guards saw her state and said nothing. And Mallen wasn't here to intervene.

That thought hurts more than I expect it to.

I should fear my father.

Anyone with sense would.

But I don't. Not in the way I used to be. Fear's gone brittle inside me, all cracked and hollow. He's broken so many parts of me that it's hard to tell which ones still feel. And maybe that's what scares him now. Not my obedience. Not my silence. But the pieces of me he can no longer reach—and the ones already sharpened into weapons.

What I feel now is the absence of Mallen. He would've stepped in—he always did, somehow, quietly, as if it was nothing. A whisper to a stable hand. A change to the day's plans. I never saw it for what it was. I never thanked him. I just assumed I was fortunate. That luck is distant now. Stolen.

Darian turns, pacing once before looking back. "He's done this before. To others."

"I know."

"No, you don't. You've been kept too sheltered to understand. Your father doesn't just punish. He designs consequences. Every strike is meant to lead somewhere. Everything is control."

"I'm not naïve."

"I never said you were."

The words fall quiet between us.

I stare down at my gloves. They're turning crimson. Blood's soaked through the fabric, smeared across my palms. It's not even mine, but it feels like it should be. Like I earned it.

My whole life, I've carried the guilt of knowing my mother's death was my fault. That my life had drained hers. That my father had used his magic to bind the darkness I'd unleashed on the world. That *he* was what kept the curse in check—that *his* cruelty was the price of my existence.

And now I see.

He didn't become a monster because of me. He always was one.

This was never my fault.

"I didn't think he'd do this," I whisper. "I thought the worst thing he wanted was control."

Darian doesn't answer right away.

He steps closer. "Let me tell you something they don't want you to know. Before the war—before the gods withdrew—your mother was the only bridge between our kingdoms. She was from Larksbind."

"I know that."

"No," he replies, quieter now. "You know where she was from. Not what that meant."

The words slam through me harder than they should. It's not just what he says—it's how he says it. Like it costs him. Like he's been carrying this too long, waiting for me to be ready to hear it. And now that I am, he's not sparing me from the truth.

"Larksbind and Starsfall balance each other," Darian says softly. "They used to exist in harmony. Until your father decided harmony wasn't enough. He wanted more territory. More power. We tried to contain him peacefully. We failed."

I stare at him, my bloodied hands aching from gripping the reins. "He attacked you."

"He nearly destroyed us," Darian confirms. "The only reason we survived was your mother."

"My mother?"

He nods. "She was from Larksbind. He loved her. Obsessively. My father said she was...content. Happy, in her own way. The truce was her idea. She believed her love for him would hold him back. So she married him. And for a while, it worked."

A wind moves through the trees, dry and sharp. My mare shivers beside me.

"But peace never lasts long in the hands of a man like your father," Darian continues, voice low. "A seer made a prophecy. She foresaw your mother's death in childbirth. Your father panicked. He tried everything to stop it—everything but letting her go. And when all else failed, he turned to Obcasus."

My heart stops.

"That's not—" I swallow. "That's not what happened."

"Yes, it is," Darian says. "You've been told a lie your entire life, but I swear to you, Azhara—I'm telling you what really happened. My father was there."

I meet his eyes, and the darkness in me stills. There's no doubt in his gaze. No hunger for leverage. Just truth. Excruciating and raw and inescapable.

"I'll swear it on the gods themselves," he says. "On the stones of Larksbind, on my blood, on whatever you ask—I'll swear it."

And I know.

I don't know how, but I do.

He's telling the truth. I feel it the way I feel the night before the sun sets.

"He used Obcasus."

"That's forbidden," I mumble. "You can't use it. No one can—"

"He tried," Darian says. "He rekindled the old magic. He threatened the gods with destruction if they didn't intervene to save her. It was madness. It nearly destroyed both kingdoms."

The reins slip from my hands.

"He unleashed the Obcasus, even though he knew the gods themselves had locked it away."

I stumble backward, eyes burning.

"He failed. Your mother died anyway. But not before you were born."

The trees blur. The ground sways, now unsteady beneath me. My mother had fought for peace, and now she was gone because my father tried to tear the heavens open to keep her.

To keep me.

He said it was my gift. My existence. He said that's what killed her.

He catches me. His arms tighten around me as I tremble, breath coming in ragged gasps.

"Breathe," he murmurs. "This isn't your fault."

But it feels like it is.

"Your father shouldn't have challenged the gods," Darian says. "He angered them when he used Obcasus and demanded their obedience. So they punished him. They stripped Starsfall of its magic—and in doing so, they punished us too. Larksbind is subtler in power, but our kingdoms are always connected. When he broke the balance, we lost our gifts as well."

"The Reaping," I whisper. "It wasn't meant to be—"

"A ritual of death?" he asks, without any bitterness in his voice. "No, it wasn't meant to be destructive. You were supposed to heal the wound he caused. Bridge the damage and teach him some humility. That is the purpose of what you contain. Your magic. Your choice. But your father twisted this into sport and a demonstration. A bloody, gilded spectacle to prove his dominion. To remind both nations who holds the leash."

I shake my head. I don't know why.

"He's lied to you your entire life—about who you are, about the Reaping, and about what happened in Starsfall."

I bring my hands up, trying to back away, but Darian doesn't let go. His arms stay tight around me. I push against him, struggling to fill my lungs with air.

"Let me go—"

"You're safe," he says, and I hate how gentle his voice is. "Just breathe. Just breathe for me."

My chest won't expand. I can't get air. My whole body's locking up, and he won't let go, I can't *breathe*—

"Easy," he says again, quieter now. "It's going to be okay."

I thrash once, hard, but he doesn't release me. The panic surges higher, sharp as knives, until it becomes too much. The fear shatters and everything beneath it pours out—hot, sharp, endless.

Tears run down my face. My sobs break from me in waves, raw and unrelenting. I don't care how I sound. I don't care what I look like. It's all unraveling now. The truth, the grief, the years of silence held like breath under water.

The crying eases, but the ache deepens. This isn't just grief—it's the shock of understanding. Like pieces of a puzzle have finally snapped into place. I remember things I'd buried. The way my maids were changed without warning. The year the shrine to my mother was suddenly forbidden. The marks on my father's hands that he never explained.

All of it meant something.

I just didn't want to see it.

Or maybe I did, and I didn't know how to name it.

Darian holds me through it. He doesn't speak again until my body stills, my tears spent, replaced by a yawning emptiness.

He only lets go once I pull back.

I sit down hard on the ground, numb, barely aware of the dry grass prickling my palms. He takes the reins from my hand and leads my horse away, tying her beside his already-secured mount.

The silence between us is thicker now. Not just grief. This is closer to recognition tinged with shame—like he sees me clearly now and knows I won't be the same.

"Are you sure?" My voice is hoarse.

"I wouldn't lie to you," he says. He doesn't waver. "I want you to know this. Even if you don't choose me. Even if you choose Mallen."

His eyes are shadowed now, their blue as dark as the ocean's depths. The wind has loosened strands of his hair, and there's sweat on his brow, but he doesn't look weary. He looks resolute. Braced against the burden of what he's shared, as if he'd do it all again if I asked. Like he'd carry every cruel truth for me if it meant I could breathe easier.

"You're a gift, Azhara. A blessing. You were meant to heal the rift your father opened. The gods gave you a power meant to mend what was broken."

"Then why does it feel like I broke it?"

"Because he made you feel that way," Darian says gently. "He raised you in the shadow of his guilt and told you it was yours. He twisted the prophecy to justify his obsession. Because when your mother died, he decided your life had to *gain* him something—or her death meant nothing."

Whatever's in my chest cracks. It's not pain. Not exactly. This is gentler. Something like the last breath before the battle begins.

"I didn't want to believe he was capable of this," I tell him. "Even when I hated him. I still needed...something. A reason. A version of him that made sense."

Darian doesn't move, doesn't speak, just waits.

"And now that I see it, I don't know how to hold it. How to carry it without it swallowing me."

He draws a slow breath. "Meaning isn't a debt. Sacrifice doesn't always bring purpose. You don't have to atone for his sins."

I close my eyes, trying to steady the tremble in my fingers. "It doesn't make sense. The Reaping makes no sense if I'm meant to repair relations between the two countries."

"Your father did more than twist it into a spectacle. The magic trapped in the ritual serves no one. It festers."

The pieces start fitting together.

"When you marry someone from Larksbind," Darian continues, "you'll restore what was broken. Heal the rift. The gods will see it as an offering. If you don't..." He doesn't finish.

I stare at the ground as the truth splinters through me. My father took from Larksbind, and now I'm the price of making it right. Not a princess. Not a prize. A reckoning. A cure.

I was never free. Just owned by different hands.

I nod, numbly.

Somewhere beneath the shock, the spiral starts. Darian hasn't mentioned my magic. Maybe he doesn't know. Maybe it's as bad as my father said it was, and he hid it out of shame. Or maybe that's another lie—a brutal, binding one—that kept me caged for years.

Whatever's inside me hums, alive and rising, reminding me it's still here. That it's waited long enough. It's been biding its time like a storm beneath still water, and now it's stirring.

And if it breaks loose, I don't know what I'll become.

Darian's arm slips around my shoulders, pulling me close. He's warm. Strong. And for a moment, I let myself lean into it. Just to breathe.

We sit in silence, surrounded by trees and fading light. I try to stitch my thoughts together.

Then Darian says, almost gently, "Mallen knows."

The words land like a knife. I go rigid. My heart stops. "What?"

"He's always known," Darian murmurs. "About the Reaping. About your father's plans. About the power in you."

CHAPTER TWENTY-TWO

I SHAKE MY HEAD. NO. HE'S WRONG. MALLEN'S PROTECTED ME. HE taught me to fight. He would *kill* my father to keep me safe. He wouldn't—he *couldn't*—be part of this.

"He's helping your father," Darian says.

"No." The word rips from me. "You're lying."

"I wish I were," he says. "But if you marry someone outside Larksbind—anyone else—the power returns to Starsfall. To whoever sits on the throne."

My stomach turns. My head spins.

My father. Or someone just like him. Someone he's placed in my path.

Darian watches me carefully, as if gauging how far he can press before I start to splinter.

"I'm sorry, Azhara. I know you care for him. But he's not who you think he is."

"He wouldn't hurt me," I whisper.

"He doesn't need to," Darian replies. "He just needs to *marry* you."

Everything inside me breaks. I leap to my feet, reeling. The clearing is too small. The trees are too close. My thoughts too loud.

"You're the same," I snap. "If he wants the throne, so do you."

Darian rises slowly, hands open. "I don't need your throne. I have my own. Please, just listen—"

But I'm already shaking my head, tears stinging my eyes. I scream at him to leave me alone. I don't know who's lying. I don't know what's true. But I *know* I can't bear this anymore.

"Don't follow me," I say without turning.

"Azhara—"

"You think if you repeat it enough, I'll believe you?" I keep walking. "That if you sound calm and sorry and noble, I'll ignore everything else?"

His footsteps crunch behind me, slow and careful.

"I don't want Starsfall," he says. "I want it to survive."

"You mean *you* want to survive."

He doesn't answer right away. I feel him just behind me now, matching my pace.

I stop suddenly and turn to face him. "You're all the same. You act like it's about protecting me. About saving the realm. But it's always power. Always strategy. And the only thing that ever changes is who's holding the prison key."

His jaw tightens, but he doesn't raise his voice. "I'm not asking you to trust me. Just to see him clearly."

"I *do*," I snap. "You think because you've known him for a few weeks that you know him better than I do? He's known me since I was a child. Trained me since I was ten. He taught me everything I know."

"Exactly," Darian says.

That word stops me cold.

"What?"

"If you were meant to be hidden—if your father wanted you out of the game—why train you to fight? Why sharpen you into a weapon if he doesn't plan to use you?"

My mouth opens, but nothing comes out.

Darian takes a step closer. Not threatening. Just...present.

"You don't forge a sword and then bury it," he says. "You draw it when you're ready to strike."

My lungs burn. My thoughts stumble, catch, refuse to land. He's not talking about my father. Not anymore.

He nods once. "You've survived. You've grown strong. And when the moment comes, he'll have someone the realm trusts. Respects. Loves."

A doll dressed in armor. A crown on a leash.

"No," I say, because I refuse to let it be true.

I turn from him again, spine straight, steps clean. My face burns and my throat tightens, but my pace is steady. The wind catches strands of my hair and drags them into my mouth. I don't push them away. I don't break stride.

Behind me, Darian's voice comes quieter now. "You said it yourself—he taught you everything. That means he knew exactly what you were becoming. What you were capable of."

I say nothing. The trees blur at the edges of my vision.

And I silently curse myself for leaving the horses behind.

"You think your father didn't know what was going on?" he presses. "That Mallen didn't report everything? When he runs your father's palace guard? The army? When he controls half the informants in Starsfall?"

"I never said he reported anything," I mutter.

"And why is he the one who selects the daemons for the first trial of the Reaping?"

I stop walking.

The forest stills around us. Not a bird calls. Not a breath moves the leaves.

"How do you know that?" I ask.

Darian's voice is low. "Because my father has spies. In the capital and major ports. In Varethorne and Nyxford. We'd be foolish not to, as long as your father's still on the throne. One of them intercepted some reports a month ago. It included details of the daemons Mallen rounded up for the Reaping."

"You've been spying? On Starsfall?" I snap. "Why would I believe anything you say to me now?"

He doesn't answer.

I stare at the path ahead, remembering. The times Mallen would come back from the forest bloodied, shaking his head when I asked where he'd been. The times he'd refused to answer me when I asked him how he caught the daemons, and ignored the warnings coiling through my gut when he told me it was necessary.

And now I wonder.

Did Mallen tell me the whole truth? Or only what he wanted me to know?

I think of the men who died in the arena. Of their blood and their screams. And of the few who made it out to be slaughtered later.

They'd known this wasn't fair. They'd known it was about breaking them.

And maybe breaking me.

The trees sway slightly in the hush, and I press my palm to my ribs, as if I can hold myself steady from the inside out.

I turn back to Darian slowly. "Why are you doing this?"

"Because you deserve to know the truth."

"I don't need saving."

"I know."

"Then stop looking at me like you want to."

His mouth presses into a line, but he doesn't look away.

I hate him, in this moment. Not because he's wrong, but because he might be right.

Because he's saying what I don't want to say aloud. What I've suspected in moments I buried.

Mallen has sat through my father's late-night councils. He knows about the prisoners who vanished. About the raids on Larksbind's ships that no one ever punished. He'd told me none of it concerned me. That I should keep my head down. That I wasn't strong enough yet to change anything.

He'd taught me to fight. Taught me to obey. Taught me to be silent unless I was commanded to act.

And I had thought that was kindness.

That it was love.

"Why not tell me this from the start?" I whisper.

Darian exhales, slow and hard. "Because I didn't want you to think I was like him."

I look up at him sharply. "How's that turning out?"

"Not ideally," he says. "But would you have believed me?"

"That was never your choice to make."

"No," he agrees. "But I didn't have much of one. Mallen was your shield. We both know I'd only have pushed you further away if I'd said anything earlier. So I kept my mouth shut."

"But you've decided it's time to shatter any illusions I have left?"

"No," he says, stepping closer. "I've decided it's time you choose for yourself."

I flinch.

It's not the words. It's the *way* he says them. Like I've never been allowed to. Like everyone else has already chosen for me.

Mallen. My father. The court. Even the realm.

"I have," I bite out. "I've chosen *every* time. To survive. To obey. To keep my head above the tide while all of you played your games underneath it."

"I know," he says, voice tight. "But you don't have to keep doing it alone."

The silence that follows is too loud. The forest presses in. I can hear his breath behind me. My own blood in my ears.

"Please," Darian says quietly. "Let me help you. Just this once."

His hand brushes mine. I don't pull away. Not immediately. The touch is tentative. Hesitant. A connection offered, not claimed. And gods, part of me wants to believe him. To believe he's different. That this isn't just another way to lead me down a path someone else already paved.

But trust is a currency I no longer have.

I turn my hand and press my fingers to his chest—gently, yet firmly—pushing him back. "Don't."

He stills.

"I'm not ready," I say. "And if you think I'll run into your arms the moment I fall out of Mallen's shadow—"

"I don't."

"Good. Because I'm not running anywhere."

The hurt flickers in his eyes—but only for a moment. Then it's gone, buried beneath that calm he wears like armor.

"I'm sorry," he says.

It sounds real. Not wounded. Not manipulative. Just...real.

I nod once, a jerky, awkward motion. My throat aches.

"I don't know," I whisper. "Whether you're trying to help or win. But I'm not choosing sides. Not tonight."

"I can live with that," he says.

I start walking again. Slower now. He keeps pace beside me, silent.

The path is narrowing. The forest grows darker.

A nightingale calls once, sharp as flint, and then falls quiet, as if it never meant for its song to be heard.

Neither of us speaks for a long while. The space between us is filled with questions that neither of us dares ask. My steps are uneven, and my heel catches on a root, my ankle twisting as heat sears through the joint. I hiss through my teeth and keep walking, though I'm dangerously close to hobbling.

Darian doesn't reach for me. Doesn't offer to steady me. Just slows his pace a fraction more, as if he understands that even kindness would scrape too raw right now.

I wrap my arms around myself, jaw tight. The ache in my ribs pulses in time with the pounding in my skull. I should've been smart. I should have ridden back to Starsfall and left Darian with the wounded horse. But I decided to walk, and now we're both picking our way through the half-wild edges of the forest with no torchlight, no trail, and too much between us to name.

The path forks ahead, the right veering steeper, stonier. My boots slip as I angle toward it, and I'm sure that this will hurt on my injured foot. Darian clears his throat softly. "That will take us along the ridge. Left loops around toward the base. Might be easier on your ankle."

I hesitate. Then take the right anyway.

He doesn't argue.

The only sound is our footfalls and the wind shifting through high branches. Every step jostles my side and makes my breath catch. But pain is simple. It's real. It doesn't wait for answers or apologies.

"What was in the reports?" I ask suddenly. "The ones your spies intercepted."

Darian glances at me, brow furrowed. "You want the full list?"

"I want to know what you do."

He's quiet for a moment. "There were details about troop movements. Trade routes. The new tariffs on ships from Rivenmere and Hawkshold—"

"Stop deflecting."

"There was a letter," he says slowly. "From one of your father's advisors. Marked confidential. It referenced the 'progress of the pairing.' Said Mallen had earned your trust. That you looked to him. That you relied on him."

My lungs turn brittle.

Darian keeps his voice low. "It said the match was proceeding better than expected. That you'd grown 'attached.' That Mallen was...keen."

I keep my eyes on the trees ahead. The leaves are thinner here. I can just make out starlight pressing through the canopy in fragments.

"He was protecting me," I murmur.

Darian doesn't answer.

I swallow, my throat burning. "He was buying me time. He thinks that if I'm strong enough—if I can fight—then I don't have to be anyone's pawn."

"Princess," Darian says gently, "very few things in life are either or. He can both love you and serve your father. I'm not questioning his emotions. Only his motives."

We crest a rise. The trees begin to thin. I see a glint of silver ahead—moonlight on stone, or water, or the edge of the road that winds out of the forest. Home is closer than I thought.

I don't want it to be.

Darian stops walking, but I keep going, slower now. Limping more openly. The adrenaline has faded and everything hurts again.

Then I hear it.

A voice—rough, low, ragged with relief and something sharper.

"Azhara?"

I freeze.

Mallen bursts out from the trees to the right, barely keeping his footing as he crashes through the underbrush. He looks wild, disheveled, his cloak askew, his hair damp with sweat. His eyes rake over me like a man who's been searching for hours. They flick to Darian, and the shift in him is immediate—tense, coiled, hand flying to the hilt of his blade.

"Did he hurt you?" he demands, surging toward me. "Tell me you're alright? Did he—?"

"No," I say quickly. "No, it's not—he didn't—"

Mallen's eyes are wild, voice trembling. "I was on the road to Nyxford when I heard. Gods, I thought—"

"I'm fine," I lie. "The horse bolted. I fell. Darian found me and made sure I got back."

Mallen rounds on Darian again, as if that should somehow be proof of guilt.

I step in between them before he can speak. "He didn't touch me," I say sharply. "He didn't hurt me. He helped."

Mallen's jaw ticks. "You shouldn't have been alone."

"I wasn't."

He looks at me then. Really looks. Takes in the bruise on my cheek, the tear in my sleeve, the dried blood at my temple. His expression crumples—just a little—and I hate how desperate I am for that to be real. That grief. That fear. That sorrow.

"You're shaking," he says softly.

"I'm tired," I snap.

He nods once, drawing in a long breath. "Come. Let's get you home. I'll call for a healer. We'll talk later."

A coil of anger tightens behind my ribs and gods, it burns. Not now. Not here. Later. Always later. Always after the damage is done.

Mallen doesn't even look at Darian again. Just wraps his cloak around my shoulders and guides me toward the path.

I glance back once.

Darian hasn't moved. He stands at the edge of the clearing, arms at his sides, gaze locked on mine. He doesn't call out. Doesn't try to follow. Not yet.

But his eyes are lit with a quiet fury.

Conviction.

CHAPTER TWENTY-THREE

Men say that Starsfall rests when its royals return.

It doesn't.

And I don't either.

The corridors whisper. The torches burn low. Shadows stretch across the walls like wounds that never close. And Mallen—he doesn't speak. Doesn't look at me. Just walks two paces ahead, every line of him wound taut with rage he's trying to contain. I should say something. I should lie again. But I'm too cold, too tired, and too unsure of my own truth to remember what version I'm supposed to be telling.

The silence breaks when he stops.

"You're limping."

"I'm fine."

He turns. Just slightly. "You're bleeding."

"It's nothing."

His gaze drops to the shredded fabric of my sleeve. His jaw hardens. "Let me see."

I shake my head.

He doesn't ask again. Just reaches for the nearest servant with a flick of his hand, voice cool and clipped: "Bring the healer. Now."

They scatter.

I don't sit. I don't speak. I just watch the back of him—broad shoulders rigid, eyes fixed on the far wall, breath barely rising. He looks like a man ready to storm a battlefield. Or break apart.

The healer arrives quickly. Too quickly. Someone must've warned him.

He bows low. His hands are steady, but his voice isn't. "My Lord. My Lady. May I…?"

Mallen gestures for him to begin.

The moment the fabric is cut, I see it in the healer's face. The shallow slashes across my arm. The bruising near my wrist. The way the skin breaks like a lie unraveling. The healer murmurs a few words I don't hear. I feel Mallen's stare on every inch of exposed skin.

He doesn't say a word. Not to me. Not to the healer. He doesn't need to. The silence says all of it. He thinks Darian hurt me. And that I let him.

"I fell," I say quietly. "The horse spooked. I got caught in the trees."

Still nothing.

The healer wraps my arm. Presses gently at my ankle.

"Sprained," he says. "Not broken."

Mallen's voice is quiet, but deliberate. "How badly?"

The healer's pause is long. "Bad enough." He pauses again. "It'll heal in a day or two."

Mallen's shoulders tense.

There's anger there. Jealousy too. A possessiveness I'm not sure I know what to do with.

I feel sick.

He wanted proof my ankle would not carry me, that I could not have fled, that Darian was not dragging me anywhere I did not choose. That I did not find a way to spend time with him. Proof from a stranger's mouth, not mine. Not to catch me in a lie, but to stop imagining one.

And the truth in that hurts more than I want to admit.

The healer bows and flees. The door clicks shut. A servant knocks, and Mallen waves them away. The room is too full of truth to let anything else in. I don't even realize I'm shaking until Mallen steps toward me. Not angry. Not cold. Just…impossibly still.

"Where did he take you?"

I flinch at the question. It shouldn't hurt. But it does.

"He didn't take me anywhere. The horse bolted. I fell. He was the only rider strong enough to keep up. Nothing else happened. I swear to you—"

"I believe you."

He says it too quickly. Too easily.

"You don't," I say.

He closes the distance between us. Not looming. Not threatening. Just present. And aching.

"I believe *you*," he says, slower this time. "I don't believe *him*."

The shift starts small. I barely notice it. And then it's sharp, and suddenly it's seismic. A shift that leaves a fracture in its wake.

It doesn't matter whether he believes me. Not if my whole sense of self hinges on which man manages to sound more convincing.

Not if I keep bending with every wind that blows stronger than me.

I am not a leaf to be carried. I'm done being a pawn in the game men play for power. It doesn't matter what Mallen says. Or what Darian claims. It matters what I do—and being broken on my own terms is better than living at the mercy of someone else's. I straighten my spine, and the breath I draw tastes different. Like something final. The sunset before a storm.

My breath catches. "He said things."

A pause.

Mallen waits.

"He said you're working with my father. That you've been lying to me. That you want the crown, and I'm the easiest way to get it. That if I choose you and we are married, you'll either continue serving him—or replace him."

Silence.

He doesn't deny it.

And gods help me, I don't know what that means.

My voice turns hollow. "Tell me he's lying."

Still, he doesn't move. Just watches me. Like he's searching my face for mercy he hasn't earned. Or some sign I might absolve him of what he *hasn't* said.

When he finally speaks, it's low. Rough. "What do you feel when he looks at you?"

The question hits like a slap. Not because of the words. But because I don't know the answer.

He sees it.

And his expression folds, slow and silent, like a wound breaking open.

"I see," he says, and turns away.

"Don't," I breathe. "Don't do that. Don't leave me alone with this."

He stops. But he doesn't turn fully.

"I told you once," he says quietly, "that I would never trap you. That I would never make you stay. That I would never ask you to choose me if your heart was somewhere else."

"It's not," I say. "Not yet."

A bitter smile flickers across his face. "That's not the reassurance you think it is."

I step toward him. My leg shakes under me.

"Darian is charming," I say. "He chooses words carefully. He looks at me like I'm the only thing in the world he wants—and I know that's not love. That's strategy."

Mallen turns his head a little further. Enough that I can see the muscle twitching in his jaw.

"He's too perfect," I say. "And he's playing a game I haven't figured out yet."

Now he turns. Now he faces me. Now his eyes burn.

"So why did you ride with him?"

Because I wanted to? Because I was lonely? Because I don't know what's real anymore? Because some part of me wanted to believe him. Just for a moment.

He steps closer.

His voice is low. "I've never lied to you, Azhara."

"But you've kept secrets."

"Yes. To keep you safe."

"How's that working out?"

He looks at me—really looks. "Considerably less well than I would like."

My breath hitches. "Just tell me."

He reaches for my hand. Doesn't take it. Instead, he waits.

"Things are moving beneath this court that would tear you apart if you even guessed at them. Your father is one of them. Darian is another. And yes—there are things I haven't told you. Because once I do, you'll be part of it. All the way in. No escape."

My hand trembles.

"And you want to be Starsfall's king," I whisper.

Not a question.

"Yes," he says. "But not because of power. Because of what I'll protect. Because of what that changes. Because of you."

I stare at him.

I'm not sure if I believe him. I want to. But that isn't the same as trust.

I turn away first. He doesn't stop me.

We lie on opposite sides of the bed, backs to each other, both lying still as if quiet could undo the damage. I don't sleep. I drift in and out, floating in a half-conscious mire of memories and fear, every heartbeat too loud, curled on the edge of the bed with my back to him. The silence between us hums with everything we're not saying.

I want him to reach for me.

I want him to stay away.

I want the truth, even if it destroys me.

When dawn smudges the windows with pale light, I sit up and swing my legs over the side of the bed. My body aches. Bruises purple my arms like reminders of choices I can't undo. I don't look at Mallen. I know he's awake. He always is when I am.

"Will you let me explain?" he asks hoarsely.

I stare at my hands. "I don't know if you want to tell me the truth."

He doesn't stop me as I walk tentatively to the basin and wash myself with the cool, clean water. Evie appears, and Mallen retreats to the further corner of the room. She helps me wash. She dresses me slowly. She braids my hair. When I'm done, he's sitting on the couch, elbows on his knees, hands steepled in front of his mouth. He looks like he hasn't slept either.

Last night sits between us like glass. The night has carved him thinner; stubble shadows his face, a bruise blooms beneath his jaw, and a strip of linen disappears under his cuff. He looks older this morning. Haunted.

I press my palms to the table to keep from crossing the space. He watches the basin still, then me, then the distance between. His fingers lift as if to reach, then fall open, empty. He does not try to touch me. And I won't comfort him. Not when I'm still bleeding inside.

He rises but stays where he is, shoulders squared, careful as if one step might startle me. He stands at the far edge of the rug, eyes searching mine.

"I lied once. You asked if I knew more than I was letting on. About your father. About what he was planning. I said no.“ He looks at me, and it hurts. “I was trying to shield you. But it was still a lie.”

The moment holds like glass. Too fragile. Too clear.

“So you don’t deny what Darian said,” I whisper. “That you’ve been following my father’s orders. That you have your own ambitions. That this—us—was never just ours.”

He swallows hard. “Please—”

“You don’t get to say that to me.” My voice is colder than I mean it to be. Truer than I want it to be.

“Azhara...”

“I’m not yours to keep in the dark.”

The words settle between us, soft as falling ash. And just as final.

“I never wanted this,” he says, voice raw. “You think I wanted to lie to you? You think I wanted to make impossible choices? You think I want to keep secrets, knowing that it hurts you?”

“No,” I say. “I think you want to win.”

That lands hard. He exhales like the air’s been knocked from him, staggered by the truth I’ve never said aloud.

“I want to save you,” he says, softer now. “And yes—I want to win. Not a throne. Not power. Your heart. Your trust. I want you to choose me. Freely. Without fear.”

“But you’re not giving me a choice,” I whisper.

His voice is a rasp. “I am.”

“No, Mallen. You’re giving me fragments. Half-truths. Carefully arranged pieces. You’re trying to walk me to a conclusion without telling me what I’m really choosing.”

His silence says enough.

I step toward the balcony, needing space. And air.

He speaks, low and desperate. “If I tell you now, it could destroy everything. Everything I’ve been working toward. Everything I’ve done to protect you from him.”

“You’re talking about the man you still serve,” I say.

He flinches. “It isn’t like that. It wasn’t.”

“But it was something,” I press. “And you don’t trust me enough to tell me.”

“I’m trying to keep you alive.”

"I don't want to live like this," I say. "Not when I can't decide what that life looks like."

He steps toward me. "Azhara—"

"No more, Mallen." My voice breaks. "No more secrets. No more lies. Either you tell me the truth, or you let me go."

He's breathing hard now, staring at me like he's trying to memorize the shape of this moment. "If I lose you—"

"You already have."

The words slice clean through him. He closes his eyes, shoulders caving inward, as if the pain might buckle him. When he opens them, the green of his eyes is unsteady—desperate, more than a little ruined.

"I have never—will never—lie to you," he says, every syllable deliberate. "Please believe me. I cannot tell you this. This would trap you, and I will never, ever do that."

"I deserve to know what's happening to me."

His voice cracks. "I do believe that. Gods help me, I do."

"Then prove it."

We stare at each other for a long time.

He doesn't speak.

I shake my head and turn away. His footsteps follow me, but they're hesitant, slow.

"I love you, Azhara," he says behind me. "I will never stop fighting for you."

"Then you should've started by fighting *with* me."

His breath catches. I don't look back.

Later, when I ask to go to the gardens, he tells me no. When I ask for the library, he refuses again, gentler this time. Every denial is another stone laid in the wall between us. His protection feels like a prison now. His silence a kind of cruelty.

When I stand by the window and stare down at Threnos, he places a hand between my shoulders.

"I love you more than I thought possible," he murmurs.

I don't answer.

He kisses the crown of my head like a benediction. "Even if you hate me, even if you never forgive me, I will protect you. I will never stop."

And then he's gone.

The guards he commands keep watch.

The city is golden in the morning sun. The spires of Starsfall's capital shimmer like they're made of glass. Threnos looks peaceful. Beautiful. But I know what it's built on and what lives beneath the stone.

When he returns in the evening and asks if I want to bathe, I nod without speaking.

He escorts me to the royal baths and stands like a sentinel as I walk the room's perimeter, checking for hidden threats I can't see. His eyes plead with me to let him stay.

I say nothing.

He leaves.

I undress slowly, peeling away layers like old skin. I sink into the water, hot and laced with crushed herbs. The heat burns, but it's a welcome pain. It reminds me that I'm still here. Still thinking. Still doubting.

The steam curls around me like mist, and I let it carry my thoughts toward the high, domed ceiling.

Darian's words repeat like a curse. Mallen wants to use you. Mallen wants to rule. Mallen will betray your father, or work with him, or become something worse.

But Darian isn't innocent either. I remember the way he said my name—like it was both a question and a promise. The memory stings more than it should.

And I'm just a girl caught in a war of shadows, with no way to tell who's telling the truth, and no time left to find out.

I sink lower into the water.

If this is what power feels like—this constant doubt, this gnawing dread—then maybe I was never meant to have it.

But I'll still fight for the right to choose.

Even if it means choosing to walk away from both of them.

Even if it means standing alone.

CHAPTER TWENTY-FOUR

THERE ARE NO CELEBRATIONS FOR THE FINAL TRIAL. STARSFALL holds its breath. The crowd is somber—tense, reverent, as though the ground itself has decided to mourn. No one has ever reached the third trial. The Reaping has never allowed it.

The steps form an amphitheater that descends in solemn rings, each tier etched into the bones of the earth, as if the land itself bears witness to every trial it consumes. Moss crawls between the stones, dark and thick as old blood, and at the lowest point, the iron gates yawn open like the jaws of some slumbering god.

And above it all looms the statue—twice my height, cloaked and faceless, one hand raised in warning, the other gripping a curved blade forever rusted by the offerings of the dead. She is the Reaping made stone, and she watches us all.

The tributes step forward beneath that eerie silence, and awe stirs like smoke through the gathered watchers. Their attention finds Darian first. He bows, grinning, drinking in their stunned devotion. He's turned their opinions inside out. Rewritten everything they believed. In a few short weeks, he's changed the kingdom. Changed me.

The Larksbind men are like carved obsidian—still, dark, unreadable. Every motion is purposeful. Assured. As if survival isn't a hope, but a fact already written.

Darian finds my gaze. That smile again. Warm, effortless, meant for me. The kind that silences the world and makes you believe in foolish things. It fits him too well. I hate how much I like it.

I descend the dais slowly. I can feel Mallen's gaze on me, scorching the skin between my shoulder blades. The weight of him is unbearable and constant. He doesn't move. Doesn't speak. Doesn't soften.

I don't turn, but I know what expression is on his face. I've seen that flicker in his eyes too often lately—longing wrapped in control, jealousy concealed by practiced calm. A silent battle behind every breath. If this is another test, I don't know what I'm meant to prove.

"Ignore him," Darian murmurs, close enough for only me to hear.

"He's staring."

"Let him. He can't stop us. And he can't hear what matters."

"Did he say anything?"

Darian's smile sharpens. "He's hoping that the labyrinth will do his work for him."

The words land heavily.

No one has ever reached the labyrinth, let alone survived it.

And if Darian does, Mallen will be waiting for him.

The trial's rules are deceptively simple: find the center, retrieve the banner.

The entrance is plain—a tunnel carved into the rock, no twists yet, no traps. But the danger isn't at the door.

They say real horrors wait beneath. That the walls are impossibly thick, enchanted, unyielding, and the paths wind and fracture like a spider's web. They say you forget time down there. Light too. And yourself.

Men say it shifts.

Not always. Not obviously. But enough. Enough to ensure no map can be trusted, no route repeated. It's almost arrogant, the way it changes—like it *knows* it doesn't have to do more than confuse you. That confusion is fatal.

Then there are the traps. Mallen said they're few—but devastating. Lethal, if he or my father have anything to do with it. The rumors whisper of what waits beneath: not just machinery or spell work, but a feral instinct curled in the dark. A presence that stalks the shifting halls with unnatural cunning, ancient and ravenous. No one knows what it is. Only that it never leaves a body behind and its terror haunts the dreams of children and men alike.

Except Mallen. He isn't afraid.

Darian, by contrast, still seems untouched by fear. He stands beside me like this is a midsummer festival, not a death sentence. His hair gleams where the sun strikes it. His smile never dims. That pale blue tunic is deliberate—it makes his eyes brighter, more innocent.

He steps closer. "You didn't think I came without a plan, did you?"

"What plan?"

"One that lets me win the Reaping and carries you clear of Starsfall. Alive. Safe. Free from your father."

I tense. The intimacy of his hand brushing my cheek is dizzying, too tender for the battlefield we're on. For a moment, there's nothing else—no crowd, no danger, just his eyes, his certainty. The way he looks at me like I'm not a prize but a future.

"You care about me," I murmur, breath caught.

He leans in, voice hushed. "Azhara, this ends with either Mallen or me alive, not both. He'll never let you go, and I won't leave you behind unless you've already chosen him. But until you do, I'll fight for you."

His words leave a sharp ache in my chest. I don't want Mallen hurt. And gods, I *know* Mallen's keeping things from me. But Darian...there's a polish to him that catches too much light. A charm too deliberate, too well-honed. A mask so smooth I can't see the cracks—but I know they're there. He always says exactly what I want to hear. And that's what makes me flinch.

But at least he's honest about wanting me.

"You promised me time."

He nods, this time slower. "And I meant it. But time's gone. The Reaping ends today. Your father—or Mallen—won't let us walk away. After the labyrinth, we leave Starsfall. Larksbind will be waiting."

My breath catches.

They're going to flee. It makes sense. They're outnumbered here. If they run, they can choose the battlefield and shape their odds. It's strategic. Smart.

I glance back—Mallen is conferring with a palace guard in low tones, jaw tight. His gaze hasn't left me. There's a wound in that look. Pain, and no longer hidden. The quiet control that has always caged him—it's fraying. And I'm the one who's pulling it loose.

"Choose me," Darian says, voice quieter now, but insistent. "Not because you're afraid. Because you want to. Because I want *you.*"

My heart slams against my ribs.

He means it. He's certain. He's *asking.*

And I'm terrified. Not of him—but of choosing. Of being wrong. Of giving my yes and watching the ground open beneath me anyway. I can't undo this. I can't run back. And yet—I want to move forward without asking permission. For once—just once—I want to choose something before it's chosen for me. I want to *want.*

I nod.

It's more than agreement. It's defiance. A vow. A quiet rebellion whispered in the breath between heartbeats. For once, I'm not a daughter or a pawn or a prize in someone else's war. I'm a girl who wants, who chooses, who claims her own ruin. And this, whatever it becomes, is mine.

Relief floods me, sharp and sweet. I've made so few decisions that were truly mine. This one is monumental—and mine alone. It tastes like freedom. It tastes like the life I've never been allowed to live.

"There'll be men ready near the exit," Darian says. "Meet me after sunset. We won't have long."

"Mallen?" My voice is barely audible.

"I'll handle him. Don't worry."

He steps back, offering a courtly bow—every inch the noble hero performing for the crowd. It's a perfect mask, crafted to hide everything we've just decided. The escape. The betrayal.

The choice.

The silence that follows swallows everything.

The world forgets how to move.

Even my own heart hesitates, as if it knows it has no right to beat for anyone now.

Tension knots in my throat. The moment fractures under its own pressure—too loud, too still. I am like a thread pulled taut past breaking, caught between the past I betrayed and the future I dared to choose. There's no turning back. No undoing this.

I've made my choice. And now, I will carry it.

I back away from Darian in a daze. I'm too numb to feel and too bewildered to think. My feet move of their own accord, despite the heaviness weighing them down and the weariness pulling at my bones like anchors in the tide.

I turn. And my eyes meet Mallen's.

He isn't jealous. He isn't angry.

He's worse than that.

He's empty. Still. Staring at me without a trace of emotion, like I'm the shattered remnants of a porcelain vase, worthy of being studied instead of understood. Like he's trying to find all the pieces of me he once knew and realizing, one by one, that I've broken them and can never be the same again.

I refuse to look away.

I walk toward him with my chin lifted, spine braced, and the smallest tremor in my hands tucked neatly into the folds of my cloak. This is what I chose. I have to remember that. I've got to if I'm going to pull this off. If I'm going to get Darian out alive.

"Princess," he says quietly. No anger. No judgment. Just that word. Like it's all I'll ever be.

"Commander." I take my place beside him and face the tributes.

The air is full of whispered prayers and unspoken fear. Their mouths shape hope like it's currency, but we all know the gods don't barter in mercy.

I whisper a prayer anyway. Not to the gods. To the part of me that still believes Darian might survive this.

Mallen watches the tributes with the same calm detachment I once mistook for strength. "Are you going to tell me what the two of you said?"

"He asked how I was after the fall," I say, keeping my gaze forward. "I wished him luck. He didn't ask me for help, and I haven't offered him any."

He nods slowly. His jaw tightens, but his posture stays rigid and cold. The only movement comes from his hands, which clench and unclench at his sides. "I hope your parting gave you what you need, Azhara."

"He might survive."

"No one survives the labyrinth," he says.

Darian and the tributes move as one, stepping through the gates and descending into the yawning tunnel beneath the arena. Their footsteps echo like drumbeats in a funeral march.

I watch the rusting iron gate swing shut behind them, and listen to the long, aching groan of metal meeting metal—an old sound, and a final one.

"That's not quite true, is it, Mallen?" I turn to him. His face darkens with each breath. "You've survived."

He freezes.

Whatever he expected me to say, it wasn't that.

He hides it well—the flash of surprise, the sudden wariness—but I see it. And more than that, I *feel* it. The truth he's buried doesn't sleep easy. It pulses beneath the surface now, waiting. Seen. Tangible.

We pass beneath stone archways carved with forgotten runes, as the scent of cold iron and caged magic lingers in Threnos. Torches flicker with blue flame, casting long shadows that stretch like specters across the streets. The passages narrow with every step, pressing inward, as if the city itself means to overhear us.

"How do you navigate the labyrinth?" I ask, keeping my tone light, almost careless.

His eyes narrow. He walks beside me as we wind our way back to the palace, toward the private wings, where the noise of the arena gives way to silence and stone quiet as a shadow. "Planning on joining him?"

I laugh—too fast, too breathless. "Hardly. Just making conversation."

Mallen doesn't respond. Not until we reach my rooms and he steps inside with me, crossing his arms as he leans against the far wall.

"You're not making small talk," he says. "You make moves."

I don't answer him. I don't know how.

Instead, I slip down beside a cabinet, keeping space between us. Just enough to breathe. Just enough to think clearly.

"What game are you playing now?" he asks, voice uncertain. Soft, almost.

"I'm not the one playing games."

He smiles and it's the saddest smile I've ever seen. "You think you've been surviving a game someone else built—but it's been yours all along. You're not the pawn, Azhara. You never have been. You're becoming the player who'll teach the board how to move."

"I want things to be different."

He nods slowly, staring at the pattern in the carpet as if it holds the answer to a question he doesn't know how to ask. He thinks for a long time. So long I stop counting the seconds. So long the ache in my chest becomes familiar.

And then he moves.

He rises and walks to me, takes my wrists in his hands, and presses his lips to my forehead with aching tenderness. My breath catches. I don't let it show.

"I have one final thing to take care of," he whispers, "but I promise—things will be different when I return. No more secrets. No more lies."

His forehead rests against mine for a heartbeat too long. And it hurts.

It *hurts.*

Because I do care.

Not in the way he wants. Not in the way he deserves. But somewhere inside me, beneath the strategy and defiance and plans spun from desperation—I care.

Far too much.

And I am about to betray him all the same.

"You need a tether to keep you sane in life," he murmurs. "You are mine. Your heart, your soul. You always will be. But in the labyrinth, I use another cord to bind me to you."

He leaves. The door clicks shut behind him.

And I let out the breath I've been holding since Darian's name passed my lips.

I pace the room, counting every step to quiet my nerves. When the sun begins to dip below the horizon, I change into my training clothes, black, silent and familiar. The velvet cloak slides over my shoulders like a promise.

I don't need the tunnels this time. Just the direct path from my chambers to the labyrinth. I've escaped the palace once—I can do it again.

Especially tonight. The guards are distracted, already dreaming of my father's feast.

I time it to perfection. Five minutes before shift change, I step into the corridor, feigning fatigue, and ask to be escorted to the baths. They groan but agree. When we arrive, I convince them I'll be fine alone. They hesitate. I smile. They leave.

The moment the door clicks behind them, I scatter decoy clothes across the floor and slip into the corridor, heart hammering.

Behind the heavy curtain, I wait, listening to the muffled beat of boots—the shift change.

Timing is everything.

Mallen taught me that.

So I use everything he gave me—every lesson, every warning, every drilled routine—against him. My guilt clings to me like sweat. But I don't let it slow me.

I move in silence. I know where the guards will be, how long their routes take, where the blind spots are.

He trained me for this. And maybe that's the cruelest part of all.

I slip through the palace like smoke, every step calculated, every shadow familiar. The path is etched into muscle memory now. I reach the concealed stair and hold my breath as I try the handle.

Please don't be locked.

It turns.

I release the breath, quiet as a prayer, and slip into the dark.

Down the narrow steps. Across the courtyard. Past the points of no return.

I run.

My lungs burn, but I don't stop. I only slow when I reach the stables. The night cloaks me, and I crouch low, watching. Waiting. No movement. No shouts.

I made it.

I grab a sword left against the wall rack near the tack room door and feel the familiar weight of it. A reassurance. A burden. A reminder. This isn't like last time. I was running away then. Trying to stop a death I didn't yet understand. But now—now I know what I'm doing. I know who I'm doing it for.

This time, I'm not running from anything.

I'm running *to* something.

To someone.

And maybe—just maybe—to the part of myself I lost along the way.

CHAPTER TWENTY-FIVE

I FLY INTO THE AMPHITHEATER. IT'S TOO QUIET.

No guards. No voices. No wind through the banners or trees. Even the night larks are silent, as if they too are holding their breath.

The hush feels wrong—like a ritual has been defiled, and the forest itself grieves. The trees loom overhead, unmoving. The night hangs dark and low, expectant, as if the sky has stooped to witness this trespass. My mind hunts for reason and comes up empty, as if the darkness has been combed smooth to hide it.

My feet still. I crouch low in the shadows, breath caught in my throat. Every instinct screams that I'm too late. That I'm too exposed. That whatever was meant to happen here has already begun without me.

My blade is already drawn. I check for my backup—still strapped to my ankle. Good. I might need it.

The iron gates gape open.

There's no torchlight. No victory flag. The brazier stands cold and unlit. That means the trial is still underway. Darian's still inside. Which means Mallen could be. Or worse—he could be waiting at the center of the labyrinth, hidden in its silence, ready to strike.

I scan the perimeter again. Still no guards. No scuffle. No signs of retreat.

Whatever is unfolding, it's unfolding below.

And it's far from finished.

The silence tears at me.

Another metallic creak slices through the night—soft, slow, like a door left to swing on its hinges. It echoes off the stone and rolls through the empty space.

I inch forward, blade angled, shoulders braced. The gate shouldn't be open. The tunnel shouldn't be calling. But it is. And my name rides in the echo.

A scream ruptures the stillness. Human. Agonized. Real.

It echoes up from the depths and slices straight through me. It's the kind of scream that stains the soul. That leaves a shadow stitched behind the eyes, a silence that never stops screaming. I press a hand to my chest like I can hold myself together through force of will alone.

I think of Darian. Of Mallen. And the creature that prowls below.

It could be anything—feral, old as ash, shaped by years of blood and solitude. Mallen said no one knew what it was.

But that's a lie.

Someone does.

They always do.

The thought makes my blood burn.

I shouldn't go in. I know that.

But I also know I can't stand here and do nothing.

Darian isn't just a tribute anymore. He's become part of my story. A choice I made with open eyes.

And Mallen—he's too dangerous to leave unwatched. Not because I fear he'll fail, but because I fear what will happen if he wins.

I draw a slow, steady breath and steel myself.

I've spent too long being handled, maneuvered, positioned like a token in someone else's game. That ends now. My future won't be granted—I'm going to take it.

I run for the gate.

The torch flares in my hand, flames shivering against the dark as I descend. The stone corridor swallows me whole. The air turns damp. Stale. Rank with the reek of buried prayers and things too long sealed. My lungs seize. My eyes water. Still, I press on.

It's longer than I expected. A slow spiral carved downward, ribbed with rust and carved names. The kind of place no light touches. The kind of place that remembers.

The tunnel ends in a fork—no forward path. Only left or right. Both cloaked in shadow.

I pause. Listening.

There's no sound. No pull.

Except—

A coil of twine rests in the dust on the left-hand path. Rough. Familiar.

A cord. A tether.

One that binds.

This is how Mallen marks his trail. I pick it up and run it between my fingers. It's ugly, utilitarian. It shouldn't matter. But it does. Because it reminds me of him.

Mallen is down here.

I find the rusted ring and lash my thread beside his. Two paths now. Two tethers. Mine loops once. Tighter. Smaller than Mallen's. But just as sharp.

I move quickly, following his line.

It winds, doubles back, cuts sharp through narrow bends. It's not designed to be navigated, only endured.

Another scream slices the dark. Lower-pitched this time. Drawn out. A requiem you sing when you know you're not going to survive.

I swallow hard and keep going. I'm too deep in to turn back.

The floor slickens with moss and veins of rot, pulsing faintly as if the earth itself is diseased. The torch sputters against the cold. The magic here is thick—old blood and older bones.

A crash splits the dark—iron shrieking against marble like a cry ripped from the throat of the labyrinth itself. Then comes shouting. Strained voices. Clashing blades. The rhythm of battle, desperate and wild.

They're fighting. All of them. Mallen must have reached the others. Unless the monster got there first.

My steps quicken. My heart hammers in my ribs like it's trying to tear its way free.

The thread tugs me onward, winding toward the chaos. I don't know what I'll find. I only know I have to get there. I have to see for myself. Know who's still breathing.

Another turn. Then another.

The air grows colder. The walls narrower. The screams louder.

My grip on my sword is wrong—too tight. I know better. I should adjust. I don't. I'm not trained for this. Not really. I was taught to survive, and to fight. But never like this.

Never for real.

The magic surges before I see them. Unbidden. Untethered. My magic is meant to be dormant—contained until the claiming is complete. But it's rising now, and it doesn't care about rules.

It's crackling beneath my skin. Not lightning. Not fire. Still cold and black. It coils through my veins like ink spilled in water—liquid shadow devouring the light. The flesh beneath my skin shimmers with it, black-gold tendrils trying to flicker at my fingertips, alive with a promise I don't yet understand.

It's never come this close before. Not this threatening. Not this alive.

It curls under my tongue. Tightens behind my eyes. Coils at the base of my spine and spreads like frost along my nerves.

I shouldn't want it. But gods help me, I do.

Because this time, it's not fear that drives it. It's fury. Purpose. Need.

The sound of battle sharpens. Someone shouts. Then silence again.

My thread veers left. I follow it. And I run.

I'm close now. Too close.

The thread jerks taut around a jagged bend. The torchlight throws shapes across the tunnel wall—shadows too large to be human. One of them moves.

I inch forward, hugging the wall.

The tunnel narrows to a small archway. Just ahead, I can hear them. Breathing. Gasping. Blades scraping stone. Every breath ahead is ragged. Wet. A gasp against the silence. Then a scrape—metal dragged too slowly. Someone's wounded. Someone's waiting. I tighten my grip and step into the mouth of the dark.

I step through the arch and let the flame die.

My eyes adjust fast.

And what I see makes my breath stop.

The center of the maze. The heart of the labyrinth. There should be a flag here—Darian should've claimed it. But the pole is empty. No colors, no sign of victory. That means he made it here. And kept going.

Mallen would know better than to strip the flag.

I pivot, checking behind me. Empty. But the space isn't safe. The air is too still. I move slowly now, every footstep careful. My sword remains drawn, balanced in my grip.

A scream pierces the air. High. Raw. It echoes too long and ends too abruptly. A crash follows—meat against stone. Another sound follows. Wet, low, choking. Someone's drowning in their own blood. That's two men dead. And not from anything quick or clean. The silence that follows is heavier than before. The kind that settles like a curse.

A figure appears.

He steps into the square, cloak dragging behind him like a shadow made flesh. He moves slowly, deliberately. The gleam of his sword drips red and fresh, the blood trailing down its edge like ink from a broken vow.

I brace. Right foot behind, weight centered, sword raised. A quiet inhale. If this is it, I won't go down passive.

"Azhara."

I freeze. My name in his voice, quiet and breaking.

"What are you doing here?" Mallen's hood hides half his face, but I see the way he tilts his head. Off-guard. Like I've struck him without raising a weapon.

"I came..." I don't finish.

He pulls the hood back. "For me?"

His voice is raw with hope. There's no mask, no suspicion. Just longing. Gods. So much longing.

He doesn't wait for my answer. He doesn't need to. His smile turns soft, reverent. Like my presence alone has rewritten the night.

I blink hard. The lie burns in my chest. I didn't come for him. Not exactly. But I didn't not come either. I hate that it's both. That my silence is a betrayal he can't see.

Still, he hasn't drawn on me. He could have, should have. I won't raise my blade unless he gives me a reason.

"Where's the monster?" I ask.

"It doesn't matter," he murmurs. His gaze doesn't waver from my face.

I don't trust him. But my magic lies quiet—watchful, unfurled—like a beast not yet stirred. No threat. No alarm. Only stillness between us, coiled and strange.

"You figured it out." He nods toward the twine in my hand. "About the labyrinth."

He steps closer. Not in threat. In relief.

I stiffen.

Mallen reaches for the twine, and his fingers brush mine. His hand is warm. Steady. The touch lingers longer than it should, and something flickers in his face—regret, recognition, a grief with my name on it.

"It's just stone and shadow," he says, quiet. "The walls don't shift. There are no traps. Men disappear in the labyrinth because they think they're supposed to. Those who enter lose themselves before they ever meet the monster."

"But there is one," I say. My voice barely carries. "A monster."

He nods once. "He doesn't attack everyone."

My throat tightens.

"Is that what I just heard?"

"Yes."

He steps closer again. His breath warms my cheek. Too close. Too much. I don't move.

"You don't have to fear him," he says softly. "Not you."

He moves faster than I expect—his arm slides around my waist, and I stagger as he pulls me with him, crossing the square in a single breath. I protest, but he doesn't answer. Just spins me out of the way and steps in front of me, crouching low with his sword raised.

I look past him, confused, breathless—and see the blur of movement charging toward us.

Mallen's body tenses. His hand reaches back, pressing against my hip to keep me still.

He's shielding me.

I drop into a low stance and raise my blade beside him. "Is it the monster?"

Footsteps thunder across the stone. But it's no creature that enters the square.

A man. Sword drawn. He halts at the last second, catching his momentum, bracing. Defensive stance. He's not attacking. He's watching me.

His gaze flicks to something behind me.

Then Darian steps from the shadows.

He doesn't rush. Doesn't raise his weapon. He walks like the square belongs to him. Each step slow, measured, deliberate—as if he's walking through a dream he knows ends in fire, and he cannot wait to light the kindling.

Relief hits me first. It's sharp, short-lived. But then it twists—suspicion, cold and creeping, washes through me. He's too composed. Moving like a man who's too sure of himself.

His gaze locks on Mallen's. "Are you going to tell her, or am I?"

Mallen shifts his stance. He doesn't answer. His shoulders rise slightly—like breath caught between fury and restraint, the kind of silence that tastes like blood before a sacrifice.

Still protecting me. Still between us.

"Tell her before I kill you," Darian says. His tone is different now. Not kind. Not clever. It's cold. Cruel. Nothing like the man who flirted in the sunlight.

"Only four remain," Mallen says, voice tight.

Darian laughs. But it's hollow. "Tell her. Or I will."

"Tell me what?" I say, and I hate the tremor in my voice.

Neither answers.

Darian turns to me. "Ask him where the monster is. Ask him how he knows the path so well. Ask him what he is."

I don't want to.

But the question sits in me like a knife twisting inward. Slow and deliberate.

I turn to Mallen, and I don't flinch. "Tell me. I deserve to know."

Mallen doesn't move. The silence stretches—tight as a drawn bow—long and painful. Then he speaks, and his voice is low and broken, and I close my eyes like it would be enough to stop the world from ending.

CHAPTER TWENTY-SIX

"There's no need for her to know," Mallen snaps. His voice is low, guttural. Not desperation—warning.

Darian steps forward, lips curled in a curve too close to a smile. His eyes find mine, watching like he's waiting for me to flinch.

I don't.

"I didn't want you to know, Azhara," Mallen continues, blade held low, but taut with tension. "When the gods bound the magic in Starsfall, they stripped away its hope. What's left had to be sealed—this place, this trial. The balance hangs on—"

"You. You're the choice. Our salvation or ruin," Darian cuts in. "That's why he wants you. Not for love—leverage. Choose him and he'll chain Starsfall's magic to the crown. He'll keep you bound to feed it."

Mallen growls—not words, just fury—and drops into a crouch, weight shifting as Darian edges closer. Neither moves yet. They circle each other in the square, blades at the ready, expressions sharp. Waiting for the right moment to tear the other apart.

Darian isn't trying to kill him yet. He's goading him. Picking at fault lines. Trying to crack the mask Mallen's held on too tightly for too long.

"You hold the power," Darian says, eyes locked on me even as his blade angles toward Mallen. "He wants it for himself. To claim the throne. To bind you to him."

"That throne means nothing to me," Mallen spits.

Darian lunges. Steel meets steel.

The impact rings through the dark—fast, clean, brutal. Mallen blocks, ripostes. Their swords blur. Feet scrape against stone. A rhythm forms and breaks as they step, slash, retreat.

Neither lands a blow. Not yet.

Another tribute moves, a flicker on the edge of the square. I shift my weight and raise my blade, watching—but Mallen's already adjusted, his stance shifting subtly to cover both threats. No flourish. No wasted movement.

"All I've done is protect you," Mallen says, not breaking form. "You know me."

I don't answer. My fingers tighten around the hilt. He doesn't look back.

Across from me, Darian's gaze flicks to mine. His expression hardens, then drops—eyes closing just for a breath. As if it costs him something to keep pressing forward.

"He's the monster," Darian says softly. Not to Mallen. To me.

A cold pressure builds in my chest. The torchlight flickers. My breath shortens.

"He comes here to gather the darkness," Darian continues, advancing. "He feeds on it. The power. The pain. It makes him strong. And it's consumed him."

My heart stutters. I force myself to meet Mallen's eyes.

He doesn't speak. But the answer is there—in the set of his jaw, the stiffness of his shoulders, the way his blade wavers for the first time.

The mask drops and behind it I see what I always should have.

Guilt.

He was never going to tell me. Never going to stop.

Mallen is the monster in the labyrinth.

He's what I've feared in every shadow and the darkness my magic couldn't bear to name.

"He's filled this place with rot," Darian says. "He'll do the same to Starsfall. To you."

Mallen's blade trembles once, and then he roars. He lunges—no control. No tactic. Just rage.

Darian meets him head-on. Steel flashes. Mallen's momentum carries him too far, his footing misjudged. He twists mid-motion, barely dodging a blade aimed to take his heart.

His feet skid. He spins and tries to recover.

Darian doesn't let him.

Strike. Block. Strike again.

Darian drives Mallen back. Step by step. His blade never slows, never hesitates. Mallen's foot grazes stone, shoulder brushing the rough curve of the labyrinth wall. Another step, and there'll be nowhere left to go.

He won't survive.

Not without killing Darian.

They clash again—metal biting metal—each strike faster, heavier. Then something shifts. Mallen pivots. Regains footing. Pressure changes. Darian's forced to yield, to give space. He's retreating now, breath shallow as Mallen surges forward.

I don't move. Not yet. It's madness in front of me. Even thinking of stepping in is lunacy. Their blades want blood, and I don't know whose they'll draw first.

A blur—Darian staggers back. Mallen throws him off, hard enough to send dust spiraling into the air. Another figure leaps in—one of the others, grabbing Mallen's arm, trying to hold him off just long enough for Darian to recover.

It works.

It shouldn't.

Mallen should've ended it.

Darian catches my eye as he straightens. He knows it. We both do.

He lifts his chin and steps toward me. Just a fraction. Just enough.

Mallen sees.

His heel slams into the other tribute's chest, sending him crashing into stone. Mallen twists, grabs Darian, and hurls him sideways. A blur of limbs and air. Darian crashes into the ground, dust clouding around him.

And then—

Mallen waits.

Sword ready. Muscles taut. But still.

He waits.

No strike. No advantage taken.

Honor. Of all things, it's that.

He should've finished it. He's trained me never to hesitate. But here he is—offering mercy.

I don't understand it, and yet, I do.

Darian drags himself to his feet and points past Mallen, past everything, to me.

"Destroy him," he calls. "End it, Azhara. That's your freedom. He'll take everything if you don't."

His voice cuts through the air like a blade of its own.

"He'll consume you. Even if he doesn't want to. He's been overcome with darkness, and it gives him no choice. That's the secret he's kept from you, that he's tried to hide all these years."

I step back. Just one. The stones feel unsteady beneath my boots.

Mallen doesn't speak. His body shifts again, poised like a coiled predator, waiting. Not for Darian. For me.

"No," I whisper.

Mallen blinks. The smallest motion. And in that moment, Darian lunges.

I move too.

Three bodies collide. The labyrinth swallows us.

Someone grabs my arm—I'm yanked the opposite way. Darian. Mallen. Both trying to fight each other. Both trying to protect me. And I'm trying to stop both from dying.

One blade whistles past my ear. Another clashes against it.

Too close. Too fast.

Mallen roars—low, guttural—and drives forward. His sword slices through the air, forcing Darian back. I'm shoved aside.

Darian hits the ground. Hard.

Mallen's blade rises.

I throw myself between them.

My sword lifts just in time, catching his. Sparks flash. The impact shudders through my bones.

Mallen stares down at me.

Disbelief. Then something darker.

His sword doesn't move.

He sees what I've done. What I've chosen.

I've saved Darian.

From him.

Mallen's jaw tightens. His eyes—once stormy green—go dark. Whatever held him together falls apart.

I don't speak. But everything in me pleads.

Not for mercy.

For him to understand.

That I didn't want this.

Darian's hand finds my shoulder—and his blade finds its mark.

It slips through the narrow space between us and slices clean across Mallen's arm.

He snarls in pain. I drive my elbow back into Darian's ribs. He gasps but doesn't stop.

"You don't have a choice!" he yells.

Mallen steps forward, bleeding, swinging. I block—barely.

He doesn't hold back.

There's nothing left of the man who trained me. Only rage. Fury. Betrayal. The anger of a man who's overcome with a darkness powerful enough to turn him into a monster.

There's no alliance left between us. Whatever tether held us together snapped the moment I stood between him and Darian. And now, I'm not an ally, I'm a target.

Steel clashes. I push off. He follows. Faster. Wilder. I brace, twist, dodge.

This is real.

And I'm not letting him win.

I drive him back, foot by foot.

Then I strike. Upward, fast. Around. I spin and pivot—pulling him with me, away from Darian.

He doesn't flinch. Meets me, strike for strike. We've done this before—but never like this. Never with blood on our blades.

"Go!" I shout to Darian. "Leave!"

Mallen surges.

I don't back down.

He hammers against me and I match it—parry, counter, drive.

He's stronger. Heavier.

But I'm faster.

And I'm done running.

I twist and kick. He stumbles. I press, blade flashing again and again. I don't let up.

He trained me for this.

And now he'll see exactly what he created.

He counters. I twist away, narrowly avoiding the blow. He wheels around—ready—but I've already stepped back, drawing him on.

He follows.

Behind him, the other tribute hauls Darian upright. He shouts something—I don't listen.

"Go!" I scream again. "Get him out!"

I keep pulling Mallen with me. Deeper into the labyrinth. Into narrower passages. With no room to dodge. He presses hard—blow after blow.

Each one closer to breaking me.

He knows. So do I.

He slams his sword down. I block—barely. His blade glances off mine with brutal precision. I stumble.

His hand seizes my wrist and twists.

Fire rips through my arm.

I hit the wall. Hard. His knee forces my legs apart. One hand clamps around my neck. Not enough to kill. Just enough to show he could.

He pauses.

"I want to know," he says. "Why him, Azhara?"

I don't answer. I won't.

It's all I have left—my silence.

His grip tightens. My lungs burn and my vision dims.

He tilts his head back. Just slightly.

That's the moment.

I take it.

My fist slams into his throat.

He reels back, coughing. I throw myself forward—fists flying. One lands. Then another.

I fight on instinct. On fury. On every unanswered question I never let myself feel. On every shattered dream, every ounce of fury I never let myself feel.

And I pour all of it into him.

He staggers. His sword drops. But I don't stop.

I drive him into the wall. My knuckles split. My shoulders ache. I slam my fist into the side of his head.

His skull hits stone. He crumples.

I freeze.

Pain hits—sharp and sudden. Devastation erupts through my chest, like it's breaking the remnants of my heart. My hands shake. I can't bring myself to check if Mallen's breathing. Blood paints the walls, his skin, and the floor beneath him. His breath rattles, a jagged scrape of noise.

He doesn't move.

I can't make myself touch him. Can't even kneel. My heart thunders. It lies, and tells me he's alive.

Because the alternative—

No.

"I didn't choose him," I whisper, voice hoarse, barely audible. Tears fall. "You made it impossible to choose you."

CHAPTER TWENTY-SEVEN

I retrace my steps through the labyrinth, the thread wound tight around my wrist. My legs move, but my body feels borrowed—raw and disconnected, like I'm bleeding out something more important than blood. My skin hums with bruises. I float and sink all at once, waves crashing over me, pulling me under.

The cold stone sweats around me, the air thick with rot and damp, and each footstep lands heavy, uneven. My limbs lag behind thought, as if I've slipped loose from myself. I can't hold onto a single emotion without ten more crashing in its wake, a storm circling tighter and tighter.

I miss him.

I want to go back for him.

I know it's too late for that. Gods, it's too late now.

I follow the thread blindly. Time doesn't move the same way in the labyrinth. It might've been hours. Might've been minutes. Every turn feels wrong. The slope steepens and I drag myself up it, one foot at a time, lungs heaving.

Then light appears—dim and flickering.

The gate.

I stagger through it into the open courtyard.

Shouts rise. The rush of movement is too fast to process. Metal clatters.

Boots thunder. I spin, ducking instinctively. A man barrels toward me and I twist just out of reach—but a second grabs my ankle and yanks.

The world tips sideways. Stone slams into my ribs.

Hands crush me to the ground.

I scream and buck, but there's no leverage. A knee pins my spine. My face scrapes against rough stone. More weight joins the first. My shoulders and wrists are clamped down, my legs immobilized.

"She's wild—"

"Hold her—"

My breath tears in and out, fast and ragged. Blood pulses in my ears. I don't know who's touching me, and I don't care—I just need them off. The panic claws up faster than I can choke it down. My magic tries to spark and then slips through my fingers like oil, useless and uncontrollable.

"We're not your enemy, Princess," a voice murmurs, too close. A man crouches to meet my eyes.

The weight eases off me, and I'm hauled upright, my knees buckling. Arms loop under mine to hold me up. My feet drag. The stone blurs beneath me. We're moving again—toward the tunnels.

"She's done," someone mutters behind me. "Barely breathing. If she killed him, she spent everything doing it."

I open my mouth to speak, and only a rasp escapes.

Arms catch me around the waist and I'm lifted again, slung over someone's shoulder like a sack of grain. My head dangles. The world rocks nauseatingly with each step. Fury sparks hot in my chest, but it burns out too quickly.

I hate this.

A wide door bangs open, and the smell of chaff and mice hits my tongue. The grain store swallows us in must and dust. A hatch yawns open, black and deep. I'm passed down through it like cargo. Another man grabs me before I can find my footing.

"Sorry," he mutters and then lifts me again. I'm too tired to curse him properly.

The second ride is worse. My shoulder bangs into his collarbone with every step. I'm relieved when the tunnel finally spills out into night. Cold air snaps against my skin. Horses shift in the shadows, stamping against the ground. The group is smaller than it should be. Not enough bodies. Time seems short.

Something's gone wrong.

A scuffle breaks out near the tree line. Darian is restrained by three men, thrashing against their grip. His face is bloodied, hair clinging to his skin. He roars something I can't make out.

His eyes lock onto mine.

The fury drains out of him, replaced by something quieter. Sadder. He nods once before he's hauled onto a horse. Someone leads a gelding toward me, reins swinging, hooves pawing.

I take a step toward it and then another. My legs tremble. My thighs are soaked in dried blood. I reach for the saddle—

"Azhara," Darian calls. His voice is rough, pleading.

I shake my head. "I can ride."

I probably can't. But I'll try.

Two men intercept. I shove at them weakly.

"I said I'm fine."

"You're clearly not," one says.

Darian's eyes are wild, desperate. "Please, Azhara. Just let me help."

I flinch at the word. Help.

"No," I say, more breath than sound. "Not like this."

I'm lifted again, too fast to stop, tossed up onto Darian's horse despite my protest. My side slams into his chest. I twist, trying to slide off, but his arm snakes around my waist and holds me still.

"You'll fall," he breathes against my temple.

"You're not strong enough to carry me."

"I am."

He nudges the horse forward before I can argue.

I press my mouth shut. The weight of his arm, the rhythm of the horse, the scent of dust and sweat—all of it crowds too close. I close my eyes, just for a moment. Not to rest. To pretend I made the right choice. Or that I still have one.

The gates vanish behind us. Trees whip past. The rhythm of the gallop rattles every bone in my spine. Darian murmurs words I don't want to hear—comforting, coaxing, soft—and I stare ahead.

I won't let myself melt.

The gallop slows as the trees thin and the shadows fall away. The horses eat the distance in silence, hooves pounding a steady rhythm into the dark earth. Trees blur past, and when the forest finally breaks, dawn stains the horizon in washed-out gray. The city lies behind us now. Its breath no longer on our necks.

But its reach? That lingers.

The others glance back too often. We all know it's only a matter of time before the hunt begins. My father won't stop. And if Mallen still breathes—he won't either. That kind of pursuit doesn't end. It only breaks when one side is gone.

The pace slows as the terrain flattens. I sag slightly, too tired to hold myself upright. Darian shifts behind me. His breath brushes the back of my neck.

"You should rest," he murmurs.

I keep my eyes fixed on the horizon, but my body betrays me. My head tilts back against his shoulder, lids drooping before I can stop them. I try to sit straighter. Try to pull from his grip. But my limbs turn heavy, numb, and unwilling.

His arm stays firm at my waist, and I hate how solid it feels.

Sleep creeps in anyway, slow and inescapable. It drags me under before I can stop it.

The world tilts again.

Someone lifts me down, and for a moment, I jolt awake, fists curling, breath caught. The face is unfamiliar. The arms, unfamiliar too. Not Darian's.

I freeze, letting the panic settle before it tips me into making a mistake. I know better. I force my breathing to slow. Force my limbs to stay still. My surroundings blur with movement—riders, trees, the distant whisper of the sea. We've made ground.

"You're safe," Darian says, riding up beside us. "You're with my second. I needed to recover my strength."

His horse keeps pace with mine. I twist slightly to see him, and the effort sends a jolt through my spine. Every muscle aches.

"You've been asleep for hours. Feeling any better?"

I grit my teeth as the man behind me shifts again, his thigh brushing mine. My body recoils before I can stop it.

"I'll ride alone," I say, voice sharper than I intend.

Darian lifts a brow, half amused. "There's the Azhara I remember."

He signals someone and a horse is brought up alongside mine. The man offers me his hand. I slap it away, glaring as I swing my leg over and transfer with more willpower than grace. My hands tremble on the reins, but I force them to stay steady. I don't care how it looks. I'm on my own now. That's what matters.

I count the riders as we move. Twenty. Most are strangers. Four I recognize. Tributes. Six are dead.

Darian rides beside me again. "How are you?"

"I've been better."

The others glance back. Conversations die. The weight of unspoken questions fills the space between hoofbeats. They want to know what happened. What I did. What I left behind.

They can wait.

I shift my weight in the saddle. The heat of pain spreads through me with every step of my horse. My joints throb, muscles pulled too tight beneath skin that doesn't fit me anymore. Something stirs beneath it all—cold, coiled, restless. The magic inside me hasn't settled. It shifts when I breathe. Prickles when I think of what was and what may come to pass.

I'm no longer the person I used to be. I don't know what's left—what's mine, what's stolen, what's ruined. But I do know this: I'm done being steered. By men, by magic, by anything that thinks it owns me.

Darian reaches for my reins, fingers brushing mine. "You were never meant to carry this weight. Not alone. Not ever."

His voice is soft. Too soft. I pull my hand back before he can hold it.

"If you're asking how I killed him, I don't know that I did."

The words taste sour. Like failure.

Darian studies me, and I can't tell if it's worry or calculation in his eyes. He smiles, too quickly, and it doesn't reach his mouth.

"I'm not worried about Mallen."

I study him sideways. "You don't need to be. I left him in no state to follow."

His expression shifts. A flicker of something. Not fear. Not grief. Something closer to solace.

"He wasn't getting up," I add, quieter now.

I stare straight ahead. The road's just a smear of dirt and dust, vanishing into morning light. I don't want to see his face. I don't want to see judgment.

"But I didn't...check."

"I see," Darian says, voice too smooth.

I hear the crack of bone against stone. Taste copper. Hear my screams echoing off the walls, though I don't remember screaming. And Mallen's silence stayed louder than any sound.

I killed a man the last time I tried to escape Starsfall. That was clean. Simple. Necessary.

But this?

This was different.

This wasn't self-defense. It wasn't fate, or magic, or justice. It was messy and personal and cruel. It was Mallen—his voice, his hands, his silence. It was me, screaming. Him, not screaming back.

It was choosing.

Darian's hand closes around mine. His palm is warm, firm.

"I assumed Mallen taught you how to kill."

"He never made me do it."

I let the silence settle over that truth. Another fracture in the armor I've barely held together.

We ride in quiet for a time, his hand still wrapped around mine. I don't pull away. Not yet. But I don't lean in either.

This isn't comfort. This is consequence.

Just a day ago, I'd chosen him. Last night, I'd defended him. Today, I'm not sure what I've done. Or why.

And gods help me, I still want Mallen to tell me I didn't have to. That it was all a test. That he'd forgive me anyway.

But he's not here.

And I made my decision.

"You shouldn't feel ashamed," Darian says gently. "You made a hard choice."

I nod, because I don't know what else to do.

"He was my friend," I say, voice catching on the word as tears slip down without permission.

Darian's jaw tightens. "No, Azhara. He wasn't."

The words cut, not because they're cruel, but because they're true—and I've known it. Gods, I've always known it.

But knowing and accepting are not the same.

He was the one who kept the monsters at bay. Who showed me where to aim and when to run. Who stood behind me like a wall no one else could see. My protector. My shadow. The one person who knew the truth and didn't look away.

He was everything in a place that gave me nothing.

And I betrayed him.

The image of his face—bloodied, stunned, hollow—won't leave me. It plays behind my eyes like a punishment. I want to scream, but all that comes is silence and salt.

"He was a monster," Darian says carefully, watching me like he's afraid to press too hard. "The sooner you can see that, the better."

My gaze drops. "He might not be dead."

The bitterness slips in before I can soften it.

Darian tenses. His fingers flex hard on the reins. For a second, he doesn't speak. Doesn't blink.

"That would be...inconvenient," he mutters, too low for anyone else to hear.

Then, as if catching himself, he softens his tone.

"Do you regret it?"

I don't answer. Not with words.

Instead, I turn forward. The road stretches on—unchanging, silent, cruel. It offers nothing but distance and dust, no absolution and certainly no answers. I can't turn back. I wouldn't even know how.

Mallen carried darkness, but he never let it drown me. He never screamed at me without reason. Never struck first. He hated Darian—yes—but that rage was never for me. All I knew was his restraint, and the way he never let me fall, even when he was the one who put me on the edge.

He taught me to fight, not so I could kill, but so I could survive. So I could become something dangerous in a world that chewed girls like me to pieces. When the palace crushed me, he was the one who stitched me back together.

He made me strong enough to betray him.

Darian reaches over, his fingers brushing mine. I let him take my hand again, even though it feels wrong. His warmth doesn't reach me.

He waits—soft, silent, patient. The opposite of Mallen in every way.

Darian doesn't press, like the answer is mine to give. He's gentle where

Mallen was relentless. Careful where Mallen cut deep. And gods, I know he's trying. He's trying to make this easier.

I shake my head, and my voice comes like splinters. "No."

Because nothing about this feels like freedom.

Darian watches me carefully, the way someone watches a candle about to go out. He expected something different. He expected relief. Gratitude. A clean break. But I'm still bleeding. Still braced for a fight that already ended.

He sees the truth, whether I say it aloud or not.

He sees the pain I shouldn't feel. The pain I shouldn't let him see. And worse—he sees the doubt.

And worse—he sees I've lied. To him.

I made my choice.

But I can't shake the feeling I buried the wrong man.

CHAPTER TWENTY-EIGHT

The manor rises from the mist like a half-remembered relic. Perched above the cliffs, it crouches in crumbling grandeur—stone walls streaked with salt, its windows dark and lifeless. Wind rattles the shutters like loose teeth. Ivy has clawed halfway up the south wing. A noble's summer retreat, long abandoned.

Now it belongs to us.

We ride through the rusting gates in silence. The iron groans open and then swings shut behind us with a finality that prickles beneath my skin. My thighs ache from the saddle, my fingers stiff and blistered from too many hours holding the reins, but I stay upright as the men dismount around me—quiet, precise, a plan already in motion. No shouted commands. No need. Darian's orders were given hours ago, and none of his soldiers question them now.

Of course they don't.

He's the last to dismount. When his boots hit the ground, I see the strain ripple through him—just for a moment. His limp catches him off guard, more pronounced than before, and he winces before smoothing it away. Then his eyes lift to mine, unreadable in the half-light. Pale as sea-glass.

"Inside," he says, quiet but steady. "You'll be safe here. We have until morning."

Safe. As if I haven't learned how dangerous that word can be.

Still, I follow him through the arched double doors into the house. The smell of age hits first—dust, old wine, the sharp tang of brine soaked into the floorboards. The kind of house that remembers everything. Footsteps. Secrets. Blood.

He gestures toward a wide corridor to the right. "You'll find the main chamber down that hall. Take whatever you need."

I nod but don't wait for him. My boots echo against the stone as I walk away from him, shoulders straight, pace even. I don't need help.

The door to the bedroom opens with a groan. Light slants through tall windows, faint and cold. The walls are papered in a fading floral pattern, corners curled like dying leaves. I strip off my gloves and drop them onto the vanity and then catch my reflection in the mirror.

For a moment, I don't recognize the girl in the mirror.

Raw cheeks. Cracked lips. Eyes that haven't looked like mine in days—wide, dark, rimmed in pain. And doubt.

This is what running looks like.

One of Darian's men knocks and then enters with a basin and cloths. His gaze lingers too long. I ignore it. I peel off the layers of dust and dried blood, scrubbing my skin until it's red and clean. When I emerge, I'm wrapped in borrowed riding clothes, my damp hair twisted into a knot. I feel lighter. Emptier.

I sit on the edge of the bed, staring again at the girl in the mirror. Trying to make sense of her. Not because I'm tired. Not because I'm hurt.

Because I can still hear the voice of the messenger who'd ridden alongside us on the road, breathless and hoarse from shouting.

I hadn't meant to hear it.

Hadn't meant to listen as the red-faced and dust-slicked rider reined in hard beside Darian.

"She didn't kill him."

The words hung there. Unearned. Impossible.

But I knew. I knew they were true the moment I heard them.

Four words. That was all it took to unmake me.

I'd told myself Mallen was dead. I'd built my escape on it. Needed to believe it. I hadn't checked his pulse. I hadn't dared. If I had—

I might have hesitated. I might have stayed.

But he lived. He lived, and he was coming.

The mirror doesn't show panic. It shows something worse.

It shows longing.

I don't look like someone who's afraid. Like someone desperate to be chosen. And I don't know what that makes me.

A liar?

Or just a girl who made one choice—and now wants to make another.

The door creaks open behind me. I don't have to look to know it's Darian. He leans in the doorway, his weight casual, his presence deliberate. Still handsome. Still a face and body gifted by the gods.

"Azhara," he says.

My name sounds different tonight. Less sure. Less rehearsed.

I don't answer. I rise and move past him without a word, the edge of my shoulder grazing his. The corridor is darker now. The house hushes around us. Every footstep echoes.

I find a sitting room at the end of the hall. Dust drapes the furniture. A cold hearth yawns at the center. I kneel and light the fire myself, coaxing the flames until they lick up and catch. The heat stings my fingers and then begins to spread.

Darian follows, but doesn't speak. Doesn't ask if he can come in. He doesn't need to. Men like him never do.

He stands by the mantel, too close to the fire, like it might soften whatever edge he's trying to hide.

"You've been quiet," he says. "Since we rode over the ridge."

"I didn't have anything to say."

"You usually do."

I shrug. The silence stretches.

"You were right not to check," he says. "At the maze. If you had—he would've used it. Turned it against you. That's what he does."

My spine stiffens. "I made a mistake."

He studies me carefully. "No, you made a decision."

"I told myself I had to. That I was saving myself. That leaving him behind was the right thing."

"And now?"

"Now I know he lived. And I ran when I shouldn't have."

He tilts his head. "I fought for you. Bled for you. Won the Reaping for you. I've planned this for years. Bribed guards. Found courtiers who weren't as loyal as they should have been. My fleet waits for us to join them on the next tide. All to take you with me and keep you safe. From Mallen. From your father."

"From the magic?"

Darian stills.

"Was this about me, Darian? Or about making sure my father doesn't get his magic back?"

"Both. I could not let your father keep power for himself. I know that's what would happen if no one claimed you. And if you choose a man from Starsfall, then the magic returns. The crown will drink it. I meant to keep that from him. But you are not a tactic. Not to me. You matter."

It is what men do not say that tells the truth. I hear it now. This was always the shape of the Reaping this year: choose Darian or choose Mallen and call one mine, while my father plans for every eventuality and tries to rig the board.

"Are you still coming with me to Larksbind?"

"I thought I would." My voice is low. "On the road, before the messenger. I told myself I'd disappear and become something new. I wanted to believe I could leave my life behind. And if it didn't work, I'd walk away."

"And now that you know?"

My fingers curl near the fire.

"I don't know what I'm doing. But I know I can't pretend anymore."

He steps forward. "You think it changes things."

"I know it does."

The words hang in the air, weighty and absolute. I watch him, waiting to see if he'll challenge them. Twist them. Wrap them in velvet and feed them back to me in prettier language.

But all he does is breathe—shallow, sharp—and step forward.

He walks toward me slowly, like he's approaching a cornered bird. "He's coming with a whole army at his back. He's not coming for love. He's coming for blood."

"No," I say quietly. "He's coming because I lied when I said I was finished. He believes I'm still worth saving."

I let the fire fill the silence, tension crackling like a wire pulled too tight. His gaze pins me. The question's coming—I already know it.

"You want to return to him?"

The question is quiet. Dangerous.

I turn toward him. "Yes."

For a moment, neither of us speaks.

"You think you can survive him?" he asks.

"I already did."

"You saw it. What he was. What he's capable of. That darkness in the labyrinth—it wasn't just the labyrinth."

"I know."

"Then why go back?"

I meet his gaze. "Because I love him."

His mouth tightens. "You don't owe him anything."

"I know."

"You think that makes it love?"

I don't answer. I let him hear the silence.

"I can give you safety," he says. "A future. I'll make you happy. You'll want for nothing. All you have to do is come with me and this will end. I'll give you everything you ever wanted, Azhara. Please."

I study him. The man who brought me here. Who's offered me escape and protection. Who wants to be chosen, but hasn't asked why I might need to choose in the first place.

And I think about the man I left behind. The one who's storming after me with an army not because of rage, but because he still thinks I'm worth the ruin. Who used to find me in the dark just to say my name like it mattered. Who pressed his forehead to mine after every fight. Who remembered I hated lilac and always carried juniper oil instead.

"You'd have me forget," I say at last.

His breath catches. "Would that be so terrible?"

The fire crackles between us. The air feels heavy.

"Yes."

He watches me closely. "You think he'll give you more than I can?"

"I think he'll never try to change me."

His jaw tightens, but he doesn't speak. The line of his throat moves as he swallows it back—whatever plea or protest he almost gave voice to. For a moment, his mask slips. Not enough to see the wound, but enough to know it's there.

He exhales slowly. "Come to Larksbind. With me."

I look at him. Really look.

"No," I say.

His silence is long and still. He doesn't ask why. He already knows.

But he says it anyway.

"You're choosing him."

"I already did," I whisper.

"In the labyrinth?"

"In every moment I didn't kill him. In every moment I've regretted it ever since. And in all those I should have given him before."

My voice trembles on the last word. Not from weakness—but from the weight of everything I should have done, and didn't. I press my hands together, grounding myself in the present, in the only thing I can still control: this choice.

"You're mistaking guilt for love."

"I know the difference."

The silence that follows is thick and heavy. He looks away first, and for a second I think he might be angry—until I realize it's an entirely different emotion. Not fury. Not hurt. Just the slow dawning of truth. The ache of knowing he was never really in the running.

Darian's gaze drops. "You're making a mistake."

"I've made worse ones."

Darian's jaw tightens. "You want a storybook ending. A broken hero chasing his perfect princess. But this isn't a love story."

"No," I say. "It's not."

He waits. "Then why go?"

"Because I want to be the one who chooses."

He flinches at that. Not visibly—but I feel it.

I wrap my arms around myself. Not for warmth. Just to hold all the pieces in. The fire is too bright now. Too close. And his voice sounds far away, like something echoing down a corridor I've already left behind.

He tries one last time. "You're not just choosing Mallen. You're choosing your father. You're giving him what he wants. Power, through you."

The words land hard. My throat tightens.

"It doesn't matter," I say. "My father wins no matter what I do. He's already found ways to take it back. Whether I choose Mallen or not. I have to face him, Darian. That's the only way this ends."

"You truly believe that?"

I nod slowly. "I do."

There's something in the stillness that follows. The way Darian looks at me—not with anger, but with resignation. He looks like a man who has taken me from the darkness of the capital to the edge of this kingdom and knows he hasn't found the light. Like he already knows what I'm going to say. Like he knew it would end this way, but hoped it wouldn't.

He moves toward me. Not with force. Not even with hope.

With sorrow.

"I could've made you happy," he says.

"I wouldn't have done the same for you."

Another silence stretches long between us.

Darian moves first. He steps back, slowly, like his body hasn't quite agreed with the decision yet. The firelight carves harsh lines across his face—cheekbones too sharp, mouth tight with restraint. For all his poise, I can feel the fracture.

Not anger. Not rejection.

Regret.

"You should sleep," he says. "It's been a long day."

I straighten. "My decision won't change after a good night's sleep. I'm going back to Threnos."

His expression doesn't change, but the tension in his jaw deepens. "You can't leave on foot. Not when it's this far."

"I'll take one of the horses."

"My men will ask questions."

"I'll make something up."

He shakes his head. "They'll talk. About me. About you. They'll think—"

"That you lost."

He tenses. "They'll certainly find it unusual."

He's built his entire identity on being clever, being clean. The one who sees three moves ahead. The one who always walks away untouched.

And now he won't.

"I didn't lie to you," he says suddenly. "About the escape. About the house. About the others—"

"But you lied about something else." I meet his gaze, steady.

His silence is answer enough.

I watch the lie unravel in his eyes. A flash of calculation and then guilt. Not the hot, brash kind. The slow, creeping kind that eats through the spine. The kind that costs someone to admit it.

"About Mallen."

Of course he did.

He wanted to win.

"I told you that the labyrinth revealed what he truly was," he says. "That the darkness you saw would consume him."

I nod.

"I wanted you to believe it. Because it made it easier for you to leave him. To walk away. I thought it would hurt you less."

He looks down at the floorboards.

I almost ask him if that's true—if he really thought it would hurt less. But the look in his eyes tells me he's convinced himself it is. And maybe that's enough. Maybe I don't need to unmake every lie just to prove he meant it.

"I needed you to be afraid of him," he says at last. "Because if you weren't —if you knew he wasn't the monster—then nothing I offered would've mattered."

"And now?"

He lifts his eyes. "Now I think the gods are watching. I know that they want you to make this choice. Clearly. With the truth laid bare. And I will anger them if I do not respect your decision."

The answer hits colder than it should.

I almost laugh, but it turns bitter in my throat. "You're telling me the truth now not because you want to, but because you're afraid of what might happen if you don't."

He doesn't argue. Gods, it's worse than if he had.

"And what is the truth, Darian?"

"He's not all darkness. Not completely. He can control it."

I swallow. "If I give him a reason to."

Darian's blue eyes burn with reluctant hope, bright and brittle like frost on steel. "Yes."

I study him for a long time. The man who offered me a way out, who stood beside me when I didn't know which way to run. Who said all the right things and still couldn't see that they weren't the things I needed. I don't hate him. I never will. But I don't trust him either. Not the way I need to trust the person I walk into fire for.

"You're not a villain, Darian," I say softly. "You're not innocent either."

He nods once. Slow. "And him?"

"He's not innocent. But he never lied about it."

I watch his shoulders sink with the weight of what could have been. The fire behind us crackles and fades, burning lower.

The moment hangs between us, full of endings that won't be said aloud. The flames have burned down to embers now, small, red, and restless. I rise slowly, as if the weight of the truth has finally settled on my shoulders. There's only one thing left to do.

"I need something from you," I say at last.

His eyes flick to mine. "What is it?"

"Not a favor. A vow."

He straightens. "You ask a lot, Princess."

"I need your silence. You'll tell no one what Mallen became in the maze. Not your men, not the Temple, not the Crown. Not even as a whisper."

He hesitates.

I hold his gaze. "You said the gods are watching. So swear it."

"I don't lie under vow," he says quietly.

"Then don't make one you can't keep."

He closes his eyes for a moment, as if listening to some voice far away. Then he says, clear and even: "I swear on the Sundered Flame and the blood that binds it. I will keep his secret."

I breathe out. The tightness in my chest begins to ease, but only just.

"You'll need to tell your men something," I say. "They'll want a reason why you left without me."

He nods once. "It has to look like my choice."

"They already assume you've claimed me. Let them believe it. Let them think you brought me here to seduce me, and once you had what you wanted, you left."

His mouth tightens. "You'd let them believe that about you?"

I lift a brow. "They already do. Why not use it?"

He doesn't answer right away.

"I'm giving you a story," I say. "One your men will believe. One that keeps your pride intact. And in return, you give me what I want."

He hesitates. "This seems an unfair bargain."

"Perhaps," I say. "But it's true."

He nods once, sharply. Agreement, but not acceptance.

"You'll sleep on the chaise and leave before dawn," I say. "Take your men. They'll think you abandoned me."

He doesn't speak. Doesn't offer to help. Doesn't beg me to stay. He just watches as I move past him, heading for the door. If the gods weren't holding him, would he choose differently?

His voice comes out soft and hoarse. "You'll go to him?"

"Yes."

"You think he'll forgive you?"

"I don't need forgiveness."

"You think it's love, what you're choosing?"

"It doesn't matter," I say. "It's the only thing that still feels real."

He nods again. A final, quiet surrender.

"I never meant to hurt you," he says.

I pause in the doorway. "You didn't."

I look back at him.

"You just didn't help me the way I needed."

And then I leave.

CHAPTER TWENTY-NINE

Darian asks again if I'll be safe.

His concern isn't feigned. He's worried—about an attack, about Mallen, about me changing my mind.

I nod once.

My throat is dry. I don't let it show. If I speak now, the wrong truth might slip out—bitter and bruised, too fragile to take back.

I can't afford doubt. Not anymore.

Mallen has every right to be angry. But I don't believe he'll hurt me.

We review the plan one last time. Darian and his men will ride east. He'll tell anyone who asks that he bedded me and then left me behind. He'll claim he unleashed my magic to protect Larksbind and left in disgust when it touched him. A hero's tale. A convenient lie. One that casts me as the ruinous enchantress while he rides free, his secrets buried with mine.

He lingers. Doesn't step back, doesn't look away. His fingers drift from my elbow to my wrist, lingering there like he wants to say more. Then he leans in—not quickly, not possessively. Just a tilt of his head, a pause that invites.

I meet him halfway and kiss his cheek. Not to invite—but to close.

His breath catches. He smiles. Not surprised. Not grateful. Just resigned.

For him, it's a lover's goodbye.

For me, it's closure.

I turn before I lose my nerve.

The cold catches in my throat as I move. Part of me wants to look back, to memorize the shape of him framed by morning light. But I don't. I won't allow myself to take anything more from him.

"Did you ever love me?" I ask, uncertain if I want to face this truth.

Darian's smile is flawless. Wounded and warm. A prince's lie.

"I love all my women, Princess."

He leaves without another word. The wind takes the sound of hoofbeats away before I regret hearing them.

I wait for the silence to turn heavy, staring at the dead fire and the rumpled bedsheet, while breathing in the scent of cedar smoke that lingers like memory. I gather my cloak, fasten the riding gloves I left folded on the table, and make my way to the stables. The horse Darian left me is fast, but still recovering from yesterday's ride. I press him into motion anyway. We pass through woods, pass the Crossroad Shrine—so they whisper—for gods who never answered but still watched.

Time stretches.

The rhythm of hooves blends with the rush of blood in my ears. My hands tremble like a lie I can't keep holding on to. I don't know if it's fear or the ghost of a choice already made.

The longer I ride, the more the dread coils. Mallen will be furious. Not reckless though. He won't strike me down in anger. But I know him. I know the way his silence bites deeper than his sword.

I just have to reach him before the mask hardens. Before the man I know is gone.

I chose this. Every step, every lie, every hand I didn't hold—I made those choices. To protect myself. To escape from Starsfall. But that doesn't undo the damage. Doesn't erase the pain of what I did to him.

Maybe he wonders if I've already forgotten it.

I don't think I ever will. But that doesn't matter now. What matters is facing what I've broken, even if he never lets me put it back together. Even if I don't deserve to.

The land begins to change. Roads widen. Grass turns to churned mud. The sound of it reaches me before anything else.

Drums.

Marching.

The army moves like memory—relentless, half-buried, impossible to outrun.

There's no cover. I don't look for any.

Instead, I pull the hood of my cloak down and ride to the center of the road. I stop and wait, spine straight, gaze unflinching across the wide plain.

The dust reaches me first.

My horse snorts, ears flicking at the sound. I tighten my grip on the reins and force my limbs to stay still. The dirt stings my eyes. Or maybe I'm blinking back what I can't let fall—not yet.

Then the army arrives.

Trumpets blare and commands echo. A line begins to form—a disciplined wall of steel and evergreen. At its front, a tall, broad-shoulder rider dismounts, his hair pulled back, his face set like stone.

Mallen.

He passes his reins to an officer, murmurs a brief command—quiet as confession, sharp as a blade tucked between ribs. They both glance my way.

And then the officer strides toward me. The man who poured wine on me at the second trial. He's younger than I remember. Older than he pretended to be. It was an act, all of it. Now, there's no pretense. Only command. Only conflict.

"Princess," he says, without bowing. "The Commander insists you come with me."

I don't move.

He reaches for my reins and I wheel my horse sharply, forcing it to rear. The officer stumbles back, rage flickering in his eyes.

"Remind the Commander he taught me not to surrender an advantage. If he wants to talk, he'll meet me halfway."

The man pales.

"Mallen said no exceptions."

"I outrank him."

For a moment, I think the officer might argue. But then his jaw clenches and he turns. Each step back to the line is reluctant, as if he's counting them out like a man walking to the gallows.

Mallen watches his approach but his eyes never leave me.

When the message reaches him, he doesn't hesitate. He steps forward—

not far, not halfway. Just enough to make the point. Just enough to force my hand.

I see it now—the way his gait stutters, his right arm held too close, the shadow developing beneath his jaw like rot that mars his skin. He doesn't mask it. He wants me to look. Wants me to know I left marks. Not just blood-deep, but bone-close. That I still matter enough to hurt him.

I press my heels to the horse's side. Slow. Intentional. Each step devours the hush between us like fire licking dry parchment.

Eyes rake across me—soldiers, strangers—and I let them. Let them witness me try to heal the wound I carved into him.

He's hurt.

He wants me to notice.

And I will not look away.

I stop when there's barely a breath of space between us.

"Princess."

His voice is low. Cold.

"Commander."

A breath shifts his mouth—not a smile, but the memory of one. A bruise creeps across his cheek like dusk swallowing the sky. Guilt lances through me. I hurt him. I had to. But still—

He steps closer.

My horse shifts and lets out a nervous breath.

"Did my father send you?"

His eyes narrow. "He did not. I came anyway."

The wind shifts and carries the distant clatter of hooves and armor, the heavy press of a hundred gazes. Neither of us looks away. Not yet. Not while this last distance remains.

A hawk shrieks overhead. The silence deepens.

Mallen doesn't move. Neither do I.

It becomes a standoff, not of weapons but will. A contest of pride, of pain.

And then he speaks.

"Get down off that damn horse, Azhara."

"Ask me as the woman with a crown and a choice, Mallen. Then I will come to you."

His gaze flicks down my body like a blade meant to draw blood, and he's too careful, too far away. What halts him isn't fury—it's distance, honed and hollow. The kind of pain that folds inward like frostbitten fingers: too numb to feel and too far gone to scream.

"You wanted me to stand; now I'm standing. You taught me to choose. I chose to come more than halfway for you, now choose for me."

His throat works like it's trying to swallow words that might splinter him from the inside. He steps close—closer—and the air between us strains, fragile as spun glass.

"Fine," he says, low. "Please."

It's not polite. It's not tender. But it costs him to say it. That's what matters.

I slide from the saddle, landing lightly, dust curling around my boots.

Mallen watches, eyes unreadable. The silence stretches again.

I drop my shoulders. "Are you angry with me?"

It sounds like a plea. The answer's already written in the way he looks at me.

"Yes."

My gaze drops.

"Did he hurt you?" Mallen asks.

I glance up.

Mallen's eyes are storms of pain barely held back, clouded with rage and fear he won't name. He cares. Too much. Enough to burn the world down if I say yes.

"No," I say, my voice carrying. "He's gone back to Larksbind. He'll tell his men he abandoned me. That way, your involvement stays buried."

Mallen's jaw twitches. He grips the bit, helping me dismount. I feel the fury rolling off him.

"Did he? Abandon you?"

"No. I let him go. I gave up my name to protect yours."

His roar fractures the air. His hand clenches, unclenches. "I never cared about mine. Yours—gods, Azhara—"

"I made my choice. You're all that matters to me."

His brows lift, eyes boring into mine. Searching. Disbelieving. Needing me to say it again, to prove it wasn't some cruel joke.

We're close now, and still too far—his breath uneven, mine held hostage between one heartbeat and the next.

I lift my chin. "You lied to me."

He looks down. "You wouldn't have believed me."

"You didn't trust me enough to try."

The silence between us stretches so long it starts to fray.

I can't speak.

"You hid from me," I manage finally. "Behind duty. Behind sacrifice. You didn't give me the chance to see you."

"You did." His laugh is broken, bitter. "I'm a monster."

"No," I whisper. My hand rises to his chest. "You make me stronger. Hold me accountable. Make me choose. You don't let me run." I swallow hard. "If that makes you a monster, then you're the one I want."

He stills beneath my hand like a man standing in the ruins of a temple—bare, waiting for the stones to fall or the gods to answer.

I press my palm flat against him. His breath hitches.

"I never stopped protecting you," he says, voice like gravel. "Even when you didn't want me to."

I exhale slowly. This shame has teeth.

"I know."

Mallen's eyes flicker. He waits. I don't know for what.

Apologies are too small. Excuses too easy. I offer neither.

Instead, I draw in a breath and step back from him.

Then I bow.

Not the shallow dip of the court. Not the languid gesture of a woman trying to charm. I fold low, one arm crossed over my chest, the other behind my back—a king's bow. The one that only the rulers of Starsfall make when they offer the highest honor to a worthy equal. A sign of humility. Of reverence. Of concession.

Gasps ripple through the line.

Mallen doesn't move.

The wind tugs at my cloak. I stay bowed, eyes fixed on the dust at my feet, and the silence bears down—taut and breathless—as if all of Starsfall holds its breath against my spine.

Let him reject it. Let him walk away. Let it end here if it must—but not for want of trying.

At last, he speaks.

"Never beneath me. Always beside me."

I rise.

He stares at me a moment longer. He stares at me like a man trying to remember the shape of mercy. Then, without a word, he reaches for me.

He lifts me into his arms, and the world disappears. His hand closes at the back of my neck, drawing me in like gravity. Our mouths find each other in a kiss that isn't soft or clean or sweet—it's bitter and bruised and full of all the things we haven't said.

And when I kiss him back, we don't offer forgiveness.

We offer surrender.

He pulls away first. His breath is uneven.

"You don't get to break my heart and pretend nothing happened."

"I'm not pretending."

His hold tightens and I lean into it. "I wanted you to choose me. Not for what I could offer. Not because I was safe or useful or ordained. I wanted it to be me. Flawed. Mortal. Me."

A breathless silence falls.

"Is that so wrong?" His voice cracks. "To want to be loved as I am?"

"You never gave me the chance."

He growls low in his throat. Desire, frustration, hurt—it's all tangled in his expression.

"I'm done fighting you," I whisper. "But I'll fight for you. Every day, every breath. I choose you, Mallen. Not for what you could be—but for who you are. Because now I finally see you."

His smile is faint. Reverent. Disbelieving.

"And I don't want my heart back," I add. "Don't even try."

He brushes a curl from my face, his thumb lingering.

"Choose me," I say. "All of me."

His eyes close for the briefest second. Then open. Dark and shining emeralds.

"Always."

My heart stumbles.

He tilts his head, and the smirk returns. Not cruel. Not mocking. Just his—familiar and alive and unbearable in how much I missed it.

"I rather like you bowing to me," he murmurs.

Then he laughs. Loud and unrestrained. And for a moment, he's golden with it—reborn, radiant, like a hymn risen whole from the ash.

He steps back. The warmth between us doesn't cool.

Mallen turns, calling the officer still waiting behind him. The man approaches with two horses. Mine and his.

Mallen swings up onto his saddle with practiced ease, though he grits his teeth as his body twists—and a wince flickers across his face, sharp as a bell's crack in a ruined cathedral.

I mount without help. His eyes catch the movement.

"We have more to talk about," he says.

I nod. "I know."

Mallen raises a brow as he pulls his horse alongside mine. He leans in and kisses me again, and I hear the cheers rise behind us this time. The sound of swords against shields. Shouts and whistles.

I don't care.

He breaks the kiss first. "Are you blushing?"

"No," I say. "But you might be."

"Careful, Princess," he teases, his voice velvet over steel. "Say one more thing like that, and I'll be claiming you before we reach the next ridge. We are thread and blade and blood, and I won't let you escape from me again."

CHAPTER THIRTY

For the second time in as many days, I'm galloping toward a mansion abandoned now that autumn's here. And it's not desperation that drives Mallen forward now—but intent.

The estate rises from the hills like a sunlit relic of privilege, its windows drunk on dusk light, reflecting the gold like a secret too beautiful to keep. Officers ride behind us, silent save for the rhythmic pounding of hooves. Mallen rides ahead now, his gaze fixed on the road, jaw set like carved stone.

We've barely spoken since we mounted our horses.

There's no need.

His body speaks for him—leaning too close, brushing my arm with deliberate carelessness when he's not riding just far enough ahead to let everyone see who brought me here. He doesn't need words to stake his claim. It's there in the line of his shoulders, the protective tension in his frame.

And I let him. Because some small, reckless part of me likes it.

I should resent that—should chafe at the idea of being claimed like territory—but there's a hush threaded through with hunger—no longer for battle, but for proof I'm still beside him. This isn't a show of conquest. It's possession, yes, but born of desperation. Of loss.

As if looking away might dissolve me back into dreams.

As if I'm still more ghost than girl in his eyes.

I've chosen to stay—but trust like his doesn't surface without scars.

Servants scatter at our arrival, their confusion swallowed by the brisk orders of the officers dismounting behind us. Within moments, the house begins to shift—its quiet halls invaded, its staff repurposed, its rooms claimed by men in uniform. Tents will rise on the outskirts, and the barns will fill with the weight of an army.

But not us.

Mallen's hand finds my waist as I dismount, the touch gentle, grounding. "The servants will run a bath," he says, his voice a low rasp. "I'll settle a few matters first. I have to make sure that Darian returns to Larksbind without declaring war and buy us time to deal with your father."

"Do you want me there?"

"Not this time," he replies, and the ghost of regret flickers across his face. "I'll tell you everything soon."

A familiar officer waits nearby—the same one who Mallen sent to bring me back. His expression is unreadable as he leads me through the echoing corridors, the hush of old stone closing in around us. The master suite yawns open before us, gilded and quiet, suffocating in its grandeur.

He checks the room quickly, his gaze never quite meeting mine. "I'll be outside if you need anything."

"You should join them. I'm not in danger."

He stops short, as if I've struck him. Slowly, he turns back, his face unreadable but tight with something like pity. "You think that's why I'm staying?"

I blink.

"He isn't guarding you. He's guarding himself. You don't see it yet, do you?"

"See what?"

The man exhales, his silence sagging under the strain of truths he won't share. "You'll understand soon. When he lets you."

"He's not like that."

"No," the officer murmurs. "He's worse when he cares."

He doesn't linger. The door closes behind him with a finality and the echo of it lodges somewhere deep—beneath the ribs, where secrets tend to settle.

Servants pour in, arms full of linens and water, scurrying like mice in the presence of an invisible god no one dares name, but all feel breathing down their necks. None look me in the eye. The room transforms around me—rugs rolled back, a brass tub dragged in, steam rising into the velvet hush.

One girl remains when the rest have gone. Her hands tremble as she reaches to help me undress.

"I'll manage."

She stares for a beat too long and then flees, her footsteps echoing down the hall like she knows I could curse the floor just by walking it.

I undress slowly, shedding layers of sweat and dust. The bath scalds my skin, but I sink into it anyway, welcoming the pain. My legs ache, my shoulders burn, and the heat seeps into the cracks I didn't know had formed. I scrub the battlefield from my skin. I comb the knots from my hair. I float, weightless, just for a moment.

And then the air changes.

"You know better than to drop your guard," Mallen growls.

I don't startle. Just open my eyes to find him standing at the foot of the tub, shirtless and furious.

Bruises ink across his chest in shades no sky has ever held—a map of my undoing etched into him like myth. The wound on his arm gapes slightly, red and raw.

"You look like hell," I say, voice quiet.

He doesn't answer. Doesn't flinch.

He's showing me what I did. He wants me to look. To remember.

"Does it hurt?"

"Only when I move," he replies. "It was worth it."

The words drop between us, heavy with everything he isn't saying.

His eyes flick lower, trailing across the surface of the water, over every visible inch of me. He sways slightly, bracing his hands on the edge of the tub. His breath is unsteady. Controlled.

"What did you discuss?"

"The future of Starsfall." He doesn't look away. "Your father and what to do about him. I've spent five years planning for this moment. We march at dawn."

My fingers drift through the water. "You're seizing Threnos?"

He nods. “It’s time. He has few soldiers left. He won’t expect a night assault.”

“And after?”

“You take what’s yours,” he says simply. “Your crown. Your kingdom. I’ll make certain no one takes it from you.”

There’s no hesitation. No pause for doubt. Just the fierce promise in his voice and the quiet, implacable rage behind it. He doesn’t speak of vengeance, but it lives in him, buried deep. And this time, it’s not for himself.

I should be afraid. He could shatter nations, and yet he kneels to no one but me. But the fear that lingers isn’t his fury—it’s how easily I ache to be chosen by it. To fold into the promises he carries like prayers clenched in his teeth.

Starsfall. A crown. A throne.

“What if I don’t want it?” I whisper, mostly to the bathwater.

He moves across the room and pours a glass of wine with one hand, never looking away.

“You can decide whether you want the throne once your father’s gone,” he says. “You can shape it how you want. We will rule as equals, Azhara. Not because of what you’ve done. Or the magic you carry. Because of who you are.”

I want to believe him.

I want it not to terrify me.

He sets the wine aside and begins removing what’s left of his clothing. There’s nothing seductive in the gesture—just quiet purpose. His back is marked by battle, not desire. His skin is darkened with blood, ash, and sweat.

He doesn’t ask if he can join me.

He just waits.

“The water’s still warm,” I offer.

He steps in. The water rises around us, rippling. I sit forward, press a cloth to the curve of his shoulder, and begin to clean him. Gently. Carefully.

His hands remain at his sides. He lets me touch him. Lets me see him.

“We are equals,” he says at last. “We always have been. Bound by more than blood or fate. Bound by our will, yours and mine.”

“You’d risk the gods’ wrath for me?”

He doesn’t hesitate. “Gladly. But this isn’t defiance. This is faith.”

I stare at my reflection on the water's surface. "In me?"

When I glance up, I half expect Mallen to look wary, but there's only quiet surprise in his expression. As if he hadn't expected tenderness. As if *he's* the one bracing to be left behind.

"I'm not afraid of you," I whisper.

He flinches like it's a lie. I reach for his hand before he can draw away.

"Not now. Not ever."

Silence unfurls between us, steeped in steam and heartbeat and the sound of water shifting like breath beneath moonlight—slow, tidal, inevitable.

"Darian said you hold Starsfall's darkness. That you gather it in the labyrinth and it will consume you. Me too, if I let it." I hold his gaze. "But that isn't true. I don't hold Starfall's light, and you're not its darkness. I don't understand how or why, but I know we balance each other. We fit."

Mallen's jaw shifts. "What else did he tell you?"

I press my palms to his chest and trace the contours of his body, slow and deliberate. My fingers knead over bruises, scar tissue, muscle. His breath stutters.

"He said you were working for my father. That in time you'd turn on him. Become worse than him. And that if I chose you, I'd be all that contains you."

I pause. Then—

"He admitted lying about what he said in the labyrinth."

Mallen tips his head back. A low sound escapes him as I dig my thumbs beneath his shoulder blades. He doesn't answer. He lets me finish, lets me serve him. His body relaxes under my hands, but his silence is louder than speech.

Then he lowers his forehead to mine. His voice is quiet, but the words slice deep.

"He's not wrong."

He doesn't say it bitterly. There's no anger in it. Just weariness. Honesty.

"He's just not right."

Mallen's hand finds mine.

"The truth lies with the gods," he murmurs. "But I know this—your magic is more than death. Your darkness is vast. And if it isn't shared, it consumes. Darian would return that power to the heavens. Strip you of it. Leave you pure."

His fingers tighten around mine.

"I would share it. Bear it with you. Carry it when you cannot."

My breath catches.

"Share it with you or surrender it with Darian," I say. "That's always been my choice."

He nods. "Did he say more about the labyrinth?"

"No."

Mallen stills. His spine aligns like a pulled thread, and the quiet around us sharpens to glass.

"Then he doesn't know," he says.

I blink. "Know what?"

He doesn't look me in the eye. His voice turns brittle.

"Azhara...the labyrinth isn't where I draw power from. It's where I go. To cage it. Myself too. When I'm losing control."

He pauses. His breath is barely a whisper.

"The darkness isn't mine."

I freeze.

Steam curls off the surface of the water, but my skin goes cold.

Mallen stares at the water like it might answer for him. "It started the night you came of age and the Reaping began. It burned through me. Like a brand. Your darkness, your magic—it needed somewhere to go. You didn't know how to contain it. So it found me."

I look down. Hazel eyes in the water's reflection. Innocent, almost. A girl with a soft mouth and unlined skin. She doesn't look like she could devour worlds.

But she could.

She has.

And she wears that ruin like a ribbon—threaded through her, binding the girl she was to the woman she's becoming.

Mallen's voice is hoarse. "You were never meant to carry it alone. But the gods...they didn't give you a choice. They didn't give me one either."

He's been doing this for years. Letting it fill him. Letting it burn. Alone.

"You never told me."

He nods, solemn. "Do you see why? I didn't want to shackle you, or your heart. I wanted you to have a choice I never had. To run. To love. And to be able to say yes with joy, not guilt."

And now I see the impossibility of it. The line he walked alone. He let me hate him. Let me think he was keeping secrets to control me—because the truth would've chained me more than any lie ever could.

"I couldn't tell you. You'd have broken yourself trying to fix it. Or worse—you'd have stayed with me out of obligation."

"What is the truth, Mallen?"

"The truth is simpler than the stories men tell," he says. "The gods asked for one thing only. Your choice. Quiet. Free. Your father refused it. He broke faith and built the Reaping to drown your choice in blood. He ordered trials that could not be won, paid for traps that did not spare, sent word to Larksbind that only the condemned should come so their hope would wither. He meant to starve you of hope until you reached twenty-five and the bargain returned the power to him. He never expected them to send Darian, and when they did, he hunted for leverage. Every death has served his theater. None of it served you."

"He chose me as the pretty answer from Starsfall. A contingency. He thought I could be held. For a while, he thought I was like him. I swear I didn't know at first. I learned the truth of it years ago and moved what I could. I built walls around your choice and taught you to stand. Not to steer you to me, but to guard. Because your choice is all that's ever mattered."

The room tilts. I see the shape of it at last. The gods wanted a single act of will. My father made a spectacle to steal it. All the banners and bells and trials were theft. Only one thing was ever meant to matter. My yes. My no. My choice.

His fingers brush mine, tentative. "I'd rather die than have your heart bound to me in chains."

My throat closes. "What did it cost you?"

He doesn't answer right away. His gaze drops to our joined hands like he's reading a memory.

"Everything," he says finally. "My gift...whatever it once was—it's gone. Burned hollow to make room for yours. There's nothing left in me but the shape of you."

I reel. How hadn't I seen it? How had I missed this sacrificial kind of love, this unspoken ruin? My vision blurs.

"All this time, I thought you were hiding yourself. But you were hiding *me*."

"You were never meant to carry it alone," he repeats. "So I did."

"And I never saw," I whisper. "I looked at you and I *never* saw."

"I didn't want you to."

I cover his hand with mine, holding it tightly. "And now?"

"Now?" He lifts his eyes, and they blaze. "Now I want to be seen. If you choose me...I want it to be real."

"I don't deserve—"

"You deserve everything." His grip tightens. "Even if it kills me."

I stare at him, blinking back tears. "You don't hate me?"

He laughs, low and disbelieving. "You think love and sacrifice don't walk hand in hand?" He draws my fingers to his mouth and presses them to his lips. "I'd carry your darkness a thousand times over. It was never a burden. Not for you."

I want to believe him. No—worse. I do believe him. That's what terrifies me.

"I'll never buy your affection," he says softly. "I mean it. I won't use pain to bind you. I won't weaponize your guilt."

His mouth finds my temple.

"Nor will I let you shrink from what you are."

A beat of silence—two, three—long enough to feel his heart against mine, erratic and echoing. Then—

"Darian doesn't understand, not entirely," he adds. "He pieced together fragments and mistook them for truth. That is why he wouldn't stop: he believed he was saving you. A man convinced he is right when he isn't is the most dangerous kind."

Mallen leans forward and traces a finger along my collarbone. My breath shudders out. His touch is reverent, but it lights a fire under my skin.

His gaze dips. His eyes burn. He sees my arousal—acknowledges it—and still waits.

"We should get out," he murmurs.

He washes his hair and then helps me from the water. His hands are gentle, wrapping me in a towel before tending to himself. I watch him dress—beautiful and solemn and wounded—and wonder how I ever thought I could live without him.

The servant girl enters, trembling. She braids my hair with shaking fingers while I sit still and let her work. In the mirror, Mallen's reflection glowers. I shoot him a look—*stop*—but he only sighs and stokes the fire like it might save him.

The girl bolts the second she's done. Mallen yells after her to bring food. I bury my face in my hands.

"You scare people," I mutter.

He shrugs. "Good. It keeps them from stealing you."

I snort. "You think you own me?"

"No. But I think you chose me. And I won't let you forget it."

He opens his arms. I go. He gathers me like a vow, his mouth finding my neck in slow benediction, each kiss scattering thought like ash.

Food arrives. Mallen thanks the servants this time, though he doesn't release me. I eat like I've been starved. He watches me with quiet amusement, and then eats too.

For a moment, it's ordinary. As if we haven't broken each other. As if the world isn't ending.

He tucks a strand of hair behind my ear, his fingers lingering. His mouth ghosts across my skin—cheek, jaw, lips. The kiss is firmer this time. Rougher. A kind of desperation laced through it, like it's cost him everything to hold back, and he's finally stopped counting the price.

"Are you sure?" he breathes.

I nod. "Yes."

He studies me, as if something inside him breaks open. Or maybe it fuses at last: the part that feared, the part that waited, the part that never stopped wanting.

"I'll never lie to you again," he says. "Even if it destroys me. Even if you turn away. I won't pretend I'm not jealous, or ruthless, or even that I'm a good man. But I am a man who'll love you without restraint, without end. I won't spare you my truth—and I won't ask you to spare me yours."

My heart lurches. "No more lies."

His gaze darkens. His hands twitch like he wants to touch me—wants to take—but he waits.

He's waited years. What's a few minutes more?

"Not even silent ones," he replies.

I reach up and run my thumb over his lower lip. He exhales sharply. His desire is barely leashed.

I climb into his lap. His hands close around my thighs, reverent and possessive. His breath hitches like he's swallowing fire.

"From either of us," I say.

And then I kiss him.

Like it's the first time.

Like it's the only time.

Because maybe it is.

CHAPTER THIRTY-ONE

Mallen deepens the kiss, his hand sliding into my hair, twisting just enough to hold me still. There's a hunger in it now—an unspoken demand—and when his body presses against mine, it's not just possession. It's a plea. A prayer.

My breath catches as he pushes me back, his hands cradling me as though he needs proof I'm still here. Still his.

My hands slide down his chest, fumbling for the hem of his tunic. He breaks the kiss, lips brushing mine with a hint of laughter, and pulls the shirt over his head.

Candlelight gilds his skin. I trace my fingers over him, slow and certain—no hesitation, no regret.

When our mouths find each other again, his hands are already tugging at the neckline of my top. Fabric slides down my shoulder, exposing bare skin to his lips. The brush of his mouth is gentle, reverent, but it leaves fire in its wake. My spine arches with a soft gasp, a laugh escaping me like a broken promise.

But then I still. My hand presses lightly against his chest.

"Mallen..."

He freezes. Not pulling away, not moving closer either.

"If we..." I murmur. "The magic will return. To Starsfall. And to my father."

His jaw tightens. His breath catches. But he doesn't flinch.

"Yes," he says.

"But you'd still do it?"

"Yes," he answers, voice low. "I chose you the moment I saw you. Or the gods chose me for you. It doesn't matter. Whatever comes, we face it together."

I glance down at him, my breath hitching—but not from fear. I smile—slow, playful, sharp as a secret—but he misses it, mistaking mischief for doubt. His eyes darken with retreat, not disappointment.

"If you're not ready, I can wait, Mallen."

I laugh, loud and reckless, and he doesn't. His arms tighten around my waist as he rises to his feet, lifting me with him. I pretend to squirm in protest, and we both play the game, knowing it's a lie.

"Azhara," he murmurs against my skin, his voice hoarse, fingers trailing downward. "I'll be gentle. This might hurt a little. At first."

He carries me to the bed and lowers me onto the sheets like I'm sacred. Then he follows, his weight pressing me down, surrounding me, his hips locking between mine. His lips find mine again, and in the dark hunger of that kiss, I lose everything but him.

Fingers work at the laces of my clothes. I reach for him, hands dragging across his skin, desperate for a tether, anything to hold me in this moment before I come undone. I'm trembling—not just with want, but with wonder, with the ache of stepping into the unknown.

Mallen stills. His gaze catches mine, searching. He sees it. The flutter of nerves I thought I'd hidden.

His mouth descends slowly, reverently, until it finds my breast. He groans, low and guttural, as his lips close around me. When his teeth graze, I cry out, and his grip on my hips tightens.

"I love the sounds you make," he whispers. "Never hide from me."

His mouth finds my breast again, slower this time, as though he's relearning me with reverence instead of hunger. The sensation coils through me like lightning, sharp and bright, and I arch into him, needing more. My leg winds around his waist, drawing him closer. He groans as our hips meet, breath catching in his throat.

"Azhara," he breathes, as if my name alone might undo him. He lifts his head, brushing his nose along my cheek. "Tell me what you want."

I guide his hand downward, and he pauses—his brow furrowed in quiet restraint. Not stopping me. Just waiting.

I meet his gaze, pulse racing. "I want you," I whisper. "Please."

Something in him splinters—not restraint, but the softest part of him, the part he never speaks of. The part that once waited in the dark and called my name.

"You never have to ask," he murmurs, reverent. "I'm already yours."

When his fingers slide between my legs, I gasp—sharp, instinctive. He stills.

"You're shaking," he murmurs.

"I want you," I say quickly. "It's just...it's more than I expected."

His hand cups me gently. "I'll take my time."

He kisses me as his fingers begin to move, slow and sure, and the world narrows to the heat rising beneath his touch. He watches every flicker of my breath, every shift in my body, like he's charting stars across my skin.

"You're beautiful," he whispers. "Gods, Azhara, I've dreamed of this. Of you."

His voice anchors me like breath to bone, and I surrender—to him, and to the truth I've tried so long to silence.

My hips lift to meet him, chasing the rhythm he sets. A moan escapes me, unguarded and raw. His expression darkens—not with lust, but with awe.

He presses deeper, his finger sliding inside. I stiffen at the sudden stretch, but he's already stilling, kissing my cheek, murmuring low comforts against my skin.

"You're doing perfect," he says. "Tell me if it's too much. I'll stop. Always."

I shake my head, breath hitching, and after a heartbeat, he begins to move again.

Each slow thrust stokes the heat inside me, every stroke unspooling what I've kept stitched behind ribs and breath and years of solitude, until it spills from me in gasps I don't try to hide. My hands grip the sheets and then his shoulders and then his hair. I lose track of what I'm clinging to—only that I need to hold on.

"Mallen—" His name breaks on a gasp. "Don't stop."

Another finger joins the first. I cry out, body clenching, but he's patient—so patient—easing me through it with steady hands and gentler words.

The heat crests higher, pressure coiling in my belly. I'm teetering on the edge, breathless, aching, every nerve strung tight.

"Let go," he whispers. "I'll catch you."

I fall.

My body seizes around him, a cry torn from my throat, and I shudder through the release, overwhelmed, undone. Tears blur my vision, and I don't know why I'm crying, only that I am, and that Mallen is there, not to rescue, not to claim—but to bear witness. To hold the edges of me when I can't.

He lifts his head slowly, rests his cheek to my thigh, and exhales like he's trying to quiet the storm in his chest. His hand stays on my hip, not possessive—anchoring. As if I'm the only thing keeping him here.

I brush his hair back, fingers trembling. He kisses the inside of my knee like a benediction.

"Are you all right?" he asks, voice hoarse.

I nod, unable to speak. My body's still pulsing from the release, nerves buzzing like lightning caught beneath skin. I've never felt anything like this—like my soul stepped out of its own body and left me breathless in the aftermath.

I'm his. I always have been.

Even if I walk away.

Even if I choose another path.

This moment—this sacred, stolen moment—is ours.

And that, I think, is what undoes him.

He rises, eyes searching mine, and whatever he sees there—relief, trust, the shape of my heart—softens his features until he looks boyish again. That same boy who knelt beside my bed, whispering my name like a prayer.

"I've dreamed of this," he says quietly. "Not like this. Not just this. I dreamed of being close to you. Waking up beside you. Hearing your voice in the dark and knowing you stayed."

My hand finds his, fingers weaving through his. I squeeze once, and he brings our joined hands to his mouth and presses a kiss to my knuckles.

"I'm here," I say.

His throat works around the emotion, and for a moment, he doesn't speak. Then, as if a storm settles in him, he reaches for the drawstring at his waist. He moves slowly, as though each breath is counted. Not for show, not to tempt—but to give me time. A moment to decide if I'll stop him.

I don't.

He pushes his trousers off and then shifts closer. Candlelight casts him in gold and shadow, every scar a story written into flesh. I trace a line above his ribs, careful of the fresh bruising. He flinches—not from pain, but from the tenderness of it.

"Does it hurt?" I ask softly.

He shakes his head. "No. It feels like I survived what I thought I wouldn't."

I lift my gaze. "Me too."

He shifts his hips, and I feel the press of him—hard and thick and terrifyingly real. My body tenses in instinct, but he doesn't move. Doesn't force. Just rests there, breathing hard, waiting for me.

I nod.

He kisses me once, long and deep, and then begins to push inside.

It's more than I expected. More than I've ever known. I gasp, clutching his shoulders. He stills instantly, his gaze locking on mine.

"I'll stop," he says, voice thick. "Tell me and I'll stop."

I shake my head. "I just need to breathe."

He lowers his forehead to mine, sweat beading at his temple as he forces himself to stay still. His control astounds me. Even trembling, he waits for me.

"I've got you," he murmurs.

My body adjusts slowly, muscles stretching to accommodate him. He's patient, brushing kisses across my cheeks, my jaw, my temple. His hand strokes my side, guiding me back to my own skin, tracing me into belonging, reminding me I am more than the body that trembles beneath him. I relax inch by inch, and only when he's sure—when I tell him—does he move again, slow and careful.

When he's fully inside me, I exhale shakily. He's deep—so deep—but not unbearable. Just full. Whole. And I'm no longer alone.

His gaze meets mine.

I pull him into another kiss.

He begins to move. Not fast. Not hard. Just a slow, rolling rhythm that lets me feel everything. It's overwhelming—emotionally more than physically. The stretch fades to heat, and then to something deeper. Something sacred.

Each thrust rocks through me, pulling breathless sounds from my throat. He groans softly, pressing his face into my neck.

"I didn't dare to dream we'd have this," he says. "Not like this."

"We do."

"Yes," he breathes. "We do."

Our bodies move together, rhythm syncing, breath for breath. My legs wrap around him, and he holds me tighter, angling his hips until each stroke makes me cry out. The pressure builds again, faster this time, sharper.

It burns too hot. Too brightly.

"It's too much," I whimper.

"You're safe," he answers, stilling. "You're mine. You were made for me, as I was made for you."

His fingers run through my hair. Pleasure builds—and disorientation too. My mind reels with sensations I don't understand. I shake my head, denying what my body is already surrendering to.

He kisses me and slows his rhythm. He's not driven by urgency nor by desperation. This is tender. Reverent. He's holding back, and every movement is measured, controlled. My body tightens around him and we find a shared breath, a shared pulse.

Mallen moves harder. Deeper. So deep it steals the air from my lungs. So deep it's impossible to hold him back. Pleasure breaks over me in waves as I arch to meet him. But beneath the hunger and heat, something begins to uncoil—vast and slow and wrong.

Not pain. Not pleasure.

Power.

My senses sharpen. They twist. They're not right. Not natural. I smell the earth outside, the iron in his blood. I hear the wind split against the window like a scream. Colors sharpen and then shift—unnatural hues that twist light into impossible shades. I see too much. Feel too much.

"I'm losing you," I gasp, clutching him.

"No," Mallen growls. "I've got you. I've always got you."

His hand catches mine, fingers threading tight, an anchor in a world come loose. His thrusts continue, steady and sure, but I'm slipping.

Gods, I'm falling.

And whatever was sealed inside me begins to wake—ancient, unyielding, mine. I didn't know the binding would break like this. Didn't know it would answer pleasure with power, devotion with death. It rises with every breath, every thrust, every beat of his heart against mine.

I arch, crying out. My skin burns with heat, but no sweat cools it. The room warps. My vision fractures. Shadows swirl at the edges, drawn out by the chaos inside me.

"Trust me," he breathes, voice ragged. "We're meant for this."

I kiss him—desperate, seeking. Our mouths collide, and everything else falls away. My soul reaches for his. Not metaphor, not poetry. Only this reality—this clashing and joining of two truths too bright to look at. They meet, tangle, fuse. The shift is violent and beautiful. It's surrender. It's the choosing of two souls.

It's the choice to never part.

And this cannot be undone.

He moves faster. My body spirals. I sob his name, writhing beneath him.

"Fuck, you're perfect," he groans.

A fault line inside me splits—lit with fire, filled with dark water—and I *fall.* My body convulses, clenching around him, crying out as my climax erupts through me like fire and ice.

But this is no simple release.

I am *breaking.*

The orgasm tears me open, rips me apart. My magic tears through the rupture, no longer bound—light and shadow colliding, screaming, alive. This is not how my power has ever moved. This is new. Singular. A breaking and a binding, both.

Darkness floods the space—thick and howling, wild and alive. It pours from me like venom, each tendril alive with memory. Mallen roars above me, his own climax crashing through, and still the shadows come.

This is the moment even the gods feared. The magic they chained. Death, not as silence—but as force. As storm.

My body shakes—hot, cold, slick. The power inside me is no longer mine. It spills out, violent and vast, and the world tilts on its axis.

I scream—for him, for myself, for whatever I'm becoming.

My magic lashes outward, unbound, a tempest of smoke and starlit ruin. Mallen seizes me again, locking his arms around my body like a shield against the gale I've unleashed.

He *holds.*

Even as I unravel, even as death surges up to take me—he holds.

Despite the chaos. Despite the power. Despite the fear.

He pulls me toward him, into him, through the storm I've unleashed.

My throat tightens as the night wraps around it. That dark tide.

It wants me to fall. To give in.

But he won't let me go.

His light—*his* light—is fierce and bright and real. It burns through the shadows, through me. His grip tightens, a lifeline, and I cling to it. To him. To *us*.

We're still one. Still tethered. Even through this.

I don't know where I end and he begins. Our bodies are joined, yes—but it's deeper than flesh. Our souls are locked in orbit, a singular gravity. We are the balance. And the world bends around us.

I breathe.

My fingers find his again and curl tight. The dark recedes. Not gone—but resting. Sated. Not the enemy. Not anymore.

It leaves me whole.

Mallen pants, his weight heavy atop mine. Our skin is slick, our breaths loud in the silence left behind. His heart beats against mine, frantic and then slowing. One rhythm. One sound.

"Do you feel it?" he whispers.

I do.

I feel Starsfall fracture around me—and inside me—and I do not look away. This is the price. This is the truth.

The world has shifted. The light is sharper. The dark more patient. Life brims at the edges—joy and grief, rage and wonder. It's all there. It always was. But now I see it.

All of it.

This is my gift.

And my curse.

"I don't want it," I whisper, tears slipping free.

He slides out of me slowly, gathers me into his arms, and cradles me like I might break again.

"You won't lose yourself," he murmurs. "I have you. I'm not letting go. This…*we*…are exactly what we're meant to be."

And then I feel it.

Not a thought. Not a whisper.

A rush—

Crashing through me like sunlight on water, a tide of emotion too pure to belong to anyone else but him. Joy floods my veins—warm as dusk light on skin, soft as temple silk. It carries awe.

It carries peace.

It carries love.

It hits so hard that it steals my breath.

"Mallen…"

His smile is a secret I almost missed. He brushes his thumb along my cheekbone, and he's there—the warmth of his skin, the stutter of his breath, the echo of his pulse where it meets mine, and the entirety of his soul.

"Now you understand," he murmurs. "This is us, Azhara. We're one. There will never be a moment, not ever again, when you are alone."

I blink back the tears that rise too fast to stop. "Did you know this would happen?"

"No," he says, and I know he's telling the truth. "I knew I carried your darkness. I thought that was what I'd do." He draws in a long breath, as if steadying himself beneath the weight of it. "But this…I didn't know I'd feel you. All of you. That you'd feel me. That we'd share not just what we are, but how we are."

He pauses, searching for the words, and a quiet tension—not fear, but the ache of a truth too intimate to speak aloud—shivers through me.

"I hold your magic inside me. Some part of your soul too, I think. Not just the dark. All of it. Life and death. Light and shadow. I don't know how to wield it yet, but it's here. And I think…I think it always will be. It won't spill like that again—not unless we break. That moment was a door—and we passed through it. What remains is fused. Contained. Ours."

I shift onto his chest and press my ear to the steady rhythm of his heart. Mallen is fierce and wild and ruthless, but this part of him is quieter. Truer. I know it now, the depth of his stillness, the peace he's rarely allowed himself.

He's safe here. With me.

He brings my knuckles to his lips, kisses them like a vow.

"There's no escape now. For either of us."

I don't want one.

Our fingers thread together as the bond hums between us—alive, radiant, and so full it's almost too much to bear. More than love or magic. It's a promise we've carried since the beginning.

His happiness flows through me again, and I understand the shape of it. He's not just content. He's whole. I gave him everything he feared he'd never have. And in return, he gives me choice. I'm chosen, and that—*that*—was what I wanted.

I breathe into his chest and speak the words against the rhythm of his heart.

"I love you."

He closes his eyes and pulls me tighter.

"I heard you," he whispers back. "And I love you too."

CHAPTER THIRTY-TWO

Pain flares down my leg as I shift my weight. I clench my jaw, refusing to give it voice, but Mallen catches the twitch at the corner of my mouth and huffs a low, knowing laugh.

Glances scrape across my skin, knowing and unkind. Every look tells the same story: why I limp, why I wince, why my thighs remember what my mouth won't say aloud.

"You can ride with me," Mallen murmurs, adjusting the reins without looking at me. "But the men will see it as weakness."

I flinch—not from the pain, but from the gentleness in his voice.

I shake my head. "Then they'll see me ride."

His silence folds back in on itself, the way it always does when kindness fails to serve its purpose. It was never a real offer. Not from the man who forged gentleness into grit and made me realize it was love.

He swings into the saddle with effortless grace. No sign that he barely slept. No indication of how many hours he spent inside me, coaxing moans and soft sobs until I fell asleep beneath him. He doesn't glance back as I bite down on a scream and haul myself up. The saddle meets my bruised thighs like a blade.

"Gods," I breathe.

He says nothing, his profile carved from dusk and stone as he stares down the road to Threnos. Intent coils in his posture. He's already left the country house behind. He's already riding to war.

"What happens now?" I ask as we pass the gates.

"The capital falls. Quickly, if we're lucky. Let's hope we're fast enough to strike before the magic makes its way back to your father."

Wind tugs at my cloak. The hills rise and fall around us, pale gold under the lowering sun. Mallen doesn't speak again, but his conviction shows in the way he moves—like the earth itself has already told him which direction to ride. Forward, always forward.

An officer eases his horse beside mine. The same one from yesterday. He's young. Still young enough to believe that war is glory and that right always wins.

"Azhara, meet Marcus," Mallen says.

The officer nods. "We storm the city before nightfall. Seize the palace before your father can dig in. The gates won't hold long, and he won't have time to regroup if we're swift."

Marcus says it like a promise already carved into stone—like he can't imagine the city resisting, can't fathom a version of this war where we don't win clean and fast.

"You're wrong," I say. "He'll burn Starsfall to the ground before he lets it go. He'll kill everyone if it buys him a day longer on the throne."

Marcus falters. Not visibly—but in the pause between words, in the twitch of his fingers against the reins. The kind of hesitation that can't be scrubbed clean, no matter how fast you recover. Mallen watches him, his eyes lingering, faint humor brushing his mouth like an impish breeze.

"Leave the man alone," Mallen mutters. "You'll terrify him."

I turn to Marcus. "Do I terrify you?"

"No, Princess. You worry me. A lot." He laughs and I arch an eyebrow at him. "You're unpredictable. I've seen you fight and seen you hold your own. But you're as likely to charge as to retreat. We're about to find out what you really are, and I'd rather know before I ride into battle with you."

Mallen growls and Marcus shakes his head at him.

"He's still trying to impress you," Marcus sighs.

"Good," I say.

His eyes flick to Mallen. "She always like this?"

"She's worse when she hasn't slept."

I laugh, and Marcus rides off, shaking his head. Mallen's smile fades as soon as we're alone. He rides like a man with one purpose. One fight. The army follows in perfect silence, boots and hooves thudding against packed earth, the rhythm of war.

The Starsfall banners don't fly above them. They haven't in years.

Mallen trained these men, shaped them in his image. They'd follow him into fire—and I know he'd walk into it for them, too. He sculpted them into discipline, into death that marches. He tried to shape me too, but my body clings to softness. My thighs ache, my spine hums with each jolt, and the echo of last night pulses through me like a secret I can't shake.

I was trained for war, but not for this.

It's stirring again—the darkness inside me. Not light, not clean magic, but the kind that slips between ribs and makes promises in the long dark hours of the night. It isn't studied. It isn't safe. It tasted midnight and it liked it. Now it waits, patient and poised, a lullaby with fangs.

I don't know how to control it.

I'm not sure I ever will.

But if my father has regained his magic, I'll have to use it.

Marcus joins us again, his words spilling like orders, almost too fast for me to keep up with as he rides beside me. He speaks like he doesn't want me to be part of this fight. Like I'm a weapon he doesn't want to use because he fears it will explode in his hands.

"Did you want to ask anything, Princess?" Marcus asks at last.

"No."

He studies me, teeth clenching. His gaze flicks to Mallen again before settling on me.

"How's your magic?"

"Dark," I say. "Death is."

His expression tightens. "I meant control. Your father may already be wielding his again."

I keep my grip steady, but the question carves through me all the same. He doesn't ask if I'm ready. He asks if I'll be the ruin that topples our army.

Mallen doesn't speak. His silence is a blade now—sharp and deliberate.

I glance between them. "You want to know if I'll use it against him."

Marcus nods once.

"If I get the chance."

Mallen's grip shifts on the reins. Only slightly. But it's enough. He trained me to read the smallest movements, the most silent tells. His restraint now is deliberate. He's afraid—*for* me, *of* me. Or maybe of what happens if I fall.

My magic wakes like a remembered dream—violent and vivid. It never whispered. Even as a child, it screamed in silence. It was never meant to soothe. Only to consume or shield, and I never knew which it would choose.

Mallen rides closer, his voice barely a breath. "You were born for this."

"Maybe," I whisper. "Or maybe I was born to die."

He turns to face me at last, eyes catching mine. A storm there—silent, aching, proud. And beneath it, something fiercer than hope. A vow made without words, burning through both of us.

"If you fall," he says softly, "I fall too."

Marcus doesn't speak again. We ride the final stretch in silence, the walls of Threnos rising like ghosts in the dusk. They used to shine with marble and flame. Now they're streaked with soot and unanswered prayers, their glory eaten hollow by time. Even the stone seems to flinch from what will happen beneath it tonight.

We're riding into a throne room soaked in old blood and older oaths. My father waits there, and whether I kill him or kneel, I won't walk away the same.

Marcus breaks the silence one last time.

"Do you have it in you to kill him?"

I meet his gaze.

"Yes."

I'm definitive. Sure. Unrepentant. The answer hangs between us like iron —rigid, brutal, unforgivable. Marcus's expression hardens. He studies me like I've spoken too fast. Too clean. As if conviction should come dressed in tears. But he's never had to stand in a room built from my father's voice and choose not to break.

"She's ready," Mallen growls. His tone is steel. Unquestioning. Protective.

"We're dead if she's not," Marcus snaps, wheeling his horse and galloping back toward the line of officers. Dust flares in his wake.

Mallen doesn't look at me.

Ahead, the capital rises from the dusky earth like a wound in the hills—white stone glowing faintly against the bruised sky. The walls shimmer—not with magic, but with memory. Light slicks the stone like sweat, like grief, like a city holding its breath. The flags above the ramparts flutter in the twilight, red and gold catching the last of the sun. They should be beautiful. Instead, they make my blood run cold.

This was my city once. My home. My prison.

It's too quiet. The breeze barely stirs the grass. The army is still. Horses shift, bridles clinking softly, soldiers adjusting gear that doesn't need adjusting. Beneath the calm, tension coils. The men know what's coming. Some wear blank expressions, others grim resolve. A few look up toward the distant towers—wondering if tonight, they'll breathe their last.

Mallen raises his hand. The movement is smooth, deliberate, and unmistakable. A pause follows—thick enough to choke on—then his hand drops, cutting the dusk in half.

Everything erupts.

Marcus bellows orders. Formations shift. Runners bolt toward flanking units. Hooves strike stone. The army flows forward like a tide breaking loose from its dam. There's a strange kind of order in it—controlled chaos, fierce and exacting. This is what Mallen's built. These are his soldiers. They don't hesitate.

I do.

I freeze—not from fear, but recognition. The stillness before the first note of a requiem. The last inhale before the sky gives way to fire. Then Mallen turns, gives me one look—nothing soft in it, just command—and I move.

"Stay close," he hisses, already urging his horse ahead.

His voice isn't anxious. It's resigned. Like he expects this to go to hell, and he's made peace with it.

We ride hard. The wind claws at my cloak. The trees fall away behind us. The road narrows and then dips. The walls of Threnos draw closer, gleaming pale and ghostly in the gloom. A crescent moon glints against the silver trim of Mallen's armor as he leads the charge—half warrior, half myth.

It sounded so simple.

Take the south gate fast, before the palace realizes what's happening. Marcus's unit would slip through the forest and open a second front on the east side. It's daring. Bold. Reckless, if anyone but Mallen were leading this attack. We're counting on speed over subtlety—and Mallen's not a commander who gambles unless he's certain the odds are in his favor.

I ride behind him, close enough to feel the churn of his horse's wake, the burn in my thighs worsening with every jolt. My fingers ache. My ribs are tight. I don't know if I'm afraid or angry or both.

Then something shifts.

Not in us—but in the world itself.

I glance up. The battlements are still. No archers. No alarms. Just the flags, limp now in the windless dusk.

Mallen slows. I match him, heart hammering.

He's seen it too.

We should be under fire by now. We should be dying. But the gate looms ahead, unbarred. Open. Two guards on either side, pacing as if it's any other night. No reinforcements. No barricades. No blood.

A shiver crawls up my spine.

It's wrong.

Everything about it screams wrong.

But we ride through anyway, slipping past the threshold like knives through silk. The moment we enter the gatehouse, our soldiers swarm forward. Mallen's voice rings sharp and commanding—orders, names, instructions shouted across the courtyard.

The city guards don't resist.

They just drop their weapons. Hands up. Expressions blank.

I pull my horse into a tight circle, watching in disbelief as men move up the stairs to secure the towers. Within minutes, the south gate is ours.

Not a single drop of blood spilled.

Not one sword dulled.

It should feel like triumph. Instead, it feels like stepping into a house that remembers its last fire.

"Mallen," I murmur.

He's already looking at me, his expression unreadable, as though his face forgot how to wear anything but silence. "I know."

Behind us, the rest of the army pours in—lines shifting, boots striking cobblestones as they fan into the city's narrow streets. Some civilians watch from windows, mouths open. Others flee and vanish into the alleyways. No one speaks. Threnos has always been a city of masks, of secrets and whispers. But tonight, it holds its breath.

Mallen dismounts. His cloak billows as he strides toward the nearest officer. "Sweep the lower districts. Check the markets, the outer garrison, and the tunnels beneath the merchant's quarter. No one moves without my order."

He's already laying snares behind his teeth, spinning plans faster than breath. I should feel safer. Instead, it feels like the calm before a curse that can't be undone is spoken.

I dismount, slow and stiff. My hands tremble as I strip off the reins—skin tingling as if the leather remembered another rider. My boots hit the ground, and pain flashes through my legs, but I stand straight. I will not show weakness. Not now.

Mallen returns. His eyes flick down to my hands and then back up. "You feel it?"

"Yes," I breathe.

The magic is here.

It coils through the streets like breath that can't be released—thick, ancient, tasting of rust and ruin. It's been waiting, sealed in stone and buried deep by gods who feared my father's hunger. But now it's broken loose. The city exhales it now, primeval and unbound, curling up from the cracks like smoke from a long-dead fire.

My skin crawls.

I strain to hear anything—movement, breath, the scrape of metal—but the silence holds.

I thought I knew these streets. I played in them. Hid in the basements, dared the tombs beneath the chapel steps. But Starsfall has changed. Its stones have shifted. Its stones no longer remember me, and the shadows have learned new names for fear.

The palace waits above us, stark against the bruised sky. Its towers rise like spears, windows dark, spires silent. No guards are visible. No lights. Just the massive metal gates and the stretch of the empty courtyard before them, slick with the sheen of old rain and older blood. I stare at the doors—tall as giants, etched with sigils long-since worn down by time and flame.

The silence presses in—dense, waiting, thick with the kind of stillness that comes before the world breaks.

Mallen steps beside me, his jaw rigid.

"You don't have to be the one to face him."

"I'm the one with magic," I say.

He frowns.

"I'm not as skilled as I should be," I admit. "But I felt it last night. It knows me. That's enough."

His expression twists—just for a breath. Regret flickers through him, as brief as candlelight catching on wet glass.

He doesn't speak.

He doesn't have to.

I see it in the way his shoulders lower, in the breath he doesn't take.

He's bracing for the version of me that might not return. For the hollowed shape of the girl he followed here.

He swallows. "You're not alone."

Before I can speak, a sound splits the night.

A single, sharp bell. Then another. Then dozens, echoing through the air like funeral chimes.

And from deep within the palace, something answers—low, shuddering, as evil flows through the ground beneath us.

Not a voice. Not a scream.

A pulse.

Old as bone and darker than sleep, it thrums up through the soles of my boots—neither sound nor breath, but a remembering.

It does not beckon. It does not beg.

It brands.

The palace gates groan open—not with haste, but with hunger.

And the night turns to war.

CHAPTER THIRTY-THREE

THE SKY IGNITES.

Fire.

Real fire.

It streaks through the vapors, arcing down like meteors. Bolts of flame crash into buildings with bone-shaking force. Stone splinters. Wood shatters. The eastern quarter erupts in a wall of searing heat.

Someone screams. A horse bolts. A falling beam knocks one of our riders sideways as the square explodes into motion.

And still the fire multiplies. Not rain—an inferno descending, a fire choosing. A hundred mouths of flame seeking breath. The city catches like dry parchment, and every street is a lit fuse, racing toward the heart.

The wind shifts, and the night darkens. A different kind of smoke appears—acrid, cloying, wrong. It coils around us like a living shroud, seeping through every breath. And too late, I realize—it isn't just fire. It's magic. Heavy, oppressive, old. It stains the air—and me with it. It gathers behind my ribs, under my tongue, where my own magic trembles.

He has it back.

My hands go still—too still. My father has his magic again. I don't know how I know. I don't care. But I feel it—steady and relentless, a drum beating with the city's blood. Not a surge. A summons. As if the palace itself is breathing, calling me back to burn.

I glance up. Through the fumes, the towers of the palace rise like jagged teeth. Close. Too close. A hush curls in my lungs, thick as oil, and it taints every breath.

"Keep moving," Mallen yells.

I wrench my horse aside just as another bolt of flame slams into the fountain behind us, sending water and stone flying in every direction. Heat scorches my face. Smoke blinds me for a moment. I breathe, and it cuts. My magic stirs—half-feral, half-mine. Death's echo, curled like a sleeping god beneath my ribs. And I don't know if I will master it or vanish inside it.

I reach for it.

It recoils.

Not in refusal, but in warning.

I'm not ready. Not yet.

Gods.

Panic skims beneath my skin like lightning. I chased this power for so long, thinking it would save me. But I was wrong. It isn't a gift—it's a language I haven't learned to speak, and every word burns my tongue. My father will be nothing like the monster I faced before. Not a man fractured and weakened by his fall, but the sorcerer who once brought kingdoms to heel. The tyrant who ruled by fire and blade. The man who made me.

I don't know if I can defeat him.

But I know that I'm prepared to die trying.

Chaos descends.

Mallen shouts. I hear his voice but not the words. My magic surges again, wild and panicked, tearing at its leash. I choke on fumes and force it down. Not yet. Not like this.

I wheel my horse, searching for Marcus—he's gone. Swallowed by smoke.

"Mallen!" I scream.

He turns toward me, ash streaking his cheek, eyes burning.

"Stay with me!" he yells.

But the world is disintegrating. Another explosion tears through the north wall of the square. Flames leap higher. The buildings are catching now—crimson tongues racing across rooftops, devouring timber, destroying homes.

I look up.

The smoke churns through the heavens like a storm. Somewhere above it, the stars are gone. The gods are blind to what's happening beneath them, and darkness wraps around me and writhes inside me, shivering against my skin. My magic wants out. It wants to answer whatever power my father has woken.

A scream tears through the night.

Not human.

Not animal.

It rises through Starsfall's capital like a jagged blade drawn across stone—a wail of power so raw it rends the air. The horses rear. The ground shudders. Buildings fall and there's no way forward. Through the gap in the buildings, a narrow street curls upward—there's an alley open to my left.

Toward the palace.

It's clear. For now.

And suddenly—so suddenly it makes my chest ache—I feel it.

Not fire.

Not dread.

But purpose.

Like the hands of the gods wrapping around my throat and dragging me forward.

A calling.

Not just to fight. To end this.

To be what I was born to be.

I don't think. I won't flinch.

I kick my horse hard and break from the square.

Flames lick my skin as I ride. Screams echo behind me, but I don't look back. I can't. Every step forward is a choice. Every heartbeat is a countdown.

Mallen's voice rings out, panicked, furious.

"Azhara!"

But I'm already gone.

Smoke claws at my throat as I charge the rise. Behind me, Starsfall burns. The screams, the crack of splintering stone, the roar of flame—they blur into a single sound: fury. Above it all, I hear Mallen shouting my name again, his voice hoarse and ragged with disbelief and rage.

He's losing me.

And gods help me, I know it. The thread between us stretches to breaking—there's panic, fury, and his fear. His mind crashes into mine like waves against a cliff. His heart hammers. I feel it—his dread, his disbelief. The way he reaches for me, again and again, as if touch alone could drag me back. But I'm already slipping through his fingers. I am breath leaving the lungs. A future unfolding. A name he no longer knows how to call without breaking.

But I can't stop. I won't.

The street narrows as I ride, flanked by tall buildings with windows like staring eyes. Fire surges overhead, leaping from roof to roof. A shutter crashes open beside me, flames pouring through. My horse startles, but I press her on, spurring harder. Every breath is poison. Every beat of my heart threatens to rupture my ribs.

I round a corner—and the world erupts.

A bolt of fire slams into the street just ahead, hurling stone and ash into the air. The shockwave hits like a slap, knocking the breath from my lungs. My mare rears, screaming, hooves lashing. I cling to the saddle, the heat scorching through my armor. Then we're through it—diving into the smoke, dodging the collapse of a stone wall to our left as it crumbles in a hail of fire and shrapnel.

My lungs burn.

My eyes water.

The darkness darkens, and for a moment, I can't see.

I ride blind, guided only by the pulse of magic thrumming in the air—the call that grips my spine and drags me forward.

My father knows I've broken from the others.

He's aiming for me now.

The fire narrows. Focused. Intentional.

He doesn't need to kill all of them. Just me.

A second strike splits the road behind me—flame arcing so near it brushes my skin with breathless heat, and my hair lifts as if startled by the nearness of death. The force slams into a storefront, and the building detonates inward, collapsing into the street. Debris pelts my armor. Something sharp slices my cheek.

Forward. Always forward.

I drive my heels into my horse's sides. She stumbles, but finds her stride again, galloping up the winding hill as buildings crack and groan around us. Another strike slams to the right—glass shatters, and the heat sears my lungs. A second on the left, close enough to melt paint from the walls. He's not just herding me. He's toying with me. Pushing me up the last street that leads to the palace gate.

But it's too late to turn back.

I must be death now.

I burst from the mouth of the alley into the upper quarter—and stop, just for a heartbeat.

The palace stands before me, black and jagged against the infernal sky. Smoke coils around its towers. The high gate is half-shattered, scorched from within. The courtyard is empty—eerily so. And yet the air thickens—brimming with hush too loud to be empty. A stillness that feels like breath held just behind a door. Something sees me. Something waits.

The path is clear.

That's the trap.

I should be afraid, but I'm not.

I ride on.

The fire behind me roars louder now, chasing me up the rise. Another explosion rips through the street behind, but I don't look. The sound is enough. Stone collapses. Flames roll through the air like waves. My horse screams, and she falters beneath me, her legs skidding on loose ash and bloodied cobble.

"Come on," I whisper, throat raw.

A shadow falls over us.

I glance up. And for a heartbeat, the world stops.

Above me, hanging in the smoke-choked sky, is a shape—no, not a shape. A figure made from smog. Wreathed in fire. Cloaked in black flame. Eyes like twin suns, burning through the haze.

My father.

No smile. No speech. Just flame.

And then the air comes undone.

Fire rains down in waves, not as bolts but as sheets—as if the heavens themselves are burning. I scream and drive my horse into a dead sprint, hooves striking sparks from the stone. The fire catches behind us, and then beside us, and then in front.

I summon my magic.

Instead of reaching for it—I demand it.

It answers. I don't understand how.

Darkness coils beneath my skin, rippling outward in a blast of raw force. The flames recoil, and falter. Not extinguished, but slowed. Just enough.

The fire burns hotter.

The night draws closer.

The darkness pushes back.

The flames surge higher—blinding, choking, absolute. Heat closes in like a hand wrapping around my neck. For a moment, I can't breathe. I can't think. The fire takes shape around me, a wall, a cage, a maw. My horse stumbles, hooves striking sparks, her scream lost in the roar.

And then, the brightness breaks.

Not outside—inside.

The world does not go still, but my fear does. The heat peels back, the fire parting not by wind, but by a will not my own.

Light arcs across my vision, silver and terrible, and the air hums with power not born of flesh or spell.

Not mine.

Not his.

A power older than names moves through me.

The light before fire was born.

It does not shield—it claims.

And the voice beneath all voices calls. The gods do not speak. They resonate. Without words, without shape, without beginning. But I know them. I feel them—ancient, endless, stretching wide across the seams of the world.

This is not mercy.

This is memory, echoing in my blood. A summons older than time.

They are not kind.

But they remember me.

And they call me forward, as if I were always theirs.

I am not burned.

I am carried.

I tear through the inferno, wind roaring, ash blinding. My cloak ignites—I rip it loose and cast it aside. Pain sears my arms where sparks catch, but I don't stop. I don't fall.

The gates are close now. Twenty lengths. Ten.

The ground shakes—another blast hits behind me. My horse screams again—but she does not stop.

The gods do not either.

We reach the courtyard. It's empty. There are no guards at their posts. No nobles on the balconies. Doors gape onto still halls. Banners hang without breath.

Just gone. Like someone cut the strings of the storm.

The silence that follows is worse than the fire. It swallows everything. My breath. My heartbeat. The scream that still echoes in my skull.

I pull hard on the reins.

We skid to a halt in the center of the courtyard.

The palace looms above, blackened and hollow-eyed. The doors are ajar. A gust of wind—or magic—slams them fully open with a groan like the belly of the earth cracking.

I dismount.

My legs almost give. I'm shaking. Covered in ash, blood, soot. My hands tremble—but I'm still standing.

I made it.

And then agony tears through me.

Behind me.

The bond.

Mallen.

He's coming. Fast. Reckless. His rage is a cacophony of pain. His grief too. His desperation. He's cut off, and finding another path. Gods, he'll make one if he has to. He's fighting like a man on the verge of losing everything, and his thoughts batter against mine like fists against a locked door—wild, bloodied, desperate. Each one lands with the weight of a truth he's too late to stop.

"Azhara, no. Stop. Please, gods, STOP."

But I already have.

I've waited too long. Lived too small.

I won't beg for freedom from men who name it love.

I'd rather burn than belong to anyone but myself.

I would rather stand alone than be loved on someone else's terms.

I'm not turning back.

I step toward the palace.

I will not kneel. I am not a tribute. And I will not offer supplication.

The air inside bites, like breath drawn through shattered crystal and broken dreams. Frost feathers across the scorched stone, and my exhale ghosts white before me. Black marble shudders beneath me, and the fire fades, its echoes clinging to my skin, to my bones.

The walls close around me—vaulted stone, marred by smoke.

The frescoes survive—half-burned saints with soot-ringed halos, their gold leaf flaking like scabs. They do not bless me. Their painted gazes follow as I pass, not in reverence, but in mourning.

And still I walk forward.

He lies ahead. My tormentor. My father.

The gate shudders again behind me.

Mallen's scream fractures the silence.

But I do not flinch.

The world behind me howls its grief. Let it.

I refuse to look back.

CHAPTER THIRTY-FOUR

THE THRONE ROOM SMELLS OF TAR AND DEATH.

The heavy doors scream shut behind me. My boots echo on the marble floor, dark with soot and cracked like a scorched desert. The banners are gone, and the vaulted ceiling is laced with smoke. Only the fire remains—burning in braziers along the walls, coiling around the throne like a serpent guarding its hoard.

He sits atop it like he belongs there. Robes scorched, crown gleaming. One hand rests on the carved armrest, the other curls lazily around the hilt of a sword propped at his side. That sword was never meant to be seen clean. I remember the stain it left on the nursery tiles. I remember the way it hummed, like it wanted to speak.

And behind him, hidden half in shadow, are the nobles he called loyal. The ones who drank his wine, smiled at his jokes, and sent their sons to taunt me. Now they cower. Not from me. Not yet.

No one moves. The fire crackles softly, like it's holding its breath.

My heartbeat isn't loud, but it's steady—like a drum before a charge. I don't feel brave. Only sharpened—like a weapon honed by its maker, ready to be tested.

I take a step and then another.

"You came," he says, voice low, warm, intimate.

The sound stops me. My chest tightens.

"I wasn't sure you would." His eyes find mine. Flame-cast and gleaming. "I thought that boy might have to drag your corpse back to me."

"I left him behind," I say.

I don't tell him Mallen tried to stop me, that he would have died for me. That he might still die for me.

"Good," my father says. "This is between you and me."

"And the men who died because you invented the Reaping," I say. "You turned my choice into a blood pageant to keep your throne. You starved Larksbind of hope and fed the sand with bodies so the magic would crawl back to your hand."

He smiles thinly. "Order costs. Power costs more."

"And you never paid any of it. You feared my choice and made others bleed for it."

He rises and the room inhales.

The fire surges—leaping from the braziers to the pillars, racing up the walls like veins gone to rot. It spills across the floor in molten rivulets, and curls behind him like wings spun from ash and vengeance.

He towers above the throne now, crowned in flame, silhouetted like the god he always pretended to be.

"They've been waiting for this moment." He gestures toward the nobles. "They are bored of waiting for my magic to return, bored of a girl playing at a choice that was never hers. They want a reminder of what power is."

I don't look at them. I don't need to.

"They respect me," he says, stepping down from the dais. "But now they need reminding of what happens to those who don't."

Another step. Another coil of fire at his heel.

"You were supposed to die."

The smile that curls his mouth is so tender it burns.

"It wasn't supposed to be her."

He doesn't move. Just watches me, like he's already won. Like this is a game he's been playing for years, and now I've finally arrived to lose it.

"But she betrayed me." His fingers stroke the pommel of his sword with reverent care, as if it's a memory he treasures. "For you."

The air thins. The world narrows. I can't breathe.

My mother's face flashes before my eyes. It's not real. I never saw it long enough to remember. I've only seen it in paintings, in portraits he once had hung like relics. I don't even have fragments of memory. No lullabies. No bedtime stories. No silk shawl stained with her perfume.

I look at him—and I *see*.

"She was going to leave. Killing you would have kept her mine."

"You poisoned her," I say, voice rising, cracking.

A pause. A single flicker of silence.

The flames rise higher and fade back down.

"I tried to save her. But she wouldn't stop fighting. For you."

I take a step forward, and the shadow ripples with me.

"Her death looked like childbirth. You let them blame me."

He spreads his arms. "Starsfall needed someone to mourn."

And now the fire wraps him again, searing the marble at his feet. The nobles flinch deeper into the shadows.

"She screamed for you," I say, and I don't know if it's true, but I want it to be. I need it to be. "While you watched her die."

His sword scrapes free of its sheath.

I raise mine to meet it.

"Once I'd hoped you'd be a worthy heir," he says. "Now I know you're a blight sent to ruin me."

I breathe, and the darkness coils through my fingers and dances up the blade like frost on steel. "Not a blight. Your ruin anyway."

He strikes.

I block and then vanish.

The darkness swallows me, draws me into its fold. I am night. I am death. I am the thing he tried to kill in the cradle—the afterbirth of ruin and miracle. Not daughter. Not shadow. Not girl. I reappear behind him, the edge of my blade slicing for his spine—but he turns, too fast, too practiced. Flame bursts from his hand and sends me flying back, slamming against the blackened pillar.

Pain bursts open in my ribs, red and bright and ringing, like a bell struck from the inside. I can't tell if they're broken. It doesn't matter.

He stalks forward, fire rolling at his heels. The shadows flee before it, but they're not gone. They're circling. Watching.

"You always knew to fear me," he says. "Even when you were small. You'd scream when I came near."

"I knew what you were," I gasp.

He raises his hand, and the fire lashes out—but I'm already moving. I dive into another shadow, and the floor buckles beneath me. The world warps, bends, *shifts*. My body snaps into nothingness and back again, not where I meant to go as I move through the dark, but close enough. I stumble out of the shade, disoriented, barely catching my balance. I swing my sword on instinct.

And this time, it catches flesh.

Blood arcs through the air. His left shoulder splits open beneath the slice, and he roars—half fury, half pain.

I fall back, breathing hard. My chest sears with every breath. He turns, haloed in flame, a man sculpted from greed and hunger.

"You think death will save you?" he spits. "You think that's power?"

"I don't need saving."

The shadows rise at my back.

He lifts both hands now, and the fire explodes.

I shield my face as the inferno crashes into me, heat licking past my guard. My hair scorches at the ends. The embroidered hem of my tunic blackens, curls, smokes. Heat claws at my throat and my chest, blistering skin where the fabric is too thin. I bite down on the scream.

My sword burns hot in my grip.

But my magic answers louder now. It doesn't recoil from the fire—it devours it.

It floods me—ancient and bone-deep, cold as untouched graves, certain as every last breath. Death, in its first language. Pure. Inevitable. And I relive the moment that she died, her soul twisting from her body and into mine, a final gift he never meant me to keep.

Her grief is my birthright. Her last breath, my first.

Not a curse.

Not a wound.

A weapon.

He doesn't know what he's made.

But he's always feared it. Always understood he would reap what he sowed.

We meet in the center of the room—fire against death, steel against shadow. His blade crashes against mine, heat flaring from the impact. I twist, parry, drop low, and slice for his legs. He leaps back, flame trailing behind him, and scorches the air between us.

We circle.

"She promised me an heir," he snarls. "For a while, I tried to make you worthy."

"I *am*."

I charge.

The darkness wraps my limbs like armor, stiffens my spine, sharpens my edge. He blocks again, and the force of it sends tremors up my arms—but I'm stronger now. Faster. My blade sings with fury.

I see every scar on his face.

I remember every word he used to cage me.

I let go of the girl who bowed her head and tried to be good.

And I let the night in.

My sword meets his again. Steel shrieks. Sparks fly. I push—harder than I should be able to—and he staggers back, mouth curling in something like surprise.

"You've learned," he says, panting.

He snarls and thrusts his blade forward, a brutal jab meant to pierce my ribs, but I'm already moving. My feet slide over ash-slick stone. The shadow draws me sideways, slipping me into darkness and out again. I strike at his flank.

But he's waiting for it.

His elbow cracks into my jaw. My head snaps sideways. Pain detonates behind my eyes, and the sword slips from my grasp. My knees hit stone. Fire blazes above me—too fast.

I roll.

His blade punches into the ground where my chest had been, molten sparks spraying my side.

"Power doesn't belong to you," he says, voice raw now, broken by rage. "It belongs to those who claim it. It belongs to me."

He snarls and lunges, blade high.

I lift mine to meet it. Our swords lock, and I hold—for a breath. Another. Then my knees buckle. He shoves harder as fire pours down his blade, scorching the steel and searing the skin of my hands.

My grip slips.

My sword clatters to the ground, and fire slams into me.

I scream.

It's not just heat. It's pain—raw, endless, *hungry*. It claws through my chest, ripping flesh from bone. I fall, but I don't feel myself hit the ground. I'm unraveling—not dying, but liquefying into flame. A girl dissolving into cinders. The fire of death consumed by another flame.

My body stops obeying. I can't move. I can't breathe.

This is it.

He steps over me, sword gleaming.

"You should have died before you were born," he whispers.

He raises his blade for the final strike.

And then—

I hear a scream that's not mine. Not in this room.

Mallen.

Not in flesh—but in soul. It breaks through me like a symphony—his anguish, his devotion, sharp as glass and soft as a prayer. I feel it through the tether forged between us, blood-sworn and sealed with devotion. A shatter made of love.

His voice tears through my skull like lightning. I don't know what he sees. I don't know if he feels my pain or the way I'm slipping—out of this world, out of this war. But the bond between us thrums like a struck chord, a live wire between our hearts. Wherever he is, the world gives way beneath him—and it sends an echo through my bones.

"Don't," he says, and I hear it not in words but in pleading.

He kneels like he's lost the sun, and his hand reaches mine through the dark.

And the night answers.

The fire dims—not around me, but within. The pain doesn't vanish, but it withdraws. Like it's being drawn from me—siphoned into him. A thread pulls taut, neither rope nor chain, but a current that cannot be stopped. His pain rushes in like tidewater into an open wound, and mine recedes. He takes the fire, and in its place, the dark expands—ripe, ravenous, and ready for the kill.

I take a breath. My lungs catch. My chest burns. But I'm breathing.

My father's sword hovers, inches from my face.

And then I look up.

Not with my eyes.

With death's.

Shadows pour from beneath the throne, from the scorched banners, from every crack and corner of the room. They seep from every crevice like spilled ink, thick and sentient. And—gods—they crown me.

And I rise—not like a girl pulling herself off the floor, but like a reckoning born from the grave.

The fire flares higher, but it wavers now. Flickers. Wounds bleed backward, and I see the truth in him now, as he sees it in me.

"You shouldn't be able to stand," he whispers.

"You shouldn't live," I say.

And I strike.

I drive the blade through him.

Not in rage, but with the certainty of a verdict long overdue. It's not fast. It's sure. Slow. A sentence passed by silence, carried in shadow.

I remember his hand on my wrist. The poison he poured as he lied. The silence that followed. The years I spent starving for kindness. For safety. For what would never come.

I *was* born for this.

He gasps.

My darkness crashes into his core—not flame meeting flame, more a new dawn rising. One that's brighter and that obliterates his existence. It unwinds him from within. His fire flickers, thrashes, and then gutters. The heat devours itself, swallowed by the whole of what I am. His magic burns bright and then breaks.

Mine does not burn.

Mine ends.

His whole body goes still. The sword falls from his grip.

The fire vanishes.

And when I pull my blade free, he crumples forward, smoke curling from his mouth like a final curse. He hits the marble with a dull, wet thud. His crown rolls from his brow, clinking down the steps of the dais.

Silence.

The nobles behind him stare. Some with mouths open. Some with tears streaming down their faces. No one moves.

The shadows hiss. The death inside me settles. And I walk forward, past his body, past his fallen sword, up the dais where the crown waits.

I bend. Lift it.

It's warm—with blood.

"I am Azhara." My voice rings through the room. "And I do not burn."

No one speaks.

But—one by one—they kneel.

Even the ones who cursed my name.

Or who thought they could live through this war without taking a side.

I plant the crown on my head.

The doors groan open before me. My father's palace is still half-burning. The walls are charred, and the halls echo with the sounds of the wounded, the weeping, the dead.

But he is gone.

I am here.

And so is Mallen.

He stumbles toward me, soot-streaked and bloodied. There's ash in his hair, a gash across one brow, a tear in his sleeve where a sword must have nicked his shoulder—but he's alive.

"Azhara—"

He breaks into a run. Not from hesitation, nor fear—just the wild desperation of a man who thought he'd lost everything and is still afraid to believe he hasn't.

I fall into him.

I don't collapse. I don't crumble.

But I step into his arms like they're the only place I've ever wanted to be.

He catches me without a word and holds me to his chest. His hands shake against my spine. Mallen presses his mouth to my temple, my hair, and my shoulder. Not as a man claiming a possession or a throne.

As one who's just been forgiven.

"You shouldn't have come alone," he whispers.

"I had to," I breathe.

"I felt you break."

"I didn't."

I pull back just enough to look at him. He's still staring at me like I'm half-shadow, half-star. Like I don't quite belong in the world anymore. Like I don't belong anywhere else but here, with him.

"I'm still me," I whisper. "Still yours."

He nods.

Then he cups my jaw, tenderly, reverently. Not kissing. Not yet. Just *touching*—like he needs to be sure I'm solid.

"I know."

And he drops to his knees.

Not in worship. Not in surrender.

But in loyalty.

He kneels before his queen.

And I touch his face, his hair, his shoulder.

Then I take his hand. And wait for him to swear. His loyalty. His devotion. His love.

Threnos is burning.

But I am alive.

And I am home.

CHAPTER THIRTY-FIVE

MARCUS AND THE SOLDIERS REACH THE THRONE ROOM, PREPARED to face the unthinkable. But instead of carnage, they find silence. My father's blood stains the floor, the crown rests in my hands, and Mallen—bruised and breathless—kneels below the dais, arms outstretched, as if in surrender to me.

The soldiers falter. Confusion ripples across their ranks.

Marcus's gaze sweeps the chamber, noting the nobles cowering on the floor. "What in the name of all the gods—?"

"Stand down," Mallen says. His voice is raw, smoke-rough, and scorched from shouting. He rises, not once taking his eyes off me. "Let them go. They're not worth the trouble."

The nobles don't wait for permission. They scatter like frightened birds, their polished shoes slipping in the blood as they rush past our soldiers.

Marcus advances. "Fire stopped raining from the heavens. What happened?"

I don't answer. Every breath feels borrowed. The crown I've claimed is heavy with every choice I didn't want to make. My father's blood stains the floor. I am not mourning him. I am mourning the girl who still thought she could leave. The weight of it all presses down, still too much to name.

So Mallen does it for me.

"She did," he says, glancing toward me with awe that hides the sharper, ragged need beneath it. "It's over."

Marcus studies me like he doesn't recognize the girl I was before. Perhaps I don't either. I meet his gaze and say nothing, refusing to explain or apologize.

Mallen steps between us and shakes his head. "It's over, Marcus."

He stops. "You've looked better."

Mallen glances at me again, and color rises in his bruised cheeks. "We all have."

Marcus lets out a slow breath. The kind that tastes of smoke and memory. His gaze flicks to the crown in my lap and then back to me, as if he's still trying to understand how I became the one to end it. I think he sees the answer in Mallen's posture. In mine too.

"Tell me she's making you ask for her hand."

My chin lifts a little. "Obviously."

Marcus bows mockingly. "You'll do fine. She'll make certain of it."

And then, mercifully, he leaves—his soldiers trailing behind him, chuckling under their breath.

The throne room empties. Silence folds in around the pillars and mosaics, thick and final. I let my sword clatter to the ground. The crown slips from my hands. I sink into the throne—not with triumph, but with the ache of survival.

Mallen doesn't move until the last echo fades.

"You scared the life out of me," he murmurs, voice rasping. "I thought I lost you."

"You were just behind me."

He approaches slowly, his steps careful. "I was. That didn't make it easier."

I reach for him, fingertips brushing his jaw. He leans into the touch like he's been starving for it.

"I'm here," I whisper.

"I saw you ride into that fire and I—" His voice breaks. "Don't ever do that again. You cannot go where I can't follow."

My eyes sting. "I wasn't trying to leave you behind."

He presses his forehead to mine. "But you would have. If it meant ending him. You would've died for this."

I don't answer. I don't need to.

His hands rise to cradle my face. "You don't need to prove anything. Not to me. Nor to yourself."

"I don't want to rule," I murmur.

"I know. But you were born to." His thumb brushes my cheek. "And you won't let it change you. You won't lose yourself."

I lean into him, every muscle aching, every thought unraveling now that it's over. He senses it, I think. He always does. His arms go around me, lifting me without effort, and I don't resist. My head finds the curve of his shoulder. My body folds into his without shame, without reservation.

We move through the halls like that, slow and silent. Soldiers bow their heads, clearing the way. He doesn't pause. Just holds me tighter.

I don't remember reaching my rooms. Our rooms now. Only the warmth of the bath, the scent of herbs, the way he washes me like I'm too precious to let go. A different kind of darkness takes me—softer than sleep, deeper than rest—and I sink into it, lulled by the hush of his hands and the heat of the water. No dreams. Just the slow release of fear I've held too long.

When I wake, I'm cradled against his chest, limbs tangled beneath soft blankets. His fingers trace the curve of my jaw, tender and rhythmic, like he never stopped touching me even while I slept.

"You're awake," he whispers.

I look up at him. His face is bruised, shadowed by exhaustion, but still—somehow—radiant.

"I'm sorry I scared you," I say.

He closes his eyes like the words hurt. "Don't apologize. Just...don't disappear on me again."

"I couldn't stop."

"I know." He exhales slowly, brushing that rebellious strand of hair behind my ear. "I should be furious. It was reckless, selfish—all of it, and more. But all I saw was you, riding into fire, and I've never loved you more."

I blink hard. "I was dying. Then you were there."

"You're never alone. Not while I breathe."

A silence falls, heavy with all we can't yet say. His hand finds mine beneath the blanket, weaving our fingers together.

"You're hurt," I say softly, noticing the stiff way he moves.

He shrugs. "Not enough to make a difference."

I trace the line of a bruise on his ribs. "It matters to me."

He catches my hand, bringing it to his lips. "And you to me."

I don't know who moves first. Maybe we both do. But suddenly our lips meet—not with hunger, but with the slow, reverent ache of two people who nearly lost everything. There's no need to rush. No need to prove anything.

When he eases me back onto the pillows, it's with the gentleness of an artist handling a masterpiece that might yet evade perfection.

His touch is careful, reverent. His kisses are soft and lingering, more comfort than passion, though the heat simmers beneath. When he brushes his thumb over my collarbone, it's not to take—it's to remind me I'm still here. Still whole.

I let myself be seen.

And Mallen—gods, Mallen never looks away.

When I flinch, his hands still. "Too much?"

"No," I breathe. "Just…slow."

He smiles. Not wicked. Not haunted by jealousy. Just a flicker full of relief and worship. Of devotion. He leans down, resting his forehead against mine.

"I love you," he says.

No demand. No expectation. Just a truth.

I press a kiss to the corner of his mouth. "Then stay. Like this."

"Always."

Desire stirs again—slow, insistent—as Mallen's mouth trails heat along my neck. His breath ghosts over my skin, and I shiver, caught between need and a more fragile want. His lips find the hollow beneath my jaw, where he lingers, pressing soft, tender kisses that make my breath hitch.

"Look at you," he murmurs, staring at me. "You undo me."

He doesn't rush.

Doesn't demand.

He lowers his head again, kissing slowly down the center of my chest as though mapping me to memory. His hand cradles my ribs, steadying me, grounding me. My back arches of its own accord when his mouth finds my breast, and I gasp—sharp, involuntary—as his tongue flicks across my nipple, gentle at first, then firmer.

I clutch at his thighs, anchoring myself. He groans, the sound low and feral, but he doesn't lose control. He simply takes his time, rolling his tongue in slow, deliberate circles until I'm panting, wordless, aching for more.

"You're trembling," he murmurs against my skin.

"Because you're cruel," I whisper, breathless.

He huffs a soft laugh and presses a kiss over my heart before continuing downward, his mouth skating across my stomach. The teasing touch sends shivers dancing over my skin. I grip his hair, not to control him but to hold myself together.

His hands smooth over my hips and down the inside of my thigh. He lifts my leg carefully, spreading me open—and I hiss, flinching as stiff muscles protest. Immediately, he slows.

"You're sore."

I nod, biting my lip, but he's already adjusting. His touch softens, soothing where he might have pushed.

Then he lowers his head.

His breath warms me. His tongue flicks against me, and my hips jerk. A moan escapes, half-shocked, half-relieved, as my body starts to unravel again.

"Good?" he murmurs.

I nod frantically.

"Relax," he says, voice velvet and steel. "Let me care for you."

He takes his time, slow circles of his tongue drawing my tension out, replacing it with heat. Pleasure builds, slow at first and then deeper, surging through me. He doesn't overpower—it's not about dominance. He's attuned to me, watching every breath, every shift of my hips.

When he finally slides a finger into me, I gasp. My body clenches around him, and he groans in response. His mouth doesn't stop. Tongue and hand working in tandem, building me back toward the edge he's not yet let me cross.

It's exquisite torture.

My hips move on their own now, grinding against his hand, chasing the pressure. He slides in a second finger, and I moan, craving more, desperate to shatter. My body begs for it.

But he slows.

I groan in frustration, writhing beneath him.

"Do you want to climax?" he asks, voice thick.

I nod, but he doesn't move faster.

"Then ask."

"Mallen..."

"Ask me."

I whimper, biting back a growl. I'm trembling, caught in the space between pleasure and denial, and he watches me there—so calm, so composed—until I finally whisper, "Please."

He smiles.

I blink up at him, lost in a haze of need, and he leans in.

"Say it, Azhara. Let go. Give this to me."

It's not about power. It never is, not with him. He wants surrender, not submission. Trust, not obedience.

And I do trust him.

"Please, Mallen," I breathe. "Please. I need you. I want—"

"Just like that."

His pace changes—faster, deeper, more intense. I cry out as the pleasure crests and crashes over me, breaking me open. Mallen watches every second, his mouth slightly parted, reverent.

"Beautiful," he murmurs as I collapse against the bed, limbs trembling.

He doesn't move right away. Just trails his hand gently over my body, grounding me, letting me come back to myself.

When I open my eyes, he's above me again, eyes burning. He strokes himself slowly, deliberately, and the want in his gaze reignites mine in an instant.

But then he pauses.

"You good?" he asks.

I nod, but a tremor stirs in my core. Fragile, unfamiliar. Like the stillness before a storm breaks. I'm not the same as I was before, and maybe he'll notice.

He sees it, hears my anxiety.

"I'll stop. Just say it."

"Don't," I whisper. "I'm choosing this. I want you."

He eases forward—his body taut, trembling—and then he's inside me, in one smooth, careful thrust.

I gasp. Not from pain, but from the overwhelming rightness of it. I feel full, complete, as though I was missing a piece I hadn't known I needed.

Mallen groans, burying his face in the crook of my neck as he starts to move. The rhythm he finds is deep and steady. Purposeful. Every motion says *I'm here. You're mine. I've got you.*

I match him, hips rising to meet his, the tension building between us with each breath, each thrust. His body presses against mine, and his hands map my skin like he's afraid he'll forget the shape of me.

"You feel like coming home," he breathes, like it amazes him.

I arch against him, moaning as he hits just the right spot. Over and over, until I can't think, can't speak. Just feel.

"You were made for me," he groans. "All of you."

I break our kiss long enough to murmur, "And you for me."

His rhythm falters and then deepens. He leans back, hands gripping my hips as he moves faster and harder, dragging me with him toward the edge. I hold on, nails digging into his shoulders, crying out as the pleasure coils tight in my belly.

"You're mine," he growls. "Say it."

"Yours," I gasp.

His eyes blaze. "Say it like you mean it."

I wrap my arms around him, pulling him down to whisper against his ear, "I was always yours."

He shudders, and I feel him hold back, waiting—always waiting for me. He won't let go until I do.

And I do.

The orgasm hits like lightning, arcing through me, leaving nothing untouched. I scream his name, barely aware of anything beyond the pleasure tearing through me. Mallen follows a heartbeat later, roaring my name as he thrusts deep and comes with a force that shakes us both. He collapses against me, chest heaving, arms trembling as he holds me close.

Neither of us speaks for a moment. The only sound is our breathing, the frantic pounding of our hearts slowly easing.

Then Mallen shifts, easing onto his side, never letting me go. He wraps his arms around me as though I might disappear if he loosens his grip.

I curl into him, one hand stroking the back of his neck, the other resting over his heart.

He kisses my temple. "Still good?"

"Better."

His smile is soft, sleepy. "You terrify me."

I blink. "What?"

"How much I love you."

I press a kiss to his collarbone.

"I'd raze kingdoms for you, Azhara." His voice is quiet. "Burn the world to keep you and tear down every star for you. And you...you could break me with a word."

I lift my head. "I wouldn't."

"But you could."

"You don't have to carry this alone anymore."

He closes his eyes and leans into my touch. "I know."

We lie tangled in each other, breath and skin and heartbeat slipping into rhythm, the afterglow dimming into stillness—quiet and steady.

His thumb rubs lazy circles on my lower back. "I like this."

"What?"

"You. In my arms. Safe. Whole."

I smile and tuck my face into his neck. I like it too. And he knows it, without me having to say it. It's in the way my fingers curl at the nape of his neck, in the warmth burning through my chest when his heartbeat drums against mine. I feel him through the bond—contentment, relief, the soft ache of wonder.

"You're safe," he murmurs, voice heavy with emotion. "Always loved."

And because it's him, I believe it.

CHAPTER THIRTY-SIX

MALLEN PACES THE LENGTH OF OUR CHAMBER, HANDS CLASPED behind his back, as if he's measuring the floorboards for war.

He's spent the week rooting out those with lingering loyalty to my father with swift and exacting precision. There were few, and they're already dead. Mallen offered no mercy, no trial. I considered intervening. But the look he gave me—grim and steady—spoke of gangrene that was too far gone for anything but amputation.

He left me the court instead. Alone. My chance to establish myself as ruler not just in title, but in presence. The nobles know my face, but not my strength. My father made sure of that. He spent years whispering poison—calling me weak, touched by death, unfit to rule. They flinch when I enter the hall. They avert their eyes. The few who witnessed me kill him understand now that I am not powerless.

But respect? That will take time.

It isn't how I want to govern.

But death holds sway over mortals, and, for now, Mallen lets the rumors spread. They say I brought untold darkness into the throne room. That the fire my father rained down burned away everything but me. That the dead listen when I speak. Some say that they obey me.

They say Mallen is the only one who steadies me—that without him, I'd burn too brightly, too wildly. That the gods were wise to demand the Reaping, to force my hand and control me. They say Darian was too perfect, too golden, that I was never meant to be his. That power has always belonged to the ones who the gods deem worthy, and that somehow, I am only worthy because of the man standing beside me.

So the lords bow more deeply to Mallen.

They respect him.

They obey him.

They call him king.

Not to my face, but often enough in the corridors. He commands the army. He conquered Starsfall. He has always been the blade, and I—until now—was the one hidden behind it.

He knows this.

It's why he's pacing now, like a man walking toward judgment.

He knows he'll be the one to crown me in the eyes of the court—even though I've already proved myself worthy. To Starsfall. To the gods. To myself.

A sigh tears from his chest. "Where is your tea?"

When Evie arrives a breath later, flustered and pale, Mallen snaps. The pot is cold. Barely steeped. He doesn't shout—but the tone of his voice is enough. She flinches and nearly drops the tray.

Marcus steps through the door before I rise.

"Enough," he says, turning to Mallen, in a voice as dry as old parchment. "You're being unreasonable."

Mallen turns, jaw tight, and slams his hand once against the sideboard. I've tolerated his scowls and the storm cloud gathering around him as he's tried to find another way to give me what I deserve. He's raged against the nobles, irritated that they still haven't accepted me for all I am, infuriated that he has to be the one to give me power.

But this? This petulance? This is beneath him.

He turns to me, eyes darker than I've seen them in days.

"You've carved your throne from ash and bone," he says.

I rise slowly, silk whispering around me. "Then let me dress for it—before I remind you what it cost me."

Marcus raises a brow. "Come on," he says to Mallen, already gripping his sleeve and hauling him backward. "Before she throws you off the balcony."

At the threshold, Mallen hesitates. "What will you wear?"

"A dress," I say, smiling. "A nice one."

Marcus drags him away before he can answer.

Evie lingers in the silence that follows, more cautious now. She knows what I can do—and what Mallen means to me. Her hands tremble as she brushes my hair into a braid and threads it with emerald pins. She spends too long on my makeup and then helps me into my gown. It's a deep green silk that shimmers with every breath, cut to expose skin I wouldn't normally show anyone but him. We cover the worst of it in jewels. The rest, I leave bare.

For Mallen.

I catch my reflection as she fastens my sandals. The woman in the mirror is no one's daughter now. She's no man's conquest. She is the queen. And if Mallen's mood frays over today, he'll have to swallow his pride and get over it.

"He'll like it," Evie says softly.

I nod, though we both know it's not the dress bothering him.

He doesn't want to kneel.

Not again. Not in front of them.

He's brushed it off every time Marcus raised the subject, but the tension in him is undeniable—like a sword not yet drawn. He'll do it. Because Starsfall will follow where he leads, and he loathes that it has to be this way. Because I asked. Because I *need* him to. And because he needs it too, even if he doesn't want to admit it. This isn't about humiliation. It isn't even about what's right.

It's about truth.

About power. And sharing it.

The knock comes. Marcus enters, takes one look at me, and forgets himself.

"You look stunning."

"You're not bowing," I say.

He grins and then corrects himself with exaggerated flair. "Majesty."

I arch a brow. "Does he have the ring?"

"He does."

My fingers trail over my jewelry. Casually. Perhaps too easily.

"He's still in a mood?"

"Oh, yes. Don't let that fool you. Mallen would kneel for you a thousand times if you asked him to. He resents it because Threnos needs to *see* it. He's your equal, Majesty, not your better, and he'll make damn sure the nobles know it."

They say that Mallen conquered Starsfall. They believe he tamed the monster locked inside it—and me. But they're wrong. I am not caged. I only learned how to dance inside the bars.

And today, I will claim what's mine.

We walk the long route through the palace, taking the same path I walked each year for a decade as I entered into a game I never wanted any part of. I played it anyway—and remade its rules. Not just to survive, but to win on my terms.

Today, I walk this path freely.

For the last time.

Today, we begin to rebuild what my father broke.

We reach the final corridor, where light fractures through the windows like spilled wine on glass. My footsteps echo—soft and ceremonial—across marble veined with memory. Every tile remembers.

The doors ahead yield without protest, opening to the altar of the Reaping: bare, wide, aching. Once a place for death. Today, it waits for a vow.

The nobles are already gathered. The square is full to bursting, every level and ledge packed with people. Banners ripple in the breeze, their colors brighter than memory. Children dart between their elders' legs, playing swordfights with sticks, their laughter piercing the murmurs of the crowd. A woman sells flowers from a worn cart, tossing blossoms like blessings into the street.

Still, Starsfall holds its breath—hope and hesitation braided so tight they bleed at the edges.

I step into view, and a hush falls over the crowd.

We descend the steps, and the crowd erupts as I raise my hands—not in praise, but in acknowledgment. The gesture they expect. Starsfall roars for freedom, for victory, for the start of a new monarch's reign. It believes itself reborn. It wants to believe we've turned the page, that history won't repeat.

The nobles speak in reverent murmurs, but their silence says more. They remember what a crowned monster looks like. They know my father is gone. What they do not know is whether we are a lull or the next disaster, wrapped in finer cloth.

They fear what lies behind the veil—war at the doorstep, ash in the well, names carved into gravestones before they've been spoken aloud.

Our reign will be different. That's the lie I breathe like a prayer. That's the truth I want and bleed toward. A time of healing and laughing. Of peace, too, if we are fortunate.

I close my eyes and reach for the magic that's returned to Starsfall. It stirs like it's waking from a winter's sleep. It flows in our rivers, floats through the air, and roots itself in the trees. It whispers beneath our feet. It threads through the kingdom, glimmering in the sunlight. I feel it now, humming just under the surface—certain, waiting, wild.

It gathers on my skin like dusk before the fall of night—too close, too quiet. It stains my breath. And when I open my eyes, the sky gleams like a fever dream. The colors too vivid, the edges too bright. Unbearably alive.

The wind moves through the trees, and they answer in elegy. The meadows smell of dust and pollen and new beginnings. Somewhere, a child laughs. Somewhere else, a bell tolls once, low and strangely solemn.

A poet will write a sonnet about this day and miss the point entirely.

My gaze finds Mallen. He waits at the base of the steps, his clothes marking him as royalty. As my equal. But it's his eyes that hold my attention—green as moss after rain, green as envy, green as memory. The same shade as mine. A mirror. A message. A vow returned.

He looks like a king.

But I'm the one in command.

He doesn't show apprehension, not to them. But his nervousness flows into me through our bond, a quiet unease threading under his control. His gaze moves down the length of me—green silk, bare skin, emeralds glinting like armor. He stops. Stares. I feel it as it shatters him.

The crowd cheers again, and I blush—but not for them. Never for them.

Only for him.

He walks toward me, gaze steady, mouth curled in a smile meant only for me. There's no script now, no performance. Just the two of us, tied together by more than memory.

By thread. By blade. By blood.

"Azhara," he says, voice quiet despite the noise.

"Mallen." My voice catches. My throat's too dry, my chest too tight.

He waits at the final step, giving me the high ground. Marcus stands at my side now, hand resting lightly on his blade. The place Mallen once guarded with silence and fire. The place he abandoned, so I could choose it for myself.

This is the final breath of the world we knew. And the first flicker of whatever might come next.

Mallen bends one knee. Just one.

He lowers his head, not because I ordered it, not because he must, but because it matters. Because we both know the court is watching. Because this lie we turn into truth matters more than comfort.

The air shifts—thin and taut as thread, as if the gods themselves are watching.

The silence that follows is complete. An eternity in a heartbeat. A breath held in expectation.

My heart beats once. Again. Too fast. My hands tremble.

I descend the last step.

His head tips back as I approach. I thread my fingers through his hair, and the world narrows to us. There is reverence in his stillness. A cacophony of unsaid things pass in silence, each more intimate than speech.

"I would kneel for you a thousand times if it meant the world sees you as I do," he says. "I am yours. Only yours. If you will have me."

I don't speak. Just smile and let all I am ripple through the bond.

He takes my hand, and I cling to him—not for ceremony, not for the crowd. For balance. For breath.

"You're meant to answer," he whispers, mouth tilted in a grin.

"You're meant to ask," I breathe, smiling back.

He laughs, free and bright. I've rarely seen him like this before—unburdened. For one exquisite second, he's not the sword, not the shadow. He's just Mallen.

"Marry me," he says. "Let me stand beside you. As your equal."

His voice carries no question—only truth laid bare. My heart stumbles anyway. I nod once, breath faltering, and he holds me, suspended, in that sliver of stillness, just long enough to feel it break.

"Yes."

The word brings silence to my soul, but it rings louder than any oath. The crowd shatters into sound. Mallen slips a ring onto my finger, and before I've fully seen it, he's lifting me like a promise, mouth on mine. The kiss bruises and breathes me into being. When we part, the world rearranges its seams to let us fit.

As equals.

The nobles bow as we pass. Not to Mallen—to me.

The message is clear.

Mallen is mine. Starsfall is mine.

Our reign begins.

The celebrations will stretch long into the night, revelry spun for the eyes of the nobles and not for ours. We'll play our parts of monarchs with aching grace, but already my bones plead for the privacy of closed doors, for a world where only our hands speak.

I sink into the throne as if it always knew the shape of me. Mallen sits beside me, watching like he's afraid this dream will vanish if he looks away. His fingers find mine and toy with the emerald ring he placed there. The stone, the exact shade of his eyes, catches the light and scatters it across the hall in fractured green sparks.

"You seemed drawn to it. That day we walked through Threnos like there was nothing but us," he murmurs, brushing his lips against my cheek. "It feels right. But if you don't like it, I'll find another."

The memory slides into place, and the truth hits like an arrow—his hand in mine as we wandered Threnos, just the two of us, laughing like the city belonged to us alone. I think that was the first time I looked at him and saw not a shadow but a future.

My breath catches. "It's perfect, Mallen," I say, and kiss him again, unsure whether I was speaking about the ring or about us. It doesn't matter.

He studies me, brow faintly furrowed. As if he senses the shift beneath my smile.

As if he's reading my mind through our connection.

"We said no more lies," I whisper.

"What are you thinking?" he asks, reaching for me. Not to fix, nor to soothe, just to touch.

I shake my head, undone by it. I love him not because he saved me, but because he never asked to. He saw the ruin in me and called it cathedral. He survived the storm of me and named it beautiful.

"You already know."

He smiles, fingers brushing mine again. The music shifts, a low pulse of strings and longing. Dancers spill across the floor in ribbons of silk and smoke, spinning light into color. Their freedom is not inherited. It is taken. Just like mine.

Starsfall rests, just for tonight.

"This is only the beginning," I murmur.

"A better one," he replies.

We will rule together—never one above the other. We'll hold the line between mercy and power, grace and fear. Mallen will protect me from our enemies, but he will never let me falter. Not even for a second. He knows weakness can be fatal in this world.

He tightens his fingers around mine. A signal.

"We could leave now," I whisper.

Midnight paints his eyes as his lips curve. "We'd have to lie," he says. "Invent a reason to vanish." A beat. "Your dress?"

I smile, remembering the trick with the red wine. This time, I know exactly what to expect. This time, I won't be the frightened girl caught in someone else's illusion. And I'll never be the pawn in someone else's game. I will never again let them move me like a piece on their board.

I will smile and spin lies until they forget they were lies at all.

That is power. That is rule.

Mallen glances at the disguised soldier. The signal passes, and already the servant begins to move.

"I love you, Azhara," Mallen says, his voice low and sure.

I meet his gaze, steady as a flame. "I love you too."

The soldier nears. I lift my chin and draw a breath—not to pray, but to become the version of me they expect to see. Silk sighs as I rise, and their gazes sharpen like teeth against bare skin.

Let them watch. Let them hunger. Let them dream of undoing me.

Let them whisper truths they dare not speak too loud. It's the words left unspoken that matter most. The words that men do not say.

I was the girl who chased freedom and became the woman who turned captivity into a crown.

I am the lie made flesh.

And I have already won.

Thank you for reading! Did you enjoy? Please add your review because nothing helps an author more and encourages readers to take a chance on a book than a review.

Don't miss more from CJ Holmes available at cjholmeswriting.com

And now, discover CAPTURED BY THE VAMPIRE KNIGHT, by City Owl Author, A.N. Payton. Turn the page for a sneak peek!

You can also sign up for the City Owl Press newsletter to receive notice of all book releases!

SNEAK PEEK OF CAPTURED BY THE VAMPIRE KNIGHT

BY A.N. PAYTON

Movement flickered at the edge of the tree line. My hand froze, inches above a cluster of green herbs. My muscles locked, refusing to turn toward the twisting phantom in the shadows. The ghostly image faded, and I sighed.

"Are you seeing it again?" Penelope reached for a yellow flower, her fingers short and thick with youth. "You're supposed to tell us if you see it again."

"I didn't see anything."

"You have to tell us before something bad happens." She studied the bud, then let it fall. Not the right one.

"Something bad doesn't always happen."

Between the weeds, under the hot sun warming our hair and the gentle rustle of wind through the trees, I knew we were both thinking about the cat. Starving, pregnant, and sick, my ghostly stalker had poured magic into the animal and healed her in a heartbeat. Now, she and the six kittens meowed and rubbed our legs whenever we left our cottage.

"That's true." Penelope brushed a strand of golden hair from her face. Sweat streaked down the sides of her hairline and dampened her locks. The heavy weight of regret sunk deep in my chest. An eight-year-old should be playing with friends in the river on such a hot day. "But it's usually bad."

Memories trudged from the depths I tried to drown them in.

A thief on the road.

The silver flash of a knife.

His heart stopping under my palm.

I pushed the thoughts away, but Penelope's face twisted as the memory ran through her mind.

"I promise to tell you if I see it again," I lied.

She bobbed her head in acceptance, and I bit my lip to hide the guilt.

Grass crept up a gently sloping hillside and disappeared into the edge of a thick forest. Yellow flowers popped up here and there, taunting us as we searched for the correct herb. The recipe for our father's medication required tansy flowers, but the blooms mirrored dandelions, wild sunflowers, and golden orbs of chamomile. My mother's spellbook displayed a single, hand-drawn image of a tansy flower, and Penelope and I took turns squinting at the page. No luck so far.

I reached for another bud, plucked it from the woody stem, and brought it close to my face. A sweet, floral smell escaped from the plant, a chemical warning to its neighbors that danger lingered nearby. The other plants quivered in the wind, unable to run.

I pulled the spellbook closer and smoothed a crinkled edge of the worn paper. The tiny flower in my hand matched the elegant sketches from my mother's pen. Finally. Only a few more and I'd be able to concoct another batch of my father's medication.

The pages shifted beneath my fingers. My brow creased. The wind could barely flutter a page at its current strength, much less move such a hearty spellbook. I lifted the book, and the ground shook under its wooden cover. The vibrations strengthened until a low rattle buzzed inside my chest. I pressed my palm to the damp grass, and the roughness scraped against me.

"Natalie?" Penelope said.

"Just a moment." The sensation intensified. The earth rocked beneath us in smooth, rhythmic motions. An earthquake?

"Natalie!"

"Penelope, I'm busy."

"Look!" Her shaking finger pointed to our little house nestled in the crook of a shallow valley.

A black and silver tide swelled through the cluster of houses composing our village. Men and women on horseback, dark clothes buckled into armor that flickered in the sunlight. Thundering horse hooves rattled the ground, enough of the creatures to shake the earth from nearly a furlong away. As the soldiers neared, war cries drifted to us, followed by a more distant sound of screaming.

The twist of fear turned in my gut.

"Vampires?" Penelope's face reddened.

"It's a raid."

“A raid?” Her throat bobbed as she swallowed. “The last time that happened...”

“I know.” I didn’t need to hear her say the words.

The soldiers flung open doors and rummaged through houses. They poured out, dragging goods and people in their wakes. The dark tide flowed closer to our perch on the hillside, and the smacks of horse hooves pounded a constant drum beating in my ears.

“Will they go to our house?”

I chewed my lip and tucked the spellbook under one arm. “I don’t know,” I answered honestly.

“We don’t have anything expensive.” Her voice sounded quiet but strong, and her little face hardened with courage much greater than her age. “And Papa’s too sick to be a soldier.”

“You’re right,” I said.

But I’m not too sick. Or too old.

Penelope wrapped her fingers around mine. I squeezed her hand as we watched the flood envelop our village.

The mass of soldiers paused at the edge of the community. Our house sat at the end of the valley, half-hidden by a swell of overgrown wheat that was once farmland but recently returned to wilderness. Two men peeled away from the rest and trotted toward it.

Penelope sucked in a breath and clutched my fingers until the tips turned white. I held hers just as hard.

More memories crept through my mind. Slick, warm blood on my fingertips. Pain in my throat as my useless chanting became screams. I shook my head. I couldn’t drown in my past failures. Penelope’s safety relied on my focus.

The men burst through our front door, and the frame buckled. My heartbeat filled my ears, blocking the shouts and horse cries. A red haze covered my vision until the only things left in the world were Penelope’s grip on my hand and the reassuring weight of my mother’s spellbook under my arm.

The pair retreated from the house almost as quickly as they’d entered. Nothing they wanted.

My breath released. The red haze slipped away.

“They’re leaving,” Penelope whispered.

"Looks like it."

One of the men swung onto his horse. A giant man, practically dwarfing his partner, with thick red hair as visible as a beacon from the slope we stood on. His monster steed reared, stomping the ground and snorting with its ears pushed back. The man jerked the reins, and the animal turned the other way.

My heartbeat slowed. They were leaving.

The redhead glanced over his shoulder. He scanned the terrain and paused, looking in our direction.

Penelope stilled at my side. "Do you think he sees us?"

One arm, buckled into silver armor, lifted and pointed at us. His partner, mounted on a smaller steed, turned our way and nodded. The two directed their mounts toward us and started up the hillside.

Butterflies beat against the confines of my stomach. Penelope's grip should have been painful, but panic numbed me. Bile clenched up my throat as my thoughts focused on the pair trekking closer.

"Can you do magic?" Penelope's voice shook more than her hand in mine.

Good question. I glanced into the distance for the hovering phantom. Nothing. Of course, when I needed it, the creature disappeared completely.

I drew a breath. Maybe I didn't need the phantom's touch to direct my power this time. Maybe it would be different.

I closed my eyes and reached for my magic. I could feel it, a fluttering entity that shared a part of my soul, but it remained wrapped in a tight spell that felt faintly like my mother.

Come on, work just this once.

I fought against the invisible cage that trapped my abilities. Mother may be dead, but the spell she cast to contain my magic remained as strong as ever. Every time I tried to purposefully wield the power, it failed to answer my call.

The spells slipped like sand through my fingers.

"No," I said.

"What do we do?"

The men galloped closer. Weapons weighed them down on one side, but their horses appeared unhindered by the massive weights on their backs. I couldn't see the vampires' eyes, but I imagined the depths filled with fury and hatred. Two hundred years of war had clouded all our gazes with the same expression.

"Run." The word fell from my lips as a combination of instinct and reality. Outrunning a vampire on or off a horse held little promise of success—but we had to try.

"What?" Penelope's eyes pinched and glistened with unshed tears.

"Run!"

I pulled her up the hill. After two or three steps, her body caught up and she sprinted beside me. We ran toward the tree line while the smacks of hooves on damp ground grew closer behind us.

The trees stretched higher as we neared. Their shade should have been a welcome respite from the heat, but it felt like an ominous shadow swallowing us up. Vampires could easily outrun us, but dodging the trees would slow them down. The wooden pillars would either be our salvation or the bars on our cage.

The wet grass turned to mud at the forest's edge. I conjured a mental map of the terrain. I'd grown up browsing these woods for ingredients for my mother's spells. I never expected that the same places where lifesaving plants grew would become a haven from vampire pursuers.

I pulled Penelope to the left, and our feet sunk into the chalky forest floor.

Someone swore. The mud would make their pursuit miserable, maybe deter them completely. Surely, two witch girls weren't worth following into the treacherous terrain.

"Did you see where they went?" asked the deep gruff of a man's voice, much closer than I expected.

"No. I'll go left. They can't be faster than us in this damn muck."

Heavy footsteps sloshed nearby. They had abandoned the horses.

I darted right, deeper into the trees. Penelope's grip on one hand and the spellbook in the other slowed my speed. Vines dripped from the overhead canopy and spilt like poison into the dirt. Animals scurried out of our way, brushing across branches and rocks, an eerie symphony for our escape.

There!

I ground my heels into the mud when I saw the downed tree. At some point, the giant had succumbed to disease or a storm and fallen to the forest floor. Years had carved away the inside of the trunk, leaving behind an empty space the perfect size for an eight-year-old.

Skidding to a halt, Penelope ran into my legs. I jerked her forward and stuffed her toward the opening of the log.

"Get in and be quiet."

She ducked into the hollow, then froze. She tried to pull herself out.

"What are you doing?" I pressed against her back, squishing her inside. "Get in there."

"There's not enough room!" she chirped. "You won't fit!"

"Of course not." The lies clung to my lips like expensive wine. "We have a better chance if we hide in different places."

Penelope hesitated, caught between fear, logic, and trust. Regret cut deep into my chest. Her brown eyes, set into her paled face, looked at me with naïveté. If I didn't stop lying to her, one day that trust would disappear.

"Okay." She wiggled into the hollowed space and settled in the darkness.

"Here, take this." I held out the spellbook, and it filled her arms, cradled against her quivering chest. "If you beat me home, put it under my bed with the others."

I stepped from the log and dragged my feet through the mud until the evidence of a second set of footprints faded away. Relief washed over me in a cold wave. Penelope was smart. She would be quiet when they came.

More curses filtered through the trees. One of the men walked beyond the clearing. It wouldn't be long until he caught me.

I bit my lip and did another scan of the area. I ached to find a place to hide, but the rocks and barren trunks offered little concealment. If I ran, the sound of my steps would give away my position.

Instead, I waited. Resolve became a noose around my neck, tightening with every moment of stillness. I fought against my flight or fight response as adrenaline coursed through my veins. My fingers shook. My breath came out ragged. Imaginary blood slipped down my fingertips. Would I meet the same fate as my mother?

The crashing grew louder, snaps of broken branches were almost on top of me. My mind filled with the sound of rushing water, a great icy river washing away logic, trapping me with only one thought: protect Penelope.

The redhead giant emerged from a thicket of clustered trees. Mud and grime marred his armor. Cuts he must have gotten from stubborn foliage healed as I watched. The skin knit together into an unbroken line, without even the hint of a scar. My mother would have been jealous.

Up close, the vampire was impressive. His massive form boasted ancestry from the gods of old. Those golden-red locks sat in neat rows, adorned with beads that glimmered in the wisps of peeking sunlight. They piled on his head like a crown, a radiant deity calling for my soul. A straight nose centered on his wide face, above full, rosy lips that broke into a smile when he raised his ocean-blue eyes and caught sight of me. Two pointed teeth shone sharper than the rest.

The frantic beat of my heart paused. My tongue turned to lead. The sweat on my skin became icy daggers, warning of the danger before me. Just like those plants I plucked from the soil, I had nowhere to run.

The intensity in his expression shifted. They flicked across my body, and my cheeks burned. I rolled my shoulders back and jerked my chin up. Laughter wrinkled the creases in the corners of his eyes. My defiance amused him.

"You're a civilian." His deep voice sounded like a stampede about to trample me.

I peeled my tongue from the roof of my mouth.

"Y-yes." I flinched at the smallness of my tone. If my power wasn't bound, I wouldn't have been so weak.

"There were two of you." He glanced around. "Where's the other one?"

"She went a different way. If you haven't found her by now, then she's already gone."

Please, Penelope, stay hidden.

He tilted his head, studying me. Something rolled across his face under the smooth mask he wore. Something dangerous.

"Come here." He beckoned with one hand while the other palmed the top of a great battle axe, almost affectionately.

I shook my head. *No way.*

"You can't be more than a hundred and twenty pounds soaking wet. What do you plan to do?"

He reached toward me, and I took a step back. His lips turned up in a grin, and a flash of silver rolled through his irises. I'd heard rumors of vampires showing emotion through their eyes. Seeing it in real life drew a shiver down my spine.

He clutched at me again, and I backed away, but he proved too fast. One hand caught a firm grip on my shoulder and the other grabbed the bottom of my chin. Though bands of muscle suggested his strength, he kept his hands soft. Tight enough that I couldn't escape, but not to leave a mark on my skin.

He lifted my face up to the hint of illumination filtering through the trees.

The smell of evergreen and mint wafted over me, taking me to the vague remains of an almost memory. A layer of surprise escaped through the fear. I expected the sharper scents of sweat and blood.

He pushed my chin up and turned me to the side. The sunlight warmed my neck, and his gaze flicked to the place where thin skin shielded my thundering pulse. I stilled, suddenly aware that this man was a bloodthirsty vampire and I was witch, and we'd been enemies for over two hundred years.

His finger brushed across my throat. "What're you doing out here by yourself?"

The depth in his voice shallowed to a soft whisper between us. Air tried to escape my lungs.

"I-I was collecting herbs." I swallowed thickly. "My father is sick. I have to make him medicine."

"Your mother doesn't care for him?"

"She's dead."

The beads in his hair chimed as he bent his head. "I'm sorry for your loss. My father passed away last year."

"I'm sorry." What else could I say? We weren't friends or even acquaintances. He had an axe on his belt and wore silver armor with marks from my people's weapons.

"Me too," he said.

He towered over me, probably six and a half feet tall, and thick in a way that said he could lift very heavy things. He looked between the mere inches of space between our bodies, and his touch under my chin softened to a gentle caress. Heat slipped between us, warming parts of me that I hadn't noticed had become chilled in the damp forest. The hand on my shoulder slid down my arm as the man's brows creased.

"What's your name?" he asked.

I opened my mouth, but the word halted on my lips.

Behind the giant, the shimmer of a shadow moved in the tree line. Rolling waves of darkness spiraled together, and the shape of a sinister phantom formed. A ghost, a specter, or whatever it was staggered into a dark cloud of existence. It stepped toward us, one hand outstretched.

"No," I whispered.

The man's brows pinched again, and he tilted his head. "I promise I won't hurt you, girl. I'm just asking your name."

The phantom didn't alter its course. It stood five steps away, continuing its pace. Four. Memories of the thief it had killed undug themselves from the shallow grave in my mind. The blood leaking from his face. The frozen scream of agony. Worse, Penelope's wide eyes spilling with tears and the horror as she backed away, not from the dead man, but from me.

"Please, don't. Not right now."

Three steps. Two. Penelope would see it all again. She would watch me kill someone, and maybe this time the scars would be too deep to heal. The thought caused more pain than death at the hands of this vampire. How many lives could I take before even my family couldn't forgive me?

"Look, I promise not to hurt you." My mind barely registered the man speaking as the shadow crept closer. "We're not here for civilians. I just want to be sure you're safe out in the woods. There could be animals or who knows what."

The phantom lingered, barely one more step to go.

"Go away," I told it.

The vampire's face darkened. His eyes snapped back to my throat. "You're not really in a position to make demands right now."

Too late. It was here.

A shadow hand pressed against the vampire's back, and ghostly fingers slipped through his skin.

Magic screamed inside me, a terrible yell of anger and power. It beat against the bonds of the spell my mother had cast years ago. The cage she created was strong, but this phantom was stronger, and it controlled me. Slivers of magic reached between the bars as the being stole my power. Magic pulled from me and jumped to the vampire. His breath caught, and the hand on my chin moved to encircle my neck.

The magic rippled over the man, tasting the salt on his skin, and it purred a happy tune in my ear. It liked him.

Goosebumps broke out across his arms, and he shivered. "If you try to do anything with that magic, I will kill you right now."

I sought his gaze. I knew he could see the fear in my eyes. I didn't know what the phantom would do. These could be his last moments.

"I'm sorry," I whispered.

"Sorry?"

The magic forged a battering ram and pounded into the vampire. It filled his body and ran an iron fist through the depths of his mind. It dragged me along, trapping our minds together. Memories, thoughts, fears, and desires swirled into my head, none of them my own.

A woman in a deep green tunic handing me my first axe.

The pain during my first battle as a witch's sword cut into my flesh. The triumph as my axe met her head.

The memories zeroed in on a man I didn't know, but one this redhead vampire knew well. *He lifted me from the horse and wrapped my wound with layers of thick bandages. He ruffled my hair, and a beam of pride streaked across his face. The man's smile mirrored my own, a perfect replica. My father.*

No, not mine. His.

A body. Bloated and gray with days of decay. The fragments of a last conversation. Betrayal, suspicion.

"Your father was murdered." The unbeckoned words poured from me. "The coroner said natural causes, but you think someone betrayed him. Your greatest fear is that you'll die without avenging your father's death."

The magic slipped away, and the phantom disappeared. For now, at least.

I sagged in the stranger's arms, exhausted.

"What was that?" The vampire jostled me.

"I don't know," I said. That was honest. I never knew what the being would make me do.

"How did you get into my head? All those memories. Did you see them too?"

I nodded.

He looked at me again, as though for the first time. My brown curls pinned into a loose ponytail, and salt crystals clung to the back of my neck from sprinting. Mud crusted the front of my dress, but my face felt mostly clean. His gaze settled on my lips, and the grip at my throat loosened.

"You're coming with me."

Surprise trapped my tongue. *Excuse me?*

The man shifted his grip to my left wrist. He pulled me the way he had come, where the distant huffs of a horse waited. It took three of his great steps for my mind to catch up.

I buried my heels into the ground. The mud slowed me, and my scarce weight became enough to halt the vampire's tracks.

"I'm not going anywhere with you," I said.

The man paused. His shoulders tensed, and he turned to me. He grew close until my chest brushed his armor, but I refused to move back. Hot anger mixed into a fire of desperation and stubbornness. He had broken into my home, chased me and my sister into the forest, and had the audacity to demand that I leave with him.

No way.

"Oh?" He tilted his head to one side. "Maybe I can change your mind."

His gaze shifted over my shoulder to the hollow log of Penelope's sanctuary.

"No!"

His stride carried him to the felled log before I could get halfway there. He plunged his reach into the cavern and pulled my sister from the space. She gave a startled scream, and he muffled the sound with his hand over her mouth.

A blade appeared against Penelope's throat. She stilled.

"I don't want to hurt her." The man's blue eyes were soft, but darkness swirled inside.

"What do you want?" I asked, but it didn't matter. I would give him anything.

"Rayhan?" a new voice yelled into the forest. The second man. "Where the hell are you?"

"Listen," the redhead, Rayhan, said. His hand did not quiver at my sister's neck. "My friend is on his way here, and he doesn't care if witches leave our presence alive or not. You get to decide. You can come with me or stay here and you'll both die."

I twisted my fingers, but I didn't have a choice. Footsteps thumped closer, one rhythmic step after another. Where was my phantom when I needed it?

Tree branches cracked as the second man drew near.

"Yes, yes. I'll go with you."

Rayhan's lips split into a toothy grin. "Wonderful."

He pushed Penelope forward, and she caught herself in the mud. Her arms trembled as she lifted her dainty chin to look at me.

"Nat?" Her voice quivered.

"Back in the log."

"Nat—"

"Now!"

Her lips pressed, but she disappeared into the damp space. A knot in my chest loosened.

Rayhan strode to me, grabbed a handful of my hair, and pulled me to my feet. I swallowed a yelp. He didn't deserve any satisfaction from my fear. I staggered to match his pace, and my scalp ached, but I strained to keep the mossy log in sight. I needed one last glimpse of Penelope. I needed to memorize her face in case...in case I never saw her again.

She didn't peek out.

I barely felt the rough edge of tree bark bite into my skin as the vampire pushed me against a narrow evergreen. I didn't know how long Rayhan planned to keep me. My father's medication was low, and Penelope couldn't make the complicated recipe yet. I bit my lip. My father wouldn't survive long without his medicine.

"If I feel any magic, I won't ask questions this time." His hot breath crossed the back of my neck. He jerked my right hand behind me, and the cold touch of silver chewed through my skin.

"Is this necessary?" I asked. "I promise I can't fight you."

"These chains are silver. They'll make it harder for you to use magic, but not impossible. Remember, I don't have a problem killing two witches if one acts up."

Penelope.

The cold metal clicked as it tightened on my wrist. Each notch was another step away from my life, my sister, my father.

Click.

"You should have thought about the consequences when you bespelled me."

Click.

"Now you're mine."

Click.

More swearing, then the trees parted, and a shorter man stepped from the foliage. Black armor stretched over his chest, highlighting eyes so dark they almost swallowed the irises. They cut across me, and his hatred threatened to imprint a physical pain on my body. I resisted the urge to flinch. One of his lips curled into a sneer.

"About time you got here, Kadence. I thought I'd have to send a rescue party," Rayhan said.

"What did you find, Rayhan?"

Rayhan's heavy hand pinned my back against the tree while the other did a quick search, revealing that I didn't carry any weapons.

"Just the one," Rayhan said. "The other got away."

"A civilian." Kadence took in my dirty dress and lack of weapons. "Leave her here."

"She's coming with us. She used magic on me. It's personal now."

Kadence narrowed his eyes. "You usually avoid taking civilians."

"You don't know what she did to me."

"We could kill her."

"Like I said, it's personal."

The two faced off. My heart thumped in my throat. I craned my neck to see both men, but only Kadence was visible from my place against the trunk. His blank face hid the hint of suspicion that his tone carried.

Finally, he shrugged. "I don't care. We need to leave before their reinforcements arrive."

"Let's go, then."

Rayhan pulled me from the tree and dragged me into the trenches of the forest. I went willingly, looking back for as long as I could. Penelope's life was far more important than mine. As fear turned the thick bile in my stomach, relief ran through my nerves. Penelope and my mother's spellbook remained safe. Only that mattered.

Nothing moved from the hollow darkness of Penelope's hiding space, but I thought I heard the sharp inhale of a smothered sob before the terrain stole my view.

Don't stop now. Keep reading with your copy of CAPTURED BY THE VAMPIRE KNIGHT, by City Owl Author, A.N. Payton.

Don't miss more from CJ Holmes available at cjholmeswriting.com

And now, discover CAPTURED BY THE VAMPIRE KNIGHT, by City Owl Author, A.N. Payton

He took her for her magic. He didn't expect her to steal his heart.

Natalie has spent her life protecting her family—raising her sister and caring for her ailing father in a world ruled by vampires. But when a brutal raid destroys her village, she strikes a desperate bargain: her freedom in exchange for their lives.

Taken by Rayhan, a powerful vampire warrior, Natalie is forced to use her unstable magic to solve the murder of his father. If she fails, she may never see her family again. But if she succeeds, the truth could be more dangerous than the killer himself.

Rayhan never meant to take a prisoner—but Natalie is no ordinary human. When she inadvertently unlocks memories he buried long ago, he realizes she may be the key to justice—and vengeance. What he didn't expect was the fire between them. Now, the woman who could destroy him might also be the only one who can save him.

As deadly secrets unravel and the killer turns their sights on Natalie, desire collides with betrayal, and trust becomes the ultimate risk.

Dark magic. Forbidden romance. A fight for survival.

Can love bloom between sworn enemies—or will it become the weapon that tears them apart?

Captured by the Vampire Knight is perfect for fans of steamy vampire romance, enemies to lovers, and magic-bound fated mates.

Please sign up for the City Owl Press newsletter for chances to win special subscriber-only contests and giveaways as well as receiving information on upcoming releases and special excerpts.

All reviews are **welcome** and **appreciated**. Please consider leaving one on your favorite social media and book buying sites.

Escape Your World. Get Lost in Ours! City Owl Press at www.cityowlpress.com.

ABOUT THE AUTHOR

CJ HOLMES writes dark fantasy romance and paranormal tales of magic, obsession, and impossible choices. Her stories follow sharp, resilient heroines and the morally grey, dangerously devoted men who would burn kingdoms for them. Expect immersive worlds, high stakes, and a thread of danger running beneath every page—shot through with dry humour and enough heat to keep you warm through even the bleakest winter.

When she isn't writing, CJ can usually be found in a café with a notebook, or wandering the UK countryside (almost always dressed for the wrong weather). If she's disappeared entirely, check the nearest bookshop: she'll be there adding to her towering TBR pile, alongside her equally book-obsessed husband.

cjholmeswriting.com

instagram.com/cjholmes_writing

facebook.com/cjholmeswriting

tiktok.com/@cjholmes_writing

ABOUT THE PUBLISHER

City Owl Press is a cutting edge indie publishing company, bringing the world of romance and speculative fiction to discerning readers.

Escape Your World. Get Lost in Ours!

www.cityowlpress.com

facebook.com/CityOwlPress
x.com/cityowlpress
instagram.com/cityowlbooks
pinterest.com/cityowlpress
tiktok.com/@cityowlpress

www.ingramcontent.com/pod-product-compliance
Lightning Source LLC
LaVergne TN
LVHW020530100826
845148LV00010B/1405
* 9 7 8 1 6 4 8 9 8 5 4 7 8 *